Also by Gillian Royes

The Sea Grape Tree

The Goat Woman of Largo Bay

The Man Who Turned Both Cheeks

Business Is Good

Sexcess: The New Gender Rules at Work

Praise for Gillian Royes and the
Shadrack Myers Mystery Series

THE SEA GRAPE TREE

"A superb detective story with richly imagined characters, *The Sea Grape Tree* is set in an island paradise where more goes on than meets the eye. This splendid third novel in Gillian Royes's Shad series, featuring the delightful bartender/neighborhood detective Shadrack 'Shad' Myers . . . keeps everyone on edge."

—Amy Hill Hearth, author of *Miss Dreamsville
and the Collier County Women's Literary Society*

"In *The Sea Grape Tree* Gillian Royes serves up a delicious rum punch of a mystery—smart and savvy, touched by her stylized prose, and mixed with beautiful settings and a host of memorable characters like Shad, the lovable town sleuth and bartender."

—Zane, *New York Times* bestselling author,
publisher, scriptwriter, and executive producer

"From page one, Royes's characters grab you. They are complex, not particularly nice, but completely human and captivating. We highly recommended *The Sea Grape Tree*."

—Troy Johnson, AALBC.com

"A gentle Jamaican mystery brimming with compassion for hardworking Shad, the amateur sleuth; his wife Beth, mother of his four children; and other vivid characters who populate this enchanting novel."

—Joan Steinau Lester, author of *Mama's Child* and
Black, White, Other: In Search of Nina Armstrong

THE MAN WHO TURNED
BOTH CHEEKS

"Royes's strong sequel to her fiction debut, 2011's *The Goat Woman of Largo Bay*, deepens the character of Shad Meyers . . . in this sensitive, thought-provoking novel."

—*Publishers Weekly*

"Royes's Jamaica is lush, stormy and stronger than the rum punch cocktails that Shad pours over ice."

—ABCNews.com

"Royes is brilliant in bringing Jamaican sun and sea, people and places to life. . . . She's equally adept with characters. . . . A cozy mystery as social commentary."

—*Kirkus Reviews*

THE GOAT WOMAN OF LARGO BAY

"Strong characters and vivid descriptive passages."

—*Kirkus Reviews*

"Poetic . . . leads to a tense climax that will have the reader engrossed to the end."

—*New York Journal of Books*

"[Royes] does an outstanding job of creating a small Jamaican village—it is so vivid that the reader feels part of the environment—and deftly shows the social and political life on the island. . . . [*The Goat Woman of Largo Bay*] is an absorbing read and one that won't be forgotten quickly."

—*Portland Book Review*

THE
RHYTHM
OF THE
AUGUST
RAIN

A Novel

GILLIAN ROYES

ATRIA PAPERBACK

NEW YORK   LONDON   TORONTO   SYDNEY   NEW DELHI

ATRIA PAPERBACK
An Imprint of Simon & Schuster, Inc.
1230 Avenue of the Americas
New York, NY 10020

First Atria Paperback edition July 2015

ATRIA PAPERBACK and colophon are trademarks of Simon & Schuster, Inc.

For information about special discounts for bulk purchases, please contact Simon & Schuster Special Sales at 1-866-506-1949 or business@simonandschuster.com.

The Simon & Schuster Speakers Bureau can bring authors to your live event. For more information or to book an event, contact the Simon & Schuster Speakers Bureau at 1-866-248-3049 or visit our website at www.simonspeakers.com.

Manufactured in the United States of America

10   9   8   7   6   5   4   3   2   1

Library of Congress Cataloging-in-Publication Data

Royes, Gillian.
  The rhythm of the August rain : a novel / Gillian Royes. —First Atria Paperback edition.
     pages ; cm. —(A Shadrack Myers mystery ; 4)
  1. Bartenders—Jamaica—Fiction. 2. Private investigators—Jamaica—Fiction. 3. Cold cases (Criminal investigation)—Fiction. 4. Jamaica—Social life and customs—Fiction. I. Title.
  PS3618.O92R49 2015
  813'–dc23   2015019812

ISBN 978-1-4767-6240-1
ISBN 978-1-4767-6241-8 (ebook)

*For Judith, who opened my eyes to
the wisdom of Bob's words*

The good times of today are the sad thoughts of tomorrow.

—ROBERT NESTA MARLEY

CHAPTER ONE

G od liked to play games with people, made the biggest
things creep into their lives when they least expected
them. If it wasn't so, Renford would have gotten a
shout-out before he climbed onto his bicycle to tell him
a drunk driver was coming down the road, and somebody
would have told Miss Maudie, hinted to her gentlelike, that
she'd won the lottery. It might have saved her the heart attack when she heard it on TV. But, no, Shad was to reflect
later, God liked to spin people around with a shock and see
if they could walk straight, like a child about to pin the tail
on the donkey. Like the boss after Shannon's call.

The news had fallen out of the clear blue sky. Shad had
been minding his own business, wiping the dust and salt
spray off the bottles behind the bar before any customers
came in. The ocean had been drumming on the cliff below
and the breeze blowing through the bar's open sides as they
always did. Even the tiny island sitting a quarter mile off-
shore hadn't been doing much of anything. The mildewed
buildings in the middle were sitting roofless and somber in
the sun, the almond tree tossing its leaves now and again.

The petite bartender had squatted down to reach the
vodka and gin bottles under the sink, and since it had been

1

a month since he'd dusted, he'd had to do more wiping than he'd expected. Beads of perspiration had popped out on his bald head, and his once-crisp white shirt was getting damp. Normally meticulous about his appearance, Shad had barely noticed. He'd been brooding about an upcoming celebration, the one that surprised every man no matter how far in advance he'd been notified. He'd just started talking himself into a positive attitude (for the sake of the children, if nothing else) when the telephone in the bar had started to ring.

"Largo Bay Restaurant and Bar," he sang out after snatching up the receiver.

"Shadrack Myers, how are you?" a woman said with an unmistakable lift to her voice.

"Shannon!" Shad inhaled sharply through the gap between his front teeth. "It's still cold in Canada, nuh?"

The woman laughed in her usual hearty way. "No, it's June, remember? It's spring here, the flowers are out and everything."

"It's nice in Jamaica, too, dry season."

"How's Beth?"

"She good, busy planning for us to marry next month. Is all she can talk about—wedding, wedding, wedding. You would think we was young, not big old people with children."

"You're getting married? That's wonderful!" The groom wagged his head in doubt. "What day in July?" she added, her voice more intense. "Maybe I'll be there."

Shad's hairless eyebrows shot up as he leaned on the counter. "You mean—you coming back to Largo Bay?"

"After fourteen years, Shad, can you believe it?"

"I better get the boss."

Shad hurried toward the parking lot, where Eric Keller was peering inside the hood of his ancient Jeep pickup with a sour face.

"Boss, your baby mother on the phone," Shad called from the safety of the restaurant, and Eric looked up, frowning. As the tall American trudged past in his old shorts and flip-flops, knobby knees slightly bent, Shad thought about giving him Shannon's news, but decided against it. Certain messages shouldn't be relayed by third parties to sixty-five-year-old men with white hair and paunches, especially when ambulances took half a day to reach this corner of Jamaica.

As Eric took the receiver back to his apartment, Shad picked up his dusting cloth, trying to recall Shannon's face, but the years had turned it into a blur above her tall, skinny body. It hurt Shad's heart to know that the fourteen years since she'd been in Largo had dimmed his memory of her, as much as she and Eric had loved each other. Their much-talked-about affair had started soon after Eric had opened his retirement dream, a cozy hotel called the Largo Bay Inn, where Shannon had been a guest. Every month thereafter for two years, she'd arrive to stay in Eric's suite, and he'd walk around beaming. Everyone had expected them to be together for the rest of their lives, but the photographer had suddenly stopped coming to Largo, leading to much speculation among the hotel employees. A year later, after she'd sent cards with photographs she'd taken herself of her new baby, the fears of the worst gossipers were confirmed.

Shannon had been missed by all of the workers and been on their minds for years after. They'd imitated her laugh, loved that she'd tried to remember everybody's name, and that she'd brought presents sometimes, once an apron for Beth and a bottle of aftershave for Shad. They would remind each other how she was always taking pictures, always carrying a camera. After she stopped coming, the photographs of Eric's daughter showed Eve as a serious, solid-looking child.

The bottle dusting finished, Shad started sponging down the refrigerator shelves, waiting for the boss's explosion of Irish temper after the call—like when he heard a liquor bottle break—because the timing of Shannon's visit couldn't be worse. But the bar owner returned and placed the receiver in its cradle, his eyes numb.

Shad stood up and slammed the fridge door shut. "She coming back."

"She told you, huh?"

The men returned to their chores, nothing more needing to be said between two people who were closer than family. Over the years, Eric and Shad had become codependents, struggling now to eke out a living from the crude roadside bar that one owned and the other ran since the demise of the hotel. Both men would have found it impossible to live without the other.

It had been seventeen eventful years since the two had met. The starting point had been when Shad arrived back in Largo with his small family after a year's stay in Kingston Penitentiary for stealing a woman's purse in Port Antonio. His grandmother had immediately found him work with her friend Old Man Job. As she reminded her grandson daily, the devil found work for idle hands; besides, he had to support her in her old age.

Old Man Job, a toothless and talented jack-of-all-trades, was building a fifteen-bedroom hotel for an American man who'd bought Mr. Sommerset's property on the point at the end of the bay, a job that called for a young man to carry cement blocks and steel beams. Twenty-year-old Shad had no interest in construction, but the only other honest work he could get in Largo Bay was fishing, which he hated with all his might for its danger and clinging stench.

"You have a girlfriend and a baby to mind," Granny had urged him. "You is a man of *responsibilities*." He had taken the construction job.

The owner of the hotel being built had been Eric, and Shad had liked him from day one.

"Looks like we'll be learning this stuff together," the big American had told him as they watched Job layering concrete blocks with mortar. True to his word, Eric had worked shoulder to shoulder with Shad digging trenches, laying footings for the steel rods, piling up blocks for the walls, doing whatever it took to create his hotel.

"I never see a white man work so hard," Shad had told Beth one evening while they were eating dinner, Granny snoring in the next room. "He say he used to sit behind a desk all day, but you wouldn't believe it, the way he work. He not proud, you know, like some of them brown people who think they too good for hard work."

When the job was done, Shad had become the hotel's bartender (learning on the job) and Eric a big deal in the little village. His exalted status came from being white and foreign, and the owner of the only real business for miles around. He was as happy as a pig in mud, he used to say.

"I dreamed of this every day before I retired," he'd told Shad as they laid steel rods for the lobby's concrete floor. "I couldn't wait to kiss that paper company good-bye."

"But you were living in New York!" Shad had protested, not imagining any place more wonderful than the skyscraper city on TV where everybody looked busy and rich.

"Listen, man, the only reason I stuck it out for thirty damn years working in human resources was so one day I could live in the Caribbean and never have to suffer through another winter. And since I couldn't live down here without working, I figured that the best way to make some money was to own a hotel." Eric had shoved a rod into place with his boot. "It'll be a cold day in hell before I work for anybody again."

Contrary to Eric's hopes, the Largo Bay Inn had never made a profit. Limited by its size and location in the isolated northeast of the island, it barely broke even every month. Ironically, although Eric had to live on a shoestring, the hotel brought prosperity to everyone else in the village. The conch divers and hair braiders and vegetable gardeners had money jingling in their pockets for a change. Employing up to thirty-five workers in the tourist season—receptionists, gardeners, cooks, and maids—the inn put food on the tables of Largo's families. This beacon of hope burned for seven good years, only to be blown out. A Category 5 hurricane sweeping across Jamaica had not only destroyed the Largo Bay Inn, but had washed away the narrow peninsula road leading from the main road to its front door. At the storm's end, the battered, roofless hotel had been left standing on a tiny island, an almond tree its only companion.

One and a half years after the storm destroyed the hotel, Eric had opened the Largo Bay Restaurant and Bar, a humble shadow of its predecessor. It wasn't a matter of choice. Having no other source of income, his retirement savings sunk into the ruined hotel, and still too young to draw Social Security, he'd finally given in to Shad's suggestion that he use the small insurance check to build a bar on the scrap of land he still owned beside the main road. The money had only been enough to construct the rough walls, concrete floor, and thatch roof that now housed the bar-cum-restaurant, Eric's compact apartment stuck onto one end.

The shabby bar was an embarrassment to the former hotelier from the opening day, leaving him in hapless despair, knowing that he had no other option. On the other hand, to Shad the bar was as sweet as it was to every thirsty tourist. His only alternative to fishing, it was his workplace and savior. In other words, the bar's owner and its bartender had been bonded by the bar and were stuck with each other like a resigned married couple.

A half hour after the call, Eric strolled in from the parking lot wiping his hands on a cloth. A lock of hair blew across his face and he thrust it away with his shoulder.

"Something is up with Shannon, I'm telling you, coming back all of a sudden like this." He looked at Shad sharply. "Did you tell her about——?"

"I don't tell her nothing, boss. I don't like *cass-cass* and gossip, you know that."

"It's a crazy coincidence, then."

"Maybe she just need a rest."

"She's working, doing an article for a magazine."

"She can write something about the new hotel we going to build, then."

Eric took a ginger ale from the fridge. "Nah, it's an article about Rastafarians."

"Pshaw, man, Rastas is old news. How she can write about Rastas and a nice hotel going up?"

"She doesn't even know about the hotel. It wouldn't matter to her, anyway."

If Eric thought that Shannon wouldn't care about the New Largo Bay Inn, as the villagers had already christened it, everyone in Largo did. It was the talk of the sixty families living from one night's catch to another. Eric and Shad were to go into the hotel business again, but with a *bigger* hotel this time, they were saying, thanks to a rich businessman named Danny Caines.

The villagers had all seen the investor from New York when he came down earlier that year. A few had even met Caines as he made the rounds in his rented car. The strapping African American had turned out to be in his midforties, younger than everyone had expected. He was a friendly type, although his relationship with a local seamstress had been a little too friendly for some. For a while during his visit, the hotel project had been in danger of dying because of the torrid affair, but in the end, despite his misgivings about cost overruns, despite the dressmaker's wrath when he thwarted her plans to marry him, Caines had decided to build the hotel after all. Even the Mafia didn't stop people from visiting Italy, he'd said with his deep laugh, and one crazy woman wasn't going to stop him.

Shad shook his head, grinning. "Shannon coming back—plenty action in July."

"That's exactly what we need," Eric said, taking a sip from the bottle and coughing.

Shad slapped him on the back. "We buying Miss Mac's land next door—"

"You're getting married—"

"—and two of your women coming down at the same time. Action, camera!" Shad couldn't help but clap his hands over his head and send out the high-pitched wail that always signaled his delight as he spun around on one heel.

"At least you don't have another woman waiting in the wings," Eric commented as he poured the ginger ale into a glass.

"Now *that* is *cass-cass*." Shad steadied himself against the counter. "They say black man like confusion, but you can match any black man, boss. You make me laugh, no joke. I hope Simone can laugh at it, too."

Simone was a woman who'd briefly lived in the ruins of the old hotel the year before. An American whose family had migrated from Jamaica when she was a small child, she'd come back seeking a place to heal, had exiled herself from her own life and camped out on the little island for two months. The boss had fallen for the mysterious woman with doelike eyes, and he'd grieved for weeks after she left Largo, but he'd stayed in touch with her and they'd planned for her return in July. And now she'd be met by Shannon, Eric's ex-girlfriend and the mother of his daughter. It sounded like one of the soap operas Shad watched on his day off, and he couldn't wait to tell Beth that *The Young and the Restless* had nothing over Largo.

The little bartender shook his head, tut-tutting. "Boss, you have too much woman in your life. You should settle down like me."

Eric sat at his do-everything table near the bar where he ate, read, and entertained his guests. "You mean after I've had a flock of children like you? No, thank you."

"Just one thing I want to ask you," Shad said, suddenly serious as he scrubbed the dust cloth clean. "With all the excitement coming up, don't get sick or nothing, I begging you. We can't afford for anything to happen to you, like how Danny Caines have no hotel experience and you the only one can manage the hotel."

Eric threw one leg over a chair. "What d'you mean *the only one?* I wouldn't take on this deal if you weren't going to be a partner, buddy." Which was the boss's way of saying that he didn't really want to build a hotel again but, indebted as he was, he had to, and Shad was to be his trump card.

In exchange for being the needed local partner, the younger man had agreed to do the real work, from running around during the construction to managing the hotel later. But that's what partners were for, Shad was convinced, especially scrape-bottom men such as him who didn't have any money or land to invest in a deal, who had few legal opportunities to get ahead. And if two American men needed an on-spot Jamaican partner for their hotel, if they wanted a young, hardworking man with a willing heart, he would be more than happy to oblige.

With five mouths to feed, Shad had not only accepted the upcoming challenge of becoming a partner but longed for it. His ambition had been nurtured from childhood when Granny had predicted that, because of his dark-dark complexion and high forehead, he would be a *busha* one day, as big as the white overseers in slavery days. Granny might be dead, but her words continued to ring in her grandson's head, and he carried with him everywhere a small plastic bag with a tablespoon of dirt from the top of her grave, his good-luck charm, to make sure her prediction came true. The new hotel was his one shot, he'd remind himself every night after he'd crept into bed beside Beth, his one chance to be somebody, even if his partners ran him into the ground while he did it.

After hanging the dust cloth over the edge of the sink, Shad looked at Eric. "Boss, where Shannon going to stay in Largo?"

"She asked me to book her into Miss Mac's."

"You forget Miss Mac not going to have the boarding-house no more? We buying the land and tearing down the house to build the hotel."

"Shit, you're right." Eric hit his forehead, white hair jerking forward. "And the closing is Friday the thirteenth. How could I forget?" He rolled his eyes up to the thatch as he tossed down the last of his drink. "There'll be no board-inghouse after that."

Shad squeezed his lips together in irritation. Known as Largo's *sniffer and snuffer* (a title bestowed by his former teacher and mentor, the said Miss Mac), the bartender knew that sometimes the boss needed help with his own sniffing and snuffing. His mind went to sleep at least half the day. "And remember, boss, Simone going to be staying in your apartment, so Shannon can't stay with you."

"I'll call her tomorrow." Eric stood up. "Maybe she'll have to stay in another town. I have to take the car to Port Maria now before the garage closes. I think it's the carbure-tor."

The next evening, after the first of the regulars had settled into their arguments, Shad watched Eric maneuver past him to take the phone into his apartment. When he emerged later, the boss's ruddy face was a shade paler and his eyes even more glazed than the day before.

"You told Shannon about Miss Mac?" Shad asked, opening a soft drink for him. Eric took the bottle and nodded. "What she say?"

"The Delgados—she'll stay with the Delgados."

"That make sense, like how Shannon and Jennifer used to be good friends before. . . ."

Shad chewed his top lip as he poured ice into a Styrofoam bucket and placed it in the fridge. Eric was staring at, not seeing, the dangling bottle opener.

"Boss, you okay? You look like a *duppy* frighten you," Shad said, trying a little levity. Eric always laughed at the mention of ghosts.

The bar owner took a gulp of his drink. "She—she's bringing Eve."

"That good news, man! Like how your son come down last year and see Jamaica, is time for the daughter now. But why she didn't tell you before that she was bringing Eve?"

Eric made his way to a stool, patting the counter like a man who was blind. "She just decided, she said."

A call from the end of the bar turned Shad's attention to his customers and a fresh bottle of white rum. As he topped them up, Eli, Solomon, and Tri sucked him into a debate about the current prime minister, the first female leader in the island's history.

"Don't tell me," Tri insisted, thumping the counter, "that a woman can run a country as good as a man, don't tell me that." Thin and sinewy, *mauger* to the locals, the aging Triumphant Arch never backed down from any political argument, the louder the better. "What you think, Shad?"

"Give the woman a chance," Eli said in his slow, rambling way. "Is only her first term and—"

"No woman should lead a country," Solomon put in. The former chef of the hotel, reduced to the bar's part-time cook, wore his usual grumpy face. "The Bible say that woman should walk behind man."

"You show me," Eli challenged him, "where in the Bible it say that, and I going to show you a man who write it."

"All I know," Shad said, "is that every woman I ever meet can think smarter and faster than a man. You forget I going to get married next month because Beth outthink me?"

When the bartender got back to his stool, Eric had left the counter, his soft drink abandoned. He'd be sitting on his verandah looking across at the island in the pale moonlight, listening to one of the Cuban radio stations as he always did at night. He never liked to sit in the bar unless he had friends over, and tonight wouldn't have been a good night, anyway, not with the way he'd looked after this second phone call.

Throwing the bottle into the garbage can, Shad mulled Eric's reaction to Shannon's news. He could understand the boss being upset yesterday about his ex-girlfriend's coming to Largo—just when Simone was visiting—but tonight he'd acted differently, completely differently, to the news that Eve was arriving, his own child. This time he was holding back, keeping his face blank, no joy, nothing in his eyes.

To Shad, a man for whom family meant everything, there would have been no better news than hearing that one of his children was coming to visit. Not that Eric had been the same kind of parent. Everyone knew he hadn't been much of a father, his two children brought up by two mothers far away in Washington, DC, and Toronto, but he was a good man down deep, and he didn't bear malice toward anybody, least of all his own children. Why then this reaction to the news that his daughter was coming? And what was the real reason Shannon was coming down after all this time?

Shad reached for a rag to wipe down the counter, knowing that the Canadian woman had won the first round. She'd thought faster and smarter than the boss.

CHAPTER TWO

Jennifer Delgado was having a *soiree*, as she liked to call her Friday-afternoon gatherings. The housekeeper, Miss Bertha, would have set out the trays of cocktail patties and miniature hot dogs with olives, Jennifer's husband, Lambert, would have handed around the first glasses of wine and scotch, and the party would be well under way, the buzz of conversation loud enough to be heard by someone—in this case, a slightly out-of-breath Eric—ascending the driveway. A clutch of guests seated on the verandah of the plantation-style home were admiring the twilight colors as he approached.

"I love the view from this porch," a stylish man in a Panama hat commented. "You can see all the way to Manchioneal Bay, can't you?"

"It looks like an artist's palette," a woman was saying in a shrill voice.

"And the red flowers of the poinciana tree go with it," another woman piped up.

After mounting the steps to the verandah, aware that his sweaty armpits were leaving rings on his shirt, Eric nodded to the group and paused to take a few breaths. If Jennifer caught him panting, she'd lecture him again about joining her gym in Port Antonio. But the climb from his bar across the road and up the driveway to the Delgados' house seemed to get longer and steeper every time he undertook it. He was aware that life and age were creeping up on him, that his knees ached when he got up in the morning and the lines on his face increased by the month, but certain markers he didn't need, such as this driveway.

On his way through the double doors into the living room, Eric greeted a couple he recognized from Port Antonio (the Plumbers? he asked himself). Inside, several more people lounged on the cushy sofas and chairs, among them Roper and Sonja, an artist and his writer girlfriend, who lived on the eastern end of the bay.

Eric shook Roper's hand, kissed Sonja's plump cheek, and asked, "Have you seen Lambert?"

"I think he's in his office with somebody," Sonja answered. Her ear-to-ear smile usually made Eric feel all was right with the world, but not this evening.

After helping himself to tonic water at the bar, Eric leaned on a column, staying out of the way of small talk. Romantic violins drifted from the speakers above him. He wasn't in the mood for a party, and he wouldn't have come if he'd had his druthers, wouldn't have shaved and pulled his hair back in a ponytail if he hadn't needed to talk to Lambert.

"At last—you're here," came the hostess's voice. Wearing a halter dress that showed off her toned arms and flat stomach, despite being a mother of two, Jennifer advanced toward him. Lambert's second wife (twenty years too young for him, Eric teased him) had always been good at making everyone feel he or she were the one guest she'd been waiting for. A transplanted interior designer from Florida, she'd been even better at enjoying life with her well-to-do Jamaican husband.

She kissed Eric on both cheeks, a habit she'd adopted after a trip to France a few years before. "You're late."

"Stuff happens."

With a bracelet-clanking hand, she pushed her blond hair back. "You're not allowed to have a long face at my parties. What's up with that?"

"Just tired, I guess." Eric swung his eyes to the corridor leading to Lambert's office. "I wonder when Lam is going to be free?"

"Why don't you ask him?"

Eric crossed the room to the corridor, shaking hands on the way with a man, an accountant, he remembered, whom Lambert had advised Eric to use and whom he'd never called. An outburst of laughter from a group of guests ricocheted off the rafters of the big room, drowning out the music.

"Hey, man, come on in," Lambert called when Eric appeared at the office door. "I was showing Doug here the plans for the Andersons' new house, the solar-powered one in St. Mary I was telling you about."

Lambert Delgado was an engineer and a product of Kingston's professional stock. A decade and a half before and newly remarried, the large mulatto had left the capital and built his home on a hill overlooking Largo. Since Eric's hotel had been the only place in the area to dine out, the Delgados had befriended the owner and they'd remained close through the years. But while Eric's fortunes had declined, Lambert's had risen, and he now handled most of the large construction jobs in eastern Portland, public and private, everyone respecting him as much for his confident authority as for his bushy mustache.

The contractor had proven to be the one person in the world—other than Shad—whom Eric would have trusted with his life. To his dying day, he'd remember how Lambert had wrapped him in a blanket when he was naked and shivering after escaping his flooded hotel during the hurricane. And he'd forever be indebted to his friend for putting him up in his home, at no cost and without complaint, for the year before the bar had been built. These favors alone made Eric beholden to the big man with the booming voice, but they didn't end there. Lambert had agreed—suggesting it himself—to build the new hotel at cost. There'd be no charge for his services.

"Largo needs it and I can afford it," he'd said, stroking one side of his mustache without blinking.

Lambert introduced him now to the man beside him, a rotund fellow who thanked the contractor for showing him the plans and departed to rejoin his wife.

"Have a seat, man," Lam said, nodding to Eric as he sat down in his desk chair. "Did you get a drink—good. How are things going?"

The leather creaked under Eric as he lowered to an armchair. "Can't complain—not too much, anyway."

"The construction permits for the hotel are all signed, and Danny sent us the first payment. We're going to start hiring the skilled laborers right after the groundbreaking. But I told you that already, didn't I?"

"Yeah, you told me, along with a million other things, none of which I can remember, of course. What do I need to do next?"

"Close on the property and sign your life away," Lambert said with the guffawing laugh that sounded like a hybrid of a Kipling character and a thumping seal, Eric had always thought. "Is Danny coming out for the closing?"

"No, Shad and I are going to be there, but they're going to courier the papers to Danny. He's coming for the groundbreaking, though. He says it'll be his first time wearing a hard hat and he's not going to miss it."

"Who's handling the groundbreaking, by the way? You'll be needing shovels and—"

"I hadn't even thought about it."

"Jennifer likes doing stuff like that. I'll ask her to do it as a gift to you guys."

"That would be great."

"How many people are you going to invite?"

Eric shrugged. "Don't ask me. Never had a groundbreaking for my old place, just started working."

"Let's see." Lambert looked at the wooden fan spinning overhead. "I'll make sure that the dozer goes in the day before—the bush will be all gone by that time, but he can make a nice flat spot for the tent. Then on the day, you or Danny can say a few words, and we'll try to get Donovan Bailey, the local member of Parliament, although it's hard to get him now that he's minister of housing. And you should have a pastor bless the project—you know Jamaicans, nothing happens without a prayer. Then after the speeches, we turn the soil: you, me, Shad, Danny, the MP. Get some photographers out there and about twenty to thirty people for refreshments after, I'd guess. Come to think of it, with free food—let's make that forty people."

"Plus two," Eric said, tightening his buttocks as he shifted in the chair. "Shannon might be here."

Lambert leaned over the mahogany desk, bushy brows high. "You're joking!"

"She has a job down here, some article to research."

"Did you tell Jen?"

"Not yet. Only one problem, though. She asked me to book her into Miss Mac's boardinghouse, but, of course, Miss Mac would have sold over to us and be gone by then."

The contractor leaned back and grinned. "And she can't stay with you."

"In fact," Eric said, cracking his neck to one side, "she suggested that she could stay here. She hates the big hotels, and she wants to be based in Largo, she says."

"She doesn't even have to ask. Jennifer would love catching up with her. Remember how they would go off shopping and swimming together? I think she even helped out once or twice in the art gallery Jennifer used to have in Ocho Rios. That was before the babies came, of course, a lot of water under the bridge since then. How long will she be here?"

"A couple of weeks, I think. She arrives on—what did she tell me?—July sixth, seventh, I think. She has a freelance contract with a magazine."

The contractor ran a hand over his wiry, gray hair. "Is she bringing Eve? It would make sense, summer holidays and everything."

"Yup."

"Splendid, splendid! Casey will be home from boarding school. They can hang out together, do the girlie thing, you know."

Eric tried to picture his daughter in Casey's bedroom with its four-poster twin beds and their pink canopies. "I guess so."

Lambert narrowed his eyes. "Why am I getting the impression that there's something—"

Eric got up and walked to the window. The sunset had

been swallowed by the tropical blackness. "Everything is wrong with this visit, Lam." Eric turned abruptly. "I almost feel as if Shannon is pulling a fast one on me, the way she did when she got pregnant. Even though she swore it was an accident, I always felt that she planned it. And of course, she never forgave me for not proposing afterward."

"That's all in the past."

"Sometimes the past collides with the present, with Simone coming down at the same time. I don't know what's going to happen, man. It's almost as if Shannon knew—"

"She'll be with us, and Simone will be with you, right? We'll keep them apart."

"This could get really—I mean, I've moved on with my life."

"I'm sure she's done the same."

"She hated me like pus—"

"Pus?"

"My mother's expression, you know what I mean." Eric sat down again and let out a hard breath. "Even when I went up to see her after she'd had Eve, it was like she'd put up a wall between us. She was living in this town house in Toronto. It had a blue door, I'll never forget, and she seemed so distant, so—different. Instead of the pretty, skinny gal dashing around taking pictures, she'd suddenly become this chubby, anxious *mother*.

"She was breast-feeding and talking to the baby the whole time. You wouldn't have thought I was the child's father, the way she was going on. She didn't even invite me to stay with her, so I took the bus from Ohio for the day because I couldn't afford a hotel. I could only stay a couple hours, but, man, were they uncomfortable. She let me hold the baby once, but the second Eve started whimpering, she snatched her out of my arms, like she didn't trust me. She didn't even ask me about my trip or anything, and I'd come all the way from Jamaica to see them."

"But you went up again, didn't you?"

"A couple of times, once a year later. The last time was after my mother's funeral. Eve was about five at the time. I remember Shannon meeting me at the door and calling Eve to come quickly. No invitation to have a drink, nothing, like I was persona non grata or something. I took Eve to the zoo and dropped her back. Not even a cup of coffee. Why she's coming back to Largo, I have no idea. I don't get it."

"Maybe she wants you to connect with Eve."

Eric straightened his shirtsleeves. "She knows I'm no good with children, I didn't want another child. I told her plain and straight. I don't know why women don't believe you when you tell them something. Claire didn't believe me either. Even before we got married, I told her and she agreed, but then she, *oops*, slipped and got pregnant with Joseph. I think when their girlfriends are having babies, it triggers their clocks to start ticking."

"You've tried your best."

"Yeah, right." Eric snorted and studied the scaly skin on the back of his hands. "Joseph straightened me out in February when he was here. He said I only put him through college because I felt guilty."

"Young people say things, you know."

"It's not like I've been a deadbeat dad or anything. I've sent money every month, and I remember to call at birthdays." Eric looked up sharply. "What are you laughing at? Most of the time, anyway, you know what I mean."

"So what's the problem?"

"It's not only Shannon—I think we could get through that—it's Eve. Apparently, Shannon was going to leave her with her mother, but now she says her mother can't *handle* Eve. She needs her father right now. I'm supposed to be the tough guy, all of a sudden."

"You're making her sound like a monster."

"I don't know anything about eleven-year-old girls, Lam—"

"Twelve, she's twelve now. In fact, I think her birthday is in July, right? She's going to be thirteen. I remember she was born a few months after Casey."

"The point is I have no earthly idea how to handle an adolescent, especially one as difficult as she sounds."

"What do you mean, *difficult*?"

Eric took a deep breath—it had to be straight up with Lam. "She was caught shoplifting a couple days ago, man." Eric examined his ragged fingernails. "Stealing cigarettes from a convenience store. My daughter's a fucking criminal."

CHAPTER THREE

The tomato vine was doing well, better than the lettuce and cucumbers. It had liked the spring warmth this year and seemed to enjoy the summer heat even better. Shannon trained the hose on the large pots of vegetables, making a mental note to remind her next-door neighbor Chantrelle to water them while she was away. Behind her, the door in the wooden fence clicked open.

"Hey there," she called without turning around. "How was the——?"

The back door to the house opened and shut. Shannon's stomach tightened into the knot that seldom unraveled these days. She moved the spray to the basil plant, kicking a branch aside, debris from last week's storm. Strands of her straight brown hair swung up and clung to her cheek and she brushed them away.

After coiling up the hose, the tall, sturdy woman walked into the kitchen, basil leaves in hand to give to her mother. Her daughter's tousled hair sprouted above the back of the sofa, in front of which the television displayed a group of loud, prancing singers.

"I was trying to ask you," her mother called, willing herself to be patient, "how your art class went."

When no answer came, Shannon entered the living room and sat on the arm of the sofa.

"I *said*, how did your art class go?"

Eve looked up from her iPad and removed her earbuds. "I didn't hear you."

"Your art class?"

The girl shrugged, eyes fixed on the screen. One shoulder of her cotton T-shirt slipped down and she tugged it up. "It was okay. We did a still life."

"Thank you." Shannon stood up and squared her shoulders. "We're going to eat soon."

Halfway through dinner, Shannon broke the silence. "Did you remember to tell the counselor you're going away in a few days?" She waited as Eve chewed her mouthful of burger to the last swallow.

"I'm not going."

"Of course you're going. We've been planning this for weeks. I've already started packing your stuff."

Her daughter looked up, sudden fire in her eyes. "And I've told you that I want to stay with Grandma."

"You're going to visit your father."

"Like he comes to visit us?" The hormones shifted again, the wounded kitten appearing as she stuffed lettuce into her mouth. "I don't even know him."

"You're coming with me and that's that."

To the curling of Eve's lips, Shannon raised her eyebrows to remind her daughter that she'd brought this on herself. She was lucky Mr. Kim hadn't pressed charges. "Your father said he was looking forward to seeing you. Besides, you'll like Jamaica. It's a very cool place, lots of beaches and mountains."

"I bet they have bugs, and you know I hate bugs."

"What do you expect? It's a tropical country—of course they have bugs. But they also have great food, great music, all kinds of stuff."

"Whatever."

Life had been like this for the last six months: silences interrupted by short-tempered answers or slammed doors. More and more, Shannon found herself watching Eve to assess her mood, controlling the tone and volume she used, weighing what to say. Whenever Eve exploded, Shannon would breathe deeply as the counselor had advised. It was a game of control and she was the adult, she'd remind herself, even if she sometimes felt like crying under the weight of it.

"I thought we could go by my office tomorrow," Shannon said. "I have to fill out some paperwork, and you can thank Angie for letting you go along with me on the trip."

"Since you're *making* me go, do I have to be nice to her?"

"At least be polite, Eve."

The conversation getting exhausting, Shannon started clearing the table. She needed a few minutes to clear her head, too, to think through yet again what she'd discussed with her editor, what would make this assignment different from the work she'd done for the magazine for the last three years—and what could put her life in danger if she didn't watch it.

When she'd signed on to work freelance for *Culture*, Shannon hadn't thought of the job as anything approaching perilous. Modeled after *National Geographic*, the magazine was designed to educate Canadians about the diverse societies crowding the globe and was now known as a journal of some merit. Angie, the middle-aged editor of *Culture*, had recruited Shannon as a photographer by allowing the then forty-six-year-old single mother to work from home. It had been the perfect opportunity to leave her newspaper job at the *Toronto Star*. On the downside, however, the magazine expected her to drop everything and fly off whenever they called. This year alone, she'd been to five different locations, including Texas, for an article on modern Tex-Mex; Australia, for an aboriginal arts festival; and the Netherlands, for the Keukenhof Tulip Festival.

Her latest assignment had come as a shock when Angie had asked her in early June to do a feature on Jamaica's Rastafarians. It was to be a double assignment with double pay. She'd be paid for the photography as well as for writing the article, since the other journalists were on summer holiday or already assigned.

"You're a good writer," Angie had said. "I've seen what you wrote for the Louisiana article when Jeff came down with food poisoning. Not bad, pretty good in fact. We want to use you more to work both sides, copy and visuals—saves us money on expenses and increases your income."

Shannon had laughed. "I guess I'll have to pull out my old journalism textbooks then."

"You'll be fine. You've never disappointed me before."

"Doing the whole article, though, that's a pretty big job."

"I thought you'd be the best person. I mean, you started going to Jamaica—"

"In 1997," Shannon had shot back, "and for two years after that."

She'd agreed to go after some inner twisting, after admitting to herself that she wanted to return to Largo Bay.

It had been too long and she'd loved the place. On her first trip to Jamaica, then a freelance photographer in her early thirties, she'd fallen in love not only with the owner of the Largo Bay Inn but with the island's scenic countryside. Her regular visits during those years had produced thousands of photographs, many of which she'd sold to travel websites, photographs she still looked at when she was feeling nostalgic.

After Eve slouched upstairs to do her homework, Shannon called Chantrelle and invited her over for one of their after-dinner chats. Fifteen minutes later, she was handing a glass of merlot across the kitchen counter to her friend.

"Suppose Eric has met someone, is even living with someone?" Chantrelle asked.

"He's a free man," Shannon replied briskly.

"Right, like you haven't been jogging every morning at the break of day, trying to get back in shape, eh?"

"Oh, stop," Shannon said, a blush coming on. "Just a few extra pounds I need to get rid of. Every bite I eat goes straight to my waist. Anyway, it wouldn't hurt to look good in a bathing suit, but I'm telling you, I have no fantasies about Eric, none whatsoever."

"You can kid yourself, but you can't kid me." Chantrelle took a sip and licked her lips. "What's so great about him, anyway?"

One side of Shannon's mouth slid up. "He's one of the nice guys—you know, authentic, down-to-earth, no airs."

"Why'd you split up then?"

"We never did, actually—after I got pregnant, he just never invited me back. Then I started working with the *Star* and I didn't have time." Shannon looked through the darkened window. "To tell you the truth, I've had this open sore called Eric Keller for fourteen years, and it needs to be cauterized. Anyway, he needs to know his daughter, whatever happens between us."

"Best not to get Eve's hopes up, don't you think?"

"He hurts her enough when he calls on her birthday and says he's coming to see her soon, but soon never comes. And his own son, Joseph, didn't even *know* he had a sister until he went down to Jamaica last year." Shannon gave a little laugh. "I didn't say he was perfect."

After fetching a bottle of olives and two forks, Shannon returned to the counter. "I'm just hoping that spending time with Eric will settle Eve down, you know?" She lowered her voice. "She seems like a lost soul. A year ago she was fine, a bit quiet, maybe, but not a child who would walk into a store and steal anything. I don't know what's come over her."

"It really seems weird."

"Unless it's the friends she's been hanging around with at the new school. I don't even know if she has any friends. She never brings them home. And *stealing*? Where did she get this idea from, to steal something? She refuses to talk about it, too. I tried to get it out of her, but they tell me I'm just to let the counselor handle it."

Popping an olive into her mouth, Shannon shook her head. "*Cigarettes*, of all things? She doesn't even smoke—at least I hope she doesn't."

"Did you tell Eric?"

"Ah-huh. He asked me if it was her first time—like he thinks his daughter is a thief and I've been hiding it from him."

"Should be interesting, the two of them getting to know each other."

"I don't expect them to bond or anything, but at least he can help keep an eye on her while I'm out working. He'll have some idea what I go through every day. I can't leave her with Mom. She seems more afraid of Eve than anything; it's like the tail wagging the dog. She lets Eve play video games the whole day if she wants to. If she tried to steal something again—"

"If ever there was a time for her father to step in, this is it."

After Chantrelle left, Shannon stretched out on the sofa to watch the news, but her mind flew back to her second meeting with her editor about the Jamaican project, the meeting that had been nagging at her for the last two weeks.

"I've been planning this for a while," Angie had said in a conspiratorial tone, leaning her ample chest over the desk, "but I didn't want to say anything to you before I had the money. Getting the editorial board's approval for an article on Rastafarians was the easy part." The older woman had lowered her reading glasses and left them dangling on their chain. "If you decide to take on the job—the whole job—I will personally *double* what the magazine is paying you for the photography and the narrative, so you'll be making four times what you normally make for a photo shoot."

Shannon had stopped breathing as she did the math: C$16,000 plus expenses. "I'm interested in hearing what *the whole job* is."

"It's not only the article, you see. I'm doubling the money because you'd also be solving a mystery that's been hanging over my head for thirty-five years. I want you to take it on because you know Jamaica better than anyone I know."

Shannon had leaned back in her chair, shaking her head. "It's been fourteen years, Angie, and I only used to make brief visits. I still have some connections there, but I—"

"Listen to me first before you decide, *please*." Angie had looked down at the onyx ring she was rubbing. "I want you to find out whatever you can about a woman named Katlyn Carrington. She was my best friend. We went through high school and college together. *Kate*-lyn, but without an *e*. Write it down."

Jotting down the name, Shannon had continued to protest. "I'm not sure I'll be able to get anywhere with it. It would be easy for a person to disappear in Jamaica and never be heard from again—all those mountains—and the country can be a difficult place for a foreigner to burrow into. Remember, I was just a photographer when I was there. Looking for a missing person is going to require more inside access than I've ever had. I can try my best, but—"

"You're my only hope," the editor had said with begging eyes, a woman who wasn't used to begging anybody for anything. "I have absolutely no contacts in Jamaica, zilch, zero."

"Tell me about her, anyway." Shannon sighed.

"She was a dancer, only twenty-seven years old, an exquisite dancer, and she wanted to start her own school here in Toronto. She wanted it to be—different, multiethnic—and since she loved Caribbean music, she decided to move to Jamaica to study traditional dance, so she could integrate it into her new studio. That was back in the seventies, when there was very little black anything here in Canada other than Afros, but Katlyn was always the idealist in our group. She loved Bob Marley, you know, and believed everyone should live together and be happy. So, off she went to Jamaica and ended up renting a room in a town called Gordon Gap. I'll never forget the name because I was dating a guy named Gordon at the time. Anyway, she wrote me a couple of times to say she was loving it, the whole experience, and she was learning a lot about the original music and dances of the island. That was in the days of pen and paper, remember, so mail took a while to go back and forth.

"She was in Gordon Gap for about six months when she started having a relationship with a man, a Rastafarian man. 'A man among men,' she wrote me. She left the house where she was staying, and nobody heard from her for almost a year. No letters, nada. Then, she turns up outside a hospital one morning, dying, literally, and her family in Toronto hears that she's . . . *dead*."

Angie voice had dived to a whisper on the last word, still incredulous after all the years. "Her parents didn't have a lot of money and they weren't very—very, well, educated, but they were just distraught. Her father flew down to get the body—but, lo and behold, the body had disappeared from the hospital morgue the night after her death."

"I can't imagine. What did he do then?"

"Well, her father wasn't the sharpest pencil in the box, you know, so he didn't get very far with the authorities down there. He just came back to Canada and I think he wrote a few letters, but nothing really came of it. Both he and Katlyn's mother grieved themselves to death after that."

"Which hospital did she show up at, do you know?"

"I think he told me once, he might have, anyway, but I cannot for the life of me remember the name now."

"What did the police have to say? They must have filed a report."

"I called the police headquarters myself, a bunch of times, but I always reached a dead end. They passed me from one department to another, one cop's desk to another. As far as I know, the police were never able to track down either the body or the person who took it. I don't know if they even tried."

"I can believe that," Shannon had said flatly, remembering when Eric had called the Port Antonio police about the robbery of a guest's wallet. The policeman had told him to interrogate the workers himself and call them back. They had no vehicle to come to the hotel, the constable had said.

Angie had shaken her head. "I seem to be the only person who even cares what happened. I tried to round up some of our former college friends to make inquiries, but they were either busy working or just didn't want to get involved. I couldn't go down because I had a young family to take care of, not to mention a job."

"What happens if I try but don't find her?"

"If you don't find her, there'll be no money, I'm afraid. I'll use it to hire a private detective or something."

Shannon, always equal to a challenge, had straightened in her chair, mentally dusting off her journalist's hat. "There must have been a postmortem, some sort of coroner's report. What did she die of?"

"Her father said it was something internal, that's what I remember. They were very private people and I didn't know them very well. He didn't seem to want to talk about it at the memorial service." Angie had started counting off points on her fingers. "There are too many questions: Where did she go when she left Gordon Gap? What exactly did she die from? Was she murdered? Was the Rastafarian man responsible for her death? What happened to her body? If there's one thing I want to find out before I die, it's what happened to Katlyn—I owe it to her—and I'm willing to pay to find out."

In answer, the photographer (now photojournalist) and single mom, had stared at her employer wordlessly, the balance in Eve's college-tuition account already increasing by C$16,000.

CHAPTER FOUR

July—the hectic month they'd all been waiting for—had arrived, the first week almost over. The closing on Miss Mac's property next to the bar was to happen in less than a week, the wedding two weeks later, and the ground-breaking the week after that. Shad had already decided that the events were coming together in some heaven-directed schedule intended to change his life forever, and whether he liked it or not, he'd have to go along for the ride.

The list of tasks seemed endless. The first one was moving Miss Mac and her possessions to her son Horace's house. Shad's best friend, Frank, had been corralled to help load up Eric's Jeep and a truck rented by Horace on Thursday coming, the day before the sale of her nine acres to the new hotel company. The other tasks Shad would take on one at a time.

Although the hotel was the priority for Shad (the turning point of his life, he'd decided), in the eyes of Beth and his four children, the wedding was by far the most important of the year's events. Everyone was getting into the act. When he walked into his living room after his Saturday-morning shift, Joella, his eldest, was trying on the brides-maid's dress her mother had sewn for her. From one of the two bedrooms came the sound of a sewing machine roaring away, the vibrations shaking the small wooden house.

"What you think, Dadda?" the seventeen-year-old asked above the noise. She twirled around to show off the full, pink skirt. "I think the top should be strapless, but Mamma say that the wedding is in a church and we must cover up. It look old-fashioned to me."

"I think you lucky to have a mother who can sew such a pretty dress, that's what I think." Shad patted her respectably covered shoulder.

In the bedroom, squeezed between the wall and the foot of the bed, Beth's nose was inches away from the whirring machine, her toes barely touching the foot pedal. One hand held down a swath of shiny blue fabric, the other fed it under the needle. Sweat was sticking the T-shirt to her plump arms, a drop trickling down her neck under the permed hair.

Shad leaned against the door and crossed his arms. "You want the fan?" he shouted above the roar. Beth nodded without looking up, and he clicked on the ceiling fan. "Like how is Saturday, you not selling in the market today?" he asked just as the machine twanged to a stop.

"You see what happen? You make the thread break." Drawing the air through her teeth in a long, disgusted suck, she wet the thread and restrung it. "I don't have time for no market today. I still have to finish Rickia's dress."

"You can't get a little time off from the library during the week to do your sewing?"

"Who going to clean the toilets for them?"

"We have plenty vegetables ready to sell, you know, tomatoes and string beans and potatoes. I been keeping them up on my day off. What you want to do with them?"

"See if you can sell them, nuh?" Beth resumed her sewing.

Before his evening shift, Shad lugged a large basket with vegetables up the Delgados' driveway. He walked to the rear of the house and opened the back door.

"Miss Bertha, you here?" he called into the quiet of the kitchen.

A large dog crossed the black and white tiles toward him wagging its tail.

"Sheba, how you doing? They give away all your puppies?" Shad patted the chocolate Lab, keeping well away. Nobody wanted a bartender with dog hair on his pants. When Sheba padded off, Shad put the basket on the counter and washed his hands, wiping his brow with the paper towel afterward. "Miss Bertha?"

"Coming, coming." The chunky housekeeper appeared in her uniform, fanning herself. After inquiries about the wedding, she settled down to sorting and counting the vegetables. "I glad you bring them. I couldn't get to the market today, I been so busy."

"Is that Shad?" said a voice from the doorway.

Shad looked up. "Shannon, is you?"

The old friends embraced, holding each other tight for a second, Shad's head reaching only to the woman's ear.

"It's been so long," Shannon said, "but you look just the same!"

"And you fill out a little," Shad said, laughing. He didn't want to say that she was lovely, lovely as ever, with her upturned nose and peachy skin, looking as if she should be milking Canadian cows. "You was kind of *mauger* before, you know."

"You're such a diplomat, Shad," she said, her smile wide and easy, the intelligent eyes looking straight at him.

"When did you come?"

"Just got here. We took a taxi because Jennifer and the kids had to go into Kingston for some medical appointments. I heard your voice, so I had to—"

"And who is that—that pretty girl?" Shad interrupted, pointing to the somber-looking adolescent at the door. "Is that Eve?"

"That's right," Shannon said with a tight smile.

In response to her mother's wave, the girl came forward, almost dragging her feet.

"Take your earbuds out, Eve, and come and meet Shad," Shannon said, gesturing.

The girl pulled the plugs out of her ears and stuffed them in her pocket. Something about the child was unhappy, he thought, her eyes down most of the time, the round face inherited from her mother made plainer by her refusal to let it smile. The blouse she wore didn't help either; it slouched off her shoulder and sank into her hunched chest.

"We glad to have you in Largo, Eve." Shad touched her arm and she pulled away, only an inch or so, and he dropped his hand. "Can you believe, I know your mother from before you was born? She used to come to the Largo Bay Inn—and we love to have her every time." The bartender started play-acting Shannon's coming into the lobby, burdened with her bags and cameras, looking for her taxi driver.

"And Rufus was always late for you, remember?" he said to Shannon.

"Like yesterday." She laughed. "And I would wait by the lobby bar with you until he came."

"You tell me about Canada and how the leaves change colors and what snow feel like on your face."

"And you'd tell me where I should take photographs. Remember that time Rufus and I went looking for this river gorge you'd told us about, and how we got lost for hours? Boy, did I let you have it the next day!"

They sat at the kitchen table while Miss Bertha went to get the money for the vegetables, and Eve slunk out the door. Shannon asked the names of the children (*four* now?) and what they were doing. She and Eve might still be here for the wedding, she added, but she wasn't sure. It depended on how much work she got done. Although it meant two more mouths to feed, Shad assured her they were invited to the wedding. Eve didn't look as if she'd eat curry goat, anyway.

Miss Bertha came back with the money. "The two of you just make yourself comfy. I going to the back to do laundry."

"Tell me what happened to the hotel, Shad," Shannon said after Miss Bertha had left. "I was looking at it from the verandah and it—it just broke my heart. It was so beautiful. It's not even part of the mainland anymore, nobody told me that. After the storm hit, I kept trying to call, but I couldn't get through for weeks. They kept saying the circuits were down. The news on TV was pretty dismal, but I had no idea . . ." She stopped, blinking hard. "When I finally got through to the Delgados, Eric was staying here, and he—he just made light of it, said there was a bit of damage which would take some time to repair, but I wasn't to worry about it. He never said a word about it becoming an island, and we never discussed it again.

"Well"—she looked away—"we don't talk much, any-way. But the next thing Jennifer said was that he was open-

39

ing a bar. I thought—I don't know what I thought—that the hotel was being repaired, slowly, maybe."

Shad started in on the dreary story that he hated to tell but she had to hear. "It was a terrible storm, terrible. When the radio tell us it was coming, Mistah Eric sent the guests to the big hotels in Port Antonio and Ocho Rios, and he told the receptionists and housekeepers to go home. The men stayed and battened down the shutters and put the furniture up on blocks. Then he told me to drive the men home that afternoon and park the Jeep in Mistah Lambert's garage."

"Why didn't Eric leave?"

"He say he have to stay in case anything happen. Early next morning, now, the wind start picking up and it was dark, dark. You could hardly see the gate in front of your house it was so dark. Then Albert start to scream—"

"Albert?"

"The hurricane—no baby in Jamaica call Albert after that. Anyway, the wind start, a hundred and eighty miles an hour, pure hellfire wind, I telling you. Everything was blowing down, shutters tearing off, branches breaking, dog and cat flying through the air. The roof come right off the house next door to me, but my house was good. I just finish putting on a new roof with the last of the money Granny leave me, so Beth, me, and the children was fine. But the village, Lord, help us, the village look terrible when we come out after it was over, almost nighttime then. Every blade of grass gone, every house near the beach get flood out."

Shannon's eyes opened wide. "Did anyone die?"

"Two people dead—Miss Queenie grandbaby when a

tree fall on her house, and an old man who didn't have much sense. But we was lucky in my house, only two windows break."

"What happened to the—the driveway to the hotel?"

"You remember Old Man Job telling the boss from long time to build a retaining wall along the driveway?"

"I remember that."

"And the boss always say he don't have no money to build no wall. For seven years, people telling him to build a wall, even Mistah Lambert—I hear him with my own ears. The driveway going to wash away, Mistah Lambert say, but the boss was too hard ears. He say his hotel strong, no storm can mash it up.

"Then come Albert, and the boss couldn't believe his eyes because he never gone through a hurricane before. The waves come up twenty feet, come right over the cliff and sweep straight through the hotel. He alone was there, and he climb on top of the reception desk to stay away from the water, so he say."

"He never thought of running away?"

"Too late, rain was falling thick, thick. He have to wait for the eye of the hurricane so he could make a dash for it."

"And did he?"

"When the eye come through, the wind and rain stop and the waves get lower. So he come down off the desk and walk outside and take a look at what happen. The roof on the dining room was gone and the roof over the other building where he was, the guest rooms and reception area, was coming off. He know he have to leave now, because the wind going to come back, and he start wading down the driveway before the second half of the hurricane hit."

The little man stood up, gesturing. "He get to the end of the guest-room building now—and the driveway *gone.* It wash away, just like Old Man Job and Mistah Lambert had said. No land was left between the hotel and the main road. He find himself on an island."

"Oh, my God."

"He decide to jump in the water and start swimming." Shad's arms churned, windmill-like, in the imaginary ocean. "He swimming, swimming, thinking he could make it, but he never realize the waves was still high. Halfway across now, the storm start to lick again behind the eye, and the waves get big again. He said he never swallow so much water in all his life, but he make it to the beach and crawl up to the main road, *naked.* He decide to come to the Delgados' house, and he fighting wind and rain now, dodging tree limb and everything, crawling up the driveway—this very driveway outside here—and he make it to the verandah and bang on the door, and Mistah Lambert pull him inside."

Shad sat down, drained, and they both looked out the kitchen window at the orphaned island. From this distance, the ocean surrounding it looked as harmless as a baby's blanket.

"And he built the bar," Shannon said, adding a sigh that mourned the old and accepted the new.

"But like his spirit die with the hotel, and he didn't have no money to build it back."

"I had no idea—"

"But time is longer than rope—you ever hear that saying? It look like we going to have another hotel now."

"*Another* hotel? Is Eric building it?"

"Is a three-partner business—the boss going to be the

managing partner, then an American man named Danny Caines going to put up the money, and me. I going to be a partner, too, and help run it. How you like that?"

After answering Shannon's questions, Shad said he had to go to work, and she walked him to the front door.

"Tell Beth hello for me," she said. "We'll have to *labrish*—isn't that the word for 'chat'? I've almost forgotten my patois."

"You better brush up on your wedding *labrish*," he said, shaking his head, "because is that Beth going to talk the whole time."

Starting down the driveway with his basket, Shad turned to wave, and Shannon waved back, her smile sad but hopeful. Off to the right, the young girl was looking through a living-room window, a frown on her farm-girl face.

CHAPTER FIVE

The four young people arrived in their open-sided Wrangler with its canvas top rolled back—as if their tans could get any darker—and ordered Red Stripes.

"From the mud on the car, looks like you've been doing a bit of driving," Eric ventured after he'd served them. He never knew how to speak to this new breed of visitors with their sun-bleached hair and braided bracelets, not an inch of fat on their bodies.

"Yeah, we've just come down from the Blue Mountains," one of the men said, tattoos from his shoulders to his wrists. "We were hoping to find some beaches where we could kite-surf, but we haven't found any yet."

"Kitesurf?"

"You know, the big wing things you surf over the water with?"

"That's a new one on me."

"It's really great in Aruba," one woman said. "They have those long, flat beaches."

Eric looked toward the parking lot. Shad was always better with these types. "Maybe you should try Negril."

"Too many tourists," the other boy said with a grin that boasted a half-broken tooth in front, a badge of kitesurfing honor, perhaps. The four left twenty long minutes and a small tip later.

Eric turned on the radio as he cleaned off the counter. A news reporter was talking about a shoot-out in Kingston's torrid Mountain View neighborhood, two gunmen killed by police, and he switched off the radio. A man could hear only so much bad news when he had no money in the bank. He was piling beer bottles into the empties crate when Shad appeared, balancing a basket on his head.

"Is that your new job, market woman?"

"Good for my posture." The bartender took down the basket. "It kept knocking me on my leg coming down from the Delgados' house."

"What were you doing up there?"

"Selling vegetables—I turn market woman now, like you say." Shad went around the partition to the kitchen and returned without the basket. He started bustling around, preparing the bar for the Saturday-evening clientele.

"You know you're late, right?"

"Sorry, boss, I started talking." Shad flashed the Bugs Bunny grin he used to get himself out of trouble. "And you know who I was talking to?"

"Let me guess." Eric turned away. "Shannon." She was finally here, not two thousand miles away anymore—but across the street and in full view of the blighted hotel. "Did you see Eve?"

"Yes."

"How was she?"

"She going to need time to get to know us."

"I better go up to Lambert's."

Eric returned to his apartment and took a shower. As

he shaved, he leaned in to the mirror, examining the new grooves around his eyes. He'd deteriorated since Shannon had last seen him. The Caribbean had a way of beating up white guys, turning their skin red and dry, but he cleaned up pretty good—even if his bar was just a shack with barstools.

Minutes after he emerged from his apartment, he saw Jennifer, Casey, Shannon, and Eve (Sheba trotting behind) crossing the road. Shad scurried away to the kitchen, as if he couldn't bear to watch.

"Hey, there," Jennifer called as they walked up the conch-lined path. She was wearing shorts and sandals, Casey on her heels, a smaller, browner version of her mother.

A step behind them, Shannon waved with a book in her hand. She looked . . . *like a woman*, Eric thought, no longer the gangly fawn he'd first met or the anxious mother he'd last seen. Her hair, which used to be short, now fell to her shoulders, a few gray strands sparkling among the brown, and she was wearing a flowing white skirt and blouse. Her long strides had a gracefulness, a self-assurance, he hadn't seen before.

"Hello, you handsome devil," Jennifer said and kissed him on both cheeks.

"Eric," Shannon said, holding the book between them as she leaned in to kiss his cheek, a cool, clean scent around her. He didn't remember her wearing perfume before.

"Good to see you," he replied.

"Hey, Uncle Eric, whazzup?" Casey bubbled.

"You know what?" Eric said after she'd hugged him. "Your father is going to have to beat off the boys soon."

Casey boasted that she'd just had her thirteenth birthday. "I'm a teenager now."

"How's boarding school?"

"Finished for the summer, that's all we need to know." She grinned.

"Eve, come say hello to your father," Shannon said, turning around.

A gloomy shadow to her mother's glowing presence, his daughter loitered behind, the torn jeans and baggy blouse matching the tangle of hair that hid one eye. She didn't look like a criminal, just a shy girl hoping to avoid attention.

"Welcome to Largo Bay, Eve." He held on to her stiff arms to give her a kiss and she leaned over to pat Sheba as soon as he released her.

"She's still getting used to the heat, I think," her mother commented.

"Good reminder," he said, "let's all have something cool to drink. I'll get Shad."

After Eric returned from the kitchen with the bartender, Solomon came shuffling in, his white chef's uniform (a souvenir from the old hotel) starched and pressed down to the fraying cuffs and collar. Holding his hat in one hand, the tall man lowered his chin and stared at the woman before him.

"Solomon!" Shannon cried.

"I don't believe it," the old man said in his rumbling voice as she hugged him. "You come back to us?"

"She's visiting." Eric introduced Solomon to Eve, grateful for the distraction.

"I know you from your picture," the old cook told Eve. She put out her hand, warding off a hug, and he shook it gravely.

"Do you still make that fabulous oxtail? I told Eve about it." Shannon said *about* in her Canadian way, and Eric felt

47

a tug in his heart that accompanied the memory of teasing her that it wasn't *a-boat*.

"Solomon is the man for oxtail," Shad confirmed.

The cook beamed, lips closed tight, and left for his kitchen duty.

"I brought something for you, Shad," Shannon said (*And nothing for me,* Eric noted), and gave the bartender the book she was holding, the hard, red cover well handled.

"*Grossman's Guide to Wines, Beers, and Spirits,*" Shad read slowly.

"The best, they tell me," she said. "Can you use it?"

"A book about keeping a bar?"

"It was my father's." Eric recalled a photograph of the bulky man he'd avoided, not wanting to explain why he wasn't marrying his daughter. "He liked to try a different drink every evening. I wanted you to have it."

Beaming at the volume, the bartender nodded. "Imagine? Your father used to hold this book in his hands just like me. Thank you, thank you."

"If you need Eric to read it to you—"

"No, no, I can read good now. Miss Mac been teaching me from last year and I can read documents and all kind of things."

Shad went behind the counter and placed his gift in the drawer he referred to as his library. He'd once shown Eric the only other book in the drawer, *The Secret World of the Private Investigator*, a gift from a hotel guest long ago, and he'd admitted that his only other book in the world was a dictionary he'd bought for the children. "I don't want them to be ignorant like me," he'd added, making a funny mouth.

A few regulars were drifting in for their Saturday-evening fixes. Eric greeted them by name, glad that Shannon could see he still had customers who respected him. He herded Shannon and her party to his table, and Shad took their drink orders.

When it came to Eve's turn, the bartender leaned toward her. "You want to try some coconut water?" he asked with a wink.

The girl looked perplexed. "What's it taste like?"

"Like manna from heaven."

She shrugged after he turned away.

"So, you're doing research into Rastafarianism," Eric said to Shannon.

"I think they call it the Rastafarian Movement now," she replied, an invisible punch to his stomach.

"Where are you going to start?"

"I want to find Rufus first. Remember him, my old taxi driver? I thought we'd drive around the area to begin with, talk to a few Rastas—"

"Rufus gone to Montego Bay," Shad called from behind the bar. "He running his father's barbershop now."

"Oh, no." Shannon wrinkled her nose in the funny way she always had. "Is there another driver I could use? I want to be free to shoot scenery and spot locations from the passenger seat."

"The only taxi driver in Largo with a decent car is Carlton," Shad responded. "But he come from Kingston. He don't know the country parts so well yet."

"What do you need exactly?" Jennifer asked.

"I'm starting from scratch since I didn't really know anything about Rastas when I came down before. Seeing them play in a band doesn't qualify, I'm afraid. I'm going to have to go into their communities, meet them where they are. And since I'm pretty green here, I need somebody who knows where Rastas live. From the research I've been doing, I've read that there are three main groups"—Shannon tapped her fingers on the table—"the Nyabinghi, the Bobo Ashanti, and the Twelve Tribes. I want to interview at least one of each, and I want to interview as many Rastas as I can find otherwise."

"Is Rasta—Rastafari a religion?" Eve asked, her eyes sliding to the ground.

"Some people think so," her father said. "Some people say it's a lifestyle and a philosophy. It's been around for a while."

The girl was slouched in her seat, still not looking at him, but he could tell she was listening, and he liked that she asked good questions. It reminded him of when they'd been at the zoo when she was five and she'd told him that kangaroos came from Australia.

"How do you know?" he'd asked her, pretending he didn't know.

"My teacher told us and she's from Australia," Eve had reported in her pert voice. "She told us about the big reef, too." He'd been tickled that she knew about kangaroos and the Great Barrier Reef, glad that she was smart—and that her mother was bringing her up.

"From what I've been reading," Shannon was telling Eve now, "the Rastafarian Movement is a combination of a spiritual, social, and economic lifestyle." Shannon pushed her daughter's hair back and Eve turned her head away. "They're opposed to greed and colonialism. It's about improving life for the poor, living together in camps to support one another, eating healthy food—"

"Not all Rastas live in camps," Jennifer said. "A lot live like regular people, in towns or on small farms. And they're not all poor, either. Things have changed a lot in the last twenty years. Some are professionals now, lawyers and doctors, some work for the government."

"And they smoke a lot of ganja," Eric said, "so get ready to inhale."

Shannon kept a straight face. "I know they use marijuana for their religious ceremonies. I don't know how much they do outside of that. I guess I'll find out."

"Are you going to smoke any?" Casey asked, grinning.

"Of course not."

Eric stifled a laugh, remembering Shannon smoking weed in his suite once, and how he'd opened the windows and turned on the fan so the staff wouldn't smell it.

"Why do they wear their hair in those—long rope things?" Eve asked.

"Dreadlocks?" her mother responded. "I was asking this guy who sells ice cream on Yonge Street, a sweet, young Rastafarian man, and he said that it had to do with his belief in Jah, that's their name for God. I guess I'll find out exactly what."

"You could start with a few Rastas here in Largo," Eric put in. "They're a bit more—they're a decent lot."

"As opposed to what?" Shannon queried.

"You know, they're used to tourists and regular people. The Rastas who live in the camps, well, sometimes they don't like people coming around. They've been known to—I could be wrong—but I've heard that they can get pretty hostile if visitors ask too many questions."

"She okay, no problem," Shad said, doling out the

drinks. "But she going to need two local people to go with her." Eric shot him a questioning look. "Is true, boss. She need somebody to drive the car and watch out for crazy taxis and buses, and she need somebody else to give the driver directions and make sure she safe. Not that anything going to happen to her, but she need some manpower with her if she going to go up into the mountains and all over."

"And you're just the manpower she needs, right?" Eric said.

"Are you moonlighting your way into another job, Shad?" Jennifer teased.

"We not going in no moonlight; daytime I talking. Like how Beth is working in Port Antonio and she not at home at lunchtime anymore, I have plenty free time in the middle of the day, right, boss? Carlton can drive her and I can help her."

Shannon looked at Eric. "What do you say, boss? Sounds like a good idea to me."

Cornered by years of guilt, Eric nodded. "Sure, I can take care of the bar while he's gone."

"I really appreciate that," Shannon said. "I could rent a car and Shad could drive it. Would that work?"

"I think the taxi driver arrangement is better," Eric said quickly. He wouldn't tell her that his employee didn't have a driver's license and probably couldn't get one with his prison record, even though Eric let him drive the Jeep.

"Should be fun," Shad said gleefully. "More fun than sitting in the bar."

Eric swallowed a sarcastic comment and turned to Eve. "Interested in helping me out while these two are gone?"

"Not pouring liquor, I hope," her mother shot back.

Another comment swallowed, Eric raised his hand. "I'll be behind the bar and she can take food orders and run them to the kitchen. No alcohol, I promise."

They all looked at Eve, who took a sip of coconut water and grimaced.

"You can keep the tips," Eric told her, and she shrugged again.

Jennifer tossed back her hair. "And the rest of the time you can spend with Casey."

"I guess," Eve replied.

"Eve's in a new school," Shannon blurted out, glancing sideways at her daughter. "I think she likes it so far—don't you?—although it's only been a year. It's really progressive, part of a chain started in Germany. They aim to develop students to be well rounded, you know, strong bodies, creative thinkers. Ninety-four percent of their graduates go on to university."

Eric tried not to think of the college payments ahead, while Jennifer and Shannon compared day schools to boarding schools. Casey followed up with a story about a midnight picnic in her dorm, the food hidden under the sheets when the monitor appeared. Everyone laughed and even Eve cracked a smile.

After the visitors left, Eric placed the empty glasses in the sink and nudged Shad's elbow. "You wormed your way nicely into that one."

"Think of it this way, boss. Shannon need somebody she can trust to go with her. The taxi driver not going to shaft her because I going to be there, and she have two men to protect her. You know it not easy for a foreign woman to move around Jamaica by herself."

"You're probably right."

"And you get to spend time with your daughter."

"She didn't seem too keen, but I hope she liked the tip idea."

"You never know with them teenagers. They keep their good feelings for their friends and let the parents see the bad ones—like they want to torment you. When Joella was twelve, she used to suck her teeth so much that Beth had to slap her one time."

"I couldn't do that, but I wish Eve was—happier, you know?"

"Next to Casey—"

"That should be interesting, the two of them together. Casey's like a debutante waiting to come out."

"A *debu*—what?"

"A little beauty queen, all pretty and giggly."

Sitting on his verandah later, Eric filled one of his pipes with the Canadian maple tobacco that always reminded him of Shannon. She'd introduced him to it when she brought it down once as a gift. In those days, she'd appear out of the blue and lean on his office door, making his heart jump. He'd tell his secretary not to disturb them, and they'd run up to his suite and start kissing before he'd shut the door. After an hour of frenzy, they'd call room service—she was always famished—so she could devour Solomon's specialty of the day. It was the affair of affairs, the best of his life, which came to a screeching halt the afternoon his lover made her announcement over dessert.

"You're pregnant?" he'd spluttered. "I thought you were on the pill."

"I must have skipped a day—"

"You don't just skip a day with birth control."

She'd looked at her spoon, laden with lime sherbet. "Well, I did."

"Are you sure you're—"

"You pee in a cup, the test comes back positive—you're sure."

"Have you thought of—you don't have to have it, you know."

She'd dropped the spoon with a clatter. "I'm keeping the baby, Eric. I'm not having an abortion."

Everything, everything had changed in that moment, the lusty passion transformed—like ice water falling on fire—by the dull reality of parenthood.

He lit the pipe, shielding it with his palm, let the wind blow out the match, and settled back in the chair. The verandah faced the ruined hotel, and tonight a quarter moon glittered off the water, the island a black rock in its midst, a stiff northeaster carrying the flapping of the leaves from the almond tree that he'd planted long ago in front of the reception area.

This was his evening ritual, looking across at his destroyed hotel, watching its ghostlike appearance and disappearance under a waxing or waning moon as each month slipped by, and it had been a comfort knowing that he still owned the isolated piece of land and its mildewed buildings, regardless of Hurricane Albert's destruction. However, he was no longer the sole owner. The island now belonged to the corporation formed earlier that year to build the new hotel, and there were plans to lease it to Horace MacKenzie for a campsite—Eric's son Joseph's idea. Renovations were to begin in a few months. Truth be told, Eric would have preferred the buildings to remain mottled, empty, and *his*, no one else's, because they housed not only the past, his glory days as the owner of the inn, but more recently they reminded him of Simone, who had lived under a tarpaulin in the roofless lobby for two months last summer.

A brave woman, or perhaps only a woman with nothing to lose, she'd stood up to Eric and Shad when they'd confronted her under the tarp, and needing the money to replace the thatch roof on the bar, Eric had ended up renting the island to her. When she'd left, he'd felt all life go out of the ruins, missed knowing he could row out to see her, missed the flickering light of her lamp he'd watch from his verandah as she moved around at night, cooking or getting ready for bed. He'd yearned for her every night ever since, thought about her as the waves crashed on the cliff beneath the porch, each tremor sending him deeper into reverie. Grieving her nightly had been the only reward to his day.

Now everything was about to change. The island was going to go through a transition and Simone was coming back—to meet Shannon and Eve. He exhaled the Canadian maple, picturing the two women sitting in the bar, Simone on his right and Shannon on his left, civilized darts flying between them, and him, of course, skewered in the middle.

CHAPTER SIX

S hannon stood up from the breakfast table. "Are you going over to your dad's today?"

"Boring." Eve was still in her nightclothes, the T-shirt she'd had on the day before and a pair of stretched-out cotton pants she always wore to bed. Her iPod was sitting on the table next to the glass of orange juice, her only concession to breakfast.

"It's up to you." Her mother took a last sip of her coffee. "I'm leaving in a few minutes. Maybe you can do something with Casey."

The wounded look was back. "I don't know these people. You can't just bring me here and dump me—"

"I couldn't leave you in Toronto either." Shannon picked up the two cameras on the table and slung them over her shoulder.

"You're always leaving me in Toronto. I don't know what's so different this time."

"You can't be trusted *this time*." To hell with the counselor. Into her safari-jacket pockets Shannon dropped a small tape recorder and her cell phone. She was getting tired of measuring her words. She had a job to do, two jobs if she had to find out about this Katlyn woman, and Eve needed to know that.

"I'll play games on my iPad," Eve grunted.

"Or help your father in the restaurant."

"Babysitting an old man all day? I don't think so."

"Well, you choose. I have to work."

"When are we going home? If it's more than a week, I'll kill myself."

"I told you, I don't know yet. I have a lot of work to do and we'll go home when it's done—and stop being so dramatic. You know how many kids would love to be in Jamaica?"

"When are you getting back?"

"Probably midafternoon." A horn tooted outside. "That's Shad and the taxi driver." Shannon planted a kiss on Eve's cheek. "Be good, or at least be nice."

On her way through the living room, Shannon looked off at the morning-hazy mountains and bays stretching in front of the verandah. She was glad to leave her daughter's sourness behind. If she could help it, she wasn't going to let Eve interfere with her pleasure at being back on the island and back in Largo—a change she'd needed more than she'd realized. She'd told Jennifer and Lambert the evening before that she was feeling her shoulders slowly descending.

"I'd forgotten that, whenever I'm here, I become like a Jamaican, kind of relaxed and easygoing," she'd said, knowing it was a half-truth, knowing she couldn't completely relax around Eve or Eric.

Cool morning air greeted her on the verandah. At the top of the driveway a small, red sedan with shiny rims sat waiting, Shad waving out the back window. After she climbed in, she was introduced to Carlton, the driver, whom Shad instructed to descend the driveway and turn right on the main road.

"We can start with a Rasta man here in Largo," Shad explained. "He know my granny from way back."

Carlton, a silent nodder, wove the car around potholes and up dirt lanes until they arrived at the base of the mountain that rose behind Largo. They stopped in front of a wooden cottage, its fresh red, yellow, and green trim singing out behind the rusty zinc fence. The man Shad had in mind wasn't home, his elderly wife reported from the door. Her long dreadlocks were tied back and she was wearing a housedress, the front of it wet.

"Can I speak to you, then?" Shannon asked, thinking it might be a good idea to start her interviews with a female. All of the books she'd researched over the last few weeks had been written by men, and she was ready for another perspective.

It took more than a little persuasion on Shad's part for the woman, Leah was her name, to be interviewed.

"I washing right now, but I try to help," she said at last, sitting down on one of the four concrete steps leading up to the house.

"Do you mind if I record you?" Shannon said, but Leah declined and the photojournalist took out her notebook.

In answer to the first question, the Rasta said that she and her husband were members of the Nyabinghi, but they didn't belong to a church. "Our God is Jah, and Jah is God of all, and Jah-Rastafari don't need no walls." She and her man had been together for thirty-eight years, and she'd become a Rasta after she met him. What seemed to interest her most was describing the *ital* food she cooked, which she pronounced *eye-tal*.

"Is spiritual food, and it must be full of *itality*. It must increase the *livity*, the strength that Rastaman get from God, and everything must be natural, natural as possible. If we drink juice, we must juice the orange with our two hands, you see me? When we cooking, we don't put in no salt, and we don't eat nothing coming out of a tin, nothing that mix up in a factory, nothing with no chemicals. We eat plenty fruit and vegetables, no pork, no meat. But we eat fish and sometimes little chicken, when we can get it. We don't eat no crab or lobster or shrimp, though, no bottom scavengers."

The conversation ended when a boy, tiny dreadlocks sprouting from his head, came to the door and said he was hungry. Shannon asked if she could take a few photographs before she left, and Leah agreed, as long as she could take them with her grandson. Shannon photographed the two standing on the step, the boy sticking out his chest, his feet at right angles.

Back on the road, Shad directed Carlton to drive to the village square.

"We have one Rasta man who fix everybody's shoes," Shad explained while wiping his brow. "I don't like to disturb him, like how he working now, but he might be able to give us a little direction."

"We're doing well for a first day, don't worry," Shannon said. "It always takes a few days to start getting into the story."

Ras Walker's shoe stand near the village square was a small bamboo shack; from its roof hung a red flag with a lion in the middle. Inside the shack, shelves were laden with shoes held together with elastic bands, one shelf reserved for new leather sandals with a stamped pattern. Three tall drums stood on the ground underneath them.

"Ras Walker, blessings!" Shad hailed the man behind

the counter, and hammer in hand, the man touched his heart in greeting. "I have a nice Canadian lady visiting us who need to talk to you. She is the baby mother for Mistah Eric and she writing about Rasta people." Shannon winced a little at the introduction, understanding for the first time what her standing in Largo was now: Eric's baby mother.

The news seemed to have an effect on the middle-aged Rastafarian, who said he could give her five minutes. He had a customer coming back shortly to pick up his shoes. With his waist-length locks and enormous smile, he'd be an excellent subject for a photograph, Shannon decided as Shad retreated to wait in the car with Carlton.

"Shad don't recommend anybody who not a good person," Walker told her, "so you must be trustable. You will overstand what I and I have to say."

"I won't take up much of your time," Shannon said, settling on the stool he offered. "I'm working for a magazine and—"

"You know anything about Rasta?"

"A little from what I've been reading."

"Is a whole different way of seeing the world, you overstand?" The man selected a tiny nail and tapped it into the sole of the shoe he was working on.

"One thing that fascinates me is the language you use. Why do you say *I and I*, or *I-man*, and *overstand*, when other people say *I* and *understand*?"

"Rasta language is not like everyman language. Some people call it *livalect*, different from dialect, you know, because I and I believe words is a powerful thing. Where you have sound, you have power. Words have a meaning higher than man. That mean"—Walker searched for another nail—"you say *I*, but we say *I and I* because we believe that a man always connected to Jah. No man stands alone, so is I and Jah, I and I, not I one."

"What about *overstand*?"

"When you say *understand* now, you using a weak word. Being *under* is weaker than being *over*, right, so Rasta say *overstand*. I and I use power words, not weak words. You must ask Shad to translate for you." Walker chuckled. "He know the language good. Is in every song he play on the radio in the bar, ask him."

While Walker continued hammering nails into the heel of the shoe, he told her that he was from St. Thomas, the parish south of Portland and over the mountains. When he was a teenager, he'd worked with some Rastafarian fishermen and had come to like their attitude toward life. He'd started growing a beard and dreadlocks, although his mother didn't approve. The men came from the hills above where the Walkers lived, from a community known as the Bongo Rastafari. The leader of the group was Prince Michael, a man Walker respected a lot because he was a wise man. When he was in his early twenties, Walker had moved to the community, and there he'd learned shoemaking. More important, he'd learned to *reason*, to debate the meaning of life and his place in it.

"We would wear white. You ever see those people? . . . No? You not on that side of the island and you don't go to Kingston, that's why. They wear turbans on their head, so you don't see the dreadlocks."

"Why do Rastas do that, grow their hair long and let it get—?" Shannon asked, waving a hand over her own head, thinking of Eve's question.

"You ever hear of Samuel one, verse eleven? They was talking about Samson. When his mother was asking Jah to give her a son, she promise that her child will serve God all the days of his life and that no razor shall come upon his head. And Jah give her a powerful son. But he meet a woman called Delilah, and she cut off him hair and cut off him strength, and he get weak after that. Rasta believe that hair is strength. Jah give us our hair, and I and I not supposed to cut it."

She nodded, juggling mentally—translating the patois, scribbling in her notebook, thinking of the next question. "Why did you leave the Bongo community?"

"It was too strictlike, and I and I more of an independent type, you know? Too much strictness tie up I and I mind and spirit."

Ras Walker bent his head to the shoe again, but Shannon had one more question. "I noticed those drums in the back." She closed her notebook. "Do you play them?"

"Sometimes. But my son play better than me. He teach drumming."

After taking photographs of the shoemaker over his metal repair boot and beside the flag, Shannon walked back to the car. She had a lot to think about, she realized, a lot more research to do, including beginning to look into Katlyn's disappearance.

"Do either of you know where Gordon Gap is?" she asked Carlton and Shad when they were under way. The two men discussed the location and decided that, no, it wasn't Gordon Town near Kingston, and, yes, it must be the village in the hills above Oracabessa, about thirty miles west of Largo.

"You know somebody up there?" Shad wanted to know.

"No, but I want to make some inquiries."

"We finish for the day?" Carlton asked.

"Yes, all done," Shannon said. "Shad, would you like to have lunch with me?"

"Sure, man, like how my kitchen at home cold now."

Before Carlton left them at Lambert's, Shannon arranged to pay him weekly, and he agreed to pick her up at ten the next morning. All was quiet in the Delgados' house when she and Shad walked in, only the wooden floors creaking under them in the midday warmth. Bertha was in the kitchen polishing silver, the chocolate Lab stretched out on the cool tiles beside her.

"Miss Jennifer take the children to Carel Beach to swim and Eve gone with them," Bertha reported. "You hungry?"

While she was making their lunch, the housekeeper talked about her own daughter, who'd been a teenager when Shannon had seen her last. "She working in a hospital in Baltimore, doing nursing. She making plenty money. I don't see her for three years now."

"Don't you miss her?" Shannon asked.

The woman looked up in surprise. "Every month she send money for me to build my own house—it worth the missing." Bertha laid out the lunch and left them in the kitchen.

"This morning—it was helpful to you?" Shad bit into his tuna sandwich.

"A good start, but there's so much history and philosophy behind the whole Rasta thing, I hope I can do it justice. There's a big difference between reading about it and talking to Rastas in person, you know."

"One interview at a time, right?"

"It's more complicated than that, though. There's something else I need to be doing at the same time."

"Just let me know and I tell Carlton to take us there."

Shannon set down her sandwich. "Remember I asked about Gordon Gap? That's my other reason for being here."

"What you mean?"

"I'm looking for—something happened to a Canadian woman over thirty years ago and my editor wants me to find out what happened to her. She came down to Jamaica to learn about the music and dance here. She was my editor's friend, and from what Angie—that's my editor—says, she was a sweet woman, in her late twenties, who was a bit naive, kind of idealistic. She came from a poor family and went to college on a scholarship, majoring in fine arts—that means like painting and dance and so on. Angie said she was really caring, always had a stray dog or cat she was taking care of, a good-hearted person. Before she came down to Jamaica, she was working in a store that sold dance clothes and she was teaching modern dance in a studio in Toronto. She'd always loved reggae music, and she started talking about coming to Jamaica to learn more about the dances down here. Her plan was to go back to Toronto and teach them."

"How she disappeared?" Shad narrowed his eyes.

"Angie doesn't know, and I could only find two brief newspaper articles in the *Globe* about her disappearance—about the disappearance of her body from a hospital morgue. The articles never mentioned which hospital."

Her listener's eyes stretched wide as he put down his sandwich. "What you mean? Her—how her body disappear?"

"That's what I'm supposed to find out. All I know for certain is that she had a Rastafarian boyfriend and left where she was living in Gordon Gap. Then she was found on the steps of some hospital very sick, and after her death her body vanished into thin air. She was an only child, so it must have hit her parents hard when they were told. The father came down, but he couldn't find out anything. Both parents have died, Angie said, but she wants to know what happened."

"What really happened to her, though?"

"She was young and foolish, I'm thinking. Maybe she fell in love with this fellow—"

"And she get caught up in something like drugs or crime."

"Something that killed her."

"And they take her body because they didn't want it examined."

"Then why did they take her to the hospital at all?" Shannon insisted. "They could have just buried the body after she died. Doesn't make sense, does it?"

Shad dabbed at his mouth with his napkin. "I asking myself, what would I do if my daughter disappear like that? I would hunt under every rock and bush, I'm telling you. But, you know, maybe the father didn't know where to start. Jamaica can be a difficult place to do any business like investigating things. The police busy all the time fighting gunmen, and they don't pay you no mind." Shad narrowed his eyes. "This kind of job call for somebody who dedicated to it, who understand how to talk to witnesses and look for clues, seen? And even if is a cold case—so they call it on TV—somebody need to finish it off, so living people can get satisfaction, you know?"

"It doesn't seem right, I agree."

"Like the dead woman just crying out for you to find her resting place, Shannon. I can hear her—you can't hear her?" He tilted his head back. "Shannon, Shad," he wailed in a high-pitched voice, "come and find me. I'm here, I'm here."

"You're a trip, Shad." Shannon shook her head and smiled.

Shad took a sip of his lemonade. "You know where in Gordon Gap she was living, though?"

"Haven't a clue, and I don't know how I'm going to get around to it, with all the research for the article I have to do and the photographs I have to take. It's a big job, eh?"

Shad pushed away from the table, looking smug. "I knew there was some reason I supposed to help you. All I doing in the car now is falling asleep, anyway, because Carlton don't talk much."

"But now there are two jobs to do. What if we have to go in different directions?"

"No problem, man. Let we just focus on looking for this lady and you can interview any Rastas you find on the way. Plenty Rastas all across Jamaica, and if she have a Rasta boyfriend like you say, my head telling me he was living in a camp near Gordon Gap. We can kill two bird with one stone."

"Gordon Gap tomorrow, then."

They discussed Shad's hourly rate for his part in the deal. He was happy for the extra money, he said, because he and Beth were spending all their money on the wedding, and with Joella going off to Titchfield High School in September, the extra cash would come in handy.

"By the way," Shannon warned him, "you're the only

person in Largo I've talked to about Katlyn—that's her name. I don't want anyone to worry about me, and I know they'd try to stop me from looking into it because it could be dangerous. I haven't told Eve because she'd probably end up telling Casey or Jennifer, you know kids. As for Eric, he's bound to try and stop us, and he's going to be negative about the whole thing, but they're paying me extra to find out about the woman, and I—I have to do it."

"And Beth going to complain that I going to dead before the wedding, so I not telling her neither."

After Shad left, Shannon went back to her room and turned on her laptop. While it was booting up, she slid open a drawer of the antique desk and removed the photo Angie had given her, the editor looking at it morosely before handing it over. The colors had faded and the serrated edges had started to curl, but nothing could hide the beauty of the young woman who stared back. She was wearing a peasant blouse and squinting into the sun, her oval face framed by long, dark hair and bangs. Under her straight nose was a tentative smile, one that hoped that the world was as kind as she was.

Shannon shook her head. *Katlyn, Katlyn,* she mused to the woman's image, *you got in over your head, didn't you?*

She slipped the photograph into her laptop bag and moved to the armchair next to the window to transcribe her notes. She had just finished sending Angie and Chantrelle emails when she heard Jennifer and the children arriving back. Wayne, the Delgados' five-year-old, was wailing about something. Eve came in a few minutes later in her bathing suit, her nose bright red and her hair more disheveled than ever.

"How was the beach?" Shannon asked.

"I learned to bodysurf."

"Did you get sunburned? You're kind of—"

"Can I use your bathroom?"

"What's the matter with yours?"

"There's a creepy-crawly thing in the tub."

A lengthy shower followed, and Shannon was about to knock on the door and tell her not to waste the hot water when her daughter emerged, toweling her hair. "Do you have any gel?"

"I have mousse—and I have an idea."

"What?"

"You might not like it at first—"

"Then don't tell me."

"How would you like to take drumming lessons?"

CHAPTER SEVEN

Shadrack Myers, otherwise a healthy man, didn't have a strong stomach, especially in the backseat of a car. The coast road at least allowed him to gaze at the ocean and gulp sea air, but the trip to Gordon Gap allowed him no escape. The uphill twists from Oracabessa had his head out the back window, trying to think of something other than his stomach, trying to keep up his side of the conversation.

"And Eve is thinking about taking classes from Ras Walker's son," Shannon was saying from the front.

"Yeah," Shad gulped. "I know his son—a nice guy, good teacher."

"I was wondering if you could set that up for me, maybe on your way home?"

"Sure, sure—"

"I can do it," Carlton said, his first words of the morning. "He live down the road from me."

"Would you?" Shannon gave the driver one of her smiles. She'd always had pretty, white teeth, Shad thought, teeth that could twist a man's arm to do anything.

To Shad's relief, around the next corner a road sign that drooped to one side welcomed them to Gordon Gap. The tiny village was too small to have a square, but offered an intersection with a bar and a grocery store. When Carlton pulled up at Shad's direction, the backseat passenger almost fell out the door.

"Feeling better, are you?" Shannon teased when she joined him outside the shop.

"Yes, man." Shad beat his chest. "Nothing like mountain air, you know."

"Now, tell me why we're going to the grocery first."

"In a little town like this, just like Largo, the postal agency is inside the grocery store, and the shopkeeper know everything that go on in the town."

Sure enough, the cranky woman inside served as both the grocery-store owner and the postal clerk.

"I hope you can help us, ma'am," Shad said. "We inquiring about a lady name—" He turned to his companion.

"Katlyn Carrington," Shannon put in.

"I don't know anybody with that name," the store owner said.

"She live here about thirty-five years ago."

Miss Randall screwed up her lips. "That was before my time, but you can speak to Mistah Thorne. He live round the corner, been here all his life."

Mr. Thorne was sitting in the shade of an ackee tree playing dominoes with three other elders. It clearly tickled the old man that he could impress his visitors and vanquish his opponents at the same time.

"You see that?" he called out as he smashed down a double three. He looked up at Shad, aged, yellow eyes shining. "What you say about that?"

"Nice, man, nice."

"We can wait in the car until you're finished," Shannon said.

"Stay right there." Thorne pointed to the man on his right. "Robinson going to take a long time to play, his eyes not too good." Robinson glared at him and back at the dominoes under his nose.

"We was wondering," Shad said, "if you remember a Canadian lady who lived here about thirty-five years ago. Her name was Katlyn."

Thorne looked up at the red ackee pods overhead. "Katlyn, Katlyn." He scrutinized Shad for a second. "What she was doing here?"

"She was living—"

"She was a dancer," Shannon interjected. "She rented a room or a house here for about six months."

"A dancer," Thorne said. "What kind of dancing you talking about?"

"Modern dance, African dance, Jamaican dance." Shannon removed the photograph, the ragged edge catching on her pocket for a second, and placed it on the table. "Here she is."

The men leaned over and peered at the picture. Robinson slapped Thorne on his arm. "That not the lady was living in Miss Gwendolyn's house?"

"She looking like one of them Peace Corps people." Thorne pronounced it *corpse*.

"Miss Gwendolyn?" Shad said. "She still there?"

"She dead from pressure," the third player, a bald-headed man, said without looking up. "She was my cousin."

"Who can I talk to, then?" Shannon asked.

"Talk to Miss Gwen's daughter," said the fourth player, a man wearing a straw hat. "She living there now."

"Yes," said Robinson. "If Miss Gwen daughter say that is she, yes, come back and see me and I tell you what I know about her."

All four men got into the act of directing them to the house, contradicting each other, pointing out where each man had messed up. Shad resorted to writing the directions, and since he seldom wrote anything, it took another five minutes to get it all down. Back in the taxi, he read his notes slowly to Carlton, who put the car in gear.

"We forgot to ask if any Rastas living around here," Shad pointed out after they'd set off.

"We're on a roll here," Shannon said. "Let's keep going."

After only two queries to pedestrians, they arrived at a steep staircase that ascended from the road. The bartender and the photographer carefully climbed the forty-three (Shad counting aloud) concrete steps leading to a wire fence, behind which was a hedge of orange hibiscus and another set of five steps leading up to a modest house. A rooster inside the fence welcomed them with a blast of crowing, and two women appeared at the front door.

"Pardon, please," Shad called, breathing heavily. "We looking for Miss Gwendolyn house."

"This the right house, but Miss Gwen dead," said the younger woman, a plump teenager in an old T-shirt. Shad tried to ignore her large breasts with their insistent nipples.

"Who you want?" the older woman said, her head covered by assorted pink rollers.

"We inquiring about a foreign lady we think used to board here. She name Katlyn."

"When she was living here?" the woman asked as she walked to the steps. "I is Miss Gwen's daughter."

"About thirty-five years ago," Shannon said.

The woman shook her head, the rollers bobbling. "That a long time ago. My mother used to rent out the back room, and we have all kind of boarders come here, from Peace Corps and everything. I was little bit then, only seven, eight years old, and I can't remember everybody."

"She was a dancer," Shad added. "She used to teach dancing at the school." A baby's cry came from inside the house.

"Mamma, you didn't take some dancing lessons one time?" the younger woman said before disappearing inside.

"I wonder—could be, you know," her mother murmured. "I don't remember who the teacher was, though. I think she was American. I only remember she was a nice woman. She teach us some Jamaican dances, *kumina* and so, and I remember we wanted to learn American dances but she teach us our own dances."

"That sounds like her," Shannon breathed in Shad's ear.

More memories were coming back to Miss Gwen's daughter. "She had long, black hair down her back," she said, putting her hand behind her. "She used to wear it in a long plait. And she was little bit, not a big woman, only a little bigger than us children—but she could dance good." Shannon showed her the photograph and the woman smiled, saying, "Yes, yes, that look like the lady."

"Do you know where she went after she left the village?"

"No, I don't, sorry."

"Do you happen to have some record, a book, perhaps, where your mother made a note of her boarders?" Shannon asked.

"Everybody keep them kind of records," Shad interjected.

Miss Gwen's daughter admitted that she still had her mother's book with the names of her guests and the amounts they paid every month. She fetched a large ledger and sat down, groaning, on the top verandah step.

"What year you say it was?" She dusted off the cover with her hand. The daughter came back with a baby in her arms.

"Her name was Katlyn Carrington," Shannon said as she and Shad mounted the verandah steps. "That would have been—let's see—"

"Nineteen seventy-seven," Shad interjected.

The woman turned the pages of the book, reading the years out loud, going back, back, smoothing pages as she went.

"See it here." She ran her finger down the column with the names, first one page, then another. "I don't see no Katy, though."

"Try Carrington," Shad suggested.

The name was under *Carrington, K.*, the woman announced. Shad craned his head sideways to read the spidery handwriting.

"She come February seventeen, and she pay twenty dollars a week." Miss Gwen's daughter looked up at her own daughter and they laughed. "Lord, that sound little bit nowadays, nuh?"

"How long did she stay?" Shannon asked.

The woman examined the ledger again. "Last time she pay was July sixteen, same year." She frowned for a second. "You know, I remember Mamma talking about a lady from Canada. It must be the same lady used to teach us dancing." Her posture stiffened. "She went back to Canada, I sure. She sent Mamma a ashtray with a leaf—but it break."

They thanked her and descended to the car, where Carlton was snoozing. "Wake up quick," Shad commanded. "Drive back to the yard where the men was playing dominoes. We need to talk to one of the men."

When they got back to Mr. Thorne's house, the domino game had ended, and according to the homeowner, Mr. Robinson had won. "He gone back to his yard with my money," Thorne added with an irritated gesture of his thumb to the house next door.

Mr. Robinson was at home in a good mood. He invited his guests into the tiny living room. "So she was the woman I was thinking of? If it was she, she taught my daughter dancing. She used to hold classes in the old community center before they build the new one."

"And her name was Katlyn?" Shannon probed as she sat down in a mahogany chair.

"I don't remember her name, but she was a nice young lady, treat everybody good, not like some foreigners who act like they know more than you."

"What happen to her after she left here?" Shad asked.

"I don't know. I only remember she was pretty, didn't wear no makeup, just natural like."

"She had a Rasta boyfriend," Shad said. "You ever see her with him?"

Robinson frowned, staring at the ashtray sunk into the arm of his chair. "Now you say that, I remember hearing something about it after she left. He was from one of the groups that settled up so." He flapped his hand in the direction of the mountain behind them. "I never met him or nothing, though."

Shad exchanged smiles with Shannon, the familiar surge of adrenaline his clue that they were onto something solid.

As they got up to leave, Mr. Robinson muttered, "If you going into them Rasta camps, you need to find a Rasta to take you in. You don't want to go into one of the camps and they don't invite you."

CHAPTER EIGHT

N ever one to leave a message, Eric was about to hang up when Simone answered.

"How you doing, Eric Keller?"

"I hadn't called in a couple of weeks, so I thought I should—"

"You don't have to make excuses."

"I'm not—so, what's new with you?"

"You're the one with the news. What's up with the new hotel, everything going well?"

"Yup. The groundbreaking is definitely Saturday—is it the third or the fourth?"

The woman gave her throaty laugh. "You're funny. You don't even know your big date?"

"I'm terrible with dates, and I've been busy, what can I tell you."

"Let's see. I'm looking it up on my phone: the first Saturday is August fourth. And by the way, the Monday after that is Jamaica's fiftieth anniversary of independence. The Jamaicans in Atlanta have been planning a big ball. I bet you didn't even *know* it was the fiftieth and you live there."

"What kind of hermit d'you think I am? They've been preparing all kinds of fun and games in the village. I think Lambert is sponsoring fireworks or something."

"I could stay over a few extra days to see that." She paused for a heartbeat, as if waiting for him to confirm. "If you still want me to come down, that is."

"Why would I be calling you if I didn't?"

"Some things can change in the blink of an eye."

"Not that, trust me. I'll be at the airport with bells on."

"You'd better be."

"How's stuff going with you?"

While she brought him up-to-date with her new foundation and the grants she was applying for—all of it sounding deathly dull to him—Eric sat on his bed looking out at the island she'd lived on only twelve months before, imagining her short, curly hair bobbing above the bushes the way it used to. He remembered his excitement every time he rowed out to see her, trying to be cool but wanting so badly to hold her skinny body in his arms. Would it still be like that when he saw her again—or would Shannon's presence change everything, Shannon, with her surprising confidence and womanly body?

"I have some more news," he said, interrupting her.

"What's that?" Simone said, her voice in a frown.

"Eve is here, my daughter."

"Your daughter from Canada?" He felt the frown disappear. "That's great! Did her mom send her down for the summer?"

"No, her mom came with her." His own forehead tightened. "She's writing an article for a magazine, doing the photography, too. They arrived a few days ago."

A brief silence, followed by a little sigh. "Everything can change in the blink of an eye, like I said."

"It doesn't change anything."

"Of course it does." She sucked air in between her

teeth—her parents had been from Jamaica, after all. "Why didn't you tell me before?"

"It was kind of sudden."

"You're kidding me, right?" He could sense her emotions ping-ponging around.

"I'm not."

"Answer me this: Are they or are they not staying with you—in your apartment?"

"They're up at the Delgados'. Shannon and Jennifer used to be good friends—back in the day."

"So you're not sleeping with her."

"Absolutely not."

"Look, I've been divorced once. I can take the truth, don't worry."

"You don't have to worry."

"Will they be there for the groundbreaking?"

"It depends how long this article takes her."

"We'll just have to deal with it if they are, but I just want you to know, I don't like drama." She'd switched to her business voice, the one she'd used to negotiate renting the island after she'd caught him snooping around her shelter in the ruins.

"But you never know what life is going to throw at you," he said, his chuckle sounding like a guilty snicker even to him.

It seemed to help, though, because she sounded slightly less terse when she spoke again. "How are the wedding plans? I wish I could be there, but this meeting in DC has me tied up. It's the best lead I have to get funds for the foundation, so I've got to be there. I hope Shad understands."

"I'm sure he will."

"Is he feeling good about the wedding? I know he—"

"Beth has him under heavy manners, no escape for him this time."

"They've been together long enough," Simone said briskly.

It was a relief to Eric when they said their good-byes. A man who would prefer to scrape donkey dung off the bottom of his shoe than tell one girlfriend about another, he was grateful, deeply grateful, that Simone had taken it as well as she had. She was no-nonsense, and he liked that about her, liked that, if she had a problem with him, she'd tell him right away. Shannon was different. Although she was more assertive now, she'd always kept things close to her chest, still left more unspoken than stated.

The conversation with Simone was not his last difficult exchange for the day. Eric knew it as soon as he saw his daughter slouching into the bar, shortly before noon, while he was preparing piña coladas for a group of tourists. She was wearing jeans and another big shirt, this one with a graffiti print.

"Looks like you've been in the sun." She slid onto a barstool and shrugged. "Not hanging out with Casey today?"

"She's watching a *Disney* movie." Eve spat out the name, her face expressionless.

"We could sure use your help. Maisie is in the kitchen cooking, but we don't have a waiter. Ready for the job?" Another shrug. "I'll take you back there and introduce you—as soon as I finish serving these guys."

When he got back, she was already off the barstool. "I want to see where you live." Her accusing eyes held his for a second.

"Sure, sure." He gestured to the door at the end of the short passageway, glad that Maisie had just straightened the place.

Eve opened the door and paused warily, as if expecting something to jump out. After a second, she entered and looked around. She needed, Eric knew, to find out how he lived, needed to intrude on his world and make herself present. He remained silent as she inspected the matchbox living room with the cheap wooden table where he counted the bar's weekly earnings with Shad, clasped the upright back of one of the dining chairs, examined the white tiles underfoot. Entering the bedroom, she looked briefly at the double bed and walked around it to the bedside table with its lamp and books.

"You read sci-fi books."

"Yes." It wasn't a lie; it just took him a year to finish one.

She let her hand rest on the large sliced shell beside the books. "I know what kind of shell this is." She stuck the other hand in her jeans pocket.

"Your mother gave it to me long ago."

"It's a nautilus. We have a couple at home." She ran one finger around the shell's circular chambers. "Do you know what they call this formation?" Another test for him, he knew, letting him know that she knew more than him, more than kangaroos now.

"The circles in the shell, you mean?"

She kept running her finger around the shell's delicate interior. "They call it a whorl."

"A whirl of whorls, huh?" His light laugh received no response as she kept focused on the shell. Typical woman, Eric concluded, unable to shift moods quickly, but it was worth a try.

She walked through the open louver doors onto the verandah. Circling the two wooden armchairs, she walked to the edge of the verandah facing the ocean, her frizzy hair sparkling in the sun. "You don't have rails."

"I like a clear view of the ocean." He couldn't afford to enclose it—and he hadn't been expecting visits from children.

She looked over the bougainvillea bushes to the kitchen window, where Maisie was busy at the sink, and sat down in one of the chairs.

Eric lowered to the other, his mind racing ahead to what could come next. "It's hot out here in the day, so I don't—"

"Is that where your hotel was?" She pointed to the island.

"Yes, a long time ago."

"And that's where the woman was living."

"Who told you?"

"Miss Bertha."

He sat back and crossed his arms. "Yes, that's where she lived. After she left, we named it after her, Simone Island."

"How long was she there?" she said, shielding her eyes as she peered at the site.

"A little over two months."

Her rose-pink nose was long and straight, the Keller nose, he noticed for the first time. "How did she get food?"

"We rowed it out to her."

"And she was all alone?" The corners of Eve's lips twitched, as if she were thinking it would be cool to live in exile.

"Except for a little dog, she called him Cammy—after her brother Cameron."

"Where is she now?"

"Back in Atlanta."

"With the dog?"

"He ran away as soon as they came back to the village. Cute little thing. He barked and woke her up once when some men went out there to hurt her, probably saved her life."

Eve looked at him hard with her blue Irish eyes with their black spokes. "Do you—are you and her, you know, having a thing?"

He swallowed. "We're good friends, if that's what you mean."

"You like her, though."

"Why'd you think so?"

"You look kind of weird when you talk about her."

He swept his hair back over his ears and stood up. "I have to get back to the bar. Those folks might need lunch. Come on, let's meet Maisie and take some orders."

CHAPTER NINE

There was nothing like mango juice dripping down your chin, especially the juice of the prized Julie mango. Jennifer had saved one from the clutches of Little Wayne and presented it to Shannon earlier. It was a beauty, with touches of pink and yellow on the skin.

"Go sit on the porch and eat it like a Jamaican," her hostess had ordered her.

Five minutes later, Shannon had changed out of her work clothes and was sitting in one of the rocking chairs on the verandah, a plate on her lap to catch drips. She stripped off the mango's skin with her teeth, working her way around in a circle, and bit into the flesh. When Shad had taught her once how *a real Jamaican* ate a mango, he'd had to wipe her nose so she could breathe.

As she chewed, the journalist thought about Katlyn, and how she'd gotten deeply into the Jamaican countryside and culture. Surely she must have loved mangoes. She'd learned the folk dances, would have learned patois in Gordon Gap, probably enjoyed the island's food. Thoughts and questions about Katlyn had begun to sit with Shannon, along with a growing respect for the woman's values. The woman in the photograph she carried around in her bag had started to become three-dimensional, four, if you included her idealistic spirit, and Shannon was starting to feel a connection with her. Two Canadian women who had fallen for a man in Jamaica; they were both risk takers with a strong sense of adventure—adventure that had gone awry for both of them, worse for the younger woman.

The biggest questions about Katlyn were still haunting Shannon. Was the cause of her death natural or not? Who was responsible? And what happened to her after she died? Shannon shuddered to think that her body could have been thrown into the ocean or tossed into a ravine. It was only right that someone should investigate her death, give her some peace, as Shad had said.

"I'm going to find out everything I can about you, Katlyn," she promised aloud. "Maybe I'll find myself in the process."

Shannon took another bite of mango, her gaze sweeping over the sloping garden in front of her, over the mango trees laden with fruit and the poinciana trees with their spreads of bright blossoms. Below the garden squatted her former lover's bar. She'd been embarrassed for him when she'd first seen it, one of the dozens of crude island bars along the coast, a far cry from the hotel. It couldn't take in much money, she was sure. The few customers that had been there on a Saturday afternoon had told her as much. Yet—and she gave him a check mark at the thought—he'd sent her child support every month for the past thirteen years and never whined about his finances.

No longer the dashing lover with a charming hotel, he

had fallen in her eyes and she was still coming to terms with the downward swoop of his life, karma she wouldn't have wished on anyone. She'd thought of compliments she could give him about the bar, but they wouldn't have been true. The only saving grace was the stunning view, but if she'd mentioned it, they would have looked over at the ruins of the hotel, and it would have brought back too many memories—for her if not for him. If not for the news that he was going to own a hotel again, she would have felt nothing but pity for him.

He'd aged since she'd last seen him. His hair had gone platinum white, the lines on his face were now trenches, and his skin looked as if it needed a ton of moisturizer. The paunch was new. He'd never been one to exercise, other than working a bit in the hotel garden, and it had caught up with him. He'd seemed almost cautious, withdrawn even, when he spoke to her, and she'd concluded that his eyesight must be failing because he'd narrowed his eyes whenever he looked at her.

Jennifer dropped to a chair beside her holding the large, yellow handbag Shannon had brought her as a gift.

"Going out?" Shannon asked.

"Nope." Jennifer opened the handbag. "Mind if I smoke?"

"I thought you'd stopped a million years ago!"

"I started when I was taking care of my mom last spring, before she died." Jennifer slid a menthol cigarette out of a pack. "The stress was so damn high, running back and forth to the hospital, dealing with doctors, screaming at nurses, meeting with lawyers, all kinds of stuff. My sister smokes and I gave in." She lit the cigarette and, snapping the lighter closed, exhaled a cone of smoke to one side. "Don't tell Lam, though. He hates it."

"Don't smoke around Eve and I won't tell Lambert."

"Done."

Shannon licked her lips. "You know what those things can do to you, right?"

"I'm cutting back."

"Promise?"

"I swear. Now let's talk about you. How's the work going?"

"Good—I think. Carlton and I went off to the Ocho Rios craft market today. I got some great shots, learned a lot, too. I found out that Rastas don't like to be called Rastafarians, but *Rastafari*, which is closer to one of the Emperor Haile Selassie's names—Ras Tafari, you know. It means a chief who is respected or feared, I found out during my interview with this really sweet woman who makes jewelry. We talked about the male-female-equality thing with Rastas."

"I thought the women were always subordinate to the men."

"I think that's changing. At least, she seemed to think so. She's pretty active in her community, plans events and all that, and she adores Haile Selassie's wife, the former empress."

"They see Selassie as a god, don't they?"

"As Jah, the one and only God."

"What do they say now that he's dead?"

Shannon dropped the mango seed on the plate and wiped her mouth with the paper towel beside her. "They don't think of him as dead since God is not supposed to die. Some don't believe he's dead; they say he's in hiding. Others say he's transitioned to a place where he can't be seen, kind of like Jesus."

"The whole culture exists under our middle-class noses, doesn't it?" Jennifer waved her cigarette. "We don't even know much about it. They're sort of mystical or something, in a different world. They don't give a damn about society, and they—they scare me a little, to tell you the truth."

"I remember being afraid of them myself when I used to come out. They looked so fierce, you know. I'd speak to one or two if they were selling me something, coconut water or craft, but I pretty much kept away. I didn't want to get into an argument with any of them."

"We see the dreadlocks, hear the language, and most of us keep a polite distance. You hear all kinds of things—"

"What kinds of things?"

"They're probably rumors, but I heard one woman was burned to death in a camp. Then there's all that marijuana smoking. They just think differently, kind of like a sect, you know. They have their beliefs and their rites and rituals, not Jim Jones or anything, but they're very set in their opinions, very sensitive—and suspicious of foreigners." Jennifer tapped ash from her cigarette over the verandah rail. "I want you to be careful, Shan."

"So far I haven't seen anything to make me worried. I still have a lot of work to do, though. I want to see this professor who's written some of the books I've been reading."

"I know you have work to do, but don't forget you're in Jamaica, sweetie. Leave some time for the beach, too."

Shannon laughed. "As long as I don't get as red as Eve."

"Is she okay?" Jennifer's botoxed brow allowed the ghost of a wrinkle. "It's hard to read her. I offered to take her shopping in Kingston with Casey, but she didn't seem interested. She's kind of—detached."

"She's fine. If she isn't slightly miserable, she's not happy."

"Does she like the waitressing bit?"

"She pretended it was boring, but *loved* the four hundred Jamaican dollars in tips. When she heard how little it was in Canadian, she wasn't too happy."

Jennifer chuckled as she put out the cigarette in a bottle extracted from the bag.

"You're pretty clever hiding your habit, aren't you?" Shannon teased.

"It's more trouble than it's worth."

"Addictions can be hard to break."

"You mean like Eric?" Jennifer dropped the bottle into her bag and clicked it shut. "I don't know who you're trying to fool. You're not through with him."

"My neighbor back home thinks the same thing."

Jennifer scrutinized Shannon through half-closed lids. "Did you ever end it, officially, I mean?"

"We never discussed it. Everything kind of faded to black, I suppose."

"My God, Shan, all these years, fourteen years and you've never—"

"Whenever we talked, it was always about Eve, about money, about his visits."

"There were only three."

"Right, well, about the three visits. Sometimes you don't have to talk about things. Neither one of us likes to—has to go into things in detail."

"Do you *want* it to be over?"

"If you're asking do I still have feelings for him, the answer is of course I—I care about him." Shannon felt like a traitor speaking about it, but it was time for honesty. "He's wise, funny, makes love passionately, demands nothing from you, and lets you be yourself—not like the younger guys." The Canadian swallowed hard as she took a couple of rocks in the chair. "He becomes your best friend, your lover, the brother you never had, everything wrapped into one—then you get pregnant."

She rubbed a bite on her leg. "But he doesn't want the child and he doesn't ask you to marry him, and you spend your pregnancy defending your decision to keep the baby, rejecting your—your friends' and family's *concern*, but wondering if you've done the right thing. And every day after that you ask yourself if you should call him, if you should give him an ultimatum, if you should apologize, if *he* should apologize. Should you fly down and confront him or should you have a lawyer draw up a document?" Shannon turned to her friend. "And you end up having the baby and cashing his checks."

"Hoping that one day—"

"I'm *not* hoping."

"You expect me to believe that you came here to do an assignment and that's all? You could have stayed in Montego Bay to do the job. Not that I'm not glad—"

"I came because—because I wanted to come back to Largo. It was an important part of my life, and I wanted Eve to know her father."

"And if it just happens that you and her father rekindle the old fire, you wouldn't mind, would you?"

"Times change, people change, Jen. I almost don't know him after all this time. There's a lot that's happened to me and to him since I was here last, from the hotel being ruined to—I feel like I barely know him anymore." Beneath them, the bar's thatch roof lay dull in the sun. "Fourteen years is a long time, maybe too long. We'll have to see."

CHAPTER TEN

They were seated like an audience waiting for something to happen, facing the empty lane on a summer afternoon, a dancehall song blasting from a radio. Joella and two teenage boys had the seats of honor on the verandah's three plastic chairs, two-year-old Joshua asleep sprawled across Joella's lap, oblivious of the noise. At their feet, Rickia and a friend sat on the top step, their arms and legs spotted with the sunlight coming through the mango tree and its fruit overhead. Five sets of eyes stared at Shad and Eve as they approached the children and his home.

"Turn down the music," Shad yelled as he opened the garden gate. "How many times I have to tell you that you making the neighbors deaf."

"You can't hear the music good if you don't turn it up," Joella parried as one of the young men bent to turn down the radio.

"I bring a guest today. You children have been saying that you want to meet Mistah Eric's daughter, so I bring her today. Her father say she can come for a little while."

Eve nodded to the crowd, her hands jammed into her jeans.

Rickia pushed up her smudgy glasses. "Hi, Eve," said

the eleven-year-old, who was always impressed by foreigners, who was going abroad to study, she'd informed her parents.

"What you guys up to?" Shad inquired after the two boys had given up their chairs to him and Eve.

"Shante and I reading, Dadda," Rickia answered, holding up a book. "Mamma borrow it from the library for me."

"Jethro, how your mother going?" Shad asked one of the boys, with short, brown dreadlocks. "I hear she not too well."

"She come out of hospital, suh. My grandmother staying with us now and taking care of her."

"And you, Winston," Shad said, gesturing with his chin to the boy holding the radio, the youth he'd found a home for several months back, "you still living with Maisie and Solomon?"

"Yes, suh, and doing a little mechanic work with Zeb."

"You hear from your father?"

"He write me from Kingston last week. He say he get a job."

"Good, good." Shad rubbed his hand over his chin, hoping to find a hair or two he could shave soon.

Joella patted the baby on his rump, observing Eve out of the corner of her eye. "She don't look like Mistah Eric."

Shad lowered his eyebrows at her. "She have her father's blue eyes, you don't see?"

"But I have my mother's mouth," Eve said, the crisp Canadian accent slicing through the Largo heat. She looked at Shad when she said it, her mouth firmer and smaller than Shannon's.

"She speak pretty, eh?" Shante commented.

"You been to Largo before?" Winston asked Eve.

She shook her head.

"How long you staying?" Joella inquired.

"I don't know. It depends on when my mother finishes a job she's doing."

"What she doing?" Rickia asked.

"Writing an article for a magazine."

"Maybe Eve can come to the wedding, Dadda," Rickia said.

"If she and her mother still here, of course," Shad replied.

"Who's getting married?" Eve asked, turning to Joella as if she expected it to be her.

Shad's face got hot and he was glad his skin hid it. "The children's mother and me."

"A wedding, that's cool," Eve said. "When is it?"

"July twenty-eighth," Joella and Rickia replied together.

"I'd like to come," Eve said to Shad.

It was the warmest she'd been to the bartender thus far, and he felt less conscious of his half-painted house with its scraggly yard. He was glad now that he'd asked Eric if he could bring her to meet his children, something he'd thought of when she'd first arrived but hadn't done, the way she'd pulled her arm away from him. The girl should see how poor Jamaicans lived, he'd decided, and then maybe she'd be grateful for her own life up in Canada and not have such a sour face. He was also glad that, at least for this first meeting, she wouldn't see Ashante, his five-year-old, who was at the school in Port Antonio where Beth took her every day. Strangers didn't understand the child's odd behavior, didn't understand autism.

A gangly, black-and-white cat wandered onto the porch. Rickia laid it belly up in the crook of her arm.

"Can I pat it?" Eve asked. Rickia nodded, and Eve knelt down and stroked the cat. "I like cats."

"You can have this one!" Joella snickered. "She eat too much."

A discussion started about what the cat, named Precious, ate and where it slept, while Shad went inside to make himself lunch. When he came back out, Joella announced that they wanted Eve to stay with them for the afternoon. "We going to walk her back to the Delgados' house before it get dark."

"Is that okay?" Eve actually looked energized, alive for the first time since he'd seen her. "I don't have anything else to do."

Shad chewed the inside of his cheek. He'd promised her father he'd take her back to the Delgados' when he returned for his evening shift. On the other hand, Joella was a responsible girl, about to start twelfth grade at Titchfield High, off to dental-tech school in Kingston the following year, and she had a reputation for handling her younger siblings with a strong, sometimes too strong, hand. All six young people were looking at him now, eyes expectant, Joella's hand stroking the baby.

"We walk her back along the beach," Rickia blurted out. "She can see the fishermen going out to fish."

"Can I please?" Eve asked. "My mother wouldn't have a problem with it."

That Eve herself wanted to stay, that she had some desire he could finally fulfill, persuaded Shad. "Make sure you have her back at the Delgados' home by six, no later, you hear me?" he told Joella.

"We look after her," Winston assured him.

Shad took his leave, glancing back over his shoulder to make sure he'd done the right thing, but the children weren't looking at him. They were talking about something—and they'd turned the music up.

When he got back to the bar, Eric was out, and Shad called the Delgados' and told Miss Bertha about Eve's change of plans. "She coming back for dinner?" the housekeeper asked.

"Yes, man. No problem."

Sunset arrived at the Largo Bay Restaurant and Bar with its usual flair of color, appreciated that evening by a busload of tourists bound for Kingston, who arrived tired and thirsty, taking the bartender away from his reading of *Grossman's Guide* and rushing him off his feet. After a few too many Planter's Punches, the customers turned to singing along with Jimmy Cliff, three of them dancing, delaying their departure until the bus driver said he'd be fired if they didn't leave for the hotel. Shad was happy to see them go despite the hefty tip, and with only the regulars left, the evening suddenly went quiet.

"You're helping Miss Mac move, right?" Eric said after he arrived back at seven o'clock. His habit was to come through every night, say hello to whoever was there, and disappear to sit on his verandah, only to be disturbed in an emergency.

"I have that under control," Shad mumbled, his finger keeping his place in the book describing *the working arrangement of an efficient bar*. "Remember we going to use the Jeep, though."

"Oh, yeah, I forgot. I was going into Port Morant to pick

up a part for the car, but I can do that next week. Zeb said there was no rush."

"Miss Mac say she want to start moving at seven o'clock on Saturday morning, the day after the closing, so I coming early for the key."

Eric slid onto the barstool opposite Shad and put both hands flat on the counter. "Pour me a scotch, please, a Johnnie Walker Black."

"I know you making joke," Shad said without moving his finger off the page. "You don't drink hard liquor since your birthday party last year."

"And the next is right now."

Eric admitted he wouldn't be able to sleep tonight without a shot. "All I can think about is Friday the thirteenth," he growled, "closing day on Miss Mac's land. I can't even wrap my head around it. It seems so final, sheesh, Miss Mac moving away . . ." The American screwed up his mouth like a purse string, trying not to get emotional, Shad could see. "I'm going to miss the old gal. She's been the best neighbor a man could have. I hate to tear her house down—I have a lot of memories in it. Remember how I stayed with her for the year while we were building the hotel? She'd have a hot meal ready for me every night, whatever I told her that morning I wanted. And she was terrific with Simone when she got off the island, weak from dehydration. It was Miss Mac who brought her back to life before she left. She's a saint, that woman, grumpy sometimes, but a saint."

Shad served him the scotch and sat down on his stool. "The price of progress, boss, but I going to miss her, too. Me and her go way back to elementary school. She never wanted me to leave school, you know, and she beg Granny to keep me in school because I was bright, but I had to leave because Granny couldn't do the embroidery work anymore, you know. I had to start fishing with Uncle Obediah to earn little something." Shad put the book away in his library drawer, his chest heavy.

"And even when I came back from the penitentiary, Miss Mac never try to make me feel worthless, you know. She just kept telling me that I must finish up my learning. And when I need to sign all them papers you and Danny gave me to be a partner, it was she who made sure I could read all the hard words, told me how to pronounce them and look them up in the dictionary. You right, we going to miss her bad."

"I just hope she's happy in Port Antonio with Horace."

"If anything, boss"—Shad smiled quietly—"she can come back and live with us in the hotel."

While Eric nursed his scotch, Shad served Tri and Solomon at the other end of the bar, they, too, bemoaning the village's loss of Meredith MacKenzie.

"Now *that* is a woman I always admire," Tri said while Shad poured white rum into his glass. "She was strict, but she teach plenty children around here, and she manage her life by herself."

Solomon agreed. "Bring up her son to be a lawyer all by herself."

"Horace still going to run the campsite on the island?" Tri asked Shad. "Didn't you tell us he was going to put up tents and rent them out?"

"Yes, he and his business partner starting work on it next month. They leasing the island from us." It was the first time the bartender had used the word *us* in reference to the new hotel, and it sounded so good he was going to use it more often from now on.

While Shad was washing up at the sink and Eric was finishing his scotch, Beth walked, almost ran, into the bar, her face twisted with worry. She never came into the bar at night except for a party, wouldn't come unless something bad had happened, and Shad held on to the edge of the sink, waiting for the news.

"Good night, Mistah Eric," she said between pants. Her eyes skidded from the boss to her baby father.

"Evening, Beth." Eric's forehead lowered over his brows, and when she kept panting, he asked what the matter was.

"Is Eve." She looked at her husband.

Shad's hand went to his scalp. He'd forgotten everything about the child. "Oh, God," he groaned.

"What about her?" Eric said, glancing at his bartender. "I thought you were going to bring her back after your lunch break. Didn't you take her up—"

"She not at the Delgados'?" Shad asked.

Beth shook her head.

"Where is she?" Eric thundered, standing up.

Beth looked up at him. "We don't exactly know, suh. She was—"

"What you mean?" Shad interrupted her. "Joella and her friends was supposed to walk her home before dark. Joella and Winston *promise* me they would look after her."

"Where is she?" Eric demanded.

"They don't know where she is." Beth's eyes implored forgiveness. "She was with them, and then they say she went with Jethro to see something. And when I get home from work, Joella tell me they hadn't come back yet. So we walk up and down looking, but nobody see them." Beth looked from Shad to Eric and back.

"The Jeep!" Eric called, yanking the keys from their nail on the wall.

"Solomon," Shad yelled over the partition behind him. "You can manage the bar for me? We gone to look for Eve."

CHAPTER ELEVEN

Eric pressed the accelerator, then the brakes, careening down Lambert's driveway, hoping Shad and Beth were hanging on in the open back of the Jeep. Beside him, Shannon was ramrod straight in the passenger seat, one hand gripping the door's armrest.

"We'll find her," she said, her hope making him feel worse. "It's a small village."

He remembered telling her once that crimes could happen easily in Jamaica—the networks of mountain roads and drug gangs and depraved youngsters could prove unyielding to an outsider. Eric grasped the wheel tighter, knowing he was overreacting, that his fear was making him irrational. By the time he hit the bottom of the driveway, he was almost calm, but then the guilt came back, followed by anger at Shad for letting him down, followed by the knowledge that he was ultimately responsible. "I'm sorry that—"

"There's nothing to worry about, I'm sure," Shannon said quickly. "She's good at taking care of herself. She's had a lot of practice." In the light under the dash, he could see Shannon's fingers gripping the tops of her thighs.

"Honestly, I thought she was with you by now. I had to go to get my—"

"And I thought she was still with you—or Shad." No judgment was in her voice, but he felt it. "Where are we going first?"

"Shad's house—she could be back there already."

Eric speeded down the empty main road and turned onto a side lane, roaring up to Shad's house, where Joella and Winston were sitting under the verandah's bare bulb. They jumped up when the Jeep stopped.

As Eric climbed out, Shannon flew to the gate. "Hi, I'm Eve's mother. Has she come back yet?"

"No, not yet," Joella said meekly.

"And they never said anything about where they were going?" Eric asked.

"No."

"What Eve and Jethro say about what they was going to do?" Shad called from the back of the pickup, throwing out his hand, chastising her. "They *must* have tell you something."

"They was talking over there"—Joella pointed to one side of the verandah—"then they come and tell us they going."

"Pshaw, man," Shad insisted and hit his knee, "you *promise* me you was going to walk her back to the Delgados'. Why you didn't do it? I think I could trust you. Now, look what—"

"Jethro said they soon come back, suh," Winston interjected. "He said he going to show her something and bring her back."

"Lord, have mercy." Shad sucked his teeth.

"Jethro have any friends?" Beth queried, leaning in front of Shad.

"He tight with Naar," Winston replied.

Naar's house was on Bartow Lane off the square, a house with two lights on either side of the verandah. When Eric blew the horn, a thin woman said that the teenager was inside watching TV. Bare-chested, the boy appeared and said a good evening and, no, he didn't know where Jethro was and hadn't seen him all day. His hair was braided tightly on one side and fluffed out on the other, as if someone was in the middle of plaiting it.

"He must be home by now," Naar added, and gave them directions.

The road to Jethro's house was behind the village, the part off the grid. Thank God, Eric breathed, clicking on his high beams, there was a half-moon tonight, the road as remote as a country road could be. The Jeep's lights stayed stubbornly low and askew, one beam showing the road right in front, the other the road up ahead, and he sucked his teeth as best an American could, irritated at himself for not fixing them. Dense foliage crowded in, hiding the thousand frogs and their belly honks. Naar's vague directions led them past a few houses, most in darkness, all nothing but lumps in the night's gloom. The road ended when the mountain rose like a black wall in front of them.

"Shit," Eric groaned. He started turning the Jeep around in the narrow space.

"It's got to be one of those houses we passed," Shannon said, putting one hand on his bare arm. It was a touch he remembered, the long fingers soft and cool.

"Let we go back and ask," Shad called. He sounded nervous, perhaps because of the darkness behind.

A few reverses and hard turns later, Eric headed up the

road, slower this time, until they arrived at a house that loomed to their right behind a low hedge. Yellow light from a lantern lit an interior room, the two front windows glowing like a Halloween pumpkin. As soon as they stopped, Shad leaped out of the back and knocked on the front door. They heard his polite inquiry when a man opened the door, a lamp glowing on a table behind him. The man pointed farther up the lane.

After Shad had jumped back into the Jeep, he leaned over Eric's shoulder. "That was Brother Michael's house. I didn't even know he live out here. He say that Jethro and his mother live a few chains down the road, a house with a wooden fence."

Shannon's hands now rested limply in her lap, as if she was forcing herself to relax. "Please, please, let her be there," she whispered. Resisting the urge to say something soothing, Eric changed into first gear and started forward, stopping at a dark cottage behind a wood fence. He kept the motor running as Shad clambered out of the Jeep.

"Don't step on no frogs," Beth called.

Shad knocked twice on the front door before someone opened a window and beamed a flashlight straight at him.

"Ay, man," Shad called, holding up an arm against the light.

"Who there?" a woman's growly voice said.

To Shad's answer, the woman coughed and spat through the window, shining the flashlight down to look at the spit. "Yes, is Jethro house," she snapped. "What you want?"

When Shad replied, the woman left the window, the light from the flashlight moving around the little house, bouncing off furniture and a framed picture of Jesus. After a few minutes, an hour to Eric, the front door creaked open. They could see the woman's head above the flashlight shaking in answer to another question from Shad, then some muffled words before she closed the door. Shad returned to Eric's side of the Jeep and slapped the door.

"That was Jethro grandma. She said he don't come home all day."

"Any idea where he is?" Eric asked.

"She don't know." Shad climbed into the back. "She say he stay out late sometimes."

"Oh, God." The soft cry from Shannon made Eric catch his breath. She buried her face in her hands and leaned toward him, releasing her fear in sobs. He put his arm around her and pulled her toward him, feeling the weight she'd been carrying—the years of bringing up Eve alone. It was as if the nights she'd stayed awake with a crying baby, the days she'd struggled with diaper bags and tantrums, the parent-teacher meetings she'd attended alone, had suddenly become real to him.

"Why is she doing this?" She was sniffling, her voice muffled by his shirt. "Where did I go wrong?"

"You haven't done anything wrong."

"It hasn't been easy," she said between sobs, turning her head so he could hear her, "but I thought I was managing. But, dammit, things have gone so wrong. She hardly talks to me, she hates my guts, I know it. Now she's started stealing, a shopkeeper is calling me, and I'm going down to get her." She turned her head into his shirt and let out a wail. "I'm a terrible mother!"

He waited for her to let it out, the noise of the Jeep's motor encircling them. When he lifted her chin, her tears dampened his hand. "Don't ever let me hear you say that again, you hear me? You're a great mother."

She sniffed. "But look what she's—"

"We'll find her, don't worry." He stroked her soft hair. She looked as fragile as on that first night he'd seen her lying on the lounge chair staring up at the stars. He kissed her wet cheek. "And she'll be safe."

Shannon sat up straight, wiping her nose with the back of her hand. "You're right."

He started back to the village square. "We're going to the police. There's nothing more we can do at this point." He turned and yelled to Shad. "I'm going to Port Antonio, to the station. You coming or you want me to drop you off?"

"We coming with you, man. My cousin is a police, remember?"

Eric swung onto a shortcut, an unpaved road that angled west toward the main road and Port Antonio, all the worse for the years since he'd taken it. Thick bushes crowded in on both sides, and he'd just slowed down for another pothole, cursing the National Works Agency under his breath for neglecting Largo's roads, when Shannon touched his arm.

"What's that?"

"What, that noise?" He braked to a stop. The thumping of drums, accompanied by discordant chanting, was coming from somewhere.

"Let's go and talk to them," Shannon urged. "Maybe they know something."

"She wouldn't be there."

"Let's do it, anyway."

Eric turned off the engine. "Hey, man," he said to Shad, "you hear that?"

"You mean the Rastas singing?"

"Is that what it is?"

"They singing a *sankey*, one of them religious songs."

"Shannon wants to check it out."

"I better come with you. Next thing I have to come find you." All four climbed out of the Jeep.

"Where's it coming from?" Shannon asked. Shad pointed to a narrow lane and started toward it holding Beth's hand. Straining to see the stones and holes, Eric followed behind, Shannon at his side. They'd only gone a few steps when she stumbled.

"You okay?"

"Thanks," she said, grabbing his outstretched hand. It had been a long time.

When they turned into the lane, they could see a dim light a couple hundred yards ahead. The chanting and drumming got louder, and Eric's heart started thumping. Breaking into a private religious ceremony was not a good idea. He'd often heard Rasta drumming at night, sometimes saw the head-wrapped Pocomania women walking to their meetings, but he'd never visited a ceremony of either religion, afraid he'd trigger accusations of disrespect or worse. Holding tight to Shannon's hand, he told himself not to be a coward. He had just as much right to be here as anyone else—but he'd let Shad do the talking. In local situations like this, it was always best to let him handle it.

The light was coming from a kerosene lantern hanging in an open hut beside the road. Sitting in a circle beating drums of all colors and sizes were about eight men, all Rastafarians, it looked like, their locks tucked into a variety of headgear. They were chanting in a slow, sad chorus:

We are worshipping our precious Jah,
Worshipping our precious Jah,
Worshipping our precious Jah,
Till the break of day.

The four newcomers stood in the glare of the lamp-light—a familiar man acknowledging them with his eyes—and waited until the last drumbeat sounded.

"You want something?" the man asked, and Eric felt the eyes of the musicians appraising them.

"Greetings, Ras Walker." Shad dipped his head to the shoemaker. "We was wondering if you—"

"Eve!" shrieked Shannon, tightening her grip on Eric's hand.

Eric's eyes raced around the drummers, settling on a slim figure seated between two teenaged boys. Their daughter looked up with startled eyes under her black cap. A smile broke over her face, her hands still resting on top of a drum.

CHAPTER TWELVE

Shannon settled into the backseat of Carlton's taxi and rolled down her shirtsleeves. Rastafarian women should cover their head and arms, the craft-market vendor had explained, and the photojournalist had made a note to wear long sleeves on future excursions.

Calm as her actions were, Shannon felt frazzled. She hadn't slept well. A stew of emotions and thoughts had kept her tossing all night, adding to her heaviness this morning. Eve, on the other hand, seemed to have had no problem and was still fast asleep when Shannon woke her at ten o'clock.

"What?" she'd groaned, turning away from her mother. "I'm sleeping."

"We're going down to your father's. We have to talk, the three of us." Her daughter hadn't answered, hadn't moved. "Get up *now*. I mean it."

When they arrived at the bar, Eve was still yawning and Shad reported that Eric was on the cliff planting a young coconut tree. Annoyed (she'd called him only an hour before and they'd agreed to talk to Eve together), Shannon had reminded herself that he'd been sweet to her the night before.

There'd only been time for the obvious questions after Eve had been found. She'd climbed into the Jeep and sat on the brake between them, the knitted cap still on her head.

"Why didn't you let anyone know where you were going?" Shannon had said through almost-gritted teeth, trying to stay in control for Eric's sake.

Eve had been talkative for a change. "Jethro was showing me his drum, and then he started teaching me, and then he invited me to come to a drumming class, and—"

"You should have let someone know," Eric had interrupted. "Your mother was worried sick."

"We weren't near a phone."

"That's no excuse," Shannon had said. "You can't just disappear like that."

"I was perfectly safe." Neither of them had wanted to counter her, at least not yet, and Shannon had been too upset to talk after they got home.

Despite her earlier phone call, Eric had looked surprised to see them when he came around the corner, and he took his time washing his hands.

"So," he'd said, sitting at their table, "what do you have to say for yourself, young lady?" He'd pulled a carved pipe and matches from his shirt pocket, a bag of tobacco from his shorts.

"Smoking isn't good for you," Eve had muttered.

"Let me worry about that." He lit the pipe. Shannon had leaned back, noting the Canadian maple, relieved she wouldn't have to go it alone this time.

"Eve, honey," he'd said after the pipe had caught, "explain how you got from Shad's house in the early afternoon to a shed in the middle of the bush in the evening."

The excitement of the night before had left their daughter, and she'd sat in her usual slouch. "I wanted to see his drum, that's all."

Eric had drawn the pipe out of his mouth. "And?"

To Eve's raised eyebrows, her father had raised his, looking like a befuddled grandparent with his white hair and pipe.

Shannon sighed and crossed her arms. "Why didn't you tell Shad's kids where you were going?"

"We weren't going to be gone for long."

"But you *were* gone for a long time," her mother argued, "and when you saw it was getting dark, you should have come right back."

"I didn't know how."

The story came out one sentence, one answer, at a time. Jethro had taken her to see his drum at a friend's house. He'd demonstrated a few strokes of the drum and she'd started practicing. When he said he was going to his drumming circle, she'd accepted his invitation to join him, believing that the village was so small they'd know where to find her.

"You're the one who wants me to take drumming lessons, anyway," Eve had added with a huff.

"Yes, but we need to know where you are and who you're with," Shannon insisted. "Last night—you didn't know those people."

Eric had cleared his throat. "Eve, you can't just—you have to be careful about the kind of people you—"

"Kind of people?"

"They're different from you. They've grown up differently. They don't have your education—"

"They're people, like us." Eve had stuck out her chin and given Eric one of her looks. "They're *Rastas*, the same people Mom is interviewing."

Eric had tapped ash out of his pipe in response.

With Carlton's arrival imminent, Shannon had summarized for Eve the dangers of going off alone in a strange place. "The point is, Eve, you can't just run off with people you don't know in an environment you don't know. I've been teaching you that since you were a little girl."

Shannon was also the one to administer the discipline: no iPod, iPad, or computer for a week. Looking quite content to let her take charge, Eric had sat sucking his pipe, and Shannon had been tempted to pluck it out of his mouth and chuck it over the cliff.

"Can I still take drumming lessons?" Eve had asked, her only question.

"From whom?" her mother had snapped.

"Bongo, Ras Walker's son."

Shannon had looked at Eric, who nodded agreement. "Yes," she'd said, "but it has to be either here or up at the house."

As soon as Carlton drove up, Shannon had escaped to the taxi, anxious to get away from both rebellious daughter and disengaged father. There had to be some reason, she told herself as she watched Shad climb into the front seat, why the ones you love are the ones who hurt you the most.

She was clear now that Eric had been, would perhaps always be, the love of her life, and although she was still unsettled about Eve's adventure, this was what had kept her awake. Revolving in her head was the intimate moment they'd shared in the Jeep. Before dawn, she'd finally conceded that, as diffident as Eric was, he was still kind and genuine, qualities she'd always loved in him. And—despite his aging body—the little smile that never left the corner of his lips, the heavy hair that fell forward despite his best efforts to sweep it back, the helpless raising of the black eyebrows still had power over her. Even looking into his cornflower-blue eyes (Eve's daily reminders to her) made her breathe a little faster. Her feelings for him were back again. Maybe they'd never left, after all.

In the front seat, Shad turned to her as Carlton sped toward Gordon Gap. "Can I tell Carlton about the Canadian woman?"

When Shannon agreed, Shad summarized for Carlton why they'd started going to Gordon Gap and ended by saying they were going back there again today. "We going to try to find some Rastas in the area, since the woman's boyfriend was a Rasta."

The road up the mountain seemed longer today, and Shannon fell asleep halfway up. She awakened, hot and damp in the long sleeves, to find they were parked outside a roadside shack, Carlton immersed in a newspaper. Shad was already deep in conversation with someone in the shack.

"You been carving a long time?" Shad was asking when Shannon walked up. Inside the lean-to, a Rastafarian was sitting on a stool holding a chisel in one hand.

"A few years now," he replied. It was hard to tell his age. He could have been in his thirties or his fifties, the firm skin of his face holding tight to its well-defined features. Coal-black dreads reached halfway down his back, tied in a thick ponytail with a scarf. The writing on his T-shirt said JAH IN FRONT. Behind him was a shelf of carvings large and small, all of them heads, most with dreadlocks, and in a corner were a broom and a machete.

"But like how times hard, the carving can carry you through, though?" Shad asked, and Shannon could see that Shad liked him, cared about him already.

"You sell your carvings and buy some good *ital* food, man, and you can feed the family." The man smiled with teeth whiter than any Canadian orthodontist could have bleached them.

Shad introduced Shannon as *the photographer lady from Canada*. "She talking to Rastafarians for a magazine. She can talk to you?"

The man shifted his gaze, his eyes almost grazing her as he gave her the once-over.

"Just a few questions," she said, a blush rising with his eyes.

He put down the chisel and tweaked his shoulders. "What kind of magazine?"

"It's called *Culture*, kind of like *National Geographic*—I don't know if you know it—but ours is for Canadian readers. We have articles about people around the world. I have one in my bag. Would you like to see it?"

"Yes, man," Shad said. "Let him see it." The man nodded and she fetched the journal from the car.

Leafing through the glossy pages, the Rasta stopped at an article about South Africa and tapped a photograph. "This is a strong man. Babylon fall before him."

"Mandela's inspired a lot of people, even in Canada. I took those photographs of him."

"True?" He was impressed, she could tell, but didn't want to show it.

She took out her notebook and rested it on the counter between two carvings. "I've heard the expression *Babylon* a lot. What does it mean for you?"

The man gave her a wary, no-trifling look. "You want information but I and I don't know your name yet."

"You're right." She pushed away from the counter. "I'm Shannon, this is Shad, and you're . . . ?"

"Ras I-Verse." In answer to an unspoken question, he continued, "You would say Uni-Verse."

She took up her notebook again. "I promise I won't keep you long."

"You want to know what Babylon mean?" He rolled the magazine tightly and got to his feet. He was taller than she'd thought, his head only a few inches below the shack's roof, and he seemed broader all of a sudden. "Babylon signify the unrighteous—like America and Canada and the Jamaican government. It mean *downpression*, the system that suppress small people, seen? Like how America is a rich country and they have poor people living on the street, no home, no food—is the whole system keep it so. That was what Brother Bob was singing about, the suffering of ordinary people, telling woman not to cry, telling the world that we should be loving, not downpressing one another."

I-Verse waved the rolled magazine toward her. "You ever listen to the words in Marley music, though? He say that we must be against Babylon, but we must fight against mental slavery first. Rasta is a *free* man, we don't bow down before Babylon." He looked like a free man, a man whose muscular arms in the sleeveless T-shirt would never be captured for long by any man or woman.

"Do you have a family?" Shannon inquired.

I-Verse glared at her, eyebrows twitching. "You want to talk about Rasta or about me?"

"I—I know family is important in your culture."

The carver laid the magazine on the counter, where it

slowly unwound. A whiff of musky body odor drifted toward her. "I and I have work to do, man."

"Only one more question, I promise. Is there a Rasta
community around here?"

A lock strayed over his shoulder when he nodded.

"Is it far from here—in the mountains?"

"She say one question and asking two." The man looked
at Shad accusingly. "What she really getting after? She want
to know if we grow weed?"

"No, man—"

"She sound like one of them drug enforcement people,
asking all kind of question about where I and I living."
I-Verse was breathing faster, moving toward the machete
in the corner. "Plenty people coming into Jamaica now, say
they writing about Rasta, then next thing you know heli-
copter flying overhead looking for weed. How I and I know
she not one of them?"

Shannon raised her hand, her heart racing, the heat from
the shirt unbearable. "I'm not DEA, CIA, or anything—"

"She want to find out about a friend," Shad said quickly,
"a woman who live with a Rasta long time ago. She don't
mean nothing by it."

"That's right," said Shannon. "I don't give a hoot
about whether you smoke weed or not. I'm working on
an article for the magazine, but I want to find out about
someone."

"What kind of person?"

"She was a Canadian woman, a dancer," Shannon answered, "who'd been living in Gordon Gap in 1977. She
had a Rastafarian boyfriend—she just disappeared."

"That was a long time—"

"We know for a fact that she died in a hospital and we want to know what happened. I want to find the man."

I-Verse shook his head. "You know his name?"

"No, I don't." Shannon rolled up her shirtsleeves.

"That can't help me." The sculptor picked up the broom and started sweeping wood shavings on the dirt floor. The back of his T-shirt read JAH BEHIND.

"What about the longtime Rasta men who live around here?" Shad suggested. "We was thinking that, like, how we just a couple miles from Gordon Gap, the man she went with might have live nearby, you know."

I-Verse leaned the broom in the corner. Picking up the chisel and a half-finished sculpture, he sat down again. "Sorry, can't help you."

"May I take a photograph of you, though?"

"Not that neither."

CHAPTER THIRTEEN

S ign there with your initials." Horace MacKenzie's impatient finger stabbed at the spot. "The first letters of your first and last names, *S* and *M*," he added, making no effort to hide his disapproval of a semiliterate partner in the hotel.

Shad followed the solicitor's instructions, signing every page he was given with a smile, making no effort to hide his satisfaction about being a partner. If Horace wanted to act as if they hadn't been in elementary school together, that they hadn't played cricket in Miss Mac's yard until dark, he wasn't worth the irritation. Not today, because this was his day, Shadrack Myers's day.

The closing on the property, however, was turning out to be more than the new partner had expected, but he was storing up every detail to tell Beth, how Horace's secretary had brought in a side table where they rested the papers after they were signed, how Horace signed each document first before handing it to Eric, who signed and handed it to Shad, who in turn handed it to Miss Mac, Horace's mother and the seller of the beachfront acreage, who added her signature, eyebrows raised above her gold-rimmed glasses, and placed it on the little table beside her. All their signatures were necessary to complete the transaction, he would tell Beth, because that was how partner business was done, and the whole solemn ritual had a circular movement, which, if interrupted, would cause everything to collapse.

One signature besides Horace's already appeared on each page that he handed to Eric, showing that the documents had been delivered to New York by courier and returned. The clear, square signature in place—*Daniel Caines* typed neatly below each—was a statement that thrilled Shad even more. Even though Eric was putting up his experience and the remains of his property along with the island and the bar, and Shad was the needed Jamaican partner, Danny's signature meant much more. It meant that the deal was absolutely, beyond a doubt, going through. Without him, the new company the three had formed back in February, the Largo Bay Grand Hotel Company Limited (the *Grand* at Danny's insistence), would evaporate.

Shad signed the next paper Eric handed him, glad he'd practiced his signature on the dinette table earlier that morning.

"You sign too plain," Beth had commented, stopping to peer over his shoulder while clearing the table after breakfast.

"What you mean?"

"If you going to be a big shot and own a company, you need to sign pretty. You have to show you know who you is."

"You don't see I signing who I is—Shadrack Myers?"

"Yes, but it don't say nothing about *you*. The way the head lady at the library write her name, Lucille Beckman, it slope to the right and go up at the end. It look like she in charge, you know."

Shad had sucked his teeth. "Is an *s* I have at the end, and it go down."

Her purse over her shoulder, Beth had shown him how to swoosh his name up at the end, and he'd practiced after she'd left because it would represent his upward future. He'd prepared himself for one swooshing signature that would show them who he was. No one had mentioned that he'd have to sign his initials and full name over and over, or that there was more than one document, and his hand was now tired, the swoosh less swish, and they were only halfway through. Sitting on his left, Miss Mac got more cheerful with each document.

"Don't forget, you moving me tomorrow," she reminded Shad, placing a form on the table. "I pack up everything already."

"I coming at seven o'clock, like you told me. Frank and Winston going to help."

"I'm lending them my Jeep, Miss Mac," Eric added. "Let me know if there's anything else I can do to help—just not lifting furniture or boxes, what with my back, you know."

Horace was silent, his eyes surveying the three from behind his desk, his immaculate linen suit and silk tie speaking for him. He was thinking about his mother moving into his big concrete home, Shad was sure, wondering how it would work out, this invasion of his privacy. Still a bachelor, he would be a good catch in Port Antonio, even if he was scrawny and his law office above a bread shop. No doubt he brought women into his house sometimes, maybe high-class women, but how would that work now with an outspoken mother living with him, a woman who spoke patois when she got vexed? Maybe he figured she could supervise the maid and his laundry, help out in the kitchen.

"Time longer than rope," Shad had assured Frank the night before. "If you wait long enough, everything come around. Horace think he better than me and better than Largo. Now he and his business partner going to rent Simone Island to run the campsite and—guess what?—is *me* he going to have to deal with. *I* going to be one of his landlords." Shad had whinnied at the thought.

"You meet his partner yet?" Frank had asked drily.

"No."

"You sign the rent agreement?"

"Not till the end of August, but it look like a sure thing. Danny say we need it, though, we need the *cash flow*." Of all the business terms Shad had recently heard, he liked that one the best, as it brought to mind a river of money flowing around them, gently enough to grab what they needed. The other terms, *business proposal*, *shares*, and *equity*, were dull in comparison, no pictures coming to mind, and he'd had to memorize them along with their meanings.

When the signing was finished, Horace stood up and shook their hands, including his mother's. "Congratulations, gentlemen"—he looked at Eric—"you now own nine acres of land."

"My father's land," Miss Mac said with a sad smile.

"Prime beach property," Eric added.

"For the new hotel," Shad finished, noticing a quick look passing between mother and son. They were all aware that the prime beach property Miss Mac had just signed over had been Horace's inheritance, his grandfather's legacy. Giving it up had been a difficult decision for his mother, but necessary, because her teacher's pension was only a few thousand Jamaican dollars a month, hardly enough for groceries, she'd always complained, and she'd had to supplement it with running a boardinghouse. But she was getting too old to cook and clean for boarders, couldn't afford the repairs on the old house anymore.

"I don't want to be a burden to my son," she'd once told Shad while he was helping her pick limes. "I selling my house so I can pay him little rent and buy my own groceries. Then I can leave him whatever leave over."

Her financial gain had become Horace's loss, and if Shad had had a better relationship with the lawyer, he would have let him know he felt his pain. If he and Beth even thought of selling his grandmother's house, Granny would be sure to come back to haunt them. He wouldn't want to trade places with Horace now for all the lawyer's offices and big houses in the world.

Gratitude was still on Shad's mind when he arrived at his house that night after work. In his hand was a bottle of cheap champagne that the boss had insisted he take to celebrate. Warming up to the occasion as he walked home, he'd anticipated waking Beth to tell her about the closing, anticipated hearing again how she'd scorned Horace's attention in high school, anticipated all manner of romping after the chatting was done. But his fantasies faded as soon as he opened his bedroom door and saw Beth hemming the familiar blue dress.

"Why you up so late?"

"I couldn't get Ashanti to settle down." Circles of exhaustion were around Beth's eyes. "She was screaming and going on. You know how she can get." Behind her, the child lay curled up asleep, a wooden spoon in her hand.

"She sleeping now."

"Yes, but I have to finish Rickia's dress."

"Finish it tomorrow, nuh?"

"I going with Maisie to Port Antonio tomorrow."

"What you have to do in Port Antonio?"

"Order flowers. I carrying a bouquet and Joella and Rickia, too, three bouquets, and we need flowers for the church." Beth knotted the thread and bit it off. "You have little money you can give me?"

"Every time I turn around is more money for this wedding." Shad sighed. He put the champagne in the fridge and carried Ashanti to her cot in the children's bedroom. "You never tell me about no flowers before," he grumbled while he changed into the sleeveless marina he slept in. "You know how much that going to cost?"

"You ever see a wedding with no flowers?"

"I come to celebrate the closing with you tonight, and is money you talking about again."

"You want me to tell you the truth, so I tell you." Beth hung the dress in the wardrobe. "I could have make up something, you know."

"And while you spending money, is me have to take the basket up to Miss Bertha's and sell your vegetables. You not thinking about that."

Beth put her hands on her hips. "Eh-eh, is not like you the only one making money now, you know."

"But you spending it as fast as you make it."

"What you think money is for? I take the job at the library so I could help pay for the wedding, you don't remember?"

"Then why you asking me for money now?"

The light stayed on in the bedroom until well after four that morning, and by that time Shad had said three times—shouting at her once—that he was sick of the damn wedding, and that when Beth showed up at the church, he wouldn't be there, and she had started to cry, her shoulders shaking soundlessly in her tiredness. He'd slept on the love seat in the living room and woken up feeling like a *heng-pon-nail*, an old shirt that had been hanging from a nail all night.

CHAPTER FOURTEEN

The beachside parking lot had one empty space and Eric pulled the Jeep in. He'd had to drive slowly because Shannon was nervous about the girls riding in the open back, and he was relieved that any parking was left by the time they got there, as late as it was.

"I'll change my clothes in the car, I don't want to get them sandy," Shannon said, surprising him with her practicality. She'd always been spontaneous back in the day—but she hadn't been a mother then either.

Eve and Casey clambered out of the back with the picnic basket. "Eve's stomach not used to pepper," Maisie had reminded him when she handed the basket over. "Make her eat the sandwiches."

The idea of a beach trip had come up the night before when Shannon had appeared on Eric's verandah, a shadow beside his chair on a moonless night. "Shad said I'd find you here."

"Nowhere else to hide," he'd nodded, his teeth gripping the pipe's stem.

"He said the closing was today. Shouldn't you be celebrating?"

From the bedroom came the Spanish words of Radio

Fidel, the show's host double-rolling the r and stretching the leader's name to the maximum as he announced an up-coming program. Eric had gone inside and turned it off.

"Have a seat," he'd said when he returned, and the two old lovers had sat in the darkness, a dancehall song seeping through the bushes from the bar, turned down by Shad, perhaps thinking of Eric and his visitor.

"It's still beautiful here, isn't it?" Shannon had ventured. "I wondered if it had changed at all, but it's just like I re-member. Except for—you know . . ."

"You can say it—except for the hotel."

They were quiet for a minute until he heard her exhale. "I thought you might leave after the hurricane."

Eric had pulled his pipe out of his mouth. "And go back to New York?"

"I don't know, go somewhere."

"There was nowhere to go." He wouldn't fall for her hint that he could have come up to Canada. "I wasn't going to sit in some little apartment and freeze my ass off in the winter. Worse if I had to work up there again, get up in the dark every day." He'd snorted when he said it, realizing after that she was doing just that, freezing her ass off in the Toronto winter, waking in the dark to get Eve ready for school. It was too late to take it back and they'd lapsed into silence again.

"Miss Bertha told us about the woman on the island," she'd said after a minute. "We were sitting in the kitchen talking about the hurricane and she told me that you had a squatter living there last year." Eric wiggled his toes in his flip-flops, guessing that this must be what she'd come about, a look-see into the Woman, but she didn't seem interested and veered away. "As sad as the story is—I mean the hurricane and the damage—as sad as it all was, I'm glad you were able to hang on in Largo, with the bar and everything. It's still an amazingly beautiful place, still peaceful, still friendly."

"It was a wreck after the storm, trees down, houses with no roofs, canoes sitting on the road." He waved the pipe. "You wouldn't believe what a mess it was."

"But they recovered, and you did, too."

"I can't say I recovered, not half of what I had, anyway."

"I know, I know, but—I'm not doing this well—I'm glad you never gave up. What I'm trying to say is, I appreciate how you kept sending the payments every month for Eve. There must have been times when you—"

"You're welcome."

"I kept criticizing you—in my head, anyway—for not coming up to visit Eve and me. I had no idea, really, of what you'd gone through."

Eric rested the dead pipe on the tiles next to his chair. "Can I get you a drink? I'm just going to fix myself one."

"A Red Stripe?"

Over her beer, Shannon had broached the subject of a beach outing the next day. "I thought I'd introduce Eve to Jamaican jerk pork from the stand where it started. She can boast to her friends when she gets back. What's the name of that beach?"

"Boston Beach." Eric examined her dark profile, the gleam on the end of the upturned nose. "You want me to take you, is that it?"

"Would you? Shad is helping Miss Mac move, so we won't be doing any work tomorrow, and Jennifer and Lam have a luncheon or something. Since I only have a couple days off, I thought it would be fun, you know, and we can take Casey along to keep Eve company. They can watch the guys cooking the pigs. She pretends not to care about stuff like that, but she does."

"And you don't want her staying home with you, nagging you to use her iPod and—"

"Precisely."

"By the time Shad gets back with the Jeep, it'll probably be closer to lunchtime—"

"No problem."

The beach was half-filled with families when they arrived with their food basket and towels, and a few people were standing around a shed at one end.

"What's going on over there?" Eve asked.

"That's where they jerk the pork," Casey explained, tossing her hair like her mother. "It was the first place on the island, that's what Daddy says."

After they'd spread their blanket and Shannon had joined them, all four went to look at the open shed in the center of the smoke. Above a long, smoldering fire, on a barbecue rack of iron bars, rested the carcasses of three pigs split in half. Each half carcass was being lovingly basted by two men naked to the waist. A third man sliced chunks off the carcasses, and a teenage boy was taking money from customers, handing over brown-paper cones of pork and thick slices of hard-dough bread.

"What's that they're putting on it?" Eve pointed to one of the basting men.

"That's the jerk sauce," Shannon said.

Her father pointed to the pepper seeds sticking to the

pork skins. "Don't even go near those. That's scotch bonnet pepper, and it makes the sauce superhot. Then they add a whole bunch of stuff, from cinnamon, ginger, nutmeg, all kinds of things, and they cook it over branches of a pimento tree. The whole thing gives it that special flavor called jerk."

"I want to taste it," Eve said, not to be deterred, chin firm. "I want to see how it really tastes."

As an indulgence to his daughter—and his own dripping saliva glands—Eric called out an order for a pound of jerk pork.

"Behold, from the first jerk stand in the world," he said, holding out the greasy cone to Eve.

This was where the story was later to diverge, depending on who was telling it. Shannon claimed that Eric ate almost the whole pound of pork, which Eric himself denied. Casey said she ate the jerk and nothing happened, and Eve boasted that she'd eaten it, too, with no ill effect. Shannon said she'd only had a taste and the sauce alone had burned her lips.

The four salty beachgoers had barely returned to Largo when Eric's stomach started heaving. He just managed to park the Jeep and make it to his bathroom in what was the opening salvo to the worst bout of the runs he'd ever had. Not only did he make innumerable trips from the bed to the toilet, but the nausea made him want to throw up at the same time. As he was to tell Lambert later, he was overtaken by a feeling of being close to death and finding death attractive. After a couple hours of agony, a second dose of Pepto-Bismol, and a glass of coconut water, the bar owner managed to doze off, moaning as he dozed. When he opened his eyes, Shannon was turning on the lamp beside him.

"Miss Maisie called to say you were in a bad way. She has to go home and she didn't want to leave you alone."

"What's happened to Shad?" he groaned.

"Busy at the bar." She pulled a chair up beside the bed and sat down.

"You got a tan," he muttered.

"How do you feel?"

"Don't ask."

"Maybe I should call the doctor." She leaned over him, the flesh between her eyebrows drawn into one deep valley. "You look awful."

"I'll be okay."

She pulled up one side of her mouth. "You don't look it."

A hot wave of nausea rolled from his bowels up to his chest. "Oh, God," he moaned, struggling to sit up, willing himself not to vomit in front of her.

"Can I get you a cup of tea or something?" she said as he staggered past.

CHAPTER FIFTEEN

S hannon put Eric's glass in the bar sink and opened the fridge. "May I have a drink?" she asked Shad.

"Yeah, man. What you want?"

She surveyed the contents of the fridge: limes and oranges, two bags of ice, neat, vertical rows of soft drinks, a shelf of beers. Its mundaneness brought her back to reality. Seeing the man she'd once idealized looking weak and pathetic had opened a flood gate of sympathy that she needed to suppress. She'd found herself plumping pillows, bringing another glass of coconut water, placing a plastic bowl next to the bed within easy reach. It had been all she could do not to wipe the dribble from his mouth after he retched.

"How'd Miss Mac's move go this morning?" she asked.

"She still have a lot of boxes and things left, but we got all the furniture. She give some to me and some to Frank. She say she can't pack all of it into Horace's house, so Beth and I have a new bed."

He placed the glass he was drying on a towel. "How's the boss doing?"

"Not good." She took a beer from the fridge. "But he's not going to admit it."

The bartender opened the bottle. "You right, but he getting soft in his old age."

"That will be the day."

"I telling you, he lost the fire in his belly, ever since the hurricane." Shannon sat on a barstool and Shad leaned toward her, lowering his voice. "Remember how he used to be so sure of what he wanted, used to argue about every little thing? Well, them days gone. Anything I want him to do now, he usually do it. And Solomon take off plenty time, always suffering from a hangover, and he still let him work here. Days gone by, he wouldn't have stand for none of that."

"Maybe he's depressed."

The bartender pushed back from the counter, horror on his face. "Depressed! He don't have nothing to depress him. He going to get a new hotel with a nice apartment, and he don't even have to put up any money. All he have to do is sit back and relax because I going to manage it for him."

Shannon took a swig. "Maybe he's lonely."

Shad shook his head hard. "With all of us around him? Nah, man. He even have a nice girl—" He broke off and spun toward the fridge.

"Girlfriend?" Shannon finished, hearing the other shoe fall. The shabby bar was the first surprise, now this.

Shad turned around to face her, pulling his lips wide. "Well, they not exactly—"

"I'm a big girl, Shad. Is she a local?" The bartender shook his head. "Who is she then?"

Shad squared his shoulders. "Best I tell you than someone else. Is the woman who was living on the island."

"*The squatter?*"

"She wasn't no ordinary, poor squatter, you know. She was a nice woman who just want to get away from everything."

Shannon sipped hard at the beer while the bartender rushed away to fill an order at a distant table. "Tell me about her," she said when he returned.

He raised both shoulders high and dropped them. "What kind of thing you want to know?"

"Her name."

"Simone."

"Is she, I don't know, big, tall, ugly . . . pretty?"

"Little bigger than Beth, not as big as you." He got busy tuning the radio to a new station. Shannon raised her eyebrows when he turned around, urging him on. "She pretty, yes, a brown-skinned woman from Jamaica. When she was five, her family move to England, then later to America."

"Why was she on the island?"

"She was grieving, grieving everything in her life. She was a big businesswoman, but you know how you reach a place sometimes when you want to stop and let the sadness catch up with you? That was where she was. The sadness catch up with her, so she come back to Jamaica to find some kind of peace. She say she was riding around in a taxi and saw the island, and she decide that was where she want to stay."

"Was she—you know, unstable?"

"Crazy? No, I wouldn't say so. She talk calm and make plenty sense. She talk the boss into renting her the island, even though it wasn't legal, like how the hotel mash up. She live there for two months like a free woman, just do whatever she feel like doing. After a while, she didn't feel like wearing clothes and she walk around the island naked."

Shannon let out a reluctant crow and raised the bottle. "Now that's a fantasy I've always had."

"And another time"—Shad chuckled—"when some guys row out one night to rape her, she shoot a gun after them and they run away. They almost drown coming back in the canoe because they didn't know how to row good. The whole village laugh after them."

Shannon took a slow sip, wanting to hate the woman and failing. "I hadn't thought of that, that someone would try to—to attack her. She must have been scared shitless."

"You know Jamaicans. They see a woman by herself . . ."

"I'm glad she knew how to defend herself."

"She a strong woman."

"Has she—has Eric seen her since then?"

"No, but she's coming in two weeks' time—for the groundbreaking."

"Two weeks?" Shannon ran a hand through her hair, untangling an unruly lock, her heart beating fast. Any remnant of sympathy she'd felt for Eric had vanished. There'd be no wiping of body fluids after this, of that she was sure.

"What day is she coming?"

"August first, Wednesday, so the boss say."

Shannon puffed out her cheeks and released them. "And I wonder when he was planning to tell me."

"Everything happening so fast at the end of the month, you know, he probably forget. The groundbreaking coming, then Danny, the investor guy, coming down with his girlfriend, and—"

"He should have told me."

Shad examined something invisible on his arm. "Is just a little visit, not like he going to get married."

"We know *that*," the Canadian woman snarled. "He's not exactly the marrying kind."

Shad picked up the glass he'd wiped before and wiped it again. "You know," he said slowly, "if it was up to any man, I don't feel there would be any wedding business. Marriage is something created by women, I sure of it. I don't think any man is the marrying kind."

"What do you mean? You're on the way up the aisle yourself."

The glass being wiped was replaced with another. "Maybe not."

"Spit it out, Shad. What's bothering you?"

Bracing himself against the counter, he gazed at the sink. "The way a woman can tie you up for the rest of your life, and she have to do it in front of a hundred people, and she have to impress the people with fancy dress and shoes. Then, guess who have to pay so the hundred people can eat and drink after to celebrate your downfall?"

"Wait a minute, hold your horses. Don't you love Beth?"

"Of course."

"And don't you want your children to know that you're committing to stay with her and with them for the rest of your life?"

"Yes, but the wedding thing—is money for this and money for that. First it was material to make dresses. Now is flowers for the church, tomorrow is something else. And we don't even get to the food and liquor—or the rings."

"Are you sure"—Shannon stood to leave—"that there isn't something else at the bottom of it, Shad?"

He breathed a hard sigh. "You know the truth? No Jamaican man like to get married. We just not used to it. Is like you give a woman the right to think for you. I don't even think American man like to get married, want to be tied down. Look at the boss. He free and single, run his own life. He have two children, but he don't marry again."

Shannon sat down heavily. "Shad, let me tell you something. What you see is just one part of the picture. You see Eric *free and single*, as you say, but you're not thinking about the mothers of his children, who pay for it. He's only free and single at our expense. We're the ones who have to do everything alone because he isn't there when we have to help the children with homework, cook dinner, discipline them—*everything*."

She knew she was raising her voice (the beer adding to the volume), hoping Eric could hear her. "What kind of life do you think that's been for Joseph's mother and for me? And don't you think the children resent his absence? They can't respect a father who's never there, who forgets their birthdays. He barely has a relationship with Joseph and Eve. You can see that for yourself."

"I see that, true. He should have—"

"Leaving me aside, think of it from his point of view." She swept her hand over the counter, almost knocking over the bottle. "He's shut people out, isolated himself. Miss Maisie, his housekeeper, has to take care of him when he has diarrhea because he doesn't even have a family member to help him."

Shad looked down, one hand on his hip, the other stroking his scalp. "I hadn't really thought—"

"Well, think about it." Shannon slapped the counter. "You said yourself that he'd lost his passion for life. I mean, just look at him, sitting alone on his verandah at night.

I bet he's thinking about the mistakes he made and the people he's hurt. No wonder he's miserable." She pushed the empty beer bottle toward him. "Free and single, my ass."

Despite her jaunty walk out of the bar, Shannon's heart was sinking as she climbed the hill to the Delgados' house. Tears welled up in her eyes, reminding her of the pain she'd felt after she'd told Eric she was pregnant and his ardor had withdrawn, like a wave pulling back from the shore. The worst, ugliest pain came when she was leaving that last time. He'd stood awkwardly in the lobby, avoiding her eyes, giving her a brief hug before she boarded the bus to the airport. She'd cried all the way to Montego Bay, her chest aching.

"Oh, God," she groaned as she approached the house, "what happened to us, Eric?" The only answer came from the night-blooming jasmine, its melancholy fragrance swamping her memories.

CHAPTER SIXTEEN

His name for the new pastor was Buffoon. Shad had heard the word once on the radio when a talk show host had labeled a politician, and he and Rickia had looked it up in the dictionary on the laminated coffee table.

"A person given to undignified behavior that causes amusement to others," the child had read out.

"That sounding just like Pastor Buckingham." Her father had laughed. The family had adopted the name, although Joella had wanted to call the minister Batman because of the oversize black sleeves of his robe, which he flapped throughout services. Beth said they were all disrespectful, that he was a good person, married to his wife like a God-fearing man.

Now observing the short, round fellow working himself into a sweat even before the sermon had started, Shad concluded that the Buffoon was nonetheless better than his predecessor, Pompous Ass. A judgmental man, he'd been replaced by the Kingston Baptists for his *misdeeds*, their name for a run-in with the law that would keep him in prison for several years.

Wiping his brow, the Buffoon waved his free hand like a magician's wand. "And now, a musical rendition from Sister Eustacia."

Soon Sister Eustacia was warbling "In the Old By and By" over the piano, a combination of screeching and banging that made Joshua, perched on Joella's knee, arch backward to find his father.

"Hang on, boy," Shad whispered. "We soon go home to Mamma."

"We should have stayed home," Joella muttered.

Beth would have taken care of things, would have remembered to bring a toy for Josh to play with—but she wasn't here today. She'd been up all night with Ashante, who'd been bothered by some unnamed fear that kept her awake and crying.

"You don't have to come to church today," Shad had suggested when Beth pulled up groggily on her elbow that morning. Miss Mac's mahogany headboard towering above had made her look even smaller in the bed.

"I have to—"

"No, you stay home. I take the other children to church so you can sleep."

She'd given him a look that said she was grateful but shouldn't even be talking to him. In the two days since his declaration that he wouldn't be at the altar when she got there, she'd barely said a word, had made him suffer the silence of her unhappiness—even as she stubbornly continued her wedding preparations. When he'd insisted again that she stay home, she'd offered little resistance.

"Mamma look like she tired," Rickia had commented after Beth dozed off. "I can stay home and watch Ashante. I keep her in our bedroom."

Buffoon got back to the too-tall podium, which cut him off at the nose, leaving him only two inches of visual clearance.

"Beautiful rendition, Sister." He flapped his wings. He smiled at the singer. "Beautiful." He turned to the congregation, fanning themselves on their folding chairs. "Give her some love, Brothers and Sisters."

They obliged, a few even calling out belated *Amen*s.

The pastor removed his glasses and wiped them on his sleeve. "*The old by and by*, what that mean?" he asked, beaming. The only answer that greeted him was the shuffling of feet. Shad looked out the open window behind the choir. Deep turquoise water lay under a bright blue sky, the waves curling, breaking in the sunshine even before they hit the shore, affirming for Shad that God was out there today.

Buckingham smiled on. "*The by and by*. It mean 'times long ago,' don't it? And we're going to talk today about some of the words of the Old Testament that tell us about some dreams that Joseph—he was a dream interpreter, you know—anybody know that, that Joseph used to interpret dreams? Is not only the obeah man can interpret dreams, you know." The pastor chuckled and a few members of the congregation joined him, the ones who visited the obeah man smiling uncertainly.

Half an hour later, Shad was still holding Joshua, shushing him, putting him down on the floor, picking him up again, patting him, wondering how much longer the child could hold out without bawling the place down. The pastor flapped and crowed, standing on tiptoe sometimes, jumping up and down a few times as he reached ecstatic heights. In the end, all that the young father remembered from the sermon was a quotation from Acts, at least he thought he remembered Pastor saying it came from Acts, words that ran around in his head long after he'd left the church.

"'Your old men will dream dreams and your young men will see visions,'" Shad repeated aloud as he poured oil into the frying pan for the family's Sunday dinner. "That what Pastor was saying today."

Beside him, Rickia was rolling a raw chicken wing in batter. "What that mean?"

"It mean that old men look back on their past and dream about it. They done live their life already." Like Mistah Eric.

"And the young men?"

Her father looked up at the grease-spattered wall. "The young men create their own visions, and they have all the time ahead of them to make their vision come true. They have to look ahead and create a future for their family." He dropped a drumstick into the frying pan.

"How come they don't say *your old women will dream dreams and your young women will see visions*, Dadda? Is only men can have visions?"

"It don't mean that women can't do it. In them days, the men was the head of everything and the women stay home."

The girl rolled out her bottom lip. "All the women in the Bible either tempting men or having babies. Men don't give them no respect."

Shad dropped two wings into the sizzling oil. "You going prove them wrong, I know, sweets." He grinned at his second child. He threw in the slices of onion and green pepper from the bowl beside him and sprinkled some thyme over them.

A dancehall song, a man bawling lyrics Shad couldn't make out, leaped from the living room. "Go tell your sister to turn down the radio, please, because her mother just waking up—and set the table for dinner."

142

Shad was turning off the gas under the chicken when Joella appeared at the kitchen door. "Dadda, a man outside want to see you."

"Come, finish frying the plantain for me while I check it out."

The man turned out to be a stocky Rastafarian wearing loose white pants and a black scarf tied around his forehead. He was standing between two tall, striped drums, one on either side of him.

"Ras Bongo, what bring you here?"

"Carlton tell me that Mistah Eric's daughter needing drumming lessons."

"I don't know how it going now because I hear she in punishment."

"She the same little girl come with Jethro to the drumming circle the other night?"

"Same one."

"She good," the man said with jerking nods, his dreadlocks swinging forward on both sides of his face. "I could use a few extra shekel. I and I going to pass by the bar and talk to her father. What you think?"

"Ask the mother first, up at the Delgados' house."

"*Irie.*"

The family was already seated at the dinette table when Shad went back inside. They were waiting for him, faces turned up, eyes down on the fried chicken and rice and peas.

Still in her nightshirt, Beth maintained order. "No dinner until we say grace," she commanded. "Ashante, take your hands out of the bowl."

"See Dadda here," Joella said. "We can say grace now."

"Where's Josh?" her father asked.

"Sleeping."

They all held hands around the table, except for Ashante, who was allowed to chew on a piece of plantain to keep her quiet.

"God," Shad prayed, "we thank you for the food you provide us, and for the money to buy it. And we ask you to bless us this week, and show us the way forward with school and the new hotel and everything. Thank you for having a loving family and taking care of each other, even when we get old. And, one special favor we asking you, make us wise and blessed in your sight—so we can see visions and make them come true."

When he opened his eyes, everyone else's eyes were on him. "What?" he asked Beth.

"See visions?"

"Why not? Is our time now." He passed the plantain to Rickia, remembering her comment about men's power over women, remembering Shannon spitting *free and single* at him. "And for you, madam"—he passed the chicken to Joella but addressed her mother—"all I have to say is this: five hundred US dollars. Is half the money Shannon giving me to take her around, but I giving it to you for the wedding. The rest I going to put to Joella's high school."

He picked up his knife and fork and cut away at the crispy chicken. "You can put what money you want towards it from your own salary, but five hundred is all I have to give—and I don't want to hear one more thing about wedding and money, you hear me?"

CHAPTER SEVENTEEN

The last twenty-four hours were the longest Eric had ever experienced. What had started as a simple case of jerk-pork revulsion had settled into fever, nausea, and an inability to keep anything down, even water. By midday Sunday, his bed was damp with sweat. He rolled from one side to the other, hoping to find a dry spot. The vibrating crash of the waves breaking beneath the cliff, usually unnoticed after all these years, made him feel worse. Nothing seemed to help, even looking at the island, which normally kept him in balance. Its strident noontime brightness was making his nerves raw.

Shannon hadn't come by this morning, although she wouldn't be working on a Sunday. He'd hoped she'd come, just to keep him company. He'd thought about her last night in the wee hours when he'd woken with a vicious headache. It would have been nice to hold on to her sturdy, womanly form when he had to climb out of bed, but he'd held on to the bed for support on his way to the toilet and groped his way back. He'd spent this morning—in between listening to the church bell clanking and the taxis honking as they turned the corner into Largo—feeling good and sorry for himself.

"I'm dying," he'd groaned to Maisie as soon as she'd appeared after church.

"No wonder, you don't drink nothing, you don't eat nothing" was her matter-of-fact response. She'd removed her blue church hat and placed it beside her handbag on his chest of drawers. The ginger ale she'd brought him had made him feel worse.

"You want me to wipe you down, clean you up a little? You might have visitors and you smell kind of . . . *fresh*." She'd wrinkled her nose, and he knew it meant he smelled like a pigsty.

"Help me to the bathroom."

While he struggled through a shower, Maisie had stood outside the bathroom door, reminding him of his life's deficiencies. "You need a woman to take care of you, Mistah Eric. All these years you manage on your own, but you know what they say, *wanti-wanti no get it, getti-getti no want it*."

"What's that mean?" Eric had asked as he dabbed his body with a towel.

"People who want something can't get it, and people who get something—you know, it just come too easy, so they don't want it."

Eric didn't answer, the drying and thinking making it impossible to talk at the same time.

"I mean to say"—Maisie's voice didn't budge from outside the door—"you have plenty nice woman and you don't even want one of them. Look how much men would like to have even one."

After he'd thrown himself back in the bed, Maisie's dark moon-face had hovered above his pillow. "I going to give you little bush tea."

"No mumbo jumbo, Maisie." He waved her away.

"A little bush tea with pepper elder and you good, man."

"I'm getting better."

"You look worse." Maisie had crossed her arms above her rounded belly. "You losing all your liquid."

"Dehydration?"

"Next thing I have to call the doctor and they give you that oral hydra-thing to drink, and it taste nasty. My niece baby had diarrhea last year, and is me have to give the child the nasty drink, but she live."

Eric had rolled over in defeat. "Okay, give me the tea."

Sipping tea later, his head propped up on two pillows and another under his knees, Eric thought about the woman's words and her reference to Simone and Shannon. The locals had never been bashful about telling him how to run his life, particularly his love life. Every few months some villager referred to one of his *lady friends* and teased him about the ease with which he attracted them. Some even goaded him to do the unspeakable.

"Why you don't just marry Simone, Mistah Eric?" Tri, draped on the bar on Christmas Eve, had asked. "Like how she still young, you can still have some *pickney* running around the place, don't it?" The old man was well into finishing a bottle of white rum, and Eric had told him to go home and sleep off the idea.

Talk of marriage always chilled Eric to his bones. His parents' marriage had been quarrelsome, and his marriage to Claire, Joseph's mother, had only been to stop her comments about her friends getting married. Since their divorce nineteen years ago, marriage had become a taboo subject for him. Claire had remarried a few months back to a surgeon, and he'd felt strangely betrayed. A Catholic, she'd said she'd never remarry, as had he, although his decision had nothing to do with religion.

Some men could stay happily married for fifty years, wouldn't know what to do if they weren't. That wasn't him, he'd told everyone, and he'd never encouraged any of his girlfriends or passing trysts to think anything to the contrary. Love affairs would end, bonds would be broken—and time had proven him right.

"I'm not into long-distance relationships," he'd told Amanda, a self-described "recovering hippie" who'd stayed at Miss Mac's boardinghouse a few years back. It was her last night in Largo, and they were lying on top of the sheets after another round of her tantric sex, which he'd insisted on calling tangled sex.

"I can come down every couple months. I'm only in Florida."

"I don't know. Maybe we should just leave it there. It's been fun, right? We wouldn't want to spoil a good memory."

She'd stood up, naked, not a small woman, not a young woman, wiping one eye with the back of her hand. "I guess this is what you do for entertainment. You find women traveling alone and sleep with them for a few nights. Passes the time, right? You know what they call men like you, Eric? *Users, teasers*." She'd pointed to the door without raising her voice. "Get the fuck out of my room."

From time to time he'd think of Amanda, with her droopy breasts and wavy, gray hair, and he'd wonder if she'd seen the wisdom of his words.

His feelings on long-term commitment hadn't changed,

and even if he'd felt inclined to tie himself down in a marriage now, no one was on the horizon. Shannon and Simone both had lives elsewhere, no matter what Maisie implied. One was comfortably settled in Toronto, and the other had never even hinted at moving back to Largo.

Simone seemed happy with the status quo. She seldom even called, and he hadn't heard from her since he'd told her that Shannon and Eve were in town. He liked that about her, that she didn't make demands or bother him. She was always busy, had even started group therapy, she'd told him a few months back. No doubt she and the group had analyzed her relationship with a man twenty years older, calling it emotional incest or some fancy term.

The age difference didn't matter in a once-a-year love affair. He'd reconciled himself to how one day Simone would find another man and it would be over. She was savvy and would know there was nothing for her in little Largo. Despite her temporary exile on the island, women like her needed a city with conveniences—therapists, airports, and technology. Only people who could live with permanent limitations could tolerate a place like this.

The thumping of a drum broke through his thoughts. It seemed to be coming from the restaurant.

"Maisie!" he called, but another round of thumping drowned him out.

He waited for a pause and called again. The woman appeared at the door, her eyes and mouth twitching. "Mistah Eric?"

"What's happening out there?"

"Your daughter taking a drumming class from Bongo, Ras Walker son. He say that Shannon tell him they were having lunch at the Delgados' and they must come down here and practice." Maisie left just as the drumming started again, this time a tentative imitation of the thumping that had gone before—Eve's response, no doubt. He put down his mug and wedged his head between two pillows. This wasn't like Shannon, sending drummers to invade his recovery.

Drowsy with bush tea, he dozed off. When he awoke, the drumming had stopped. He could hear voices: first Maisie's, then Eve's. His stomach felt calmer—the tea had worked—and he was hungry. He sat up slowly, testing his head for the ache (gone) and his bowels (only slightly queasy).

Someone outside started singing in a high, slightly off-key voice, the rhythm pronounced, the lyrics repetitive. He walked creakily through his living room and padded past the kitchen where Maisie was working. Arriving at the bar counter, he held on to steady himself. His daughter was standing at the side of the restaurant, singing with her back to him. He couldn't make out the words of the song at first but eventually caught them.

She was chanting, "Shaking to the rhythm of the *August rain*," over and over, hopping from one bare foot to the other, stamping her foot three times at the end of each verse.

"What's *that* all about?" Eric said, interrupting her.

Eve blushed as soon as she saw him. "It's a—just a verse—something Bongo taught me, so I can practice my drumming to it."

"Do it again."

The girl shrugged. "It's kind of silly."

"I want to see it."

Facing the ocean again, she started the song, stomping to the last few beats.

Shaking to the rhythm of the Au-gust rain,
Shaking to the rhythm of the Au-gust rain.

She chanted it louder each time, hopping with her hands on her hips, and Eric applauded when she finished. Eve turned to look at him and clapped, giving a yelp like a happy puppy.

CHAPTER EIGHTEEN

S hannon raised reluctant eyes from her iPhone. "He's not there?"

"I-Verse sick today," Shad said as he jumped back into the car, escaping the misty rain.

"There's someone else there?"

She stuck her phone back in her bag, trying to put out of her mind the multitude of emails that had downloaded after they'd left Largo. It had already been a trying morning, and they were still at ground zero about Katlyn. A visit to Port Morant Hospital had yielded no information. Apart from getting rained on as they ran to and from the taxi, they'd been told by a lethargic secretary that she didn't know where the old records were kept. They must have been thrown out long ago. Everything was wrong with the hospital, the woman had complained as if they cared, pointing to something on her computer monitor. The machines in the X-ray department were worn-out. They were almost as old as the records Shannon was looking for. And the hospital had two operating theaters, but only one anesthetic machine, and the equipment they had in the operating theater was so old—

"And the new equipment is too expensive, we know,"

Shad had assured her, interrupting the monologue before they rushed out through the downpour, a rainy season warning.

Her frustration making her more determined, Shannon had instructed Carlton to go back to I-Verse's shack. He was their only connection to a Rastafarian camp so far, and maybe, just maybe, this time he'd open up and tell them something about the communities around Gordon Gap. If he didn't, they'd have to find another Rasta in the area who'd be more helpful.

Shannon jumped out of the car, shielding her head with her camera bag, and dashed toward the shack. I-Verse was nowhere around, and his stool was now occupied by a woman in a long, patterned dress. On her lap, a baby played with one of the sculptures. The woman, young, perhaps in her midtwenties, had thick, blond dreadlocks coiled above her tanned face.

Shannon ran around to the narrow opening at the back of the shack and ducked inside. "Hello, we were hoping to find I-Verse."

Blue eyes looked back at her. "He not here and he don't say nothing," the woman replied with a shake of the dread-lock-coiled head.

"We've come a long way—from Largo Bay on the east end."

"You going to have to come back tomorrow." A Southern accent hung over the patois like live-oak moss. The baby waved the sculpture and placed it on top of its curly, brown hair, looking up at the visitor, a golden-brown child with green eyes.

"Boy or girl?"

"Boy." The woman touched one of her hoop earrings. "You buying something?"

"I hadn't planned to, but—they're so beautiful, maybe I will." Shannon chose a bust of a man with a woebegone expression. "I'll take this one." A lovely gift for Chantrelle.

The woman gave her a quick smile as if it went with the purchase. "Fifty US."

"That's a little high, don't you think?" Shannon liked how it felt in her hand, the smoothness of the man's face and the roughness of his dreadlocks reassuring. The rain started pounding on the zinc roof.

"It take a long time to carve," the woman yelled over the racket.

"Did I-Verse carve this?"

The woman took the carving, looked at the bottom, and shook her head.

"I have the money in the car," Shannon said above the racket. "We'll have to wait until the rain dies down a bit."

The baby looked up at the roof and cried out, and the woman said something to him in a low voice.

"My name is Shannon, by the way. I should introduce myself—if I'm going to be standing around in your place like this."

"I'm Akasha."

"That's beautiful. Does it mean something?"

The American Rasta tipped her head. "It mean 'open air, space.'" She frowned again. "Like freedom."

The raindrops slowed, falling farther apart in space and time into the muddy puddles now surrounding the hut. Shannon started toward the opening. "I'll get the money out of the car."

After she'd returned and paid for the sculpture—a little haggling until they got to $35—the woman looked up from making change. "Where you come from?"

"Toronto. I'm working here."

"You a photographer?" Akasha said, gesturing with her chin to the camera bag as she handed over the change.

"Yes."

"You take a picture of me and the baby and send it to me?" Shifting the baby to her other hip, the woman exhaled sharply, a criticism of someone. "I don't have no pictures to send my mother."

"As long as I can use one for my article, I can give you one." The woman nodded and Shannon took out a camera, squaring the two in the LCD screen. "Where does your mother live?"

"Alabama."

It was a short portrait session, the young woman with a stiff smile and the baby cooing. When Shannon checked the shots, she could see that they would be gorgeous photographs of mother and son, their colorful garments and glowing skins radiating life and health. Akasha approved of the pictures, turning the baby around to see them.

"Let me have your email address and I can send them to you."

"We don't have no email. You can print them and send them to me at an address?"

"Of course." The address turned out to be a post office box in I-Verse's name, not as helpful as Shannon would have liked, but an opening nonetheless. "Are you I-Verse's wife?" she asked, putting the camera away, and Akasha said yes. "You make beautiful babies."

"So everybody say." The woman looked pleased.

"Where did you two meet—if you don't mind me asking? You don't often see—you know—you don't see a lot of foreign Rastas."

"We met in Negril." The young mother placed a basket on the stool. "I was working at a bar—Nick's Café, you know it?—and he was my manager there."

Shannon tried and failed to picture I-Verse pacifying a complaining tourist. "Were you a Rasta before you met him?"

"Yes, ten years now."

The rain poured down with renewed energy as Akasha packed up the sculpture. With the baby on one hip, she started wrapping it with one hand, rolling it in crumpled squares of newspaper and placing it in the basket.

"Can I hold him while you do that?"

The young woman handed the child over.

The guttural roar of a motorbike approached, veered toward the back of the shed, and cut off. A Rastafarian man in a yellow rain jacket ducked inside. "Rain coming down again like dog and cat." He laughed. "I-Verse ask me to come for you." A big man with big teeth, he had a scar on his forehead peeping out under the dripping hood.

When he raised one eyebrow at Shannon, Akasha said, "She just buy a statue."

"You pack up yet?"

"Just finishing."

"We can't leave now," he said. "Rain too heavy for the baby."

Shannon turned to Akasha with a warm smile. "Can we give you a ride home in the car?"

CHAPTER NINETEEN

S had crossed his arms in front of the seat belt, the Rasta woman and Shannon chatting away in the back of the taxi. The musky oil the woman had on was stinking up the whole car, making him sick to his stomach, and he couldn't open the window because it was raining too hard. Worse still, his hope of returning to Largo in time to see the bulldozer clear Miss Mac's land was evaporating. It would be after dark by the time they got back and work would have stopped.

Carlton was having a bad time of it, too. While they were waiting in the steamy car outside the sculpture shack, he'd been telling Shad about his love life, or the lack of it, and said he'd finally gotten a date with a nice girl and was supposed to meet her at three o'clock. So now he was driving through the rain with his jaw muscles tight. He'd already told Shad he was 'fraid Rastas, so he'd be worried, too, about driving into one of their camps.

"How'd you get interested in Rastafari?" Shannon was asking Akasha, pretending to be casual, Shad could tell, but really interviewing the woman.

"In high school in Birmingham, one of my friends was a Rasta and he tell me about it."

"What did you like about it?"

The woman sighed. "Rasta believe in living a healthy, good life, you know. They heart in the right place."

"What did your parents think?"

The baby crowed and the woman played with his hand. "My father—he don't like it—and my mother—she follow my father. They is Baptists." Her patois sounded phony to Shad, as if she was laying it on too thick. "I don't go home for a long time." The quiet that settled over the car was interrupted only by the chirps of the child.

The sheets of rain stopped suddenly and Shad opened his window. They were driving farther into the hills, not like the tall Blue Mountains behind Largo, but the rolling knolls in the middle of the island. Cedar and mahogany trees lined the narrow road, releasing large drops of water onto the windshield.

"Is far now?" Shad asked.

"About two mile," the woman answered.

Beth had never trusted white Rastas, said they had their own countries and cultures to follow, and they should be happy with that. "And I don't know why they want to dreadlocks up they good, good hair," she'd once said. "God didn't give them no hair for locks."

As the rain came to a stop, the road descended into a valley, the stretch of asphalt lined by bamboo. "Coming up here." The woman pointed over Shad's shoulder. "See the gate there?"

To their left was a closed iron gate beside which were red, yellow, and green flags drooping from bamboo sticks. The dirt road inside the gate disappeared behind eucalyptus trees, looking as if they belonged in a movie with their ghoulish, gray leaves and bark.

"You want us to drive in?" Shad queried, testing the waters.

"Yes, like how the baby and the basket heavy."

Carlton halted in front of the gate and Shad opened it. After he'd climbed back into the car, he turned around. "Maybe we can find somebody—"

"Tell me something, Akasha," Shannon interrupted. "Do you have some people who've been here for thirty-five years or so?"

The woman blinked a few times. "Maybe."

A twisting quarter of a mile on, the eucalyptus-lined driveway ended at several small concrete-block buildings. A pickup truck was parked at the entrance to the settlement, and Carlton stopped beside it.

"Thank you for the drive." Akasha opened the car door. She heaved the basket onto her shoulder and got out.

"I'll mail you the photos," Shannon said.

"Thank you for that. And I going to ask them now for you."

She returned after a while, walking behind three Rastafarian men, one of them a cross-looking I-Verse, a kerchief tied around his throat, a tam on his head. Shad could see Carlton's hands tighten on the steering wheel. The three men walked side by side in long, loose garments, the old man to the right of I-Verse thin and short. His shiny face was deeply lined, and from a receded hairline hung locks that were almost white. He was carrying a brown book of some kind, as if he'd been reading and didn't want to stop. The third man was large, very large, a delicately crocheted tam with a red, zigzag pattern topping thick locks and curious eyes.

"Act friendly," Shad muttered to Carlton, and started smiling as the group approached.

I-Verse walked around to Shad's side of the car. The two men stood behind him, Akasha stopping in front of the car. Smelling of eucalyptus oil, the tall carver put his hand on the car door like a man in charge.

"I and I don't tell you not to bother us?" he said to Shad sharply.

"The dead woman's family want to know what happen to her. If one of your children disappear, you wouldn't want to know what happen?"

I-Verse's eyes swung from the little bartender to Akasha, and his forehead eased a little. "What you really want? You say you writing an article for a Canadian magazine, but you—"

"We need to speak to a Rastafarian who's been around Gordon Gap a long time," Shannon said as she leaned between the front seats.

"You want to meet one of the brethren who around a long time." I-Verse turned slowly to the old man behind him. "See one here, he name Ras Redemption."

The elderly man stepped forward, he and I-Verse crowding the window. "Who want to talk to I-man?"

"Greetings," said Shad. "A lady from Canada—her name Shannon—she in the back—want to ask about a friend of hers—"

"Not exactly a friend of mine," Shannon corrected him.

"—who long time ago used to live with a Rasta man. I name Shad, and this is Carlton. She want to just have little time with you, won't take long."

The three men looked at each other with silent messages, while Akasha swung the baby back and forth.

"Come, nuh?" Redemption said abruptly. He started

walking back to the buildings, and the other two men followed him.

"You ready?" Shad asked Shannon.

"Can I bring my cameras?"

"Leave them for now. Let me do the talking, you hear?"

"I have to ask him questions, so I have to do the talking, too."

Akasha walked up to the driver's window, patting the baby on the back, her eyes on the retreating trio. "You coming or what?"

Carlton sank a few inches lower in his seat. "I staying here."

"We coming, we coming," Shad said, and he and Shannon climbed out, following Akasha as she jumped over the puddles in the compound. The place looked bare and unembroidered, as if every penny went into food and shelter. A few men and women with locks of different lengths had come out after the rain, some attending to a cooking shed with a brick stove. They stopped what they were doing to examine the visitors. Inside an open building with a table of unfinished sculptures, two youths were carving and chatting.

"Irie," Shad hailed them when they looked up. The young men nodded, one touching his heart, and followed them with their eyes.

When Akasha came to a cottage, she gestured that they should enter. Several pairs of sandals were clustered around the entrance, and they took off their sneakers, Shannon almost toppling over. Shad lined up their muddy shoes side by side.

"They not going to bite you," Akasha whispered before leaving them.

The small room they entered was crowded enough without adding two more people to the clutter. Posters covered the walls with images of Marcus Garvey and the late Ethiopian emperor, and the low table in the middle was laden with candles, books, and ashtrays. Hanging over the sagging sofa was an ornate silver cross, and sitting cross-legged on it was Redemption, lighting a giant, cone-shaped spliff. I-Verse was seated on a chair near him, the third man absent, and Shad and Shannon were waved to two stools. After the host had taken a long pull and held his breath, he exhaled a sweet-smelling cloud and gave the joint to I-Verse, who did the same. Shad took the spliff from him and inhaled as much as he dared, the scratching in his throat almost making him cough, before handing the cone to Shannon while he held the smoke in his mouth.

She stared at the joint. "I don't think—"

"Just a little," Shad said, one eyebrow lifted in warning as he exhaled, and she took it carefully between her fingers.

"All right." She closed her eyes as she inhaled a tiny puff.

Shad swallowed the burning in his throat. "Is good weed this."

"The best." The old man slapped his knee.

"Ras Redemption, how long you live up this side?"

"Almost forty years now."

"You might can help us then. You ever see or hear of a foreign woman name—" Shad looked at the journalist, the weed making all names disappear.

"Katlyn. She lived in Gordon Gap for a while."

Shad cleared his throat, a reminder to Shannon to let him lead the conversation. "This was about—"

"Thirty-five years ago." Shannon gulped on her second

little pull. Frowning, Shad gestured toward the sofa and she handed the joint over.

Redemption sucked hard on the spliff, making a deep, throaty sound that seemed about to split his small body. "This sweet lambsbread, man." He looked at the spliff. After he passed the ganja to I-Verse, the old man leaned back on the sofa, his eyes on the ceiling, and questioned Shannon. How old was the woman? What was she doing in Jamaica?

"They call her anything besides—what you call her?"

"Katlyn." Shannon took the photograph out of her bag and passed it to Redemption.

The old Rasta stared at the picture for a while, his face morphing from caginess to controlled surprise. The creases beside his mouth got deeper, his eyes narrower. Finally, he threw the photograph on the table and put his feet flat on the floor. "I and I might have something for you."

"Anything you know—"

"I going to need little help, though," the man added, the Rasta vocabulary abandoned.

"What kind of help?" Shad could feel his pulse speed up, hear his words slow down. The room was feeling close and hostile, the weed swarming his brain.

"I need some bills to help me."

Shannon looked at Shad with vague, pink eyes.

"Money," Shad told her, looking behind him, measuring the distance to the door.

"You—you want me to *pay* you for the information?" she said to Redemption as she tried to sit straighter.

"How much?" Shad asked.

"Pshaw, man," I-Verse said on the inhale, spliff in hand,

"she have plenty money. She not working for a big magazine?" No smoke came out of his mouth, as if it had been absorbed by his bloodstream.

"I don't have it on me, but if—"

"You want information, you pay the bills." The old man sucked in the remains of the joint. "Come on Sunday. We having a Nyabinghi."

CHAPTER TWENTY

The yellow behemoth clawed at the earth, noisily seeking treasure—and charging a fortune to do so, Eric was sure.

"You ever want to drive a bulldozer?" Shad shouted.

"Never," Eric shouted back.

It was the first day of work clearing Miss Mac's land, heavy rains having held back the start.

"You can't go into the job with water filling up every trench you dig," Lambert had explained on Monday morning. "It's bad luck to start on a rainy day, anyway."

The next morning, soon after the sun had dawned in a clear blue sky, Eric had been jarred awake by Shad's banging on his door. "Time for action, boss," his new partner had yelled.

When they'd arrived at the site, Lambert was already addressing a cluster of villagers beside the road, each one carrying a machete and a stick. He was introducing the foreman, a stranger to the village, a serious-looking man wearing delicate metal glasses and heavy work boots.

"And you see this man, Mistah Roberts?" Lambert had been saying in patois, pointing to the foreman. "He know what he doing, so don't question him. He a fair man, give you a fair day's wages, and you won't have no argument with him if you do your work like he say. But if you have a problem, go to him, don't come to me. I don't want to see nobody come up to my house to complain about Mistah Roberts or tell me about this or that. Mistah Roberts is your boss and I am Mistah Roberts's boss. You have a problem, you see him. That how it go."

Roberts had stepped forward and given instructions for the first day's chopping of brush and grass. Teams were assigned, locations on the property pointed out.

"But first," the foreman had said, pulling a quart of white rum from his pocket, "the libations."

Lambert had gestured to Eric and Shad to come closer. "Either one of you want to say a few words before we start?" Eric had shaken his head, wary of superstition since his altar-boy days helping to change wafers into the body of Christ. Beside him, Shad had nodded eagerly.

The foreman led the group halfway down the unpaved driveway to Miss Mac's empty house and, after the workers gathered in a circle around him, poured the contents of the bottle onto the dirt.

"Blessings to the ancestors," one woman said to nods and mutters.

Shad had stepped forward. "Please bow your heads." Hats were removed, heads were lowered.

"Oh, good and gracious and *beneficent* God," the bartender had prayed with fervor, "as we proceed on our mission to make Largo Bay the beautifullest place in Jamaica, we ask You to be with us, keeping all the workers them safe and everything good, because we know, God, that You is the One who make us to build this hotel right here, right now. We been suffering for the last years since the old hotel gone, and You know that now is our chance. We ask all Your blessings on this construction, God, that Mistah Lambert may guide everything good, and that the foreman know what he doing, and that the rain hold up long enough to build it on time. Thank You for this opportunity to dream dreams and make visions come true, God, in this our Savior Jesus Christ name. Amen."

After the chattering workers had dispersed, Lambert had said a word to Roberts, then walked over to where Eric and Shad were standing. "I should put you two to work," the big man had said with his ho-ho-ho. "Toughen you up a little."

"When hell freezes over," Eric had said. "Been there, done that, with the old hotel."

Lambert had paced a few steps. "Everything's set to go, except for—"

Just then, a truck had roared around the corner and pulled up, a sunflower-bright bulldozer on its flatbed. The contractor had leaped into action, walking the operator through the job. After that, the men's eyes had been riveted by the machine as it reversed off the truck, the big treads dropping dried mud from the last job. Half an hour later, the dozer was creating a ruckus and a driveway into the heart of the property.

Eric had been ready to leave, could smell his coffee already, but he knew that Shad would want to watch the action. It was always like that with Shad. If history was to be made, something new was to be seen, he had to be part of it.

"I always want to drive a tractor," Shad said after they'd found a tree to lean on where they could hear their own voices. "Nobody can stop you when you driving one of them things."

Eric had a flashback. "I remember when the bulldozer came to clear the land for the first hotel. The old guy who was driving it had to pee all the time, kept leaving it and going into the bushes. Now that I think about it, maybe he was just extending his hours, making more money. Funny, I never thought of that before."

"I wasn't there then. Old Man Job hire me after that, when you was getting ready to dig the foundation."

"Yeah, that's right."

Shad pinched his starched jeans higher and squatted down. "Speaking of money, boss, I want to talk to you about something."

"No raise coming, buddy. Sorry."

"You forget I add up the money, boss, or subtract, is more like. No, is something else. I was thinking we could make some money from my wedding."

Eric looked down at Shad, the man's eyes glued to the dozer, beads of sweat already glistening on the chocolate scalp. "What you talking about? Weddings don't *make* money, man, they *cost* money."

"But I was thinking that, instead of a regular reception, we could hold a pay party. We could call it Shad's Rock-steady Reception. Play some Millie Small and Desmond Dekker, you know, old-time reggae."

"Wait a minute." Eric pushed away from the tree. "You're thinking of getting married in the church, then telling the guests to come back to the bar and *pay* for the reception?"

Shad rubbed his chin. "You think they would vex?"

"You're damn straight they'd be vexed. You don't charge people to come to your wedding."

"But they wouldn't have to spend no money on gifts. They just pay at the door."

"You talked this over with Beth?"

"Not yet."

Eric looked at the machine reversing over a small mound. Shad's schemes were not usually harebrained. "What's up, the wedding getting too expensive?"

Shad stood up, straightening his jeans. "The wedding expensive, boss, but is the ring business. I want to give Beth two nice rings, one with a diamond."

Two villagers approached, thwacking away at the bushes with their machetes, leaning on their sticks for support, and Eric and Shad returned to the bar, where the conversation continued over coffee. The pay party, they finally agreed, would be held one week *before* the wedding, the coming Saturday, and Shad would get his cousin's husband to be DJ.

"That way you'll have time to buy the rings before the wedding," Eric suggested.

"And we can split the profits, boss, fifty-fifty."

"No way, this is your idea and your wedding. Just don't destroy the place or hand me a bill at the end of it. Pay the cost for whatever liquor you use, and the rental is my wedding gift."

The name for the party, the groom-to-be insisted, had to remain Shad's Rocksteady Reception. "The words flow nice," he affirmed.

Halfway through reading the *Daily Gleaner* later, Eric looked at Shad washing dish towels at the sink. "Tell me something, has Shannon gotten any closer to finding that Canadian woman?"

"An old Rasta man tell her to come to a Nyabinghi on Sunday coming. He say he can help her."

"A Nya—"

"Like a church service, but a Rasta ceremony, plenty drums and food."

A tremor rose up Eric's spine and he shook out the newspaper to straighten it. "I don't like the sound of it. I don't like her going up there. All kinds of things could go wrong, you know that. Next thing, with all the ganja—"

"I going with her, don't worry, and Carlton." Shad rubbed his ear with his shoulder as if a mosquito were bothering him. "Who tell you about the Canadian woman, boss?"

"Eve told me."

It felt good to say that his daughter had confided something that her mother hadn't. Ever since she'd danced for him to Bongo's ditty, and maybe because he'd clapped, Eve had started peeling back the layers with her father. First she'd asked him, mumbling, biting her lip, if she could take all her drumming lessons at the bar. The next day she'd asked if she could have lunch with him after her lessons. The first lunch was painfully silent, but he'd waited for her to start talking, keeping his own mouth shut until she'd opened hers. She'd come with a box under her arm the following day and asked if he'd play Scrabble with her.

"My teacher—Miss Simmons—said we're to play at least ten games—to keep our brain synapses running over the summer or something," Eve had said after she'd taken her first seven letters.

"You mean to keep you away from those awful video

games you were telling me about," her father retorted as he examined his rack, sure she was going to beat him.

"Everybody plays video games. They help your reflexes."

"Reflexes to be trigger-happy, you mean, all that violence. In my day all we had was good old movies. We didn't even have a TV at home until I was in my teens."

"What do you call those cowboy-and-Indian movies? People used to die in them all the time."

"Yeah, but you didn't see any blood."

"Still violence," Eve had countered under her breath.

He loved her spunk, loved that she was undaunted by their difference in age or by his being her father, even if he didn't feel like a father. She had a solidity about her, a maturity to her pancake face that looked older than her years, and now that she was looking up more, her eyes—his blue eyes—said that her word was her bond.

Halfway through the game the day before, she'd thrown him for a loop. "Mom is doing some detective work here, you know."

"What detective—I thought she was writing an article."

"She is, but she's looking for some woman, too." The story had come out. Eve had walked into Shannon's bedroom to find her staring at an old photograph of the woman. "She said Angie, that's her editor, asked her to find out about the woman. She was here a long time ago, but she never went back home to Canada." The girl had gone back to the game unperturbed.

"How come you never said anything about her looking for some woman who'd disappeared?" Eric asked Shad now, trying not to make it sound like an accusation. "I mean, something as serious as that—"

"Shannon didn't want nobody to worry about her."

"I just hope you all know what you're doing." Eric sniffed loudly, nostrils flaring. "It's been a long time and you know Jamaica. It sounds like a hopeless case."

"Maybe not so hopeless, boss. That's why we going to see an old Rasta on Sunday."

"If I didn't know that my going with you could be a liability, I would go, believe me."

"Boss, don't worry yourself," Shad said, whining a little to pacify. "Everything cool, man, everything under control."

"Yeah, right."

CHAPTER TWENTY-ONE

Descending one slow step at a time, Shannon felt her dread rising with the noontime heat from the driveway. She tugged at her ponytail, making sure it fit smoothly through the hole in her baseball cap. In the last few days she'd tried to live with the reality that Eric had a girlfriend, that her relationship with him now was nothing more than being the mother of his child. She'd been angry to begin with, sending Bongo and Eve to the restaurant to drum, wanting to hurt him as much as he'd hurt her. The hardest part had been admitting to herself that she'd hoped, the tiny tendrils still clinging to her heart, that something would be triggered by the three of them coming together with this trip.

"You should've told me he was involved with the woman on the island, whatever her name is," she'd told Jennifer the afternoon before, her voice tinged with betrayal.

"I didn't know what—what his status was—if he and Simone were still . . . ," Jennifer had said, leaning forward in the verandah chair, an unlit cigarette between two fingers. "I was hoping it wouldn't really matter."

"We have a child together. Didn't you think I'd want to know?"

GILLIAN ROYES

"I thought—"

"You knew they had a relationship when she was here, didn't you?"

Jennifer cupped her hands and lit the cigarette. "Everybody knew by the time she left."

"Doesn't he talk about her?"

"You know Eric—tight-lipped."

Waving the smoke away, Shannon frowned. "What's she like? Tell me the truth." It had become an interrogation, no time for diplomatic curiosity.

"She's divorced, worked in advertising in Atlanta. Nice, nobody's fool, though."

"Is she really coming for the groundbreaking like Shad said? You're taking care of the guest list, you should know."

"Lambert told me she was coming."

"And you never said anything."

"I didn't want to carry tales, Shan." Jennifer pulled at her cigarette. "They're best friends, you know."

"I don't get the logic."

"Honestly? I thought you'd be gone before the groundbreaking." Jennifer had looked up at the verandah's eaves where a large purple-and-white orchid was fluttering in the breeze. "If anything, Eric should have told you himself, although I don't know why I'd expect him to. He doesn't clean up his messes very well, does he?"

Shannon kept her eyes on the railing to avoid looking at the island. "If she's coming to the groundbreaking, that can only mean they're still involved."

"She could be coming to give her support. Her brother Cameron came up with the idea for the hotel when he came down to find her last year. He's a commercial real estate

174

guy and he brokered the deal with some client of his, a man named Danny Caines, who wanted to own a hotel in Jamaica. I mean, if it hadn't been for Simone, there'd be no new hotel."

Jennifer's last words formed themselves into an excruciating thought that Shannon had taken back to her bedroom, the thought that Simone had helped Eric rebuild his life—and she, Shannon, had not. During his most painful, needy time, she had done nothing. A few guilty hours later she'd balanced it out by assuring herself that she'd given Eric a daughter, and a daughter was far more valuable than a hotel. And besides (this she had to focus on repeatedly before it sank in), he was entitled to date whom he wished, as was she.

It wasn't as if she'd been celibate in the intervening years. There'd been a few affairs, which had ended when she insisted they take it to a higher level. Eve needed a family, she'd say, even as the men were shrinking away. While talking with Chantrelle one day, she'd realized that she used the tactic to end her relationships, most with unavailable men or men who couldn't commit, because she didn't really want them. The most recent had lasted four years. It was with a younger man from Alberta, an engineer with a mining company who came to Toronto twice a month. But her fondness for Thomas was nothing like the way she'd fallen for Eric, the zing of infatuation keeping her awake the first night she met him.

She still remembered every detail of that night when she'd been on the hotel's verandah looking at the stars, when Eric had introduced himself and they'd talked for two hours, the electricity between them making the night air hum around her ears. But, no, Tom she'd trusted and had been willing to build on that. When she sang her song about getting married, it had ended yet again, and for the last year she'd been content being alone.

Earlier that day, Shannon had decided that it was time to speak her mind to Eric. She was older, more mature, and certainly able to tell him, calmly, that she knew his secret, and she would make light of how she and Simone might bump into each other. But the old Jeep wasn't in the parking lot when she crossed the road, and she let the pasted-on smile relax. When she rounded the hedge, however, there he was, seated behind the bar across from three customers, making her breath catch in her throat.

"Hey," he sang out when she stepped onto the concrete floor, "long time no see." She knew it was only a greeting to impress the tourists, who swung their heads around to see whom he was talking to.

Shannon took off her sunglasses. "Hi, is Shad around?"

"No, he's off to Ocho Rios to buy decorations for his party."

"I didn't know he was having a party," she said, aware that the newcomers were taking note of her clothes, her accent.

"It's on Saturday night," Eric said, addressing the young couple and elderly woman across from him. "If you're still in the area, you should check it out."

The man fished in his shorts for his wallet. "We're on our way to Ocho Rios ourselves." He placed a credit card on the counter. "Y'all have fun, though."

After they left, Eric offered her a drink and she asked for a Guinness. "That's right, you always liked it."

Because it makes me feel bold, she wanted to say.

He placed the dark beer on a coaster in front of her. "Is Eve coming over?"

"She's gone rafting with Jennifer and the kids."

"Has she shown you her latest trick?" He sat down on Shad's stool, smiling broadly as if he hadn't a care in the world.

"What trick?" She took a sip.

"Sucking her teeth. Shad taught her the last time she was here." Eric laughed, slapping his thigh. "You should have seen her, trying to pull the air in between her teeth and moving her mouth all over the place."

"Yes, she came back and showed us."

"She's enjoying herself, don't you think?"

"I hope so. I had to drag her here kicking and screaming."

"It's a different story now, though, learning the drums and everything. She's even been trying to speak patois. You should hear her mimicking Shad and Maisie." Eric was tickled, she could tell, as if he'd created a new life for Eve.

"Heard the patois, too."

"I've been meaning to talk to you about the—you know—the thing about her taking the cigarettes. I don't want to say anything to her about it."

"There's nothing more to say to her. She was caught by the shop owner. He threatened to call the police, but he called me instead and decided not to report it to the police, thank God. The counselor said we shouldn't talk about it with her yet."

"Has she told you why—what made her do it?"

"Nope, tight-lipped girl." She took another swig of courage. "Like her father."

Eric pulled his hair back, a pucker between his brows. "What's *that* supposed to mean?"

"Nothing."

"I don't know who you're calling tight-lipped." He stood up and straightened his shirt. "It's not like you've come clean about this *detective* work I'm hearing about."

Her head jerked back. "What detective work?"

"I hear that you're not only doing this magazine stuff, but you've been looking for some—for some woman who went missing."

The zing she felt this time made heat pour through her face. "She's not missing. She's dead."

"*Dead?* That's even worse. Why don't they hire a detective?"

"The—it's not a big deal. She had a relationship with a Rastafarian man and I'm just asking a few questions as I move around for the article."

"And you're going to some compound for some ceremony thing, I hear."

"I'm just going to take a few photographs, ask a few questions."

"You have any idea how dangerous it is, going to a Rasta compound asking questions?"

"You talk about Rastafarians as if—as if they're *aliens* or something."

"You know exactly what I mean; you said the same thing to Eve yourself. They're different from you and me, and some of them don't like white people."

"I haven't had any trouble—"

"I've lived here a long time and—"

"I can take care of myself, thank you, Eric!" she said,

trying and failing to lower her voice. "I've been doing very well so far. What do you think I'm doing every day? I've been flying all over the world to make a living, so I can raise *our* daughter." The words were flying out of her mouth, emboldened by the lonely years.

"I don't want anything to happen to you." He looked around the empty bar. "There've been incidents where . . . You don't want to end up like—like the woman you're looking for."

"It's part of my *job*, Eric. What you want me to do, tell my boss that I won't take the assignment? How can I do that? I need the money for Eve to go to college—"

"And if you're going to take care of Eve, you need to keep safe. That's my point."

"You don't trust me, is *that* your point?"

"Of course I trust you."

"Thank you very much." She hoped he read the sarcasm in her eyes.

"You're trying to make me feel guilty, aren't you?"

"You *should* feel frigging guilty."

"Oh, right." He slapped the fridge. "Here it comes."

"It makes sense, don't you think? All of a sudden, you're Mr. Concerned, worried about my welfare. Did you worry about me when I was trekking across the outback of Australia or—or in the bazaar in Morocco? Did you even know where I was most of the time? I've been managing with no help from you, thank you very much. Not so much as a card on my birthday, not even at Christmas. Two calls a year and you're worried about me? Give me a break, Eric!"

He opened the fridge door. "I'm thinking about Eve, too, if anything—"

"Eve?" she shrieked at his back. "When have you ever cared what happens to her? Thirteen years and you've seen your daughter three times, three fucking times in her entire life!"

"I couldn't—"

"Did you even remember it's her birthday next week?"

"Of course I did." He turned around, his cheeks shiny.

"She's going to be thirteen, Eric, in case you forgot. Thirteen years and you've never even invited her to your home. You're her father, or did you forget? Don't you think she'd want to know who you are? I had to bring her down for her to see you!"

He spread his arms. "Don't you see how I live? I don't have a hotel anymore."

"That's no excuse and you know it."

"But I send you the money—"

"I give you that, but it's your presence that's important, Eric. Joseph said the same thing when he called the first time. Both of your children don't even *know* you."

"Is that what this is all about? You walk in here looking like a dark cloud, and now you're throwing this at me, just like how Joseph threw all that—that negative stuff at me when he was here."

"What did you expect? That we'd appear, all sweetness and light, and nothing would come up about—"

"Where was she going to stay? I only have one bedroom, for chrissake!"

"If you'd wanted to see her, you'd have found somewhere, Jennifer's or somewhere. But the truth is—"

"The truth is that I didn't have the money to send for her or come visit—if you even want to know the truth."

"But you could at least have *called*—"

The roar of a machine flung itself between them. They looked toward the noise and the sudden peace it brought. "The bulldozer next door," he shouted, gesturing.

She nodded and yelled back, "We can hear it from the house." Each word was tight and clear, her heart still racing. She wasn't done with him.

CHAPTER TWENTY-TWO

H ow it look?" Shad said. He stroked the black satin lapels and the salesman winced.

Maisie adjusted the brim of her straw hat for a better view. "You looking sweet, man."

Snatching up some plastic flowers from a vase, Shad thrust them into the hand of the salesman and pretended to walk him down the aisle, dum-dumming all the way to the store's front door.

"I hope Beth look happier than him." Maisie giggled.

"One day," Shad said, feeling it, knowing it, "I going to own my own tuxedo. I not going to just rent it. I going to wear it to the hotel's New Year's Eve parties, the way Mistah Eric used to."

"You can take it off now," the salesman snapped.

"How much it cost if I take it for three days?"

"Ninety thousand for the weekend." The man eased Shad's arms out of the jacket.

"I don't want to buy it, you know, star. Is only *borrow* I going to borrow it."

"Ninety, and if you dirty it up, is more for cleaning."

Shad shrugged out of the jacket and paid in cash (insisting on a discount and getting none). He'd pick it up the coming Friday, he told the attendant.

When he and Maisie were in the Jeep again, heading out of the Ocho Rios back street, he sighed deeply. "Miss Maisie, so much good things happening to me that I getting scared."

"You mean, the wedding?"

"No, man, I talking about the hotel."

"What you mean? The wedding is a big thing! Everybody in Largo waiting for it."

"The wedding big, yes, but nothing going to change after that—except that Beth's money jar going to be empty." He honked at two taxis stopped in the middle of the road, the drivers chatting. "Is the hotel that keeping me awake at night, man. The more I hear the tractor next door and the more I see the land being cleared, the more I worrying. It make me realize that the new hotel coming for true. All the talk over the last year, and suddenly it happening."

"You work hard for it, all these years working in the hotel, then in the bar. You deserve it."

"You know how my life going to change? No more quiet life—pure aggravation after that."

"But is Mistah Eric going to run it."

"Mistah Eric!" Shad snorted. "The only running he doing is running out of steam. Is *me* going to be steam and engine and engineer."

"You wait. Once it open—"

"You don't see what I saying? It different now. I is a partner, I *responsible* this time."

"But wait." Maisie pulled her chin back into her neck. "Is not you responsible for seven years now? Is not you who tell Mistah Eric to build the bar when the hotel gone? Is not you stocking inventory and keeping ledger and holding welcome party for the investor man? Is not you organizing party in the bar?"

"Pshaw, man, that easy. Hotel business is different. I going to have to go to conferences at the Tourist Board, and I not no big-shot man with education and passport. You ever hear of a poor man like me becoming a hotel manager?"

The old lady stared at him, her moon face beautiful in its righteousness. "All you have to do is remember what Jesus say: 'In the world you have tribulation, but take courage.' You is a good man, Shad, and you like to help people. Everybody going to help you, don't worry. Why you think Solomon and him friends come leaning up on your counter every night? Why people coming to your parties? Is because they like you, they respect you."

"They might respect me, but they can't help me with a big business like that. You talking twenty bedrooms, lobby with receptionists, dining room, swimming pool, beach, two bars—and you have to keep forty, fifty guests happy all the time. When they not sleeping, they want good food and hot sun. Nights, they want entertainment. They want to know Jamaica, the Jamaica they see on them advertisements on TV."

"You will find things for them to do, man. You always full of ideas."

Shad drove on, his mind working faster than his foot as he braked around the back streets' tight corners. "And all the workers them, working in housekeeping and bar and kitchen and garden, how I going to manage them?"

"You don't manage Solomon and me now?"

"Yes, but is fifty-plus workers we talking about hiring."

"What you don't know, you will learn."

Shad bumped into the parking lot of a strip mall. "Is not that shop we going to? The Party Shoppe, so is called, right?"

Maisie nodded with conviction. "Yes, but I telling you, if Jesus on your side, nothing can go wrong."

"Suppose He not on my side?" Shad chuckled. "Maybe He don't like the tourist business, like how Jamaica is a different place from what the TV selling. They telling people abroad how is one love, one heart, and they come and find people harassing them to buy ganja and braid them hair. Jesus don't like no lying business, and I not the best candidate for Jesus, anyway, like how I was a thief."

"That was in your youth, man. You done save and baptize now. You go to church every Sunday, even help Pastor fix up the church, give it a fresh coat of paint and everything. Nobody asking you to be perfect, just to do your best."

Shad thought of the Buffoon flapping his wings. "Maybe you right, even the minister not perfect."

After they'd finished shopping (she for blue decorations for Beth's shower, he for silver balloons for his party), Shad headed east back to Largo. A few miles before the turning to Gordon Gap, Maisie put her hand on Shad's arm.

"You mind if we stop by my cousin's house just five minutes? She kind of sickly and I don't see her for a long time."

"No problem, man. Where she live?"

"Up here so, not far from the main."

Shad turned the Jeep onto the road Maisie indicated, then turned onto a side road and stopped in front of a small house, its narrow front yard crowded with flowering bushes.

When they walked up the short path to the house, Shad

pointed to a bush close to the verandah wall, its furry, red flower looking like a cat's tail.

"What they call that one again? My grandmother used to grow it in the yard, but it dead now."

"They call it kiss-me-over-the-garden-gate."

"That's right." Shad whinnied with delight. He loved the old-fashioned sound of it, and he could hear his grandmother roll it around in her mouth when she said it. "You think your cousin will give me a clipping to plant in the yard? I could put it right where the old bush used to be."

No sound came from the house when they climbed the porch steps. "She must be in her bed." Maisie called a loud *howdy-doo*. A weak voice echoed back and she disappeared inside while Shad sat on an aluminum folding chair on the porch.

His eyelids had just started to close when he was roused by a whirring sound. A tiny doctor bird had zoomed up to the passionflower vine shrouding the porch and was sticking its beak into a flower. With its long tail and iridescent, blue-green body, it reminded Shad of why, as a boy, he'd always loved hummingbirds, even if he couldn't catch one.

"Excuse me, please," a voice said, and Shad peered between the heart-shaped leaves of the vine. Standing at the bottom of the steps was a young man holding a basket. "Miss Mattie living here?" His short dreadlocks almost covered his eyes; a Rasta novice.

"Miss Mattie is the sick lady?"

"My mother ask me to bring her some soup."

"She inside with a friend of mine." The youth went into the house and returned without the basket.

"Tell me something," Shad said before the boy could descend the steps. "You know any Rasta camps around here?"

The teenager's eyes narrowed. "Why you want to know?"

"I inquiring for a friend of mine. My name is Shad, sorry, I should have said."

The young man's name was Unity. "They have plenty camps." He rubbed a pimple on his nose. "The Nyabinghi camp, the place where the wood-carvers live, and then some brethren live just below them. They have a big farm, growing vegetables and thing."

"They been there a long time?"

"I think so."

"How you get to that camp?"

"Little before the Nyabinghi camp, you turn right."

Maisie appeared with a pair of clippers in her hand. "Time to cut bush."

CHAPTER TWENTY-THREE

I n the two weeks since Eve had arrived in Largo, Eric had learned a lot about her. Just playing Scrabble had taught him that his daughter was competitive and funny: when she won, she'd do her rain dance, making everyone around her laugh. Another discovery was that she had a quick retort to every comment, usually delivered in a flat voice. She also reacted as strongly to her environment as her father. If the bulldozer roared close to the bar, they both got distracted and the Scrabble scores were low. She was moody, and on a couple occasions she was almost as morose as when she'd first arrived from Canada.

"What's the problem?" he asked her on Friday afternoon as he placed the word *zealous* on the board, a double-word play. He'd been feeling lucky today.

After trying to shrug it off, Eve conceded that she and her mother had had words. "She's gotten weird."

"She has a lot on her mind." Eric drew six new letters from the bag. "But then, your mother always takes on a lot. Maybe sometimes she can't handle it all."

"Like me?"

"Of course not. I mean she was always a—a multitasker, you know. She likes to have several things on the fire at the same time. I don't know how she does it. She probably gets exhausted with all the things she has to do, gets weird, you know."

Eve's stolid face looked more adult than usual. "You're saying I'm a burden."

"Where'd you get this burden business?"

"If I'm not a burden, why don't you want me here?"

Eric put down his rack of letters and looked into her "Keller-blue eyes," as his mother would have described them. "Of course I want you here. Look at us, we're playing Scrabble, for goodness' sake. I wouldn't do that for just anybody, you know."

"Yeah, but you never invited me down to Jamaica. Mom had to—"

"The short version?" he asked with raised brows. "No money, no space."

She lifted the right side of her mouth like her mother.

"I haven't been the greatest dad, I know." His eyes fell to his letters.

"You haven't been a dad at all."

"Absolutely true."

"You owe me. You know that, don't you?"

He pushed the letters away. "I tell you what. Your birthday's coming up. Let's plan something."

She couldn't hide her smile. "You remembered."

"You didn't think I'd remember? What do you want to do?"

"Go snorkeling. Mom doesn't have time to take me, and Aunty Jennifer hates deep water."

"It's a deal. What day do you want to go?"

"On my birthday, that's Wednesday." She looked at him

with her eyes half-closed, as if she knew he hadn't remembered the date.

"Wednesday it is."

"And another thing." She laid out the letters for *zany*. "I want you to promise that you'll call once a week—when we get back."

He nodded. "A little expensive, but you're worth it."

"If you had a computer, we could—"

"Who says I don't have a computer? My hotel partner, Danny, gave me one as a gift when he came down."

"You have a computer!" Eve pushed back her chair. "Are you on the Internet?"

"Yeah, I don't use it, though."

"You're kidding."

"I only know how to turn it on, but—"

That was all Eve had to hear. She made him fish out the laptop and insisted on showing him how to send emails, instructing him to write someone an email. Grunting that he never should have told her, he looked up the email address on a letter from Danny Caines and tapped out a greeting, adding that everyone was looking forward to his arrival for the groundbreaking. Eve showed him how to send off the letter and entered her email address into his contacts; then she opened her Facebook page as he stood behind her chair.

"What in the world—?" He leaned over her shoulder. "You have all this—all this stuff about yourself—for the whole world to see?"

"Everybody does it."

He inspected the photographs, a few of her making faces, a dog, a goldfish, a skinny girl laughing, a boy with greasy hair grimacing to show off his braces, two girls with arms wrapped around each other. They all seemed to be wearing black.

"Who *are* these people?"

"That's Randy, and that's Mariana and Shanti, and—"

"Do they steal cigarettes, too?" The thought had sprung from his lips uncensored, and he straightened as soon as he said it.

Eve looked at him, brows low over her eyes. "You, too?"

"What do you expect? I'm your father, I care about you." And he knew what it was to steal when you wanted something, even if it was only a *Captain Marvel* comic book that your mother said she couldn't afford, although your father spent money on beer every night.

Her face dark and furious, Eve logged off and slammed the laptop closed.

"You shouldn't be stealing cigarettes and you know it." He stepped back to let her pass.

She turned at the door. "I hate you, both of you." She was gone before he could think of a follow-up.

Back in the bar, Eric slid the Scrabble letters into their bag. There were no customers, the norm for early afternoon, a good thing since all he could think about now was Eve and her crime. It had been easier in his time. His mother had forced him to go to confession and had sat outside the confessional until he'd finished describing his sin to the priest. Ten Hail Marys later, he'd felt like a criminal and she'd been relieved.

A slight headache was creeping around his temples, brought on by remembering they weren't supposed to talk to Eve about her indiscretion. He stashed the Scrabble box on top of the refrigerator and took two aspirin from the bottle inside. Damned if he'd go along with some wimpy counselor's advice. Shannon could tiptoe around the child if she wanted to, but he had every right to speak his mind.

He brought the computer to the bar counter and jabbed at the power button, half-hoping it wouldn't turn on. A few lights on the machine flickered, then glowed steadily, and he wiggled around on the barstool to get comfortable. After a few wrong clicks, he logged on to the Internet. He had letters in his in-box from people and companies he'd never heard of. He dug around in the bar's drawer, the one with the invoices and receipts. After pulling out a business card, he entered the email address. In the blank space below he wrote:

> *Dear Simone, I'm sending you an email. I just wrote Danny Caines too, which shows it's never too late to teach an old dog new tricks. Ha ha*
>
> *The bulldozer has been making a racket next door and work has started on the land. Lambert tells me that the construction might start a couple weeks late because of some building certificate he still has to get. Anyway we're going to do the groundbreaking as planned. Jennifer is arranging it. I thought we'd just need shovels and hard hats, but it sounds a little more than that. I guess you'll see for yourself.*
>
> *My daughter is still here and has me playing Scrabble and writing emails. She is really good on the computer too with her own website and everything. No brakes on her mouth, though, like all these modern kids. In the old days, they would have taken out the belt. I'm trying to be patient. I may not be the best father in the world, but I can try, right?*
>
> *Tomorrow night Shad is having a party in the bar to make some money to buy Beth her engagement and wedding rings.*

He's real excited about it (the party, not the rings).
    That's about it. I'm going to check back and see if you
answer this letter. Ha ha ha
    Eric

He pressed SEND, pressed it the way Eve had shown him—and everything disappeared. A blank screen stared back at him, ignoring his curses.

CHAPTER TWENTY-FOUR

A rat's maze, Shannon kept thinking, as Carlton wove his way through the back roads of downtown Kingston, trying to stay away from the clogged main arteries. It was the journalist's first time in the capital, although she knew the North Coast well, and she'd looked forward to meeting the university professor and seeing Kingston.

She'd assumed that a large Caribbean town—a city, really, with a million people—would have some semblance of history, gracious old homes, sidewalks shaded by overhanging trees, wide boulevards, even a downtown with cobblestones, maybe sailboats in the harbor. Instead, she was looking at lanes that reminded her of bazaars in Old Delhi with its clutter of small shops and sidewalk vendors. The hawking and spitting of the coconut vendor pushing the cart next to the car, the loud jumble of angry, laughing, questioning voices, made her pull back from the door as the car squeezed its way through.

"Kingston just alive, you don't find?" Hortense said from the back, her words smiling. Carlton's new girlfriend had asked to come along for the ride into the city.

He'd apologized in advance to Shannon with the woman

by his side. "She going to Matches Lane. I not charging you extra, don't worry."

Hortense, short and round, too young for Carlton, had added that she wanted her cousin to do her hair and nails. "Is for the wedding. Carlton invite me and I want to look nice."

The trip to Matthews Lane, according to the sign, near Kingston Harbour, meant plunging into the liveliest and loudest thicket of the city. Glimpses of a harbor without sailboats were squeezed between the vendors' electric-blue tarpaulin awnings. At the entrance to the lane, a policeman in a bulletproof vest stood with legs apart, swinging his baton.

"Move along," he told Carlton.

"Just dropping off, Officer." Carlton pulled over to let Hortense out, and Shannon said she'd like to get out and stretch her legs.

"Three hours is about all I can take in a car," she said, rubbing her back, stiff from the drive from Largo.

"You want to get your hair done?" Hortense inquired, suddenly brittle. "They don't do white people hair."

"I'd like to take some photographs."

"They don't want no photographs neither."

"Leave her," Carlton said. "She a photographer."

Hortense got out of the car and slammed the door. "Follow me, then—and don't take no pictures unless you ask people first."

Ambling behind Hortense, Shannon gazed at the open-air beauty salons lining the pedestrian lane. Women and a few men were painting nails and braiding hair on each side, the smell of chemicals high in the air. She took a couple shots—after asking permission—of a woman painting a swirling, abstract design in lime green and blue for one customer, each stroke of the brush landing perfectly on the acrylic nail. Ignoring the chaos around her, the manicurist was bent over her work with a focused frown like any artist.

By the time Shannon caught up with Hortense, the young woman was already seated on a stool under a tarp, a plastic bib around her neck. The hairdresser-cousin was introduced, a stocky woman with long, straight hair who requested that her photo be taken. Shannon took a few shots of the smiling woman as she started undoing Hortense's braids without looking.

"You come?" a nasal voice said behind them. A young man, blue jeans low around his hips, sauntered toward Hortense and put a possessive hand on her arm. "I think you was going to get here earlier."

"I couldn't come earlier. I come with this lady." Hortense looked at Shannon nervously.

The youth glanced at Shannon and turned back to Hortense. "How long you staying this time? You staying for the party tonight?"

The girl dropped her eyes. "I not staying."

"I don't know why you have to go and leave Kingston."

"I tell you, I can't find no work here." Hortense sucked her teeth.

Shannon put the cap on her lens. "I better be going. Do you want us to call before we pick you up?"

"Yes, thank you," Hortense answered with sudden politeness.

When Shannon got back to the corner of the lane, both

Carlton and the policeman had disappeared. Clutching her Canon camera to her chest, feeling conspicuous all of a sudden, the journalist looked up and down the crowded street, willing the taxi to appear.

"You looking for action?" someone said in her ear, making her jump. A man in his early twenties grinned at her, two gold teeth shining in the top row. "Me can help you, you know." He brushed back shiny dreads.

"I don't need any help, thank you." She raised her camera. "Unless you're a real Rastafarian. Then I'd take your picture."

"Yeah, man, I the real deal."

"What community do you belong to?"

"I do my own thing, man. You looking"—at which point the American accent started—"like you could do with some company. Where you coming from?"

Carlton's taxi screeched to a halt beside her. Shannon shrugged apologetically and jumped into the car.

"Pshaw," Carlton said as he pulled away, "all them kind of people—"

"He said he was a Rasta."

"He not no Rasta. He just a *rent-a-dread*, a prostitute trying to look like a Rasta." Carlton sucked his teeth. "The tourist women like to sleep with Rasta, so they say."

The drive uptown to the university went through the Parade and Cross Roads neighborhoods, Carlton giving the names of the intersections they passed through. With Shad absent, he seemed to have jumped into the role of talkative guide. "I'm a Kingston man. I learn to drive taxi here."

"Why'd you leave the city, then?"

"Some of these town criminals get into your taxi and

don't want to pay the fare. When you ask them for it, they pop you off. Or they come into the taxi to rob you and they kill you so you can't identify them. A friend of mine die that way, I don't want to follow him."

In the north of the city, the houses and buildings got larger, the spaces between them wider. Shannon had been expecting the press of small Japanese cars to thin out, the winner-take-all style to soften with the high-rises of upper Kingston. But the traffic got worse, if anything, and she wasn't prepared for the pall of smog visible against the mountains.

"This is Hope Road," Carlton said, swerving to avoid a taxi as he emerged onto a busy four-lane road.

"If we can survive it."

"This part good, man. People have more manners up here."

"Who's that?" She pointed to a man on the sidewalk. His long, white gown was sashed at the waist, and he was holding brooms over his shoulder, his turbaned head held high.

"That's a Bongo. They come from St. Thomas."

"Ras Walker was a Bongo." Shannon looked back at the man. "I guess that's why he gave his son the name."

The University of the West Indies was nestled in the foothills east of the city. Uniformed guards at the front gate gave them directions to the professor's office in the social sciences building—a square, white structure with cedar louvers—one of many scattered between large trees.

The professor wasn't in yet, the office secretary said. "We have an appointment," Shannon replied.

"Jamaica time," Carlton said, and retreated to the car.

Richard Ransom appeared ten minutes later with a pile of books in his arms. Following him into his office, Shannon made a mental adjustment. She'd been sure that an expert on Rastafarians would be a Rastafarian himself, one of the new professionals in the group. He would be elderly and very academic. She was wrong on all counts.

A good-looking man with a flat belly and toned limbs, he had close-cropped hair matched by an equally neat mustache and beard. Shannon could picture him in shorts, running around the campus's circular road at dawn, beads of sweat on his unlined forehead.

"Please, have a seat." With his chin he indicated the solitary guest chair, his voice pitched lower than she would have thought. After placing the books on a shelf, the lecturer sat in the captain's chair behind his desk and leaned it backward. *"Culture,"* he said with a wry smile, "featuring Rastafarians, eh? That's impressive."

"We try to move around the world." Shannon rummaged in her bag for her camera and recorder. "It was Jamaica's turn."

"How can I help you?" He spoke with the accent of the educated Jamaican, Standard English colored by the island lilt, the charm of it playing with her head. She started her tape recorder along with the questions, the answers revealing a thoughtful man who'd already done two decades of research on Rastafarians. Not that it made him an expert, he added modestly.

"Where did it originate?" Shannon asked. "I mean, the whole Rastafarian philosophy and lifestyle?"

"The philosophy came first, the way it always does with socioreligious or political groups." His monologue told the story of a perfect storm at the turn of the twentieth century, a series of revivalist preachers, in combination with the inspirational lectures and writings of the leader from St. Ann's Bay, Marcus Garvey, all calling on the black man to have pride in Africa as the motherland.

"The most popular preacher was a man called Bedward, a fascinating man. He'd traveled to Panama to work on the Canal and come back to Jamaica. He used to draw crowds of people down by the river not far from here." Ransom looked out the window as if he longed to witness a sermon himself. "His favorite topic was the black man's oppression. The authorities arrested him, of course, and put him in the mental hospital. But as soon as he came out, he was back to the sermons. What was particularly powerful was that he linked himself to Garvey. They were both sent, he claimed, to lead their followers out of Israel to the Promised Land, that land being Africa, of course."

Groups of Bedwardites, as they called themselves, started to form, objectors to mainstream culture, religious in their practices of prayer, fasting, and healing. "These were some of the earliest communities of—of zealots, I guess you could call them; other people would call them mystics. After the revivalists came groups, still heavily religious, who objected to the British colonial government that controlled Jamaica. They held up Africa as a sort of utopia, and because of the Old Testament references, the country that was most looked to was Ethiopia. Its ruler, the Emperor Haile Selassie, or Ras Tafari, became an icon and eventually took on the mantle of a god to groups that started calling themselves Rastafarians, followers of Ras Tafari.

"After the 1930s, 1940s, some of these groups started

ritualizing the smoking of marijuana, the growing of the hair, and so forth. These were things that were outside of the norm of the society, and it branded them as revolution-aries." Ransom's voice rolled on with its academic cadence as if he were delivering a lecture. She had come to the font, it seemed, and he was enjoying watching her drink from his knowledge.

Lifting her camera while he talked, Shannon took a few shots of the man's ringless fingers—the nail on one pinkie longer than the others—between which he rolled a gold pen. When she zoomed in on his face and clicked, she could see that his eyelashes curled backward, almost in circles, and that his lips were outlined by a thin chocolate line.

"Is there still any prejudice against them?" Shannon asked, sliding her camera back in the bag, on her right hand the gold band her parents had given her to hide their em-barrassment at having a pregnant, single daughter.

"There's been discrimination against Rastas from way back. It's been a long, hard road to this point. Beatings, arrests, they've been through it all, particularly when they first started. The British didn't know what to do with them other than make them outlaws."

"Rather like the Maroons at first."

"Except that the Maroons were fighters and the Rastas weren't. They believed in peace, even if their language is—strong sometimes."

"But was there any connection between the Rastas and the Maroons? Have they inspired them?"

"Jamaica's Maroons escaped from plantations during slavery, as we all know, but what is not known as well is that they made a peace agreement with the British government, who hadn't been able to subdue them. That agreement stated that the Maroons would capture any runaway slave and *return* him to the British—and that they did. They even started hunting runaway slaves for the planters." Ransom's eyebrows had shot up while he said it, taking it personally.

"So the Maroons—"

"The Maroons have a sort of iconic reputation in Jamaica. They're seen as brave and—and combative—victors, you know, who defeated the British army. I guess they'd be called terrorists today."

"And the Rastafarians—"

"They have mixed feelings about the Maroons. On the one hand, they see them as heroes, but, on the other, they're seen as traitors to the slaves."

Ransom presented Shannon with two of his books and she thanked him, suppressing a desire to tell him that she owned both, had read every word and underlined several.

"I hope you have something on the Nyabinghi," she said, turning to the flyleaf of one.

"A chapter or two."

"Great, I'll read them before I go to a ceremony they've invited me to on Sunday night," she said, knowing she'd impress him, knowing he'd be diplomatic enough not to say it was a big deal because she was a white foreigner. Instead, he inquired about what group it was and where they were located.

"I've been to several Nyabinghis, but I've never been to the Gordon Gap camp," he'd said while she was zipping up her bag to leave. He was standing, the curled eyelashes blinking rapidly. "I'd like to join you on Sunday night— that is, if you don't mind."

CHAPTER TWENTY-FIVE

"Y ou not going to church?" Beth asked for the second time.

Shad pulled the sheet over his head. "Leave me alone."

"Just because your party bust, it don't mean you should vex with God, you know." Her flip-flops slapped the floorboards as she departed.

Shad rolled over and sighed. The party hadn't been a bust, it had been a catastrophe. Like a bad omen, the DJ hadn't arrived at eight o'clock as agreed, which didn't matter because no one had bought a ticket by nine o'clock when he finally showed up. Only a few teenagers were hanging around in the parking lot, looking for action with sly smiles, offering to help move the equipment *for a small change.* Before long music was blasting out of the speakers Bragga had positioned in the four corners of the bar, their vibrations making the silver balloons shiver. Free of charge in the parking lot, the teenagers had bounced up and down in time to the music.

"Is a good thing Mistah Eric sleeping up at Lambert's house tonight," Shad had commented to the only paying guests, Frank and his girlfriend Marjorie, who'd brought another couple. "The noise would have kill him."

When Beth had emerged from the kitchen with a tray of sardine sandwiches, she'd looked around the bar. "I hope you didn't spend big money, because it look like you not going to get it back."

"Pshaw, man," Shad had responded, his heart sinking by the minute. "People come late to these parties, man. Come midnight, they showing up."

"We can use the decorations for the wedding," she'd said, a little too happily. Just then, the DJ put on "My Boy Lollipop," and Shad took Beth's hand and swung her onto the dance floor, doing his own version of the knee-knocking rocksteady, singing along with Millie Small, trying to lift his own spirits.

By eleven o'clock, the chairs were still neatly tucked into their tables, and the two couples were the only occupants of a lone table. At twelve, they asked for their money back.

"I can't give it to you, man," Shad had protested, shouting above Justin Hinds singing "The Higher the Monkey Climbs," the notes ricocheting off the concrete floor. "You already stay and enjoy the music. Like how I have to pay the DJ."

"But is no party this," Frank complained. "We just sit—"

"You could have dance."

"It depressing to dance alone, man."

"I don't know why nobody come," Shad had said, throwing himself into a chair. "They always come to my parties."

"If the wedding wasn't next week, everybody would have come," Frank said.

"What you mean?"

"Everybody say they waiting for the wedding, because

they can eat and dance at the reception free. So Miss Brown tell me, anyway. She say nine hundred dollars hard to come by, and she don't have to pay nothing next Saturday."

"*Bumba claat.*" Shad allowed himself the curse word Granny had slapped him for once. "You see my trial? My own wedding ruin my party."

"The timing just wrong," Frank had reasoned. "They have one dress and one suit to go to the wedding, and they don't want to dirty it up before."

At one o'clock, the dance floor was still shining and the boys in the parking lot had left. Shad handed over J\$12,000 to Bragga, the 50 percent discount meaning nothing now. It was all money down the drain, tip money that he usually used to pay the electric or medical bills, hard-earned money. Beth had helped him cut down the balloons and the streamers, which she carefully deflated and folded while her future husband downed two Alka-Seltzers.

Shad looked now at the sliver of morning between the drawn curtains. A mosquito whined past his ear and he pulled the sheet back over his head. The failure of the party had left him with a headache and a hole in his stomach, a hole that preferred the rosy darkness of the sheet to any light the day could offer.

The failed party was a sure sign—he felt it in his bones—that his influence in Largo had waned. People used to flock to his parties in the old days, the last one two years ago when they'd had to shut down the DJ at two o'clock instead of four because so many people had shown up. The parking lot had been full of bopping, flirting youths, and two drunks had started a fight. Even when Shad had turned off the music and announced over the mike that the police were coming, the bar continued to be crowded with drinkers, chatting, smoking, laughing, buying one, two, three for the road.

The joke was that he hadn't even prepared for that party. For this one, he and Bragga had gone over by phone on Thursday the list of classics Shad wanted played—Stranger Cole, Derrick Morgan, Winston Samuels, all the rocksteady greats, and later, during his break, he'd run around the village announcing the party, telling everybody they must come. Friday, he'd bought the cans of sardines, loaves of bread, slices of cheese, for the sandwiches. Early yesterday he was already at the bar scrubbing down the floor with the stiff broom and a bucket of sudsy water. The lawn above the cliff had been cut by noon, the organizing and decorating of the bar finished by four. Everything had been perfect—for nothing. And worst yet, he'd lost his investment money in the wedding rings.

Beth's sandals came back and stopped at the foot of the bed. "You remember that this afternoon is my bridal shower? You promise you would look after the younger children. Joella and me leaving here at—"

"I can't," Shad muttered from the pink comfort of the sheet.

"You can't what?"

"Look after the children."

There was a silence, followed by the drawing in of air through small, wide nostrils. "How long I tell you that Maisie having a shower for me?"

"I going to a Nyabinghi—"

"What I supposed to do with the children?" She had on the voice that came with arms akimbo. "I can't tell Joella that she have to stay home and watch the children, like how she planning for one week now what she going to wear to the shower."

"I have to work."

"If you didn't waste your money on that party—"

"I have to go with Shannon. She paying me."

"She pay you yet?"

"Not yet, but it soon come." He pulled the sheet higher. "Take them all with you, nuh?" Beth ripped off the sheet and threw it onto her side of the bed. "Pshaw, man." He rolled onto his side and hugged his knees.

"Like you not listening to me."

"Take them and get Joella to help you."

"What you talking about? The bride can't take all her *pickney* to her shower! First of all, Maisie don't have enough food to feed all of them, like how they eat down house. Second of all, Joshua just starting to walk and he pulling down everything and Miss Maisie house neat like magazine. Third of all, Ashante going to throw a tantrum because she don't like too much strange people around her." The arms went to the hips. "A woman can't even get little cooperation so she can go to her own bridal shower, is that you telling me?"

"I promise Shannon."

"And who is me, jellyfish? You don't promise me, too? As soon as Maisie tell me she having bridal shower, I ask you and you say yes, you would look after them."

Rickia saved him. "Daddy," she called from the bedroom door, still in her nightgown, "Bongo want to see you. He say you left a message for him to come."

CHAPTER TWENTY-SIX

The restaurant was spotless, the early-morning sun streaking across the polished floor, and Eric was a little disappointed that he'd been wrong. He'd steeled himself to return to a postparty mess of dirty floors and dangling decorations. Instead, everything looked as clean as when he'd left the evening before. Shad must have stayed late cleaning up, probably left shortly before dawn. It must have been a hell of a party, though, because the music had blared up the hill to Lambert's house, and he'd only gotten to sleep after putting his pillow over his head.

He'd had trouble falling asleep, anyway. He'd lost another Scrabble game with Eve after dinner, causing his daughter to do her victory dance, this time to the applause of her mother and all the Delgados. It unsettled him to lose to her in front of them. He pretended he didn't care, but it showed that he knew less than an adolescent.

The game had started before dinner. Eve had suggested it, as if she wanted to forget her parting shot the day before, the hate she'd spewed out. After her third play, she'd mentioned her birthday. "And you're taking me—"

"—snorkeling." He'd nodded. "I didn't forget."

"Where are you going?" Shannon had asked in a light voice from the sofa.

"Sugar Bay, because the reef comes in close."

"I remember," she'd said, almost to herself, two words into which were clearly funneled the memories of their snorkeling together at Sugar Bay, making out under a tree once and being frightened, she laughing hysterically, after a coconut dropped near her towel. Dinner couldn't come quickly enough after that.

Thank God, Shannon, too, had put aside her anger since their quarrel, or her quarrel with him, and she was now cool but civil, at least in public. For him, the argument had been a turning point in their relationship. He'd seen a new side of her, a rage that had never before surfaced. It had made him think twice about accepting Jennifer's invitation for him to spend the night.

"You've got to come," his neighbor had implored. "The noise from the party will drive you nuts."

Conflict is better avoided had been Eric's mantra for all his life, and he'd refused, not wanting to face the two women who'd just told him off. But, later, the thought of Shad's party blasting reggae music into his apartment had driven him to accept the offer, and he'd arrived at sunset with a pillow under his arm.

After the Scrabble game, the adults had dined on the back patio at the table Miss Bertha had set with candles, lamb chops, and wine. Soon after they got started, Sheba had padded out and thrown herself down on the stone pavers beside Shannon.

"I love this dog." Shannon had leaned over to pat its brown belly.

"How's your work going?" Eric had asked, an attempt at détente.

"Fine." She'd looked up from Sheba almost reluctantly. "I went into Kingston yesterday to interview an expert on Rastafarian history, *the* expert, I guess."

"Who's that?"

"Richard Ransom, a professor at UWI, interesting man."

Not only had Eric never heard of the so-called expert, but he hadn't liked the way she'd said it. And he didn't like that Shannon had described the professor in such glowing terms that it had brought attention to her lips, which had curved into a coy smile in the candlelight.

"How so?" he'd grunted.

"He's the go-to person, I guess, for all things Rastafarian. He's traced their roots back a hundred and fifty years, back to the Maroons and Garvey."

"I read his columns in the *Observer*," Lambert had said. "He's a pretty good writer."

"What's he like?" Jennifer inquired. "They never show his photograph."

"Younger than I'd thought, midforties, I'd say, slim build, comfortable in his own skin." Shannon had looked at Jennifer with half-closed lids. " Nice, toffee-colored skin, too." The two women had laughed and Lambert had raised his eyebrows at Eric.

"Did you tell him about the Nyabinghi ceremony?" Eric had asked, spearing a lamb chop.

"I did."

"He warned you against going, didn't he?"

"Quite the opposite. He's coming with us."

That had galled him the most as he tossed in the Delgados' four-poster bed last night, the reggae music coming in the window reminding him that he wasn't getting anything out of Shad's party either. Shannon had a date, call it what you want, with the man. He'd seen the look in her eyes when she'd talked about him, too. It was lust, undoubtedly, lust for a man at least four years her junior. Thank God, Eve hadn't been around to hear her mother going on about *nice toffee skin*. He hadn't stayed for breakfast but had risen early, trudged down the hill, and taken a cold shower. It had made him feel better, although none of his usual ditties had come to him today.

The *Daily Gleaner* hadn't been delivered yet when he sauntered into the empty bar with his coffee and hard dough bread thick with marmalade. For lack of anything better to do, he sat sipping and chomping, waving to the children going to Sunday school, the little girls with hair neatly held with a dozen clips, the boys in their starched shirts.

Bored by nine o'clock, he sat his computer on the counter and checked his email. Two letters awaited him. Danny Caines asked about the clearing of the land, and Simone wrote that she was getting ready to make her presentation in DC. He answered both with one finger, saying the same thing: all was on target for the groundbreaking, the site was almost cleared off except for some large trees, and he was looking forward to seeing them.

Shad appeared just after noon. He was wearing the black pants he always wore to church, his head down as he trudged toward the building.

"You're in early," Eric commented when the bartender approached the bar. "I would have thought you'd be sleeping in." A stoic mouth was the only response. "A hard night, eh, bud?"

Shad shrugged. "How's business, boss?"

"The usual Sunday—one coffee and a sandwich, both mine." Eric made a funny mouth of his own.

Shad opened the fridge. "I going to have a Coke."

"I gather all isn't well."

Popping the top off the soda bottle, Shad sat down beside him. "You could say that." He took a long sip of his drink. "I come after church to tell you I can't pay the money back from the liquor—not right away—although is only one bottle of rum and some ginger ale. You can take it out of my pay next week."

"That bad, eh?"

Eric's bartender took another sip, swallowed, and bared his teeth. "Nobody come."

"Nobody—forget the rum, then. Let's make it your wedding present, that and the rental."

"I wish I could pay it, since that was our agreement, you know. I always like to follow my word." The little man shook his head. "Times tough right now, too. I have to pay Miss Bannister to look after the children while Beth gone to her bridal shower. I can't wait until this wedding business finish."

"What happened with the party, though? You always have such great—"

"Frank say they didn't come because they coming to the wedding for free. You ever hear such a thing? Is pure freeness Jamaicans like, I telling you. I having a good-good party with food and everything, and they couldn't come and pay a few dollars." Shad sucked his teeth, pulling the air slowly from back to front in a long, disgusted suck.

"Don't worry about it, bud." Eric patted him on the arm. "But I can't write off the liquor when it comes to the wedding reception."

"No, man, I paying you for that. I was going to buy the wedding liquor with some of the money from the party—but you know what? I was lying in my bed this morning and I decide that the wedding guests not going to see no scotch, whiskey, vodka, none of that. They think they coming for freeness, but just punch they getting, with rum and without rum. I been reading a recipe in the book Shannon give me, and I want to try it out, a daiquiri with white rum. And I going to water it down with ginger ale, too."

Eric couldn't hold back a laugh. "You're kind of bitter, aren't you?"

"You *raas claat* right about that."

"Who's doing the music?"

"You forget Ford, the trumpet man from New York, is coming back? Before he left last time, he promise me he would play for free at the reception."

"That's right, I forgot." An image of the tall, quiet trumpeter came back. He'd been staying with Roper Watson, the artist who lived on the eastern end of the village. When Ford had played at the bar one night, he'd blown them all away with "My Mother's Eyes," his own mother's favorite, he'd said.

Shad rubbed his scalp. "I looking for a guitarist, though. Ford say he need a guitarist and a drummer. I find the drummer already."

"What about your cousin? Didn't he play guitar last time when Ford played?"

"He gone foreign. He marry an American girl and get a

green card, but he left his guitar with me. He say he going to buy a better one in Philadelphia."

Eric rubbed his stubbly chin, rubbed it hard. His heart was pumping in his chest already, like the old days. "I tell you what, man. If you can't find somebody to play guitar, I'll stand in."

"*You*, boss?" Shad's eyes bulged as his mouth dropped open. "You can't play guitar."

"All I need is a little practice."

"When last you play?"

"High school, but I was real good. We used to play for proms and weddings." It had actually been two proms and a rehearsal dinner, almost a wedding, making the young Eric entertain the idea of Hard Nights going professional, until the other band members started talking about marriage or college or office jobs and he hadn't been able to talk them out of it. "Trust me, I can play."

The bartender shook his head and nodded at the same time, mixing it up. "I want to believe you, boss, but—"

"Just lend me Junior's guitar so I can practice."

"In one week?"

"In one week."

"I tell you what, man—I will give you the guitar and you practice up. Then let me hear you."

"Deal—now let's get that guitar."

Giving Shad a ride home, Eric talked nonstop, the old rocker in him coming alive again. He described his band's gigs at a bar in Shaker Heights (not mentioning it was the Danny Boy, where his father was a regular, or that the band members were underage). When they got to Shad's house and the black leather case was placed on the passenger seat,

Eric opened it, a Pandora's box, with care. Inside was an old Yamaha, exactly like the one his brother David had played, not an expensive guitar but a solid one. Eric had always yearned for a Yamaha. The Pantheon he'd bought cheap from a guy at school had always sounded tinny to his ears and needed an amp to sound decent, except that he couldn't afford an amp.

"You're coming to work at the usual time?" he asked Shad as he ran his fingers across the strings. "I need to start practicing."

"I coming after lunch, around three o'clock. Then I have to go with Shannon to the Nyabinghi thing—"

"I forgot about that."

"We probably going around six. Bongo coming with us, he going to meet me at the bar."

"See you later then." Eric closed the case gently. He slapped the gearshift into reverse and roared backward to the main road.

CHAPTER TWENTY-SEVEN

The dream was so lucid that she'd written it down when she first woke up. She'd seen two pairs of glasses, both metallic, both asymmetrical. Nothing like the readers she bought at the drugstore, these were works of art. The first pair was embellished with flowers and vines that wound around the frame. A straight, thin bar ran horizontally across the middle of the right lens. The second pair was simpler, its lenses clear and the frame geometric, bronze strips above and below the right lens, narrowing to the left lens, almost forming a triangle.

"What do you think it means?" she asked Jennifer, who was perched on the bed, watching her pack her camera bag. "One pair was floral and the other modern and clean."

"Do they always have to mean something? I've never been one for dreams."

"My feeling is that it means—let's see, the first one is about nature, perhaps Jamaica. And the right eye was really decorated. Anything on the right side of your body is supposed to represent the masculine, so I think—"

"Who says?"

"I can't remember where I got it from, but I think the right eye is Eric and the past."

"But there's a bar running across the right lens."

"Maybe that's Eric blocking me."

"What about the other pair?"

"Those were more—I don't know, like Toronto, maybe. Chic, straight lines, like the future."

The second pair, she'd realized while eating a banana that morning, was about making a shift, the shift she'd felt when she'd stood up to Eric for the first time. The words that had been turning over in her head for years had finally been released.

"And you could see clearly out of those second glasses, the modern ones?"

"I could. They were still asymmetrical, heavy on the right side with thin strips at different angles. I think they were both about the creative part of me."

"The first one is creativity in Jamaica, but held back by Eric."

"The other is about being creative up north, I think, where I'm freer, more contemporary."

Jennifer leaned back on her elbows. "I wish I had dreams like that."

"What kind do you have?"

"They're always about whatever I'm doing at the time, you know. Like last night I dreamed that I was at a ground-breaking for some big building, but, dammit"—Jennifer snorted—"the shovels hadn't arrived in time, so everyone was standing around not knowing what to do. I started to panic."

"Oh, God, no." Shannon straightened, laughing. "What happened then?"

"They all started looking at me and pointing. I know it's about the hotel groundbreaking."

"It's going to be fine. You're so good at event planning."

"I know, but I still have a million things to do. The member of Parliament hasn't confirmed that he's coming yet. The good news is that the champagne has arrived already, and I've found a caterer, but he's in Port Antonio, so I have to arrange transportation." Jennifer sighed and swept her fingers through her hair. "The shovels and hard hats are fine, though. They're already in the garage."

"If push comes to shove, you can just have them dig the holes, drink champagne, and go home."

"No use digging holes if there's no publicity afterward."

"You don't have a photographer?"

"He said he had a wedding and they're paying more, so he ducked out." Jennifer turned to her, biting her lip. "Feel like taking his place?"

"I've never done a groundbreaking in my life."

"All you have to do is point and shoot."

Shannon sat down hard on the bed. "I'd love to help you, Jen, but I'm hoping to wrap things up tonight."

She'd already told Jennifer about her search for information about Katlyn, since Eve had already told Eric, but she'd played down the importance of the mission, not wanting to worry her or Lambert. "I have a feeling that this old Rasta, Ras Redemption, has the answers I need about Katlyn. When I showed him her photograph, it definitely triggered something. You could see it on his face. Something tells me that I'm going to have everything finished in one or two days and get out of here before the groundbreaking."

"To avoid Simone, you mean." Jennifer circled the bed and put one arm around her friend's shoulders. With the other, she tucked Shannon's hair behind her ear. "Sooner or later you're going to have to face her, hon, or some other woman."

"I'd rather not, thank you." Shannon pulled away and walked to the window, to the view of the bay and the hills beyond. She rested her hands on the windowsill. "God, I love this place, this crazy little town, and I might never see it again. It's so beautiful."

"Then stay for a couple more weeks. The wedding is going to be fun, and you've got to remind me to bring the shovels the weekend after."

"It's tempting, but I can see it now." Shannon squared her fingers to frame an imaginary picture. "Simone hanging on Eric's arm, Eric dying with embarrassment, Eve furious with him for being with another woman, and me looking like Little Miss Left Behind." She shook her head. "I don't think so."

"So what? You're smart and beautiful. Maybe you'll meet someone—"

"Like who, Beth's uncle from Port Antonio? Let's be realistic here." Shannon picked up her bag, collected another with her purse and tape recorder inside. "I better get started. Professor Ransom is meeting us at the bar in ten minutes."

"That's right," Jennifer said with a slow smile, "the one with the toffee-colored skin."

Shannon headed for the door. "Oh, come on, Jen. I was just joking around."

"Many a truth is spoken in jest, my love." The hostess slipped her arm through Shannon's as they walked down the corridor. "But maybe Dr. Ransom would like to come to a country wedding—for research purposes, of course."

CHAPTER TWENTY-EIGHT

W hat was it about the emperor, Haile Selassie, you know, that made them *worship* him?" Shannon asked in the backseat.

Shad turned around and laughed. "He little but he *tallawah*. Small but strong—like me."

The professor wasn't laughing. "Selassie represented the power of the black man, that he could be the leader of a large country in Africa."

Ransom took himself too seriously, Shad decided, maybe he was nervous. When he'd appeared in the bar's parking lot in his nice new Volvo, he'd parked first in one spot and then in another. A neat man in jeans and sneakers, he'd looked uncertain as he approached the counter, and a tourist couple at the end of the counter had turned to stare at him.

"Am I in the right place?" His voice was like a radio announcer's, deep and smooth, commanding attention. "I'm supposed to meet a Canadian woman here."

"Shannon?" Shad had asked.

"That's the name." He'd shaken Shad's hand as he introduced himself, something few people did with a bartender. "Richard Ransom."

"Shad Myers."

"And Shannon—"

"She coming soon, she never late."

Just then the boss came out of his apartment, where he'd been playing chords and bars on the guitar. "A customer?" he'd asked Shad, and got a ginger ale out of the fridge. "Aren't you going to serve him?"

"He looking for Shannon."

Eric had popped open the soda and looked at the man, now wiping his forehead. "You're the professor from the university." Eric had shaken his hand across the counter. "Eric Keller."

Shad wondered about all the handshaking taking place and why the boss hadn't mentioned that he owned the bar.

With the couple at the end of the bar eavesdropping, not looking but not talking, Eric had started asking about the trip to Gordon Gap, his voice loud as he asked the questions, not like himself at all. Ransom had answered that he didn't know much about the area or the Rastas there and that's why he'd come.

"You want something cool to drink?" Shad had asked.

"Maybe a—"

"A Planter's Punch?" the bartender guessed. You could tell a lot from what people drank, he'd always thought, so it had to work the other way around, guessing their drink from how they looked. Ransom was a Planter's Punch man, cool, sophisticated, but not too heavy on the liquor.

"I was going to say a glass of water, but that sounds much better," Ransom agreed.

"You sure you don't want some lunch?" Eric asked. "The chef is in the kitchen, ready when you are."

"A Planter's Punch is fine, thank you. I had lunch on the

way." The professor had sat at the counter and watched Shad take out the ingredients: grenadine, bitters, curaçao, club soda, and juices. "What about the rum?"

Shad had taken a bottle off the shelf. "I use my family's rum, Myers rum, man."

"Your family?" Ransom said politely, not the kind to say Shad wouldn't have relatives who owned a rum factory.

"He's a comedian," Eric had chimed in.

Shad had chuckled. "Them is the rich Myerses. I come from the poor ones."

"I don't think they even make it in Jamaica anymore," Eric said, elbows on the counter.

"I heard a Puerto Rican group bought them out," Ransom said as Shad plopped a maraschino cherry on top of the concoction.

"Just what the professor ordered, right?" Shad said as the man sipped the drink.

"I've forgotten the long drive already."

When Shannon walked into the bar, Eve beside her, Ransom's face had brightened.

"Hi, Shad, hi, Dad." It was the first time Eve was wearing a dress, shapeless, but a dress nonetheless.

"Hi, honey." Eric had come around the counter to give her a hug. "You're coming to help me and Solomon this afternoon, eh?"

"Yup."

"This is Dr. Ransom. He's a famous authority on Rastafarians." Eric had turned to the professor, one arm still around Eve's shoulders. "This is our daughter, Eve."

"Pleased to meet you," Ransom had said, shaking her hand. His eyes flicked questioningly from Eve to Shannon.

"I see you found the place," Shannon had said crisply.

"Yes, I passed it and had to double back. I'd never noticed it before. It's sort of . . ." Ransom had covered the insult with a long sip of his punch.

"I glad you're coming with us," Shad had said. "Carlton, the driver, like to stay in the car. I ask a Rasta guy, Bongo, to come with us because I felt it would be good for three of us to go inside together, you know, but Bongo tell me this afternoon that he can't come. He say that since he in a different Rasta group, he don't want to be disrespectful and go to a Nyabinghi without an invitation."

"Probably a good thing," Ransom had agreed, just as Carlton came to a stop outside the restaurant.

"You can manage things here?" Shad had asked Eric.

"I'm helping him," Eve had said, and they'd all laughed.

"Everything ready for you, boss. I cut up the limes and oranges—and ice in the freezer. The tourist people have four Red Stripes, but they don't pay yet."

Shad had hustled to the taxi after the other two, looking forward to the drive to Gordon Gap, even if it made him a little carsick. There'd been pure stress all day, something Shad hadn't needed after the flopped party, which still hovered over him. Beth had insisted he go to church with the family, and he'd sat through the dull service dreading telling the boss that he couldn't pay him for the liquor. Then he'd rushed to the bar with the bad news, driven with Eric back to his house for the guitar, taken the younger children to Miss Bannister after extracting her fee from Beth's money jar (which she'd complained about the whole time he was eating lunch), and then run back to the bar to set things up for Eric before he left. A Sunday-evening drive through quiet countryside, the sun lowering gently behind the western hills, should settle his soul.

"Anybody know why they're having this Nyabinghi?" the professor was asking, tossing it out to the group like a school quiz.

"Don't they have them periodically?" Shannon answered.

"This one is to celebrate the emperor's birthday tomorrow, July twenty-third. That's one of the four Rasta holidays."

While they chatted, Shad touched his elbow to Carlton's. "What up with you?"

"Nutten," Carlton said, staring straight ahead.

"When people say *nutten*, they really mean *plenty*. Your jaw looking stiff today, like something running on your nerves. Is either woman or money business."

Carlton's lips quivered.

"Is a woman then," Shad acknowledged. "If it was money, you'd be frowning. I never see a man who don't frown when it come to money."

The quiver became a weary smile. "You is the detective."

"Is something about your new girl, the one you was telling me about?"

Carlton looked out his window. "She gone back to Kingston."

"I thought you was looking a work for her."

"I find one for her in Port Morant, cleaning a woman's house. Easy job because the woman live alone and gone to work in the days."

"She start already?"

"She start messing around, you mean. I notice every time she get out of Largo and get phone service, she calling and leaving message for somebody. And sometimes she get a call and she tell them she working, but she don't want to tell me who she talking to. 'Is a friend,' she say. Then yesterday I walk into the kitchen to find her. She was using the people phone, but like she was quarreling with somebody, a man it sound like. And I hear her saying, 'If you love me, you have to trust me,' is so she was saying." Carlton sucked his teeth. "When she see me, she look like a *duppy* frighten her. She slam down the phone."

"Her conscience bother her."

"I tell she—"

"Carlton, you've gone too far," Shannon said from the back. "I think you passed the road to Gordon Gap."

"Pshaw, man," the taxi driver muttered as he braked to a stop. "You see how a woman can take your mind off your work?"

ow's the drumming going?" Eric asked when Eve returned from serving curry goat to two women.

"Okay." She started writing out the invoice and looked up. "Did you know that the drum represents the heartbeat to Rastas?"

"I didn't know that." He was squeezing oranges for fresh orange juice. Someone usually wanted juice on Sundays, and although no call had come for it yet, he wanted to be prepared. He could always drink it later. "And did you know that I play the guitar?"

"You don't play—"

"I'm telling you, and I've been practicing."

From the kitchen came a crash and a curse. Solomon had been in a cooking frenzy all afternoon, chopping garlic, thyme, and scallions, banging pots around, answering criticism by saying he was practicing for Shad's wedding reception next weekend. Two batches of fried chicken and three versions of curry goat had been on the stove when Eric had last visited the kitchen. The old chef had been standing in the middle of the room slurping from a spoon. Never one to read a recipe or admit that he couldn't read, he always relied on his seasoned tongue.

"The curry goat still not the way I like it," he'd snarled. Fifty years of white rum had finally killed the man's taste buds, Eric had decided before retreating to the bar.

Thankfully, there'd been more customers than usual. Though only six o'clock, five tables had already ordered, and Eve had been trotting back and forth to the kitchen, slapping her drink orders on the bar counter like a pro. Eric wished he had a video camera to capture her counting and recounting money from her departed customers, matching it with the invoices, stashing her tips in the pocket on her chest, and giving him the balance for the cash drawer.

"Making quite a haul, huh?"

She nodded, patting her pocket before rushing to a table.

Eric gazed off at the island with its ruins, looking mysterious now in the gray cloak of early evening. He usually rowed over once or twice a year to inspect the condition of the ruins and the grounds, more often when Simone was out there. A couple weeks to go and she'd be here. Would things be the same? Would *she* be the same? She sounded a little different on the phone since she'd gone back to Atlanta, more cheerful, not as sardonic. He flipped on the switch next to the refrigerator, bringing to life one lightbulb above the bar and two above the restaurant. Running his hand over his ponytail, trying to distract himself from thinking of Simone's running into Shannon, he made a note to stop by the beauty salon for a trim. *Thick and nice,* his hairdresser, Rose, would comment as she brushed it.

He watched Eve's back in the baggy dress, her slightly bowed shoulders reminding him of his mother. She was going to be tall like her parents, had already stretched up while she was here, he was sure. He was glad she was working with him tonight, seemed to have either forgotten his rude comment about her friends or gotten over it. Her directness, her honesty, was thirst quenching, like springwater to a man tired of alcohol.

Chatting to some customers, thanking them for the tip, she was waving, telling them to come back. A smile lit up her face when she returned to the counter. "You should see the tip those people left me. I feel kind of guilty taking this money away from you."

"As long as they pay my bill, I'm good."

"They bought a lot of food, four thousand five hundred dollars!" She added the tip to the money in her pocket and washed her hands at the sink.

Eric folded his arms. "What are you going to do with your money?"

"Buy some souvenirs, I guess."

"For yourself?"

"Yes—and a friend."

"Boy or girl?"

"Girl, of course. We don't—we're not tight, but we're friends."

"No boyfriend?"

She sniffed, trying hard to control her mouth while she dried her hands. "Why'd you think that?"

"You're kind of cute—and you're thirteen this week. Shouldn't I expect it?"

"I'm cute?"

"Of course you are. You have gorgeous blue eyes, a nice—athletic figure, and your hair is shiny like your mom's."

"It's frizzy here."

"Everybody's hair is frizzy here."

"I have to clear that table." She dashed off.

"Do you know," she asked at her next break, "why my name is Eve?"

"Your mother chose it."

"She wanted my name to start with an *e*, like yours."

"She never told me that."

"There's a lot you don't know," Eve said with a look of old-soul wisdom. "You didn't know the name of that shell—"

"I know you like a certain boy."

Her eyes popped wide. "I like a boy?"

"I saw you walking with Jethro yesterday. You thought you could just sneak past the bar, didn't you?"

She blushed a shade pinker than her sunburn. "We were going up to the house to practice drumming, that's all. We're just friends."

"I saw how you looked at him. You were giving him that—that look that girls have when they like a boy—you know, all attentive with a big smile on your face." Eric remembered how Jethro had looked at his daughter as they walked along, his dreadlocks shaking as he talked, and how he'd started gesturing with one arm, the other wrapped around a drum. Although it was a bald-faced lie that he'd seen Eve smile, because she was turned away from the bar, he'd been able to tell she was fully engrossed, nodding, as they made the turn into Lambert's driveway.

He'd wanted to call out and interrupt them. Instead, when he'd gone up later to the Delgados' to spend the night, he'd asked Eve if she'd help him out on Sunday afternoon when her mother and Shad went off to Gordon Gap. It would give him a chance to say something. He'd say nothing to Shannon, who'd accuse him of being anti-Rastafarian, fitting him into the slot of the aging conservative.

Up to the instant he'd seen the two young people together, Eric had thought of his daughter as a permanent child, her detached cynicism when she'd first arrived as a childish game. His abrupt reframing of Eve as a teenager had begun minutes after watching the two young people walk up the driveway. He began to remember what he'd been like himself at that age, randy, trying to get girls to like him, rubbing against Nadine O'Connor behind the high school athletic building.

The image of Jethro working his way into Eve's underwear kept coming back to him, adding to his restless night in the Delgados' bed. In one version of the scene he'd pictured their hands drifting off the drums and onto each other. Another scene had them lying in the bushes; in another, pressed together behind a shed. Then the horrible thought of Eve's being pregnant—had she even started menstruating?—had made him resolve to say something.

"Jethro's nice," Eve said with her standard shrug.

"He's also already gotten you into trouble, don't forget."

"We're not *doing* anything, Dad, if that's what you're worried about."

"I didn't say anything—I mean—nothing that any father wouldn't say. He's a couple years older than you, isn't he, and you know what boys—"

"Don't even go there."

"I meant that he's not—you have to be careful."

"We're not—"

"He's from a poor family, I saw where his mother lives, and he sees you as a rich white girl. He's probably looking for what he can get, you know what I mean?"

"I'm not a rich white girl."

"To him you are."

"A customer is calling me," she snapped, and stalked away.

Eric sighed, closing his eyes. *Sheesh, a man couldn't win for losing.*

CHAPTER THIRTY

T he dark, silent seconds were measured by the clackety-clack of the windshield wipers as Carlton drove through the village of Gordon Gap. Shannon patted her purse holding the envelope with J$18,000 in cash, US$200, as Redemption had said. She'd gone with Carlton to an ATM in Port Antonio to withdraw it, and the fat, white envelope had made her nervous. Eighteen thousand bills looked a lot more than two hundred. She'd stored it in her bedside table, checking on it morning and evening to make sure it hadn't gone anywhere.

It had been sunny in Largo when they left, but the weather here changed quickly from one part of the island to another, from one hour to the next, as unpredictable as its inhabitants. Carlton had asked if he could stop off in a village on the way to give his cousin some mangoes, and the three had had to wait in the car for half an hour after he disappeared inside.

Shad had passed the time asking Ransom questions about where he was from and what family (no relation to the Ransoms in Ocho Rios, he was from Kingston) and how he came to be a professor (through scholarships and universities in London). It had started to rain just before Carlton jumped back into the car without an apology. By the time they'd reached the road to Gordon Gap, darkness had fallen, and the passengers' silent stares were paralleling the head-light beams.

Shannon rubbed an itch on her back against the car seat. Spatters of water were sneaking through the inch-opened window onto the long sleeve of her shirt, but she was too warm to close it. Beside her, Ransom sat looking toward the bellows of frogs. He seemed the only relaxed one in the car, didn't seem worried about what the evening might bring, and his presence reassured her. She'd begun to doubt if being paid four times what she normally re-ceived was worth all the trouble, but now she was feeling better. Being with the most respected scholar of Rastafari couldn't hurt.

She reached into her purse and felt the envelope. The money for Redemption was her personal donation to the quest. Expenses were included in what Angie was paying her, but the bribe would be worth it to get to the bottom of the business. No information on Katlyn, no payment from Angie. Equally important was getting out before Eric's girlfriend arrived in Largo. She already had reams of notes and hundreds of photographs, enough to put an insightful article together at home in Toronto; the only thing needed for her departure from Jamaica was Redemp-tion's input.

"What you think," asked Shad, turning in his seat, "if we pay a little visit to another camp on the way? It's a Rasta farm, and I hear—"

"I thought Ras Redemption was going to help us," Shannon said.

"We can't put all the farm eggs in one basket." Shad grinned at his own humor.

Shannon looked at Ransom, who'd been briefed on Katlyn earlier in the drive. He tipped his head, as if he thought it would be worthwhile. "Just a few minutes then," she said.

Shad told Carlton to turn onto an unpaved road before I-Verse's camp, and they bumped along for half a mile.

"You sure this is it?" Carlton said.

"I not a hundred percent sure," Shad replied in a low voice, audible in the back.

It was even darker here, the overgrowth and trees narrowing the already narrow road. Outside, the screeching of crickets had turned to a steady drone.

"I don't know," Ransom put in. "We don't know where we're going, it's dark, and it's raining. Maybe you should do this another day."

"Have to," Carlton said, stopping suddenly. Ahead of them, the lights showed a gully full of rushing muddy water.

"Let's go to the Nyabinghi, then," Shad said.

"Thank you," Shannon whispered to Ransom after they'd gotten back to the main road.

He put his hand on top of hers and squeezed it lightly. "I could hear what you were thinking." He didn't lift his hand and she didn't move hers, the warm comfort spreading from his hand to hers.

"By the way," she said, "I have a few facts to ask you about that are not in your books."

"You've been reading them."

"I read them already—in Canada."

They laughed together, making the hand-touching easier.

Outside, the rain had stopped. "We reach," Shad said. The gates to the camp were open tonight, and as they wound along the drive to the compound, the car lights picked out the eucalyptus trees towering over them like dripping sentries. Around the corner, a row of kerosene torches low to the ground announced the celebration, and in front of the first building, a large flag hung soggily from a bamboo pole.

A cluster of young men stood at the clearing in front of the buildings, some talking, some drawing on spliffs, turning one by one to look at the approaching car. The torches lit their faces from below, making them look like skulls, their chins and cheeks gleaming yellow. When Shad rolled down his window, the sound of drumming throbbed into the car, and Carlton leaned over the wheel as he crawled to a stop.

"*Rawtid!*" Shad exclaimed.

"A big night," Ransom agreed.

One man, dreadlocks in a bun on top of his head, stepped over to the car and placed his hand on the driver's window. "What your business here, brethren?" he said, clearly the gatekeeper.

"They coming to—" Carlton started.

"Ras Redemption invite us to the Nyabinghi," Shad explained, leaning in front of Carlton. "Is not the first time we come."

The gatekeeper called to another man, said something about Redemption, and the other man started toward the buildings.

The professor let go of Shannon's hand and stuck his head out the window. "I'm Richard Ransom—from the university."

The man with the topknot looked puzzled. "You coming to study us?"

"I come to partake, man, *nuff respect*," Ransom replied, switching to a middle-class patois.

A post-rain breeze drifted into the car along with the drumbeats. The men kept looking at them, at Shannon longer, and she shivered. She wanted to reach for Ransom's hand, but each of the car's occupants was sitting upright in a silo of space. A minibus braked to a stop beside them, and a dozen Rastas stepped out, men in baggy pants, females wearing flowing dresses with colorful headgear. They greeted the men and walked inside.

The gatekeeper kept his hand on Carlton's open window, only releasing it when I-Verse walked toward them. "Yes, you can let them in," the tall wood-carver announced. In his embroidered white shirt and yellow turban he looked elegant among the youths.

"Park here," the gatekeeper instructed Carlton, "and walk inside."

"I staying in the car," the driver replied.

Settling the camera bag on one shoulder and her purse on the other, Shannon stepped out of the car and joined Shad and Ransom beside I-Verse.

"This Mistah Ransom, the professor from UWI," Shad said to I-Verse, gesturing to Ransom, who bobbed his head at the introduction.

"The Ransom who write all them books?" I-Verse asked, the scent of marijuana bursting from his lips. "Welcome,

welcome, brethren, some nice reasoning with I and I tonight." The Rasta started toward the buildings, and the men at the gate parted to let them through.

Shannon felt the wash of eyes as they passed, and she took an extra step to catch up with Ransom. "Stay close to me."

"Joined at the hip," he said under his breath.

CHAPTER THIRTY-ONE

With each step they took, the drumming got louder, the haze of ganja smoke making it seem more insistent. From behind a building came the glow of a fire. A full moon had just risen above the trees, banishing the compound's bedraggled daytime look and turning it into a dramatic scene lit by torches. It reminded Shad of a film he'd taken Beth to see in Port Antonio for her birthday, the one about an ancient kingdom that was really in the future, except there was no electricity and everything looked old-fashioned, just like these Rastas.

Dozens of people swarmed the grounds in graceful outfits and turbans trimmed with variations of red, yellow, and green. Some moved around the outdoor kitchen; some walked toward the center of the compound carrying bowls. Men called instructions to women; women called instructions to children.

"Greetings," Akasha said, waving as they passed the kitchen. She looked pretty in a red head wrap, rows of beads around her neck.

"I and I getting ready for the feast," I-Verse explained to the visitors.

"*Ital* food, good food that," the professor replied.

"You hungry?" the Rasta asked Shad. "Is organic, so they call it in America."

The group rounded a building to find a robust fire, six feet across, roaring in the middle of the compound. On either side of the fire were two long tables covered by white tablecloths and laid with bowls and silverware. Platters of food already sat in the center of each, and more food was being added. Encircling the whole area were torches on bamboo poles, and to one side was a large tree. Framed photographs of the emperor hung from the lowest branches of the tree, the panes of glass glimmering above the six men drumming in a semicircle below.

"Take a seat." I-Verse gestured to a bench at one of the tables.

"Is Redemption here?" Shannon asked.

"Redemption busy now, reasoning with some brethren."

She smiled without showing her teeth. "We had some business to attend to, remember?"

"Little patience, your turn coming." I-Verse turned to Ransom. "Time for sacred herb. Everything taste better after a little smoke, right, Professor?"

Ransom looked up at the man, blinking rapidly. "Yeah, man."

The drummers started singing, a wailing about *taking us home* that went along with a rat-a-tat rhythm and a higher-pitched drum. Before departing, I-Verse placed a spliff in Ransom's hand as if he were the elder, the one to start the smoking, and Ransom glanced at his companions, eyebrows lifted helplessly, before placing the four-inch joint in his mouth. Shad wondered what Ransom was going to do—a man from Kingston used to being behind a desk—until the man took such a strong pull of the spliff, seeds popping, that his eyes crossed. Maybe it was part of his job, so he had plenty practice, Shad decided.

Shad took the joint and, after giving it a suck, offered it to Shannon.

"I'm working," she hissed.

Akasha, the baby lashed to her chest with a sash, motioned them to join the circle that was forming around the fire. "Praise time."

I-Verse appeared and gestured to the drummers to stop. They laid their drums down and joined the circle. I-Verse grabbed the hands of Shad and Ransom and raised them, his woodworker's palms hard and scratchy, and everyone raised their joined hands.

"Jah, the Beloved, the Wise," he called above the crick-crack of the fire, "your brethren come to you to ask blessings—blessings on the food, on the queens who made it, and on the feast. And I and I come before our emperor, the Most High Jah Rastafari, knowing you are everywhere around us. Your brethren walk before you in humility and follow your guidance, because wisdom is forgotten and overstanding is lost. Just as this fire represents the key to your presence, the judgment of the Almighty, may it also cleanse us all of wrongdoing. Jah and man, I and I, will keep all bad mind away from the door, now and forever more."

"Jah Rastafari!" the group shouted.

"Eating time," I-Verse said, releasing their hands.

Shad stared into the fire, the ganja making the crackling of the branches louder, the colors more vivid. He'd never noticed the greens and purples in flames before. A fire could hypnotize a man just as the sea did sometimes, but fire was like anger, the ocean like peace, and he preferred the latter.

By the time he made his way back to the bench, little room was left. "Give a man a seat, nuh?" he said to the teenager beside Shannon.

"Nuff respect," the youth responded, and made space for the visitor. Chatter and laughter were building, spoons and forks clanking against bowls, the windy roar of the fire in the center.

Shannon touched Shad with her elbow, her purse clamped under her arm. "Should I ask I-Verse about Redemption again?"

A plate of stewed eggplant was calling to Shad. "Soon come, soon come," he soothed as he spooned it into his bowl. "Like the man said, little patience. Eat something first."

Shannon threw him an exasperated look and reached for the fish that Ransom had put down, an aroma of onions and thyme steaming from the dish.

I-Verse returned to Ransom's side. "Redemption want you to join the reasoning."

The professor looked at Shannon. "Do you mind? I won't be gone long." When she nodded, he picked up his bowl and followed I-Verse.

"Redemption was supposed to see *me*," Shannon muttered to Shad. "I thought that was why we're here."

"Reasoning is a man thing." Shad helped himself to the fish.

"A *man* thing?"

"They gone to talk about Rasta beliefs. When he ready to talk business, he will come to you."

"When he wants to talk money, you mean."

"He probably don't know much, anyway."

Shannon's open mouth revealed half-munched fish. "He said he could help!"

"He keeping you in suspense, making you glad to get any crumb he can throw you."

"Don't you think he's the man who—you know, the one Katlyn went off with? Something definitely registered with him when he saw her picture."

"I think he taking advantage of you."

"Don't even go there, not after all this trouble, taking out money, coming to this thing, having that old man over there staring at me."

"Who, him? He just an old-timer, some of them don't trust white people."

"He keeps looking at me like—he's giving me the creeps with that stringy beard."

"You a guest, man, Redemption invite you. He can't do you nothing."

When the bowls were cleared, someone passed Shad a joint, and he took one puff and then another. Shannon looked at it, wavering, but passed it on. Bread pudding was placed on the table.

"You not eating dessert?" Shad asked the teenager.

"No, my mother don't make it. I and I don't eat food she don't make."

"She must cook good then, because the eggplant was sweet and you eat that. Which one is your mother?"

"See her over there." The youth pointed to a chubby woman in a yellow-and-black turban. "I-Verse wife."

Shad frowned. "I thought Akasha was his wife."

"Akasha his second wife. My mother is his first."

"Two wife? How that work, star?"

The young man gave a half snort, half laugh. "Most of the time it okay."

Shad whinnied. "I not going to try it with my baby mother, pure trouble that, fire-and-brimstone kind of trouble."

"Were you born in this camp?" Shannon asked.

"Yes. The camp was here long time, though."

"How long?" Shad asked.

"Thirty years. We celebrate our anniversary last year."

The drumming had started again, this time louder, more urgent, calling the gathering from the tables.

"Round the fire," the lead drummer called.

"Round the fire," two women echoed, clapping and moving toward the center.

"Fire time, fire time," a man chanted. Most of the diners joined them, the children's hands held firmly as they approached the blaze with their parents.

The drummers started thumping out a tune, and the others sang, clapped, some with their heads bowed, the moonlight shimmering off the white shirts and tams.

> *Babylon is falling,*
> *Babylon is falling.*
> *Jah children leaving,*
> *They leaving for Zion.*

A nudge in Shad's side from Shannon. "This looks like something we should join. What do you think?"

"If they want us to join them, they'll ask us, nuh?"

The group around the fire was getting bigger, people drawn from behind buildings. The song changed to another.

Feet shuffled from side to side. Voices rose and fell, some melodious, some plaintive. When the chanting stopped at intervals, the shuffling of feet and beating of drums filled the night air. The heavy scent of cannabis hung over the new chant that followed, a brisker tune with a strong beat, almost like a Marley tune. Shad's head was starting to expand, the fire appearing larger and closer to him. He looked toward Redemption's house for the professor.

"Oh, yes, oh, Jah," a man in a big woolen tam shouted. He twirled a few times, clapping his thighs. Two women joined him, their arms wide, their white skirts spreading like flowers as they spun, the fire crackling orange behind them.

"I have to get this," Shannon whispered. "It'll be a great shot for the article."

"You—you can't—don't—" Shad tried to gesture, but his elbows were glued to the table.

"I'll make sure they don't see me. I won't use the flash." Pulling a camera from her bag, she stood up slowly and stepped over the bench.

"Shannon, no," Shad warned hoarsely, but his words were drowned out by the drumming. He watched as Shannon circled around the back of the tree, holding the camera behind her. No one seemed to notice. All eyes were on the whirling dancers. Unable to move, unwilling to bring attention to Shannon, Shad watched her slide behind a bush, her lower body hidden. She raised the camera and focused, and he could see her finger pressing the button one, two, three times. Suddenly, a scream went up.

"Babylon—she a spy!" the man with the stringy beard was shouting, pointing at the bush.

"Who? Who?" Urgent cries came from those sober

enough to understand, glassy looks from those who weren't, while the drumming thumped on.

"The woman—the white woman," the man shouted, pointing at Shannon as she stepped out from her hiding place. He shouted for the drummers to stop and they paused, looking puzzled.

"I'm sorry—I was just—" she protested, trying to smile.

"She not troubling nobody," Shad yelled, and scrambled to stand up. If he could make them understand, everything would be fine. If he couldn't, it would end badly, he knew.

"I and I know she was up to something," the old man kept saying, over and over.

A woman ran to Shannon and held her arm. "Is a tape recorder you have?"

"Leave her alone," Shad said, stumbling over to them.

"Don't worry, I won't do it again," Shannon blurted. She was backing toward the bench, pulling the woman with her.

"Ask Redemption!" Shad urged. "She come from a magazine. He invite her."

"Babylon!" the old man screeched, his eye sockets black under the moonlight.

"Leave her, leave her!" Shad yelled. "She don't do nothing."

"If the woman so pure, throw her in the fire, then," the woman holding Shannon yelled back. "Like Shadrach, Meshach, and Abednego, prove she can't burn."

"I telling you, she don't mean no harm. I should know, because I name Shadrack."

"You name Shadrack?" The old man crouched down a little. "Jump in the fire with she, then. Fire will show faith, the fire of judgment." The crowd was circling them, the bonfire flashing between their bodies.

"She taking picture," a voice called. "She must be CIA!"

Shannon pulled her arm away from the woman and the Rastas followed her and Shad around the table, shouting that they were traitors, calling them downpressors.

"Get Ras Redemption!" Shannon cried, snatching up her bag.

"He invite us," Shad explained yet again, his tongue feeling thick. "I telling you."

"A devil woman that! Bloodfire for she!"

"Babylon must burn!"

"Richard!" the Canadian called toward Redemption's house.

"Mistah Ransom!" Shad shouted, but the louder they cried, the louder the mob shouted and the more venomous their eyes.

CHAPTER THIRTY-TWO

Trying to ignore the twinge in his back, Eric heaved one side of the toilet bowl up and slid the tile underneath. Simone shouldn't have to sit on a rocking toilet when she came. He'd tolerated it himself for the past six months, groaning every time he sat on it. Too small, too low, too cheap, the toilet would have to go soon—even if he had to build another hotel to get one. His family might have shared one bathroom in Cleveland back in the day, but times had changed, and he asserted to the mirror as he washed his hands, if he couldn't afford a toilet that didn't embarrass him or make his arthritic knees act up, then life wasn't worth living.

Back on the bartender's stool behind the bar, Eric found a scab on his forearm and scratched it away. He hadn't minded taking the Sunday-evening shift so Shad could go with Shannon. It had given him time to contemplate the nature of a man's life where a toilet and three women could create pure havoc. The toilet problem he would solve in time. He wasn't so sure about the women. Simone, Shannon, and Eve had come, initially, anyway—without invitation—straight into a life that was otherwise peaceful if boring, creating a tangle of emotions—

"Another whites," came a call from the end of the bar. Eric poured the rum and walked it to Tri, who was still laughing at a joke.

"Boss man," Tri asked after he'd taken a sip, "what you call a woman who have two men at one time—one in Largo and one in Kingston?"

"A woman you run from," Eric replied, and returned to his perch, the old fisherman's words ringing in his ears. Having more than one woman always confused him, made him slip up. Women could handle it, some women, anyway.

Shannon was different. She'd always been straight with him, told him from the beginning that she was a one-man girl and didn't have a boyfriend. Simone he wasn't sure of. For all he knew, she could have a man in Atlanta. She didn't seem like a game-playing woman, one who'd waste your time getting ready for her visit, breaking your back to steady a rocking toilet, buying new sheets for your bed. But, now that he thought about it (the twinge in his back joined by a twinge in his stomach), maybe that was the reason for her infrequent calls and nonchalant attitude. She had a man in Atlanta.

Her detachment had suited him at first. It had, after all, been his suggestion that they shouldn't communicate after she left. He'd called her despite himself, even invited her to the groundbreaking, but they'd never discussed monogamy. Did she or did she not have another man? The question mark clung to him, making him queasy.

He was about to get the computer to write her when Carlton's car screeched to a halt outside, accompanied by the smell of burning rubber. Shad and Shannon got out and, after the car drove away, walked into the bar glumly.

"What happened to the professor?" Eric asked, chuckling. "Got lost?"

Shad came around the counter and offered Shannon a drink. "A vodka, straight," she said after throwing a black bag on the counter. "And make it a double."

"What's going on, Shan? A *double*?"

Her face was flushed, and he had to wait until she'd had a sip of her drink. "We had to leave him," she said, so low that Eric had to lean in when she repeated it.

"Boss," Shad explained as he helped himself to coconut water, "the Rastas chase us out of the place."

"Shit." Eric slammed his fist on the counter. "I knew something like this was going to happen."

Shannon nodded with her eyes closed. "It was my fault." She finished the drink in one swig, throwing her head back, grimacing when she put the glass down.

"Another double," she told Shad with a tremble to her lips. "I'll pay for it."

"You don't have to pay for it," Eric said, "but you're going to get drunk if you don't watch it."

"I want to get drunk."

"You're coming with me," Eric said after Shad had given her the drink. He led her by the elbow to his apartment and into a verandah chair. "Tell me what happened."

That was the night that Eric and Shannon shared a bed for the first time in fourteen years. Not that he'd taken advantage of her, although, not being used to strong liquor, she was almost too drunk to make sense after the second double. It was just that she couldn't go home alone in that state, and he was too tired after her lengthy, stumbling description of the evening's events to walk her up the hill to the Delgados'. She'd be embarrassed to let them and Eve see her in that condition, anyway.

It had been easier to help her to his bed, tears dripping down her cheeks, where he took off her muddy sneakers before she flopped back on the sheets. Then it seemed necessary to remove her long-sleeved shirt, so he'd unbuttoned it, rolling her over halfway to ease her arms out, trying to avoid touching the bra with the small breasts that now drooped to the sides. And since he dared not undress her further, he'd adjusted her until her head was on a pillow and her legs in their jeans under the sheet.

The moonlight was to blame. Eric had watched the silvery touches to her lips and her eyelids leaking their shiny tears as she'd talked, and it had made him think of when they'd first met. Her thick hair had sparkled while she related what had happened at the Nyabinghi, the moonlight picking out the white strands, and when she'd ended on a wail about feeling responsible if anything happened to Ransom, Eric had reached over and rubbed her arm.

"He can take care of himself," he'd assured her, not caring if the man could or not. She'd kept lamenting that Ransom had gone somewhere to do something—she didn't seem to know what—and finally wound down to a soft sobbing, almost falling asleep on her own words, mumbling about getting back to Eve.

"You're not going anywhere in that condition," he'd said, and she didn't resist his throwing his arm around her waist and helping her to the bedroom.

She'd fallen asleep before he got into bed. Her snores had started off softly, gradually rising in volume, with interspersed snorts, much as she used to. He'd gotten little rest, thinking about her in his bed (*after all this time!*) and what would happen next. In the middle of the night, he'd felt like having sex. When the urge died down, he'd started to worry about what she would say when she woke up, what Eve would say, what the Delgados would say, each one needing a good half hour of anxiety. Close to morning, he'd considered what the other woman in his life might say if she knew, and the excuses he created kept him awake for another half hour, deciding it was better not to say anything to Simone—or ask her if she had another man.

It seemed only minutes later that he awoke in bright sunlight and rolled over onto his side. Shannon was lying faceup in the same position he'd laid her in, but she'd pulled the sheet up to her chin and was staring at the ceiling. Sunlight slanted through the louvers onto the sheet. Beyond the window, the island was waking up, the branches of the almond tree swaying in the morning breeze.

"What the fuck am I doing here?" she murmured as if she were talking to herself.

"Sleeping, I hope."

She turned with a worried frown. "Did anything—"

"No, it didn't."

"Good." She rubbed her forehead. "I have a headache."

"It's no wonder."

"And I feel like a total idiot."

"Why?"

She squeezed her eyes shut, as if she'd been thinking hard since she woke up. "How many reasons do you want?" she groaned. "I shouldn't have taken out my camera during the ceremony. That was just plain dumb, dumb, *dumb*. I don't know what I was thinking—after all I've read and heard. A professional photographer doesn't just walk into a sacred ceremony and start shooting without permission. I thought I could get away with it because I have before, but I shouldn't have tried. I wasn't even there to work on the article. I was there to find out about Katlyn, and now I've probably ruined my chances of getting any more information, dammit."

She opened her eyes. "Then I shouldn't have gotten drunk, and I sure as hell shouldn't have ended up in bed with you."

"You were sleeping it off."

"I shouldn't have taken this assignment. I don't mind doing the article, but I never should have agreed to look for this woman."

"Shoulda, woulda, coulda—"

"And for sure I shouldn't have come to Largo."

"Now *that* I disagree with."

She was looking up at the ceiling again, blinking rapidly. "Maybe I should have just stayed in Kingston or Ocho Rios and done the research for the article. Coming back to Largo—"

"I'm glad you came."

"We've butted into your life—"

"You brought Eve."

She breathed into a pause. "Is that the only reason?"

"No."

The minute that followed felt like an hour, and he dared not move. One word from him could change everything: his future, her future, Eve's future. He had arrived at the fork, at the major decision he'd avoided for so long—and he couldn't keep being a lone wolf (Maisie's words alive in his head).

Shannon reached over and rubbed his cheek with her knuckle. Her silent question drew her into him, and she started crying against his shoulder, but this time he thought she was crying for times past, hopes unfulfilled. He wanted to dam up her tears, wanted to tell her it was him, all him, his fault. He stroked her hair and the crying slowed.

"Sometimes," she said, sniffing, "I feel like I've made such a mess of my life, getting pregnant, being a lousy parent—"

"You've been the better parent by far."

She gave a hard snuffle. "I knew you didn't want children, but you never said one mean word to me when I told you I was pregnant. And you sent me money even when you didn't have any. You haven't been a great parent, true, but you're still a great guy." She raised her lips to his chin, then to his lips, kissing him with those fluttering, little kisses that he used to love. She had told him what he needed to hear, and of course he couldn't hurt her feelings by telling her no, or he didn't want to.

CHAPTER THIRTY-THREE

Shannon nuzzled into Eric's cheek, breathing in the sour-earthy smell she recalled on lonely Toronto nights. Wondering if she was doing the right thing, she kissed him again and again, the tears drying on her face.

It had happened almost accidentally, she knew, but he'd initiated it. He'd put her in his bed, slept with her the whole night, and reached over, his hand colliding with her arm, to embrace her. He wanted to be with her at last, she could tell, hardly been able to keep his eyes off her whenever they were together. Either he'd realized that he loved her more than Simone or that he wanted to be with her because they had a child together. This, this would be the moment that would decide if she'd live in Largo or he with them—or if she'd place him forever in a pigeonhole that said *Eve's father*.

He kissed her, twisting his tongue around hers the way she'd always liked, and she kissed him back. Then she pulled away a few inches. "Are you sure?"

He looked over her shoulder as he unhooked her bra. The dryness of his hand on her breasts, the clumsy way he ran his hand up and down the side of her neck, were so familiar, so welcome—like a wave coming back to shore—it almost made her cry. Instead, she kissed him, running her hand over his chest and stomach. She rubbed the hairs on his chest, now gray, and the paunch that was new to her. But he was still Eric, older, wiser, and the man she loved. She guided his hand down and unzipped her jeans for him. It felt so right, the way he stroked her, getting her excited in seconds.

She started pulling down his boxers, but he gripped her wrist. "Wait a minute."

"What's the matter?"

He was looking away and she turned his face to look at her. "We don't have to, you know."

"It's not that."

She grinned. "Don't tell me you're shy." She reached inside his shorts. Unfamiliar, shrunken folds met her fingers, the hard verve of years past melted into baby softness.

"I'm sorry." He sighed, pulled her hand out.

"You don't have to apologize." They blundered through who was sorrier than who while they lay in an embarrassed embrace.

Back at the Delgados' an hour later, Shannon was frying an egg when Jennifer walked into the kitchen barefoot, her green housecoat tied around the waist with a sash.

"Good morning, sunshine. Have you seen Miss Bertha?"

"She said something about getting the children dressed for something."

"Yeah, we're going into Ocho Rios to spend the day with friends. Eve said she'd like to come along. Is that all right?"

"Sure." It would be nice having the house to herself. She could work on her notes and photographs, would have the space to go through the parachute drop that had already started, her hope of a future with Eric unraveling even as she'd buttoned up her blouse beside the bed.

"You're disappointed," he'd said, still under the sheets, his indignity hidden.

"It's perfectly normal, happens all the time."

"I don't want you to think—"

"Please, don't worry about me. I'm fine." She'd tucked in her blouse, avoiding his eyes and the truth they'd speak.

"I'm glad you spent the night. It felt like old times."

"I was a mess. Thank you—really." She'd glanced at him briefly as she slipped her feet into her loafers.

"I wonder what Eve thinks," he'd ventured.

"She's still sleeping, if I know her." She'd tried to smile as she left and cried as she climbed the driveway back to the Delgados'.

Jennifer padded to the refrigerator. "I was waiting up for you last night, but I faded. When did you come in?"

Shannon turned away. "I spent the night at Eric's."

Her friend poured orange juice into a glass and sat at the kitchen table. "Want to talk about it?"

"Not really." Shannon turned off the gas and held her head for a second. "God, I feel awful. I drank too much."

Jennifer tapped her fingers on the glass. "So you spent the night with Eric—but what happened to your professor friend?"

"We left him at the Rasta camp, but his car was gone this morning from Eric's parking lot. He must have come back."

The story of the previous night was retold over breakfast. At the end of it, Jennifer sat back with alarmed eyes. "You might have to rethink this whole investigation. This could be really, really dangerous."

"I feel like giving up, honestly, but something about Katlyn's story keeps pulling me to find out more. If something like that had happened to me, I'd want someone to find me—or my body, in this case, wouldn't you?" Shannon shuddered. "I hate to think what happened to her. She sounds like she was a really sweet girl, you know. Terrible way to end up. Not to mention that I'm being paid a fair amount to find her. I just can't seem to get anywhere with it, though.

"Shad thinks this Redemption man, the old Rasta, doesn't know anything, that he's just playing with me to make some money. I was hoping he was Katlyn's lover—he's old enough—and that he'd just cough up the facts. Too simple, I suppose. Especially since his camp hasn't been there long enough, only thirty years, and Katlyn disappeared thirty-five years ago." Shannon slumped in her chair, almost relieved, and flicked her fingers open. "I might have to go home empty-handed."

"You wouldn't want to cut your trip short, though, would you? Not with Shad's wedding coming up. And Eric and Eve—I know you don't want to talk about Eric, Shan—but he and Eve are getting along so well. It would be a pity to rush back. Eve needs her father." Jennifer tilted her head in question, a woman who always had hope. "And maybe now that you've spent the night with him—"

"He's too old for me, anyway."

"Lambert's older than me."

"Yeah, but Eric is older than God."

"You didn't seem to think that last night when you slept with him."

"Emphasis on the word *slept*."

"I thought—"

"I had too much to drink and he put me to bed. That was it."

Jennifer took a deep breath, regrouping. "Well, it's not like you don't have options, is it? Ransom wouldn't have come all this way from Kingston if he didn't like you."

Shannon sighed. "After reassuring me that we would be *joined at the hip* during the ceremony, that he would be my protector, it took him about a millisecond to leave us so he could *reason* with Redemption. I think his going with us last night had everything to do with his work and pretty much nothing to do with me. But I'll call him this morning to see if he's okay."

Bertha waddled into the kitchen. "Miss Jennifer, you want me to give the children breakfast before you leave?"

"Good idea. I'll bathe while you do that." The mistress of the house stood and tightened her sash. "See that Miss Shannon gets a nice lunch and don't disturb her, please. She could do with some rest."

CHAPTER THIRTY-FOUR

It seemed as if every one of Shad's days off was spent doing some kind of work, and the Monday before his wedding was even worse. He checked on Miss Claudie about the cake, picked oranges from Miss Armstrong's tree for the reception's fruit salad, and cleaned the house from top to bottom in preparation for the arrival of Beth's sister on Friday.

While wiping the mirror in the bathroom with newspaper, a thought occurred to him that made him rush through the rest of the cleaning. He showered, walked down the road to the bar, and asked Eric, who was fiddling with the computer behind the bar, if he could borrow the Jeep.

"It needs gas," the boss said glumly.

"I going to put some in."

Eric frowned at the computer again. "Do you know how to get on to the Internet? I've forgotten."

"You plug into the telephone line yet?"

"Of course I plugged in."

Shad rounded the counter and pointed at the screen. "Eve tell me you have to touch this round thing with the arrow."

"Can you get in for me?"

The bartender took the keys off the nail where they always hung. "I gone, boss." Halfway across the restaurant, he turned back. "You know when they tearing down Miss Mac's house?"

"Wednesday, Lambert said."

"I not going to miss it. I have to say a prayer for Miss Mac and all she do for me. You have to thank God, you know, before you pull down a house with all them memories."

The Jeep was as ornery as ever, and Shad had to wipe off the battery terminals before it would start, salt and corrosion affecting all Largo's vehicles. Once the car started, he washed his hands, cleaning his short fingernails, before starting on his errand. Driving past the Annotto Bay fire station, a small bowl of mangoes his only companion, the sometime detective admitted to himself that he hadn't been much of a detective this time around. Because of the closing on the new hotel, preparations for the wedding, and the failed party, he'd let Shannon do most of the work hunting down Katlyn.

He thought about his past ventures: saving Simone from political thugs, hunting down Joseph's would-be murderers, rescuing Danny's girlfriend from the clutches of drug dealers. Nothing had distracted him then. Today, he would make up for his recent negligence and do a little detective work on his own. He recalled a phrase from *The Secret World of the Private Investigator*, written by Ellis J. Oakland, a man much admired by Shad. The best investigators, Oakland said, *follow their hunches*. When he'd first read it, Shad had thought that a hunch was something on a crippled man's back and had asked Beth's opinion.

"A hunch mean what your mind telling you," she'd explained.

Shad had been able to relate to that right away. He always followed his hunches when he guessed a customer's drink, but now his mind was telling him that, since he'd promised Shannon he'd help her solve the Katlyn business, he should do some work on it today. Beth might not want him to do any detective work after they got married, but something had been nagging at him, and he wanted to work on it on his last day off as a single man. By midafternoon, he'd found his way to the road where Maisie's cousin lived.

"Miss Mattie!" Shad called from the gate. Clutching the bowl of fruit, he knocked on the number plate with a stone. An elderly woman peeked out from behind the vine screening the porch.

"Who that?" she said with narrowed eyes.

"Is Shad, ma'am, the man who bring your cousin Miss Maisie of Largo Bay. She send some mangoes for you."

Half an hour later, having drunk a glass of lemonade and discussed the elderly woman's lumbago, Shad inquired about the young Rasta whose mother had sent food while Mattie was sick. "His name was Unity, a nice young man, good manners. I want him to help me find something he was telling me about."

"He live next to Mammee's Bakery, about ten chains up the road."

After thanking her for his clipping of the kiss-me-over-the-garden-gate, Shad took his leave and started driving up the road, remembering the chant in school: a chain is a hundred feet, ten chains are a thousand. Before long, the smell of baking bread started making him hungry, and he stopped outside a small shop.

"Unity live around here?" he asked the teenage girl who handed him two patties and a plantain tart.

"Next door." The girl lowered her face and suppressed a smile. "The house have a orange door."

"Like you know what behind the orange door." Shad winked.

Sure enough, Unity, dreadlocks concealed under a skull-cap, opened the door. Shad reminded him of their earlier meeting. "You can come with me to find the Rasta farm you was telling me about? My mind just tell me to visit them."

"I was going to wash my—"

"I pay you ten US."

"Deal," the youth replied, a next-generation Rasta.

By the time they'd climbed the road to Gordon Gap, the sun was going down, and after they passed through the town, Shad turned on the Jeep's crooked lights.

"Right here," Unity directed when they approached a dirt road. It was the same road that Carlton had tried to drive down, but the surging water of the night before was now only a trickle and the Jeep lurched down the gully bank and up the other side with little difficulty. The road ahead was heavily overgrown, and tall bushes started beating against the windshield.

"You see anything?" the young man said, peering into the darkness. His question was answered in a few minutes when Shad jerked the Jeep to a halt beside two houses, both brightly lit within. Shad knocked on the door of the larger house.

"Good night," he said to the Rastafarian woman who

opened the door. He introduced himself. The short, erect woman, Sister Aziza, she told him, looked up at him with glowing skin and wise eyes. She was wary at first, but softened when she heard the story about Katlyn's demise.

"We trying to find out what happened to her," Shad said.

"I remember reading something in the paper about it long ago." Sister Aziza invited him to come in. "It's a story that's stuck in my mind ever since." Candles shimmered from every table in the room, and the scent of something minty drifted through the house, coming from either the candles or the pot on the stove in the corner. "And her parents never found her body? That's a real shame."

Aziza was a middle-class woman by her accent and furnishings. The candlelight made her look younger than her age, Shad was sure. She wasn't from Gordon Gap originally. Aziza and her husband, formerly lawyers in Kingston's Twelve Tribes community, had retired to the area fifteen years before to start an organic farm. Her husband had died six years ago, but she'd stayed on.

"People eating so much garbage, fast food and all kinds of thing, nowadays." She touched the scarf covering her gray locks. "We wanted to learn how to farm and pass on good growing and eating habits, you know. We never had any children, so I'm going to leave this farm to the young people here."

"I know the life not easy, but is a valuable thing to do," Shad agreed. "Good for the country."

"Yes, like our legacy." She had something trustworthy about her, good in a lawyer and a farmer.

"How did you end up here? It's a long way from Kingston."

Aziza rose to check the pot on the stove. "We were driving around looking for land," she said over her shoulder. "We wanted to buy something in this area because it was fertile and—and Rasta friendly, you know. There's a long history of Rastas farming up here. It's not everywhere you can find that. Somebody told us there was an abandoned farm further up the hill, so I went to look at it. And we found this man living in a shack up there, all by himself—a hermit—looked like he didn't have two sticks to rub together. My husband asked him if the land was for sale, and he said no, but he had some down here. Just like that." Aziza sat down, waving Shad to do the same.

"We found out he was from Kingston, and he'd been a Rasta from the time when police used to beat up Rastamen and throw them in prison, back in the 1950s. That was when it was illegal to be Rasta. He was one of the men who started the Pinnacle camp—you ever hear of Pinnacle?" Shad shook his head. "Back then, everybody was afraid of Rastas. People used to call them *madmen*, you know. They had all this angry talk and wild hair, refusing to do what the English people wanted. The old Rasta had been part of an early group in the Kingston ghettos, but the police were always harassing them. They moved to the mountains nearby in Sligoville and set up a camp they called Pinnacle.

"Up to five hundred, a thousand, brethren came together in Sligoville. Then police raided the place and burned it down and locked up the leaders. When this man got out of jail, he and his followers set up a camp here. They were the first on this mountain."

Shad's nostrils flared, scenting something other than mint. "Where he was living when you last seen him?"

"Up at the top of the road, you can't go any further than that. They were trying to hide from the police, you know. I think the old hermit had inherited the land from his parents."

"He still alive?"

"He must be dead by now."

"And his name was . . . ?"

"People called him Dread. His birth name was on the deed, Adolphus MacMillan. We bought the land with cash, and he marked his name with an *X* on the sale agreement. It was all legal, you know." She laughed, slapping her robe. "We were lawyers, after all, and we didn't want anybody to accuse us of—anything illegal."

Shad thanked the woman and returned to the car. "We going up the road," he told Unity.

Past I-Verse's gate and five miles on, Unity said he wanted to wash his hair before it got too late. "Soon come," the bartender replied, knowing well that soon wasn't coming for a while.

The narrow, twisting road ended a few hundred yards farther on at a small, dark shack surrounded by thick bushes. "This must be it, star."

"I have to come with you?"

"What you think I paying you for?" Shad creaked the car door open. "I don't like to come to these kind of places alone. Time to big up like a man."

The moon was three-quarters full, enough to help Shad find his way around the undergrowth behind the shack, Unity breathing heavily behind him. A ghostly building, its shuttered window covered by vines, suddenly appeared to their left.

"*Raas claat!*" the youth whispered loudly.

"Look like it empty." Rounding the structure, they saw a circle of abandoned houses, a dozen or more. "Plenty people was living here one time," Shad commented.

They moved slowly, hunkered down, stepping over and around the tall grass between the houses. At the back of the yard, hiding behind the empty buildings, was a cottage from which a weak light emerged.

"I good, boy," Shad muttered. "Somebody still there."

The yellow light of a kerosene lantern glowed behind a tattered curtain, more holes than cloth. Gesturing to his companion to go around the back of the house, Shad tiptoed to the front door. The smell of thyme poured out of the shack's window.

"Anyone home?" He knocked, knocked again on the thin wooden door.

The only sound was the tinkle of a spoon being placed in a pot.

Taking his handkerchief out of his pants pocket, Shad wiped his forehead. "I looking for a gentleman name Dread," he called.

The door opened an inch. "Who you?" a voice croaked.

"Excuse me, please. My name Shadrack Myers. I had a friend . . ." He trailed off as the door opened slowly, allowing the odors of seasoning and sweat to pour through. The large, dark shape of a man humped with age stood before him. He was leaning on a stick as tall as he, the lamplight behind him, and lumpy, dangling dreadlocks fell to his knees.

"I asking about a woman—"

"I don't know no woman," the man growled, and slammed the door.

"A Canadian woman," Shad called.

The door opened a little, stopped. "What you say?" The rumbling voice could have come from a tomb.

"I asking about a woman who disappear—"

The door was yanked open. "I look like a murderer?" The man raised the stick.

Shad stumbled backward and fell to the ground. "Wait!" Shad yelled. "I just asking—"

"Who send you?" Over the Rasta's shoulder, something glinted above the torn curtain. "You is police, right?" He raised the stick again, but this time someone held it and pushed the old man and his stick back into the house.

"Leave him, brethren!" Unity shouted. "The man don't do you nothing. Is so you think Jah want you to act?" After the fellow slammed the door, Unity held out his hand to Shad. "I man enough for you now?"

CHAPTER THIRTY-FIVE

E ric stood on the edge of the low dune and waved his
arms. "Don't go out so far," he called.

Eve waved before bodysurfing with Casey back to
the beach. As soon as their feet touched sand, they headed
back to meet the next wave.

It had been a long morning for her father, and he was already looking forward to the lunch Jennifer had promised.
The day had started early because snorkeling was best done
before nine, he'd assured Eve.

"You ready?" he'd asked her when she came out of the
Delgados' door that morning.

"You forgot to wish me happy birthday," she'd chided
him when she reached his car window, and he'd started
singing the birthday song.

"It's okay, Dad. You can skip that part."

"I thought you wanted me to—"

"Is that my birthday present on the seat?" She'd torn open
the gift, trying on the mask of the snorkeling set inside. "Can
Casey come with us?" she gurgled through the mask.

"Of course."

Eve had run into the house, and her father had waited in
the Jeep until he could wait no longer.

In the kitchen he'd found Miss Bertha cooking what looked like an elaborate omelet, Sheba at her feet. "Mistah Eric, you want a johnnycake? I just cook some."

He'd munched away at the fried bread and inquired about her son Isaac, who'd worked at the hotel as a gardener.

"He too frisky, I telling you. His sister is the steady one, but he have one woman after another. He already have three children by three different woman, and he only twenty-seven. What you think about that?"

"I hope he can support them."

"Pshaw, is the cock crowing all you men." The woman had sucked her teeth.

Eric had blushed a deep crimson, glad she'd turned her back. The phrase *erectile dysfunction*—the poetic words hiding the terrible meaning—had haunted Eric since Shannon's hasty departure on Monday morning. It had been weighing down his forehead as if he were carrying a metal sign tacked to it with the initials ED. He was now officially impotent, he kept telling himself, something he'd heard his mother calling his alcoholic father through the thin bedroom walls. He'd never had a problem before, and he'd always smirked at the ads in magazines touting cures. Just the year before, sex had come easily with Simone, and there'd been no need to think about it in the chaste months since. But here it was at last: he couldn't get it up.

The only person he could share his dilemma with was Lambert, but Eric was too ashamed to bring it up. His best friend had a lusty sex life himself. Cringing already at the cost of seeing his urologist, Eric had spent Monday afternoon fiddling with the computer, determined to get answers. That night he'd discovered Google. On Tuesday, when Shad wasn't looking, he'd visited websites that gave him the information he was seeking.

Impotence, according to one site, was caused by alcohol, medications, or chronic illness; none of these applied to him. Eric had read on, one finger on the screen, that impotence could be a signal of heart disease. Another website said he should protect his erection by eating healthy produce (all those mentioned unavailable in Jamaica), avoiding fatty foods (the core of his diet), and controlling obesity, high blood pressure, and high cholesterol (all of which he probably had, he was sure). By the time he got to warnings to curb smoking and get regular exercise, a feeling of doom had descended and he'd gone to bed depressed.

"Isaac too randy," Miss Bertha had continued, spooning more fried bread into the basket. "He must be taking Spanish fly or something."

"Spanish fly?"

"Is a thing that make men—you know—give them plenty juice. Make them get it up and stay up. So they say, anyway."

Eric had just gotten up the nerve to ask where one would buy this miracle medicine when Eve and Casey rushed into the kitchen with their gear, Jennifer right behind.

"We're having a little birthday party for Eve this afternoon," Jennifer had pretend-whispered. "You should come."

"I'd love to."

"And, of course, we'll have lunch waiting for you when you get back from the beach."

The snorkeling at Sugar Bay had been more fun than he'd thought it would be. He and Casey had helped Eve put on her mask and fins, and the three of them had paddled around the cove's coral outcroppings, signaling each other underwater when they spotted a colorful parrot fish, or once a stingray lying on the sand. When the waves picked up, they'd stopped snorkeling and the girls had opted to body-surf. He'd sat on his towel under the same coconut tree where he and Shannon had made out long ago, and he'd been reminded, yet again, of their disastrous night in bed. Only after he'd bought three lobster patties from a man walking on the beach did Eric realize that, if he went to the birthday party, he'd have to meet up with Shannon.

On the drive back home, with Eve and Casey squeezed into the passenger seat, Eric decided that he'd have to go to the birthday party and face his shame. He wasn't sick, he had no pressing appointments, and he'd look like a moron if he didn't go to his daughter's birthday party. Plus Shannon would think him a coward. When they got back to the Delgados', he ambled into the kitchen behind the girls. The first person they ran into was Shannon, lifting cookies off a baking sheet.

"Can we have some?" Casey asked.

"Please, don't. They're for the birthday party."

"I was just wondering what time the—the party was," Eric stammered when she glanced up at him, the memory of Monday morning creating a fog between them.

Her voice was even, no emotion. "About four o'clock."

"Righto." He rushed back to the Jeep without lunch.

At the bar, Shad was wiping glasses and setting them on a towel.

"Didn't Solomon relieve you?" Eric asked. "Isn't it your break time?"

"Boss, I stay here with Miss Mac while they was tearing

down her house." The bartender shook his head. "She start to cry, and I almost cry myself. Is a sad, sad thing when you see your house mash up like that. The old roof just give way, then the walls come down, easy, easy. You would never think that they stand up to all them hurricanes." He sniffed hard. "They should have said a few words before, though. The bulldozer have no respect, man. All them years she live there and bring up her son, all them people who stay in her boardinghouse, all the time we used to sit in her kitchen and talk—just gone with the dust when they smash it. I decide that I don't want to learn to drive a bulldozer. It don't know the difference between right and wrong."

Eric murmured his sympathies and walked down the conch-lined path to what had been the house next door. The nine acres of land that had belonged to Miss Mac now lay bare, a few cedar and mahogany trees standing over the wasteland. In the middle of the property was a pile of concrete chunks and old beams: Miss Mac's demolished three-bedroom house. Although the land now belonged to the Largo Bay Grand Hotel Company—the name already making him uncomfortable—it still belonged to his former landlady, Miss Mac, in Eric's mind. True, she'd wanted to sell her house and land, she'd been saying so for years now, but that didn't change her stamp on it or fill the emptiness she'd left behind.

As Eric stared at the rubble with a heavy heart, a fat, brown rat ran up a beam lying askew. When it got to the end, the creature turned its head—sensing an observer—and locked beady eyes with the new owner.

"Get ready, bud," Eric announced. "Your life is about to change."

CHAPTER THIRTY-SIX

B low them all out!" Shannon urged the birthday girl.

"Make a wish," Rickia added as Eve blew out the thirteen candles, sweeping her head around the square cake with her name in the middle.

"Don't tell us the wish or it won't come true," Casey said.

"I wasn't going to tell, anyway." Eve was wearing an orange dress that Casey had given her, and her hair was swept away from her face in a fluffy ponytail. She looked older to Shannon all of a sudden, her face longer and calmer, its former sulkiness almost absent.

"Don't the senior citizens get cake first?" Lambert called from the adjoining living room.

"Coming right up," Jennifer said, carving into the cake.

The first slice went to Eve, who held it up and crowed, "Chocolate, my fave."

"I better not have any," Shannon heard Eric say behind her. He had come to the party on time, and he and Lambert had retreated to the sofa, a safe distance from the women and the seven children clamoring around the table.

Shannon handed Joella a slice of cake for Baby Josh, standing shakily clutching his sister's skirt, the dead stamp of Shad in his little jeans and sneakers. Behind them, Shannon heard Lambert lower his booming voice, saying something about a *lack of testosterone*. Eric's reply was too muffled to hear. Intrigued, she cut two large slices of cake and walked them to the men, determined to show Eric she didn't care if he had a lack of testosterone or not. Lambert thanked her when he took his plate, and Eric mumbled something, turning as pink as the rosebuds on his cake.

As she spooned out ice cream for Rickia, Shannon knew—felt it for the first time in the depths of her—that there was no going back to what could have been with Eric. Red flags were flapping all over the place. He hadn't pursued her, hadn't told her about his girlfriend, and—the biggest flag of all—he couldn't get it up when they were making out.

The feeling that the relationship was over had been coming on since she'd left him on Monday morning, and she'd spent the rest of the day feeling despondent. But Tuesday was a new day, and she'd resolved to focus on the tasks she had to complete before leaving the island, helped by the news that Shad had sprung on her.

"I met an interesting lady Rasta," he'd said when he called at midday. "The one we start to visit the night of the Nyabinghi, but the road was blocked, remember? Aziza is her name. Anyway, she tell me about the man she and her husband bought their land from, an old man who live by himself. I went to visit him."

He'd related his encounter with the angry Rasta and clucked his tongue. "Not a nice man, not a nice man at all."

"Did he know anything?"

"He just vex. He thought I was police."

"I guess we should rule him out."

"Yeah, no woman would want him," Shad had quietly mused. "Something funny, though."

"What do you mean?"

"When he open the door, I see something strange. I see a piece of glass, like a diamond hanging on a string in front of the window."

"That doesn't mean anything."

"I never see nothing like that in a Rasta house yet." The would-be sleuth paused. "Anyway, we still don't know what Ras Redemption was going to tell you."

Shannon had lifted her lip. "I really don't want to go back. I'm pretty sure they don't want me back—and I don't trust him."

"And I can't help you now. I have to do all kind of thing before the wedding, pick up flowers, suit. Mistah Eric lending me the Jeep." And the following week, before the groundbreaking, he explained, he had to collect people from the airport. She wondered if he meant Simone.

Not long after, Miss Bertha had called Shannon to the phone again. Richard Ransom was returning her phone call from Monday. He apologized for calling back a day late; he'd been entertaining a visiting colleague from Scotland. He didn't use any pronouns.

"I heard you left the Nyabinghi in a hurry," he added in his radio voice, this time with a soft laugh.

"I'm sorry we had to leave—"

"What happened?"

"It was my fault. I took out a camera, and the folks around us weren't happy. Stupid mistake, one I'll never make again."

"I'd never have known about it if I hadn't asked where you were. One of the drummers told me you'd gone because of some *confusion*—that's what he called it—and I-Verse got me a ride down the mountain. When I left, everybody was celebrating. You wouldn't have known that any drama had gone on."

"How did you get back to Largo? I saw that your car was gone—" She broke off, about to reveal that she'd seen his car missing from the car park early Monday morning.

"I took a taxi when I got down to the main road."

"That's a relief. I felt terrible leaving you, but things got a bit hairy. I thought I was going to be burned at the stake."

"I hardly think so, although I'm not surprised you got some verbal threats. They're suspicious of outsiders, you know, for good reason. They've been outcasts for so long. But they're a peaceful bunch, Rastas; they really don't want any trouble." His deep voice rumbled into a laugh. "I'm sorry to tell you, but burning a foreign journalist would bring them far more attention than it would be worth."

"You're probably right, but what about Katlyn?" Shannon inquired, the journalist in her scavenging for any crumb he'd gained from Redemption. "I wonder if she was ever threatened. I'm glad to hear the Nyabinghi would never have actually harmed me, but maybe she wasn't so lucky."

"Redemption never mentioned a word about her. He only wanted to reason with me, best me at Rastafarian philosophy."

Shannon updated him on Shad's visit to Sister Aziza and the man named Dread. "I'm sorry I never had a chance to talk to Ras Redemption," she added, a little dig.

"He might be worth another visit."

276

"I'll have to think about that."

"You know, I was thinking about another community I know that's not far from Gordon Gap. It's in a place called Heron Hill. I did some research there a few years ago. Maybe we can go up there one day. They might know something."

"Whatever I do, I need to do it soon. I want to get out of here by the middle of next week the latest. Shad can't help me, though. He's busy getting ready for his wedding Saturday afternoon." She'd wondered if it was too big a hint.

"Getting married, huh?" Ransom had said, accompanied by the sound of pages turning, as if he was consulting a diary. "I could help you Saturday morning. That's the only time I can do it, because I'm having company after that."

"Would you?" She'd grinned into the phone, deciding that she could deal with this man—even if the company was female.

Eve's birthday party moved on to the opening of gifts: a book from Shad's children and a return ticket to Jamaica from the Delgado family, at which Eric had looked a little chagrined about Lambert's helping him out again. Eve had hugged everyone, saying she would read the book on the plane back to Canada—and then come back next year.

Shannon's gift had been opened at the crack of dawn when Eve shook her awake. "It's my birthday."

"Happy birthday," her mother had moaned as Eve jumped into her bed, the first time in years. "I know you're here for your gift." She'd chuckled as she kissed her daughter.

The teenager had pulled away. "I bet I can guess what you're giving me."

They'd laughed when they both looked at the tall drum with the bow sitting in a corner.

It had already gotten dark and the party was winding down by the time Beth appeared for her children.

"You have to have some cake and ice cream," Jennifer insisted.

"Might as well build up my strength for the wedding."

"Want to see my drum?" Eve asked her guest, and rushed out of the room without getting an answer.

Jennifer cut a slice of cake for Beth. Shannon was spooning ice cream on top when the room went black.

"Lights gone!" a child shouted. Everyone started talking in the darkness.

"Don't get excited," Lambert called above the hubbub. "I'll turn on the generator."

"I going to eat my cake," an invisible Beth said with a laugh.

"We have candles around here somewhere," Jennifer said.

Shannon felt her way around the dining table to get Eve, who wouldn't be used to electricity outages, and had just reached the opening to the corridor when she bumped into a large figure with a sour-earthy smell.

"It's just me." Eric grabbed her arm. She started to pull away, but he held her firmly. "Shh." He gave her a hard kiss, the kind that a woman feels to her toes.

CHAPTER THIRTY-SEVEN

Shifting his weight on the old barstool, Shad tried not to compare the Quality Life Bar with his own bar, but some things he couldn't ignore, such as shaky chairs for the customers. The small bar in the square was better known for the cheapness of its rum than for its comfort, and although his grandmother had been a friend of the owner, Shad could count the number of times he'd visited the bar on one hand.

"You mean all you going to drink is Coca-Cola?" Tri said. "Is one time a man get married, if he even do that, and the least you can do is take a decent drink."

"Is your stud party, man," Solomon agreed, his tongue already heavy. "Time to loosen up."

"Stud party?" Frank repeated, standing at the end of the bar over a Red Stripe. "Is *stag* party, you don't know that?"

"Stag party, stud party, man party, don't matter," the chef grumbled.

Super-blue, the bartender, held up the rum bottle. "Who want more?"

"Put some in his Coke, nuh?" Tri urged, and the bartender started to pour rum into Shad's glass.

The guest of honor pulled his glass away. "I soft-drinking like Winston, keeping him company."

Winston raised his pineapple soda to Shad, the man who had fathered him when his own father had left. "Thank you, suh."

Tri had come up with the idea for the stag party one night a couple weeks back. He'd told them that in America the men celebrated before the wedding, he'd seen it on TV. "Is to big-up the husband, help him say good-bye to his happy, single days."

"Look how long I living with Beth and I still happy," Shad had replied. "I don't need no stag party to say good-bye to happiness."

"Pshaw, man, we giving you a little send-off," Tri had declared. "Just accept it, nuh?"

The town bar next to the cricket pitch would be the venue, and *only five man* would be invited, the elder had assured Shad. "Is not no free-for-all. I not paying for every man jack to come and drink liquor."

The fluorescent bulb above the bar cast a greenish glare on the men's faces and long shadows on the linoleum floor. Frank started boasting about the horse races last Saturday when he'd gone to Mas Abe's betting shop in Port Antonio and won over J$1,000 (and still wanted his money back from the rocksteady party that night, Shad noted). A couple of customers in the bar joined in the conversation with their own gambling stories.

Not a gambler since his youth, Shad stared at the pinup calendar behind the bar. A pretty girl leaned on a tree trunk, her skin glowing as if it had been rubbed with coconut oil, like Sister Aziza's face. Shad drifted away, thinking of how high he'd gotten at the Nyabinghi, wishing he hadn't indulged in the weed he'd been offered. It had only made him panic when, maybe, things weren't quite as bad as they felt at the time. He wondered if Aziza smoked ganja. She didn't look as if she did. Dread probably did, which would explain his crazy response to the visit. Shad thought again of the glass pendant above the old man's curtain, which had reminded him of the diamond he wanted to buy Beth one day, the ring she deserved.

Winston nudged Shad. "You want little music?"

"Yes, man, turn it on."

The teenager put the radio on the bar counter and tuned it to a woman singing a slow, sexy song. "You like Lady Saw?"

"'Lady Truthfully'?" Shad grinned. "What man don't like that song?"

"Turn it down," Eli pleaded.

"Turn it down, yesh," Solomon said, raising his glass. "We have to give Shad a eulogy."

Tri hit the counter, doubling over with laughter. "You burying him?"

"You mean a toast!" Eli exclaimed.

Frank raised his glass. "I want to toast him, yes. I want to toast the man who making our life hell."

"What you mean?" Shad pulled back.

"All the woman in Largo nagging they boyfriend to marry them," Frank said. "You don't hear?"

"Miss Olive tell me she want we to marry before we dead," Tri said, sucking his teeth.

Eli leaned in. "Minna say if Beth can get wedding ring, she want one, too."

"And Maisie start up now," Solomon said.

"I sorry, gents, but the wedding not even my decision."

Shad shook his head. "Is Beth who want it, and she not happy until it done. And when she happy, I happy. Only one thing going to change—no more harassment about wedding."

"That what you think," said Frank.

"Ring on finger, chain on foot," Eli added, and Winston snickered.

"I don't care if she a angel before," Tri said. "She turn into a devil after."

And then it came back, a picture in a black frame on a wall, he couldn't remember whose wall it was. But it was a picture of a woman standing on tiptoe, one leg high in the air behind her, and on her back she had huge, white wings like an angel—a dancing angel.

CHAPTER THIRTY-EIGHT

Remember, I'll be there on Wednesday. *This* Wednesday, mind you." She was laughing at him already, at his forgetfulness, his age, he could tell.

"How could I forget? August first." Eric had never liked the month of August, with its heavy rains and mosquitoes, and this time it was bringing the tra-la-la of the groundbreaking—and the dreaded meeting of the two women.

"It's going to be quite a week," Simone said. "Up here in DC until Tuesday, then back to Atlanta for one night, unpack and repack, and on the plane to Montego Bay the next day."

"You'll be ready to collapse when you arrive."

"If there's anyone sleeping in your bed"—a titter hid her gibe—"you'll have to ask them to leave."

"My bed is empty, I told you."

"If your daughter's still there, I'd love to meet her."

"You're asking if her mother's here."

"How well you know me."

"They're still here. Shannon hasn't said when she's leaving."

"I'll be cool, don't worry." Simone sniffed sharply. "Have you seen them a lot?"

"Eve's been helping out in the restaurant, and we went snorkeling for her birthday."

"That's great. What about her mother?"

"I see her sometimes, not as often. I saw her at Eve's birthday party on Wednesday."

"I guess she's soaking up that Jamaican sunshine while she's writing her article."

"I'm not hearing a tinge of jealousy, am I?" Eric pulled the stool closer to the phone, anxious to turn the conversation away from Shannon, the one who'd been on his mind the last few days. His former lover's lips, the soft skin of her face and arms, had been haunting him since they'd embraced in bed. In between fretting about his libido, he'd kept wondering what it would have been like if they'd had sex. She'd wanted him, he knew it—and he'd failed her.

Being at the party had been torturous at first, and Shannon had ignored him much of the time. She'd gone off to the TV room with board games for the older children, while Jennifer had taken care of the younger ones. He'd sat with Lambert and they'd ruminated on the hotel project for a solid hour until Eric had switched to talking about his discovery of Google. Just then, the children and their supervisors had reassembled around the dining table for the blowing out of the candles, Shannon's long legs calling to him under her shorts. For some reason he still didn't understand, he'd chosen that moment to make a joke with his friend about all the ads on the Internet for Viagra and Cialis.

"You'd think every American man was suffering from— you know," he'd chuckled.

"I think all that stress in the States is leading to exhaustion, lack of testosterone," Lambert had intoned.

"If you ask me, the baby boomers are trying too hard to stay young," Eric had mumbled.

When Shannon brought them cake, leaning over to hand him his plate, he'd been given a quick view of the breasts he'd stroked only two days before. Forgetting his comment that he wouldn't have any cake, remembering the fluttering kisses she'd given him, he'd felt a quiver in his groin when he took the plate.

As soon as the lights went off and before he could even think, he'd gone straight to where he'd last seen her, almost tripping over two excited children. Not finding her, he'd moved toward the corridor, knowing she'd be thinking of Eve. He'd found her, held on to her arm, needing forgiveness for his failed libido, and kissed her hard enough to prove that younger, toffee-skinned men had nothing over him.

"Of course, I'm jealous!" Simone burst out laughing. "You're thousands of miles away on a tropical beach with— I'm sure—the beautiful mother of your child. What's not to be jealous about?"

"I didn't know you cared that much."

An exasperated snort. "Why would I be coming down to Largo if I didn't care? We've had this conversation before, Eric. You're a pretty hot guy—know it, own it."

"That part's hard."

"And speaking of hard, you're a great lover."

He reddened, not knowing what to say, not wanting the only customer in the place, a woman in a beige suit (a bank auditor, she'd said), to hear anything about his private life. Her head was bent over the cow-foot soup Solomon had left in the fridge and Eric had warmed up.

"I can't speak too long. Shad is running around in the Jeep doing stuff for the wedding, so I'm holding the fort."

"It's tomorrow, right? He must be freaking out."

"Like a chicken with his head cut off."

"Did he buy the rings?"

"The party he held was a flop, so he didn't make the money to buy them. He's gone off to buy a small silver band. Better than nothing, he says." The auditor was signaling him and he nodded at her. "How's the weather in DC?"

"Hot as Hades, especially downtown. Thank God for air-conditioning."

"Keep cool until I see you then—August the fourth, right?"

"Are you—?"

"Just joking, just joking."

CHAPTER THIRTY-NINE

Shannon arrived at the bottom of the Delgados' driveway at the exact moment the sun was rising over the hills. A rooster crowed, then another and another in a cacophony of awakening. Shielding her eyes, she looked up the road for Ransom's car. The only sign of life was a woman with a basket on her head walking toward the square; a scrawny dog in the middle of the road was eyeing the basket. The journalist leaned against the gatepost with her bags. Across the road, the sun-drenched bar sat silent, the chairs stacked on one side. The hedges around the parking lot were freshly, if unevenly, clipped—Eric's contribution, no doubt, to the wedding reception that afternoon.

She'd never understand the father of her child. Just when she'd given up on him, he'd do something unexpected, such as kissing her in the dark and then disappearing, muttering about helping Lambert with the generator. The kiss had excited her, given a jump start to her dying hope.

The silver Volvo pulled up beside her. "You're right on time."

Ransom grinned. "My bad habit."

"Am I forgiven for abandoning you?" She stood outside his window, pretending to cringe.

"Only if you'll forgive *me*."

"We were supposed to be joined at the hip, weren't we?"

As Shannon settled her bags in the rear seat of the car, Ransom explained that he hadn't wanted to insult Redemption, the community's elder, by not joining him for a reasoning, especially since he hadn't officially been invited to the Nyabinghi. "Then *I* would have been burned at the stake." They both laughed, both relieved. "I think he knows and trusts me now, though."

"And that's a good thing for me."

"Do you know where Carlton lives?"

" 'Up the road, left at the mango tree, and look for a yellow house'—Shad's exact words."

They picked up Carlton in front of a brown house and set off for Gordon Gap. The taxi driver had agreed the day before to act as extra security in the absence of the bartender. "You don't have to drive," Shannon had explained. "The professor is driving."

"I have to be back by three for the wedding."

"Me, too. I'll make sure we're back."

Before leaving the house that morning, she'd laid out the dress and shoes she'd brought for the wedding, wondering if her own time-faded dream of marrying on the beach in Largo would ever come to fruition.

"First stop," Ransom said, "is the group I told you about in Heron Hill—if that's okay with you. It's on the way."

The Nyabinghi camp in Heron Hill was in the mountains several miles before the Gordon Gap road, and it took a while getting to it. Remembering her promise to Carlton that they'd be back in time for the wedding, Shannon could feel his discomfort behind her all the way. She was relieved to see the farming community appear, and her hopes rose as she looked over the well-established fields and buildings that must surely have been older than three decades. After being introduced by Ransom to the elder in charge, a middle-aged man with a long, thick beard, she wasted no time asking about Katlyn—only to be disappointed.

"I and I don't really encourage foreign Rastas up here," the leader told her. "They come down, all excited about living off the land and being Rasta, but in one or two years, they gone back. They get homesick. No foreign Rasta ever live here."

"Have you heard of a Canadian woman who was dating—living with—a Rasta man thirty-five years ago?"

"I and I wouldn't rightly know." The leader stroked his beard.

Shannon asked—as respectfully as she could—if she could take a photograph of him with Ransom and, when they both agreed, posed them in front of the entrance to the camp, no visit to be wasted.

"Next stop, Ras Redemption, right?" Richard confirmed as they climbed into the Volvo.

"Hopefully, the last stop," Shannon said, "so we can get back by noon."

They got to the shed where the community's sculptures were sold by late morning. The teenager in attendance said he thought Redemption would be home, and they drove to the compound, stopping in the clearing next to the houses. Shannon added a floppy hat to the sunglasses she was wearing, her self-conscious disguise after Sunday's debacle. The camera bag left in the car beside Carlton, she set off with Ransom through the nearly empty yard.

"Is Ras Redemption here?" he asked a statuesque woman staring at them.

"You is the professor from the university, right?" The woman squinted at Shannon. "And she is the woman who come with you last Sunday." The woman cast an eye over the photographer's hands, holding nothing but an envelope. "But she don't bring no camera this time."

"No camera this time," Shannon repeated, looking quickly at Ransom, and the woman pointed to Redemption's cottage. "I think I got the all clear because of you," Shannon murmured as they walked toward the house.

"You're the celebrity."

"And still a white foreigner."

"Greetings!" Ransom called when they arrived at the open door. Ras Redemption appeared in a striped pajama bottom and a T-shirt.

"You come back," he said casually, waving them in while he took up his seat on the sofa. "Make we have little reasoning." He sounded clear and sober. "You ever see this book?" he asked Shannon, pointing to the brown book on the coffee table, the same book he'd been holding on her first visit.

"Tell me about it." She removed a pile of newspapers from a stool, now used to the protocol of light conversation before substance.

"It call *The Kebra Nagast*," the Rasta said, looking at her but trying to impress Ransom. "Is like our Bible. You should read it, like how you going to write about Rastafari. You must know the truth."

She twisted her head to read the spine. "*The Lost Bible of Rastafarian Wisdom and Faith*, eh?"

"They say the sources come from the Old Testament," Ransom added, "from Egyptian and Ethiopian texts."

"I'll make sure to mention it in my article." She cleared her throat. "Ras Redemption, I'm sorry I didn't see you when I was here last."

"I and I hear you run for your life." The Rastafarian held down the quivering corners of his mouth. "Nothing was going to happen to you, you overstand?"

"It didn't feel like that at the time."

"Little misunderstanding was all," Ransom said.

Shannon raised one eyebrow a fraction at him before turning back to her host. "I still want to talk to you about the Canadian woman. You said you could help me."

"And you can help me?" He leaned his head back on the sofa, looking at her through lowered lids. "Big magazines pay money for interviews, right? Just because Rasta live humble, it don't mean we can't do business, too."

"Yes, I brought it." She laid the fat envelope on the coffee table between them. "You can count it."

He eyed the envelope. "No need."

"Please tell me what you know. There are people in Canada who still care about Katlyn." Shannon took a deep breath, tightening and untightening one fist. "Did you know her—the woman in the photograph I showed you?"

Redemption straightened his head, a sudden sadness in his eyes. He took his time opening a brass box on the table before him, rolling a fat joint, and lighting it. Shannon watched him, prepared to wait, even if she had to miss the wedding, because something was here, despite Shad's misgivings. After inhaling, Redemption offered Ransom the joint.

The professor declined. "I'm driving."

The Rasta took another pull, exhaled, and stared at the joint. "We never call her no Katlyn. We call her Kay. We was living in another place and we was all young then."

Shannon's heart started pounding in her chest.

"I and I met her in the grocery shop one day and we start talking." He looked up, the mouth smiling, the eyes still cheerless. "She want to learn *kumina* dancing, she say. We used to do it around the fire—African dancing from slavery times, we don't do it much anymore—and she say she want to learn Rasta drumming and singing. I invite her to come to the camp for a Nyabinghi and she love it. Then I start teaching her Rasta ways, teaching her the language, lending her books and so. She see the truth and she become Rasta. She change her name, call herself Akila. It mean 'wisdom,' and that was what she wanted. Her hair start to locks up"—he waved one hand over his head—"and she start to spend plenty time in the camp, visit me all the time. We become good friends, you know what I mean?"

His gaze traveled from Shannon to Ransom, the smile fading. "But I was too young for her. She need a more—a older man. She was a bigger woman to me and she had travel around and everything, so we stop. . . ." He shook his head and took another puff. "You want some?"

"Yes, please." Shannon took the spliff, her thank-you to him for giving her the truth to take back. It also signaled her acceptance, she'd later realize, of Rastafari. They were just people, people who loved and lost, like Redemption, like her.

When she inhaled, she held her breath too long, and the smoke shot out in a bout of coughing. Ransom patted her on the back.

"Do you know what happened to her?" she wheezed.

The elderly man rubbed his knees, maybe his arthritis. "We never quarrel or nothing, and she kept coming back to the camp, teaching the children and so. The leader of the yard start to talk to her, a big man, ten years or so older than her. The land we was living on was his family land, so he was the leader. Next thing, Akila move into the camp and start living in his house with him. It break my heart, but I happy for her, because she was a good woman. She take care of him, cook for him, clean his house, and wash his clothes, and she decorate the house pretty-pretty with her own things.

"Everybody like her. She teach the children something she call *square dance*, which look like our quadrille, and they used to dance for us sometimes. And she teach reading and writing in the little school we had for the *pickney*. Everything was nice for a while. But it look like the life too hard for her. She not used to outhouse and washing clothes with her hand and sleeping on old mattress, you could see it. A few months later, she get sick with running belly and lose plenty weight—"

"Running belly?" Shannon queried.

"Diarrhea," Ransom said under his breath.

"And we call the Rasta doctor, a woman who give us herb and tonic when we sick, and she give her medicine, but she don't get better. She draw down so thin she couldn't walk, so she stay in the house and the women cook for her and for him." Redemption took the joint from Shannon's outstretched hand.

"Next thing we know, she and the man gone and the house lock up. Then he come back one night when we sleeping, and after that he just shut himself up in the house. Don't talk to nobody. We never see her, so we know she gone left him. When he have to come out to get little water or food, if we say something to him, he turn mean. Any little thing and he start to quarrel with us, and when we remind him that Rasta man is a peaceful man, he curse us off and tell us to leave if we don't like it. He start calling us *Babylon*. That come like a bad word to us, and one by one, we leave the place. One of the brethren rent a piece of land over here, and we build up a new yard with new rules and new leaders. We stop farming so much and start carving sculptures, because I used to carve, so I teach the younger ones."

Shannon leaned forward, the ganja messing with her head already, remembering she had to be the professional. "Did you ever—ever see Akila again?"

"Never see her again."

"Hear anything about her after that?"

Redemption shook his head.

"Is her Rasta friend still alive?" Ransom asked.

"He must be dead long time, brethren."

"Where was the camp?" the journalist asked.

The elderly man gave the directions. "But it cover up with bush now."

"What was the man's name?" the professor said.

"Ras Zadock, but we start calling him Dread after he start calling us Babylon."

Shannon sat up straight, trying to remember something. "I think that's helpful."

"Walk good, then."

"Thank you, brother man," Ransom said as he stood up.

"I and I don't like no secrets," the old man answered, reaching for the envelope.

CHAPTER FORTY

The tuxedo seemed to be a different size. "Maybe I lose weight since I try it on," Shad said.

"Like you swimming in it." Frank poked a white carnation into the groom's lapel.

"Nothing I can do about it now." Shad shrugged his shoulders to fit. "And the best man supposed to make me feel good, not tell me the suit too big."

"I just talking the truth."

"Some truth you supposed to hide."

"Come, friend, time to go."

"Yes, boy." Shad threw his head back, laughing as he clapped and spun on one heel. "Like a lamb to the slaughter."

"I glad you so happy," Frank commented with a curled lip. "Marjorie buying magazines with wedding gowns already."

The two men jogged down the steps of Frank's house, where Shad had stayed the night, and started the short walk to the church. Beth had insisted that the bride and the groom shouldn't see each other for a night and a day before the wedding, and besides, her sister and brother-in-law needed the bed.

"Remember to pick up the ice for the reception," Shad reminded Frank. "And Miss Maisie need help taking the fruit salad to the bar."

"How you expect me to pick up ice *and* fruit salad?"

Shad was about to offer a solution when he saw the silver Volvo flying down the road past them. The car screeched to a halt and reversed—Carlton in the driver's seat.

When it came parallel, Shad called out, "Where the professor?" He could see Carlton's desperate eyes as he rolled down the passenger window.

"Trouble—plenty—plenty trouble, man!" the taxi driver babbled.

Shad ran to the window. The professor was lying with his eyes closed on the backseat. One of his sneakers had come off and his foot hung over the seat, lifeless in its sock.

"We was up in Gordon Gap—Shannon and the professor and me—and we—we go to a place—"

"Where I-Verse and Redemption—?"

"We went there first, then—then we went to another place way up in the bush, at the end of the road, and the two of them went in and I stay in the Volvo—and after one hour I went to find them. And all the buildings them was empty except one little house, and I look through the window and I see Mistah Ransom on the ground like he sleeping, so I pick him up and carry him to the car."

"And Shannon?"

"Shannon gone. I call out and—and I even walk around, but nobody else there."

"Take Ransom to the hospital," the groom said, jumping into the passenger seat. "Drop me at the church first, though, to tell them I can't come."

"What about the wedding?" the best man said from the sidewalk.

"We can marry tomorrow."

"And Beth going to kill me today," Frank said, squeezing into the back beside the inert professor.

A quarter mile farther on, a line of four cars on one side of the road announced the church, the doorway now adorned with streamers and balloons. Beth's sister and daughters were laughing on the front steps, and the Delgado family was walking up the short pathway with Eric and Eve.

"Don't wait for us," Shad instructed Carlton. "If anything, I using the Jeep. Go straight to the hospital."

Shad hopped out after the car had coasted to a stop, Frank on his heels. "Going right now," the taxi driver said, and shot off.

"Glad to see you're on time," Eric called. Everyone turned around, smiling to see the groom and best man arriving.

"We have a problem, boss," Shad said.

"I know. Shannon is late so we had to leave her."

"Is a bigger problem than that."

"Is it something to do with Mom?" Eve whispered.

"What's the matter?" Lambert said.

"I going inside to break the news." Frank rushed into the church.

"Jennifer," Shad asked, "can you help Beth plan the wedding for tomorrow?"

"It can't be tomorrow," Jennifer protested. "That's Miss Louise's funeral, Bertha's aunt."

"Tell Beth I sorry, but is emergency this."

"What's wrong?" Eve whined, biting a nail. "Daddy?"

"I told her not to—" Eric started.

"I know where she is," Shad said. "We just have to go and get her."

"We're coming with you," Lambert said, and looked at Eric. "Let's go in my car."

"Good," Shad said. "The Volvo gone somewhere else."

"Where's Mom?" Eve cried, a tear starting down one cheek.

"We'll find her," Eric reassured her.

Jennifer wrapped her arms around the girl. "I'm sure she's okay, honey." Jennifer nodded to Shad. "I'll talk to Beth."

"Come on, guys," Lambert urged. When they were out of earshot, he murmured, "Let's stop at the house for my gun."

The drive to Gordon Gap seemed long, made longer by the air-conditioned silence in the Range Rover. Eric clutched the overhead handle while Lambert drove like a maniac. In Port Antonio, Shad unknotted his black tie and put it in his pocket. In Annotto Bay, he freed the top buttons of his shirt. At the turning to Gordon Gap, he shrugged off the rented jacket, folded it beside him, and rolled up his shirtsleeves. The light was starting to fade as they climbed the hill, and Shad leaned back on the headrest, saying a prayer for Shannon and adding another that Beth would forgive him.

"Where exactly are we going?" Lambert asked as he accelerated the Rover past the empty sculpture shack.

"It sounding like she went to an old Rasta camp that I went to on Monday," Shad reported. "Carlton found Mistah Ransom there. He look like he dead."

"Ransom was—dead?" Eric said, turning around, his knuckles white on the overhead handlebar.

"Where is he now?" Lambert asked.

"Carlton taking him to the hospital."

"Turn here," Shad instructed Lambert. "We need to pick up another man." Lambert drove down the driveway while Eric muttered dire warnings.

As soon as the car stopped, Shad jumped out of the SUV and ran into the Nyabinghi compound, crickets claiming the darkness around him. One of the cooks in the kitchen gave him directions, and he found I-Verse, fresh from taking a shower, and explained the situation (Ransom now dead, by Shad's description).

The Rasta immediately agreed to go with them. "I and I hear about Dread, but everybody say he die long time. Maybe is somebody else living up there."

Back in the car, Shad introduced the sculptor to the men in the front while Lambert headed to the road. "Like you was going somewhere nice, the way you all dress up," the sculptor commented.

"We was going to a wedding," the bridegroom said, swallowing hard. "My wedding."

He told Lambert to turn left up the hill. "Just keep driving."

The abandoned camp came into sight at the dead end. "Park here," Shad murmured.

"There's nobody here, man," Eric commented. "It's black as pitch."

"I telling you, that was where Shannon disappear. Carlton describe it and I been here myself. I meant to tell her little more I remember, a picture I see on a wall, but she find the place already."

"Let we split up," I-Verse suggested. "I bring a flashlight."

Lambert took a sleek, gray gun out of the glove compartment.

"I hate this part," Eric groaned, and opened his door.

"Follow me," Shad ordered. "I know where he live."

CHAPTER FORTY-ONE

Shannon felt as if she were coming up for air, swimming upward through the bellows of frogs. She opened her eyes a slit and willed herself not to panic—even if she was in a strange place, lying outdoors, and it was night, too dark to see anything but a few stars. She could feel the cool grit of dirt under her hands and heels, smell the greenness around her.

Shuffling footsteps were approaching, the thump-thump of a stick keeping time with her pounding heart. Yellow light danced around the bushes. She shut her eyes as the footsteps came closer.

"Wake up, my beauty," a rough voice said. He wanted to be called Zadock, not Dread, he'd told her and Ransom. His stinking warmth was above her now and she could see the lamplight through closed lids.

"Wake up!" he barked.

"What—what happened?" she murmured, opening her eyes, not looking up.

"You sleep a little." The man towered over her with his stick and lamp.

She sat up slowly and brushed off her hands. A buzz filled her head at the temples. She blinked hard, trying to clear it. He must have drugged them with the bush tea he'd offered—*a little welcome present*, he'd called it. Mixed with the cannabis, it had knocked her out cold for several hours. In front of her were the filthy, old pants she remembered. Fresh dirt clung to the torn edges.

"Where am I?"

"You don't know where you is?"

She rubbed her forehead with the back of her hand. "No."

"You must have forget."

Her sandals were beside her, placed by the man, no doubt, and she slipped her feet in, trying to control the shaking, willing her racing heart to slow down.

Oh, God, she prayed, *please don't make him too crazy, please don't let me cry.* It was her fault again, her fault for suggesting a visit to the old camp before returning to Largo.

"We might as well," she'd urged her companions.

Richard had had his doubts. If he was as violent as Shad had said, maybe she should come back another day with more people, he suggested. Carlton had wanted to turn back. But Shannon had kept thinking that she wanted to get this search over with, wanted to get out of Largo and Jamaica as soon as possible, had to see the man now. They were so close.

"If he's that old, he can't be too dangerous," she'd urged Richard, who'd finally agreed to go to Dread's camp.

Shannon looked around slowly. They were in a small clearing surrounded by bushes. They must be close to Zadock's house, since he'd be too old to carry her far. Where was Richard now? What had Zadock done to him?

"You have to take me back," she said as crisply as she

could. "Dr. Ransom is waiting for me." She started to stand up, and he pushed her gently back to the ground. "You can't make me stay."

His smile displayed the few teeth left in his head, glinting yellow in the lamplight. "You forget is *you* come looking for me. I didn't come to you." He set the glass lamp on the ground and lowered with a moan next to her, the stink of him closing in.

She leaned away, not too far. "Why did you bring me here?"

"You don't remember?" He squinted at her, the lamp beneath making his mole-patched face gruesome. "Remember, this was where we first make love?"

Shannon's heart leaped to her throat. He thought she was someone else—Katlyn, perhaps? "I don't—I don't remember."

The man seemed puzzled, almost hurt. "You don't remember how we used to come up sometimes and smoke little *sensi* and have a *picnic*, you used to call it? You like it here because it have a nice view. You can't see the view now because it too dark, but you used to love it up here. I think you would remember—that bringing you here would make you remember everything."

Shannon shook her head. "I don't remember."

"It will come back." He gathered the straggly, gray dreadlocks around his face and pushed them back.

She stood up quickly and strode to the edge of the clearing. The weak moonlight showed a valley sloping down to what must be the ocean with a couple distant lights, not much to go by, and no path out of the clearing.

She returned to stand over him. "You can't keep me here."

Only a cackle answered her as Zadock set down his stick.

She lowered herself a couple feet from him. The man was confused, clearly delusional, but probably harmless. If she could get him to talk, maybe she could get him to take her back.

"What do you want from me?"

"I bring little food so we can have a picnic, like the old days. We too old for sexing now, but we can still eat." He brushed off his hands and took a crumpled bag of crackers out of a pocket. From another he took a plastic bag and started opening it, revealing a lump of cheese.

"If we have a picnic, can we go back?" She'd eaten worse.

Crumbs fell onto Zadock's dirt-blackened shirt as he bit into a cracker. "Take time, man."

Redemption's revelation had been worth the $200: Zadock was, without doubt, Katlyn's lover. After Shannon had knocked at his door and called his name, the old Rasta had opened almost immediately. His height and the thick, black moles that intertwined across his cheeks had frightened her at first and she'd taken a step back. But he'd invited them gruffly into the one-room shack and told them to sit down, talking to them, talking to himself, even talking to the stick he was leaning on. Yes, he was Dread, he'd said, but call him Zadock. He didn't know how they'd found him, but he was glad they'd come. He didn't use Rasta jargon, perhaps from being alone so long, and he'd mumbled in patois as he fussed around a two-burner stove, the smell of kerosene swamping the room.

While he made tea, Shannon had looked around the home at the faded paintings of angels, fairies, and dancers that hung on the walls, one of them looking like Isadora

Duncan on tiptoe, another of an angel balancing on one leg, the other extended. She'd felt transported back in time to meet Katlyn, and she could almost feel the Canadian's presence around her imprinted in the pictures, the dirty cushions she'd probably tie-dyed herself, and the ragged chiffon curtains that were once blue and green. She pictured the young woman in the peasant blouse hanging the pendant over the window, the crystal that was still bright beneath a rusty dragonfly.

Shannon reached for a cracker. If she could engage Zadock long enough, Carlton and Richard would surely find her. The cracker was dry in her mouth, no saliva to soften it.

"You still sweet, my queen, and you getting gray like me." Zadock reached out and patted her hair and she ducked.

"My name is Shannon, you know that, right?"

He smiled, chewing cheese with his mouth open. "You come back with a different name, but your voice give you away. I know you was Akila when you call my name at the door."

"My voice might sound like hers, but—"

"You come back like you say you was going to. You don't look the same and your name is different, but you speak the same. You the same sweet girl. You think I don't know you? You used to believe in all this reincarnation business, and I used to tell you is foolishness." He was in a reverie now, chewing and gazing at nothing. "You say you was going to come back in another body. You say you would find me and we would stay together. I used to tell you to hush your mouth—but you come back, just like you said. You never lie to me, you was always good to me. You always say I was the *love of your life*." He gave a low, coarse laugh.

"It was raining plenty when you move up here end of August, and we used to love up in the little bed when the rain was falling, you remember now? And next morning you would cook my porridge with nutmeg and cinnamon, just the way I like it. You was a good-good wife, even though you say you miss your family and friend. I sorry you couldn't write them no letter or send them no photograph. You say you don't want to tell them you turn Rasta because they would make you go home or send police to find you. But you say one day you would take me up to Canada to meet them, remember?"

"But I got sick." Better to identify, she figured, give him less to worry about.

"You wouldn't let me take you down to the hospital because you was afraid they arrest me. You ask for the Rasta doctor and you let her treat you with them herbs. You say you put yourself in Jah hands." His lips and voice quivered. "Nobody cook for me after you get sick and die, you know. They all leave me. I would starve here if it not for the boy who get me a few things from the grocery. I still have little money left from the land I sell, and is that I give him. I tell him not to tell nobody that he see me or Jah will strike him dead and he believe me.

"I know if anybody see me, they going to arrest me. They going to say that I kill you, I cause you to dead. They going lock me up and throw away the key. Worse, they could hang me."

"Why didn't you—"

"You gone and get *sick*," he insisted, swinging toward

her, the moles of his face inches away, making her heart leap to her throat. "*Nothing* I could do for you. You stop dancing, stop teaching the children, stop eating. I try everything, all the bush tea and coconut water and herb the Ras doctor bring, and even that couldn't help you. All I beg Jah to save you, and you still get sicker. Nothing could stop the running belly, all blood start to come out of you. I wipe you up and clean you up, but you still have it coming down and you still don't want to go to hospital. *Babylon,* you say." His age-reddened eyes glistened in the lamplight, water gathering on the lower lids.

"I'm sorry." She was.

"You tell me where you want me to bury you"—he coughed and spat—"and that where I bury you."

Shannon's voice went low. "It was you. Where did you bury me?"

"But I didn't, no, no, *no,*" he proclaimed with a vigorous shake of the head. "I didn't want you to dead. I carry you down to St. Ann's Bay Hospital in a friend taxi one night when you was so weak and poorly you wouldn't even wake up. I was hoping they could do something. But I had to leave you because I know they was going to arrest me if they know I bring you. They hate Rasta, and you was an upper-class woman and they would have lock me up, like how they lock me up and send me to the madhouse after they burn down Pinnacle. Next thing they going to say that I poison a white woman and charge me with murder."

He brushed the crumbs off his shirt, matter-of-fact all of a sudden. "So we put you in front of the hospital, and I put your purse with you so they would know who you was, with your passport and everything. I stay far and watch you lying on the steps until they pick you up. I hoping they can save you, even though you tell me yourself that you was going to dead."

"How did you find out she—I had died?"

"I go back to the hospital the next day and I see a nurse leaving. I ask her if she know what happen to the foreign woman and she tell me you was dead."

"And you took the body?"

Zadock looked down at the old pieces of tire and twine that made up his sandals. "I cry, you see, cry and cry, like my heart break. But you make me promise that I must bury you under the Julie mango tree, because you love Julie mangoes and you could see the sea from there, and you show me the spot." He sat up straight with his justification, still blameless. "I have to get your body, have to get it."

"How—how did you do it?"

With a triumphant smile, the old man snorted. "Who Jah bless, no man curse. I take all my money, twenty-three dollars—big money them days—to pay one night-shift guy who carry the stretchers, and he bring the body out the back door that night on a stretcher with a sheet over you. We put you in the taxi, and we drive and come back while it was still night, so nobody see us bring you inside the house. I wrap you up in the pretty spread you always like, the one with the flowers. The next night now, I dig the grave right where you say you want me to bury you, and I come back for you and bury you. I have a funeral for you, just me one, and I ask Jah to take care of you since I not there to do it."

The cheese finished, he rolled up the bag of crackers. "But life hard since you gone, everybody leave me."

"Will you show me where you buried—?"

"I going dead, but you know that already. I don't need no doctor to tell me. I have pain morning time, afternoon time, nighttime. I ready to die, the sooner the better." Leaning on his stick, he groaned his way to standing.

"After that little man come asking if I know a Canadian woman, I know you was coming back. He like John the Baptist, telling me you was coming. I realize you know that is my time now to dead, and you coming to take me back to wherever you come from, so I ready for you when you knock on my door. But I have to get rid of the university man with you, so I mix up the bush tea I use when the pain come on bad and I can't sleep. When the two of you fall asleep now, I did bring you up here to rest little bit. And while you was sleeping, I get things ready for us, so we can leave and go back to your home. I want to do it decent like, so I make things nice, and I do it before I get too sick and don't have the strength."

He bent down and picked up the lamp. "You want to see our burial ground? Come, I will show you."

CHAPTER FORTY-TWO

N obody lives here," Eric whispered as he knelt beside Lambert. The light from I-Verse's flashlight bobbed up and down between the compound's weeds and houses, coffins of darkness.

"We have to wait until they give us the all clear." Lambert held the gun upright and ready.

A mosquito whined around Eric's ear and he slapped his cheek. "You're making me nervous with that thing."

"I'll only use it if I have to."

The flashlight went out. In the pale light of the moon they could make out the shadows of Shad and I-Verse sidling along the wall of a house, advancing to a window. The flashlight popped back on and was directed into the house. After a minute, the light was turned upward before it went out again.

"The signal," Lambert said, and they hurried across the bushy yard to join the advance team.

"The man not here," Shad whispered.

"The window open, though," I-Verse said. "Like somebody living there."

"Shine the light inside again," Eric said. "Maybe we'll see something."

I-Verse pulled the ratty curtain aside and directed the light into the house. The one-room shack had a dirty mattress, a few pieces of furniture, and several framed pictures on the walls. Two enamel cups sat on the crude table in the middle.

"Interesting decor," Lambert noted.

"I see something on the floor," Shad hissed.

I-Verse ran the flashlight around the floor. A black purse with a long strap sat beside one of the chairs.

"That's Shannon's!" Eric exclaimed. She'd had it the night she'd gotten drunk and he'd put it on the bedside table.

"I think you're right," Lambert agreed.

The four men looked at each other.

"They around here somewhere." I-Verse turned off the flashlight. "They not far, like how he don't have no car and don't go nowhere. If is Dread, he too old, anyway."

"Stand still," Shad said. "Let we listen good."

There was nothing to be heard but the creaking of bamboo.

"We have to spread out," I-Verse said.

"If you go so"—Shad directed Lambert and Eric, pointing to the front of the shack—"we will go so." He nodded to the rear of the house and started off.

"I don't like us splitting up," Eric said. "If anything happens—"

"Hence the gun," Lambert snapped as they rounded the house, its door shut. Visible in the gloom on the other side were two long buildings, their roofs fallen in.

"Looks like they had a farm here or something," Eric commented. "This must have been—"

Lambert put his hand out, shushing him. "I hear something." Distant voices floated through the night, no words clear.

"Where's it coming from, Lam?"

"Over there." Lambert pointed straight ahead, and Eric screwed up his forehead to make out the dull forms of trees and hills. The voices had stopped, but there was something else. "You see that? It looks like a—"

"—a light."

They started toward the glow, the contractor in front, plowing through the bushes behind the buildings. The light seemed to be moving up a hill, and they followed as best they could, pushing bushes and weeds aside with hands and feet.

Soon they were walking up a slope, Eric's leather shoes sliding backward on the soft earth. "I wonder where Shad is," he muttered as he pushed at some guinea grass. "Maybe that's only the Rasta guy's flashlight."

"I don't think so. They went in another direction."

Fifteen minutes farther uphill, Eric halted. "Is it," he said between breaths, "has the light—stopped moving?"

"I think you're right—and we've gained on them."

They crouched down to cover the hundred yards separating them from the light. As they approached, they could hear voices filtering through the vegetation—a man's rumble followed by a woman's low comments.

"That's Shannon, I'm sure," Eric whispered. The two men crept closer, the light finally visible in splices through the tall grass.

". . . a view of the sea like you wanted," the man was saying, his voice growly and insistent.

"Can we go back now?" Shannon was pleading with a small tremor. "I'm tired."

Her companion gave a short laugh. "You don't have to worry about that where we going."

Eric parted the grass. He could make out the backs of two people, Shannon and a man in a filthy shirt, his long dreadlocks blocking out the light he was holding. They were standing over a mound covered by flowers and grass.

"See how I bury you nice?" the man said, sweeping a lamp over the mound, the other hand leaning on a stick as tall as his head. "You always like lilies, so I plant them on top."

"Very nice, you did a nice job." Each of Shannon's words was clear but trembling. "Let's go now, you've shown me Katlyn's—my grave."

"I want you to write a letter, so we can tell people where they to bury us, nuh?" The man moved closer to her. "Then when our time come, they can bury us here, me and you. They don't even have to dig no grave."

"How will they know—"

"The boy will find the letter."

Tugging at Eric's arm, Lambert whispered, "On the count of three. One, two, three!

Hands in the air!" he shouted as he ran toward the Rastafarian, pointing his gun, Eric stumbling behind. The big man and Shannon spun around.

"Babylon!" Zadock screamed, lifting the staff.

"Stop!" Shannon shouted—too late.

Lambert, flailing, went headfirst, Eric on top of him. Dirt showered down as they fell into the deep, narrow hole, the smell of fresh earth smothering them.

"What the—?" Eric squawked.

"Where's my gun?" Lambert said.

Eric's hand touched the gun and he gave it to Lambert as they struggled up, brushing themselves off. The top of the hole was a few inches above their heads, lamplight burnishing the leaves of the overhanging mango tree.

"Get us out of here!" Lambert shouted.

"Serve you right," the unseen man called. "You coming to trick us and Jah trick you."

"Shannon, you okay?" Eric yelled.

A cackle met their shouts, followed by the sounds of a struggle. The lamplight jerked around.

"You're hurting me!" Shannon cried.

"Stop hurting her!" Eric shouted.

"You mustn't go near them," warned the man in a soft growl. "Is the same people who tear down Pinnacle. They come to arrest me. They won't give us no peace."

Eric strained to look over the top of the hole. He could see the heads of the strange duo a few feet away, the lamp turning them into Halloween masks. Shannon was looking at the old man with worried eyes. His face was close to hers, as if he were holding her tight.

"You think you so bad," the old man rumbled, nodding to Eric. "But I not going to let you kill us. We going to kill ourselves."

"I don't want to kill you," Lambert called. "Just let go of the woman—"

"She dead, anyway," the Rasta chortled, and yanked Shannon out of sight. "Is our next grave you sitting in. She going to dead twice."

"He's crazy," Eric hissed.

"Get up on my knee," Lambert said in a low voice. "Can you climb out?"

"I think so." Eric stood on his friend's leg and put his hands on the edge of the hole, now at chest height.

"Don't try nothing!" the lunatic yelled, brandishing his stick, clutching Shannon tighter. Eric jumped down and the two men crouched as the stick thrashed above.

"I going to hit off the head of the first one who climb out!" the old man screamed.

"No, you're not!" Lambert shouted back, and fired into the mango tree.

CHAPTER FORTY-THREE

W e walking in circles," Shad said irritably as I-Verse's flashlight showed yet another stand of prickly grass ahead. His tuxedo pants were snagged already, and he was wondering how much they'd make him pay for the damaged suit.

"Jah will guide us, man," I-Verse said, humming a song in time to his steps.

"You calm, boy."

"Nothing worth stressing up over, even this." The big man beat back the grass to allow Shad to follow and continued humming as he started forward again.

"What you singing? I know plenty music, but I don't know that one."

"*I-Ternal Fire*, Capleton sing it."

"Sound nice. I must play it in the bar."

"Pshaw, man, all good Jamaica music created by Rastafari. I wonder what the country would do without us."

"Is not all Jamaica music write by Rasta." Shad stopped and shook a stone out of his new shoe. "What about—"

"Starting with Bob Marley, come right down, star. Peter Tosh, Bunny Wailer, Mutabaruka, Gregory Isaacs, Dennis Brown, Barrington Levy—"

"True, is plenty." Shad caught up with I-Verse. "How come so much Rasta is musicians?"

"Rasta music is the voice of poor people, of all down-pressed. That why the music gone far now, all to Japan and Africa, everywhere. Is universal music with universal messages. When music speak for the downpressed, Jah make it go all around the world. I and I music is conscious music, it make people think, make hearts open."

I-Verse stopped walking and turned off the flashlight. "Where Dread house?"

"Behind us, I think."

The Rastafarian pulled a spliff out of his pocket. "A little weed going to help this journey."

"You crazy, man. We can't be taking no weed break now."

"Little herbal essence give us mental *livity* to find them, man. This good stuff, from Orange Hill." I-Verse lit the joint with a lighter, took a long pull, and held his breath. When he finally exhaled, a sweet cloud surrounded them and Shad took a guilty gulp. "So is true you was going to married today?"

The would-be bridegroom pulled up the pleats of his pants and squatted down. "My girlfriend vex all now. Guests come from England and America for it." He pictured the disappointed faces of Danny, the investor, his red-haired English girlfriend Sarah, and Ford, the trumpeter, who'd come all the way from New York. Although Shad had been prepared to pick them up from the airport, they'd arrived in Largo on Thursday in a rented car Danny had driven from Montego Bay. It wasn't going to be fun facing them when he got back.

I-Verse laughed on an exhale. "Maybe you not supposed to marry."

"You don't know my girlfriend."

"*Satta*, man, calm yourself. Next thing—"

An explosion rang out. "What that?" Shad cried, jumping to his feet. "Is not a gunshot?"

"Must be your friend."

"Don't turn on the flashlight."

They plunged into thicker foliage toward the sound, I-Verse beating the bushes away with the flashlight, their eyes getting used to the pale moonlight. They were walking up a hill now, the ocean to their right.

"Wait." Shad pointed. "You see a light coming from up so?"

"I see it, yes."

"Put out the spliff, man. Next thing they see us."

The sculptor threw down the joint and stepped on it. "I and I tell you a little weed would help us."

They continued walking uphill toward the light, pushing through the bushes, until Shad touched I-Verse's shoulder. "You hear somebody talking?"

"Not far now."

Stooping down, they crept closer and parted the weeds. The scene in front of them was lit by a lamp on the ground. Shannon and Dread were in the middle of a clearing, he behind her holding his stick across her throat. She was trying to push the stick away, her breathing labored, but the old Rasta was holding it firmly with both hands. They were standing in front of a raised flowerbed and facing a rectangular hole, the dirt from which was piled to one side.

"Is not a grave that?" Shad whispered, nodding to the hole. "Like he going to bury her in it."

"Throw up the gun!" the old man was calling toward the hole. "I going to kill her and then I kill myself. I know Jah send you because it our time now, and I sick of pain. But I not going to let no Babylon soldier kill me."

Eyes closed, Shannon pushed at the stick again, her attempts futile.

A shout rang out from the hole. "Rastaman," an unseen voice called, "you won't get away with this."

"*Backside!*" Shad hissed. "Lambert down in the hole."

"You say you going to kill the woman." It was Eric's voice. "Tell you what, trade me for her."

"I not trading nothing," Shannon's captor shouted. "And you sound like you from Canada, too. You is police from Canada, you think I don't know? The two of you is police come to get me. Well, I too smart for you now. This don't have nothing to do with you. She and I going together. She know it already, that why she come back. I telling you, throw up the gun."

"Don't!" Shannon squeaked, her arms flailing.

"What you telling him?" Dread's voice was low. "If we have a gun, we can die quicker, then you can take me back with you."

"I'll give you the gun," Lambert called. "But you have to come and get it."

"Then you going to shoot me and take the woman. You think I stupid?"

"You have to let her go," said Eric.

"I know all of you is Babylon," Zadock shouted. "You going to kill me or lock me up, like when you burn down

Pinnacle, but I get away from you then, and I going to get away from you now. She and me going to fly up to where she come from, and after that you can climb out of the hole. But you must promise to bury us when it done."

"Is madness that," Shad whispered.

"Live alone too long," I-Verse said, shaking his head.

"If you don't give me the gun," Dread shouted, "I going to strangle her first, then you can kill me when you come out." He pulled tighter with the stick while Shannon gagged and whirled her arms, trying to hit him.

"Stop that!" Eric called.

"He going to kill her, man," Shad whispered. "We have to do something."

I-Verse stood up. "Rasta don't kill *nobody!*" he shouted, sending the flashlight sailing through the air. It smashed into the old man's forehead, making him spin with the blow, his dreadlocks flaring wide as he fell. While I-Verse ran and pulled Shannon away from his grasp, Shad rushed to the side of the hole.

Eric's chalk-white face looked up. "Thank God."

Standing close to him, Lambert held the revolver upright. "Take the gun." He threw it to Shad, who caught it and swung toward the man lying on the ground.

"Don't move!" Shad called, waving the gun *CSI*-style. "I got you covered." The Rasta looked up, dazed, and felt around for his stick, while I-Verse helped Eric and then Lambert out of the grave.

"Shannon," Eric cried, running to her, "are you okay?" Hands to her throat, Shannon staggered and fell on the mound behind her, gasping for air and crushing the flowers.

CHAPTER FORTY-FOUR

D id they charge us extra for the drum, Mom?" Eve asked, looking up from the boarding pass in her hand. She was wearing the lime-green T-shirt she'd bought in Ocho Rios as a souvenir, matching it with a band that held back her hair. The color looked good with her tan, she'd said.

"No, they didn't charge us for the drum." Shannon patted her own souvenir, the black-and-blue from Zadock's stick, covered by a scarf.

Every sofa and seat in the in-transit lounge was taken, even though it was midweek. The flight to Atlanta, the first leg of their journey, was filled, the clerk had told them at the check-in counter. "Jamaicans like to travel in the summer," she'd said as she attached a FRAGILE sticker to the drum. "We can't take the winter, we have thin blood."

Eric had stood a few feet away fidgeting with the keys to Lambert's Rover, borrowed for the trip to the airport, even though Shannon had said they could take a taxi. Jennifer had told her that Simone was coming in on the same flight, and the news that dropping them off was a matter of convenience had been met with a bitter laugh from Shannon, releasing the last thread of hope from her heart.

Much as she'd have liked to, she couldn't say that Eric had treated her poorly during her visit. He'd been kind throughout and even more solicitous since the Zadock incident. She'd always be grateful that he'd offered to trade himself for her and would never forget how, leaving the old Rasta sitting on the ground, he and Shad had linked their arms through hers and rushed her down the hill and through the abandoned camp. They'd followed I-Verse's flashlight in front, guiding her around bushes, catching her when she tripped, Lambert behind them with his gun. Driving back, Eric had made her lie with her head on his lap, and he'd stroked her hair every now and again while she, shivering, had kept her eyes closed.

"Don't drive so fast," she'd asked Lam once, and Eric had repeated the request, as if it were his own.

Not once had he said, *I told you so*. Even when he'd carried her into the house and placed her on the bed—Eve clinging to her arm, Jennifer asking what had happened— he'd never made her feel foolish or guilty. While the women fetched an ice pack for her throat and massaged her feet, he'd shrunk back and finally left.

The next afternoon, Sunday, she'd been about to take a nap when he'd appeared at the door. Eve, lying beside her mother, had seen him first. "Come in, Dad."

He'd stood looking down at Shannon with a crooked smile. "Welcome back to Jamaica, kiddo," he'd said. She'd given a laugh that hurt her throat, but she'd liked that the comment had harked back to their past, to the name he used to call her in the early years of their affair, and she'd felt a surge of love for him. And in one of those clear-air bolts of lightning, the insight one gets after a shock, she realized that she had been as guilty of pushing Eric away as he had been of her—their estrangement had been mutually created.

To begin with, she'd wanted to get pregnant despite his clear statement that he didn't want another child, and she'd found excuses not to take her birth control pills (dark spots on the back of her hands). When he hadn't reacted happily to her news, when he hadn't suggested that she move down to Largo with the baby, her anger had created a barrier of frost between them. She'd stayed away on purpose, taking his money and not calling him, trying to hurt him from a distance—but it had backfired.

From the foot of the bed, he'd asked how she was feeling, and she'd replied in monosyllables, her throat hurting too much to talk. When she'd rolled over onto her left side, Eve had curled up behind her. "Like two spoons," her daughter had said, stroking her arm, a different girl from the one who'd arrived on the island.

She'd already told her mother how much she'd worried about her. "I thought something horrible had happened to you, that you wouldn't come back," she'd said while she was massaging her mother's feet, ready to cry.

"Nothing's going to happen to me," Shannon had whispered.

"I'm sorry I'm so awful sometimes." When her mother had said nothing, the girl had continued, squeezing her mother's feet tight as she talked, "You've been gone so much—all the traveling, I missed you so much. I know you do dangerous things when you're working, and I don't know what would happen to me if—if—and Dad didn't seem to care about me, either. I thought he wouldn't want me if—and—and Grandma just watches television when you leave me with her. I know I've been a mess, but I just wanted you to—to—be home. I'm sorry—"

"A fresh start, how about that?" her mother had wheezed, and they'd slept together that night.

While Eric stood looking down at them as two spoons and chuckling, Eve had urged him to lie down with them. She was trying for a reunion, a healing, Shannon could tell, and her heart ached for their daughter. To Shannon's surprise, he'd walked around and lain down on the bed behind Eve, covering the awkwardness with talk of Zadock and their adventure.

"Your mom is a trouper, I'm telling you. I think the old man was in love with her."

Shannon had cleared her throat. "Your dad was very brave."

"What did you do?" Eve asked him.

"I helped Uncle Lambert."

"I'm glad," Eve said. "You know, you're not like how I expected you to be."

"What were you expecting?"

"A total asshole."

"Eve!" Shannon had growled.

"Well, it's the truth."

"And?" Eric asked.

"You're pretty cool."

"That's big praise, coming from you." Shannon could hear him relishing the compliment, having surpassed his expectations of his parenting skills.

"Can I come back next year?" Eve asked.

"You have a ticket, don't you?" He rolled over toward them. Three spoons.

"Dad, do you know what we are?" Eve had suddenly said, her voice carrying a broad smile. "We're a whorl, like that nautilus shell Mom gave you."

"You're right," he'd said after a second. "We're a whorl." He'd followed with words that burned into Shannon's mind, that day and every day thereafter. "Better than that, we're a *family*. Your mother and I may not ever be together, but we are your parents and we love you. Nothing will change that. And that means I will always care for you, and you're welcome to come and visit anytime. I'll do whatever I can to make it happen. And now that I'm going to have a fancy hotel again, you'll be staying in a fancy suite next time."

"I can deal with that," Eve had quietly commented.

Despite the shadow that had descended upon her, Shannon heard herself saying the unimaginable. "We love you, Eric," she'd whispered, for Eve's sake, of course, not his.

"I love you both," he'd answered right away, reaching to pat Shannon's arm and then Eve's.

The message had been clear. The romance was at an end, her bitterness toward him contributing to her loss and another woman's gain. While he hadn't had the guts to speak to her directly, at least she knew where she stood. From here on, they were to be a family and nothing more, the love between them *agape, not erotica*, as her father, a historian at York University, used to say.

Shannon breathed in the new normal, the pain in her chest settling in for a stay, while Eve reminded her father he was to write at least once a week.

"I want to know everything that happens in Largo. Casey is going to let me know when Sheba has puppies again, so you don't need to tell me that."

"You're forcing me to do emails."

They could try skyping, Eve had suggested and had to explain what that meant. They would be in touch, he agreed, every single week, because he wanted to hear about her drumming lessons in Toronto and how she was doing in school.

"And no more shoplifting or anything like it, you hear me, young lady? Or no trip to Jamaica for you next summer."

"I hear you," Eve had muttered, and Shannon had managed a smile into her pillow.

After he left, she'd asked Eve to get her some of Miss Bertha's lemongrass tea for her throat, and while Eve was gone, Shannon had allowed herself a few moments to accept the finality of Eric's statement, allowed a few tears to grieve the end of their love affair. One door had closed, but a window of truth had opened: they were to be a family, a separated family. Like Zadock, she thought, she'd have to live with the cruel reality of separation from the love of her life.

Shuddering at the memory of the stick at her throat and his unwanted intimacy, she'd written Angie a long email about him later on Sunday, downplaying the previous day's drama, but telling her what she'd pieced together with Shad's help:

Katlyn fell in love with a Rastafarian and they were man and wife in the very best sense. She became a Rastafarian herself, even changed her name, and knowing that her parents would never understand or approve of her radical new direction, she stopped writing everyone after she left Gordon Gap. Her lover had been akin to a terrorist in his day, when it was illegal to be

Rastafarian. He'd been locked up after the police had broken up
Pinnacle, his community near Kingston, and he'd spent time in
prison and a mental hospital.

Shannon recounted how Katlyn had refused to go to
a doctor when she got diarrhea, how Zadock had tried to
treat her himself and finally took her to the hospital, hoping to save her, and kept hidden because of his fear of the
authorities.

He had no rights as her common-law husband to claim her body
or bury her where she wanted to be buried, and he would prob-
ably have been under suspicion of murder with his record and a
foreign woman involved.

Poverty, cultural history, and isolation had caused
Katlyn's death, Shannon had added. But Zadock had
spent all his money to get her body back, and he'd buried
her in her favorite bedspread exactly where she'd asked to
be buried. For thirty-five years thereafter he'd kept every
memento that reminded him of her—and longed for her
return.

By the time she sent the email, Shannon knew why she'd
gone easy on the lunatic who'd almost choked her to death.
It was out of respect for Katlyn, who had found a love that
had more meaning to her than her own family and friends,
and for Akila, who wouldn't have wanted an evil word said
about her lover. Based on what Redemption and the heart-
sick Zadock had said, the last year of the dancer's life had
been filled with a new philosophy and a loyalty so deep that
she wouldn't leave the Rastafarian community or betray

Zadock when she got sick. Her death had been a sacrifice for him, and his life had been a commemoration of hers.

"Just as I thought," Shannon had told Jennifer huskily as they sat on the patio that evening. "Finding the answers to Katlyn's death has—it's clarified what I want my own future to be."

"Obviously not with Eric," Jennifer had said over her soup.

"No, it's not. But I know now that I want to be loved the way Zadock loved Katlyn, steady and true. Not this on-again, off-again thing I've had from Eric all these years, which just leaves me off-balance, never knowing where I stand."

"You're worth a lot more, girl."

"I want to be the *beloved*, you know what I mean, of a man who adores me." The journalist had been a little embarrassed by her own immodesty, but it didn't stop her. "I want to be loved from the top of my gray hairs to my big toe with the fungus." She raised her wineglass. "I want to be the last name the man whispers before he dies."

"Amen."

They'd clinked glasses.

On Monday morning she'd asked Jennifer to find out what St. Ann's Bay Hospital had on their records about Katlyn. A call to a physician friend of the Delgados' was rewarded a few hours later: Katlyn Carrington had died of amoebic dysentery with attendant dehydration. Her body had disappeared, and the Jamaican authorities had never found out who the body snatcher was. And they wouldn't be hearing it from her, Shannon decided, so that Akila, as the Rastafarian she'd become, could continue to rest in peace under her Julie mango tree with the ocean view. The young woman's short, idealistic life deserved nothing less, Shannon would tell Angie, and if she wanted to see the spot, Shad could show it to her.

Richard Ransom had called later that morning with apologies for not having returned Shannon's call on Sunday. He'd been entertaining a colleague from the Netherlands who'd come into town (again not using a pronoun) and hadn't had a spare moment to call until then.

"What happened to you?" she'd asked. "They said you'd gone already when we got back—"

"I woke up in the Port Antonio Hospital. Carlton was sitting beside me. They gave me a cup of coffee and I was fine after a couple hours. I didn't even wait to see the doctor."

"How'd you get back to Kingston?"

"I dropped Carlton in Largo and went on home. What happened with you?"

She gave him the short version, her voice straining.

"Oh, my God, I had no idea!" he'd exclaimed. "Carlton told me everything was *under control*. If I'd known, I would have driven straight back."

"You couldn't have done anything, but the mystery of Katlyn's death and disappearing body has finally been cleared up."

"Does that mean you're going back to Toronto?"

"We couldn't get a direct flight, so we're going through Atlanta on Wednesday. We've started packing up."

"I'm sorry we won't—"

"You've helped so much already, Richard."

"I didn't do much, just got in your way and into trouble."

"Stick with me at your peril." Shannon laughed, and he with her. "Abandoned the first time, drugged the second."

"Giving me stories to tell."

"I'm glad you came with us, though, and the information you gave me was terrific."

"Quite welcome."

"I have a few follow-up questions, but I'll email them, if that's okay?"

"Sure, anything you want to know." He'd paused as if he was gathering courage. "I might be coming up to Toronto in October, by the way. There's a conference I want to attend."

"You have to call me when you come. Do you have my phone number?" They'd exchanged contact numbers, and he promised to send her an email with dates.

"I'm looking forward to reading your article," he'd added. "Actually, I'm looking forward to seeing you."

She'd felt warm inside when she hung up, and she'd measured Ransom—kind, good-looking, intelligent, interested in her and not ashamed to show it—a definite possibility. She wasn't sure he was the type to fall madly in love with her, what with his social life, but if she saw him in October, she'd find out.

Feeling hopeful about Ransom, swapping stories with Jennifer, eating Miss Bertha's soups and porridges had put Shannon in a reasonable frame of mind by the time Eric picked them up to go to the airport on Wednesday morning. He'd dressed in long pants and put on aftershave, and he seemed extra chipper on the drive.

"Where you off to next?" he'd asked her at a rest stop while Eve was in the bathroom. "They assign you anything yet? I hope it's not as—"

"I'm quitting my job."

"What do you mean?"

She'd looked down at her guava juice, jiggling her straw in the glass. "My old editor at the *Star* wants me back—and I think Eve would be better off if I was home more."

"Might be a good idea. Although you've done a fine job with her so far."

"I want to do better."

"Me, too." He'd lowered his eyes as their daughter approached.

At the airport, he'd turned solicitous again, waiting while they checked in and walking with them to Immigration carrying Shannon's bags. The hugs and farewells exchanged were warm and brief. Maybe she'd come back to Jamaica one day, Shannon had thought as she waved at her daughter's father behind them, but she'd bring a boyfriend with her next time—or have him meet her at the airport. Standing in the security line, she'd taken a moment to recognize the pain in the middle of her being, the pain she knew would get less with time and other distractions.

The in-transit lounge was getting more crowded, standing room only for late arrivals, and groups of people had congregated around the cafeteria at the back.

"I'm going to get something to drink," Shannon announced. "You want anything?"

Eve looked up from her iPad and raised her lip. "Coconut water?"

"I know you're kidding."

Shannon bought two bottles of water and gave one to Eve. Restless, she walked the length of the lounge and back. She was looking out of the hall's plate-glass windows when their plane glided up to its breezeway. Fifteen minutes later, the first arriving passengers were heading to Immigration down a passageway outside the lounge. A glass wall, across which was a horizontal stripe of yellow, green, and black, the colors of the Jamaican flag, separated the departing from the arriving.

Shannon found a space between two potted palms to inspect the passengers. Her heart started pounding, dreading the inevitable, and a wave of heat crept up her torso. *My first hot flash,* she thought with a grim smile, *the end of my youth, right on time.* With her chest and neck glowing with sweat, she finished her bottle of water and resumed her watch.

A middle-aged couple holding hands was followed by bustling businessmen and businesswomen clutching briefcases and dragging bags. Tourists in shorts and jeans, young mothers holding babies, college students, returning locals, filed past.

"These the people from our plane?" Eve asked at her shoulder.

"Yeah, I think so. Did you leave our stuff——?"

"The couple beside us said they'd keep an eye on it." Eve put her arm around her mother's waist, and Shannon around her daughter's, and the two examined the passengers streaming past.

"I had a dream about this," Shannon said. "I was looking through this pair of glasses that had plants and vines around the frames, and a bar across the lenses, like it was my past in Jamaica. Then there was another pair that——"

"Don't go weird on me, Mom. I was just starting to like you."

An elegant woman was walking toward them pulling a carry-on bag, a woman Shannon knew at once. Slim and petite, she had slanted eyes and her short hair was black, not a gray hair in sight. She wore her clothes well: a long-sleeved T-shirt, skinny jeans, and low-heeled sandals. Dangling, gold earrings swung from her ears as she walked, with an ease to her lips, ready to charm the Immigration and customs officers.

"She's pretty," Eve said.

"She is, isn't she?"

This exchange, the arrival of Eric's new love and the departure of the old, had a smooth, psychic rhythm. Shannon placed her hand flat on the glass separating her from Simone, the woman who'd scared away two men with her gun, who'd gone naked because she felt like it. The new arrival looked straight at her and hesitated for a second—a flicker in her eyes as she glanced at Eve—before hurrying on to those who awaited her.

CHAPTER FORTY-FIVE

The rain drummed down on the thatch roof, the first of the August rains. Eve would have done her dance if she were here. When he got up, Eric decided, he'd write her an email telling her it was raining, and he'd say that he missed her. It might earn a mental shrug, but he'd do it, anyway.

Beside him, Simone was still asleep, her naked back turned to him. The tawny stepping-stones of her spine curved from her hips to her neck on the pillow. He pulled the sheet up to her shoulders and dropped it like a snow-flake so it wouldn't wake her. She was *exhausted*, she'd said when she arrived, although she hadn't looked it.

When she stepped out of Immigration, he'd had to look twice to recognize her. She'd put on weight since she'd left Largo, no longer the gaunt woman waving out the window as her brother drove them away. The baggy shorts and faded T-shirt that had been her uniform on the island had been replaced by an outfit from a fashion magazine, the shiny gray top and tight black pants looking chic and sexy.

She'd walked up to him, glowing, earrings swinging, and stuck out her hand. "I don't think I know this hand-some man."

"Come here, you." He'd hugged her close, pleased that she'd noticed his shirt and long pants.

"Aren't you going to kiss me?"

He'd answered by whispering something in her ear, and she'd laughed out loud.

On the way back in the Rover, they'd talked, the year apart making conversation sporadic at first. Halfway through the drive, she'd tossed out the question he was ready to answer. "Has your ex left yet?"

"Went out on your flight, as a matter of fact."

"I thought so."

His altar-boy guilt about the women's playing musical plane seats had melted away. He'd been tempted to say something to Shannon on the drive to the airport, but he'd reminded himself that sleeping dogs were best left alone. She'd been through enough already. A reminder of the other woman in his life was uncalled for just when she was leaving the island.

It was cowardly, he knew, his cowardice coming from mixed emotions. Seeing Shannon again had brought up some of the old feelings, and his dilemma had gotten worse when he saw Zadock manhandling her. He'd wanted to kill the man with his bare hands, had been figuring out how to do it when I-Verse's flashlight had slammed into Zadock's head. On the drive back to Largo, he'd wanted to protect her for the rest of his life.

The following morning, Sunday, he decided to bounce it off his bartender.

"Great work last night," he'd commented when Shad walked into the bar. "Good thing we took I-Verse, eh?" When Shad had answered with a nod, Eric had rattled on,

"I never had much to do with Rastas before, the whole white-man bugaboo, I guess. They stay away from me and I stay away from them. Ras Walker fixes my shoes, of course, but that's business, you know, and he's kind of like part of the scenery. I'd never gotten up close and personal before this. The whole evening was really an eye-opener for me. This loony Zadock guy thinking me and Lambert were the police and we'd destroyed his old camp? Oh, man. He would have killed Shannon if he'd had a chance. Crazy guy, he'll probably die up there all alone one day. You have to feel for him, living like a hermit. No wonder he's gone bonkers."

"I called Bellevue, the mental hospital," Shad said glumly. "They sending police to pick him up. I didn't tell them nothing about what happened, though."

"Good thinking. Shannon's not going to press charges, but somebody needs to keep him away from people." Eric had drained his coffee cup. "But that I-Verse, I'm telling you. Here I am, practically shitting in my pants, and he comes along and saves the day. He doesn't even need a gun, just a flashlight, like some superhero."

"Rastas just people, boss—good and greedy, hero and crazy—just people who believe in God and want to lift up the poor. People think that Rasta is different from them, but is not true. They want the same things we want: house, food, safety. They just go about it different. Rasta want to change the world, so they start with themselves."

"You're starting to sound like them. You thinking of going Rasta?"

Shad had rubbed his scalp. "I like my bald head too much."

"Every other young man seems to have dreadlocks nowadays, even in the States."

Shad opened the fridge to start preparing the bar for service. "The music, the food, the language, it catch on—and young people like the one-love culture."

"One love? Look how they treated Shannon at the Nyabinghi!"

"They were 'fraid of Shannon. If you had police flying helicopters over you and drug enforcement people burning up your weed, weed you use in your religion, you wouldn't get suspicious of every stranger, especially when they taking photographs?"

"They're mighty touchy, though." Eric had picked up the newspaper. "You told Beth about last night?"

"She don't want to hear nothing."

"The wedding, you mean?"

The bartender hadn't answered, just kept cutting up limes and oranges, the knife held tight in his hand.

"You still getting married?"

"If I can get out of the doghouse."

"That's bad."

After a minute of trying to read the newspaper, Eric had put it down. "I'm thinking of asking Shannon to—you know—for us to live together."

Shad had looked up with a frown. "You moving up to Canada, boss, like how you hate the cold? And you can't leave the new hotel just like that."

"Oh, no, I wouldn't live in Canada. I was thinking they could come and live down here. We could put Eve in the same school that Casey goes to."

Shad waved the knife across his neck. "But—you up to

here with debt, don't even have money to support yourself. It going to take at least one year to build the hotel, and you going to be sucking salt the whole time, and when that finish, it going to take time to make any money off of it."

"I have my Social Security starting next month, and Shannon can work."

"You already say your Security check not going to pay you much." The bartender frowned. "And what work you think Shannon going to find in Largo Bay? She can get good work in Canada, and she would have to keep it because you don't have any money to support her. So she going to be gone, working to keep Eve in boarding school and college. Most of the time, both of them not even going to be here, and you going to be right back where you are now, alone, but deeper in debt." Shad had tut-tutted over the limes. "And, another thing, Eve don't need to go to no boarding school now. She come down here with a sour face, like she angry, and she just start to relax now and enjoy life. You can't put her in no boarding school, man."

"Why you so negative all of a sudden? I give you some good news and—"

"Because marriage is a serious business, boss. You hear me? Is a *business*. It not something you just decide to do one day. You don't take *every* somebody you love to your bed and bosom. A man must think about it careful first, see if it's a good thing to do. Marriage is about people planning their happiness, and you have to be able to make enough money to provide for your children. Both people have to pull together, that what Beth teach me. She cleaning toilets so we can pull together for the children sake—and to pay for the wedding." Shad had gone back to his slicing and sighed. "Even though her money gone now."

The sledgehammer of Shad's words had hit Eric, and he'd walked down to the beach with the truth of it. Boarding school cost a pretty penny, according to Lambert, and the little primary school in Largo had nothing to offer Eve, who had free visits to museums and zoos in Toronto.

A fishing village had nothing to offer Shannon, either, but an occasional break from her work. She was at the peak of her career. In ten or fifteen years, perhaps, she would slow down, but she still had mountains to climb, notches to carve on her belt. If she moved down to Largo, editors would call someone nearer at hand, and he knew Shannon loved her work, had to have a notebook or a camera with her. But if he asked her, he knew, she'd move down and try to find some kind of work. He'd be closer to Eve, even if she was in boarding school, and she'd have Casey for company, anyway. They'd be a family, something he hadn't had much of growing up. He had to do this.

When Eric returned to the bar, his bartender had continued talking as if Eric hadn't left the room. "And another thing, boss," Shad said as he swept a broom over the cobwebs on a beam overhead, "I not feeling like you really love Shannon."

Eric had stopped in the middle of the empty restaurant. "Whoa, that's kind of private, don't you think, buddy?"

"Love is not a private thing, boss, unless you hiding it. Beth say is good to talk it out—and women know them sort of things."

Eric had sat, a little disoriented, at a table he never used. He'd looked at his hand and spread his fingers. "Shannon is a good woman and I'm lucky to have her in my life. I'm glad she had Eve, and she's done her best to bring her up well. I'm grateful that she loves me, crazy as I am, and she wants Eve to love me. I've always admired how she's fought her way up in her profession. That's not easy, you know, in North America. I sure don't have that type of drive. She's a good mother and a woman of character, that's how I'd sum it up."

Shad leaned on the broom. "You know, boss, I hearing that you glad and you grateful and you admire her, but you never say nothing about love."

Eric had blinked once, blinked twice, and walked to his apartment. There he'd sat in another chair, this time at his dining table. Shad was right again, dammit. He hadn't said anything about love. You didn't take someone as your life partner because you felt gratitude and admiration. And try as he might, all he felt when he thought of Shannon was the warmth of a comforting stove, not the burning of a hot, wild fire.

He'd stood up and walked to the verandah. A warm stove didn't turn a man on. That must have been the cause of his wilting when they were in bed together. He'd been blaming himself, his age, his health, but that had nothing to do with it. He no longer undressed her in his mind, didn't long for her touch and her kiss. Having a child together wasn't a good enough reason to commit to her, and it wouldn't be fair to saddle her with an impoverished, old man who lusted after another woman.

That afternoon he'd climbed the hill to the Delgados' house, ready to settle the marriage question once and for all, the question he'd seen in Shannon's eyes since her arrival. She'd tried to hide it, but she'd come down to find out how he felt, probably gotten drunk to end up in his bed. She must have been disappointed when he couldn't make love to her and confused by his kiss in the dark. The loving feeling he'd had for her after Zadock's assault had simmered down to a genuine caring—and that was all.

Speaking the truth had been easier than he'd thought. With Eve on the bed between them, he'd felt at a safe distance from Shannon. He'd been able to include them both in his words, leaving his daughter understanding his commitment to her, and her mother not expecting anything more. It had gone well, he'd thought afterward, and the drive to the airport a few days later had been almost anticlimactic.

All the way to Montego Bay, even as he made small talk with Shannon, Simone's face had stayed in front of him. He'd had to hide his excitement and keep the conversation light, although he really wanted to shout out the Jeep's window that his woman was coming back, the woman he imagined in his arms when he listened to the Cuban stations, imagined dancing the tango with in a Havana nightclub, even if he didn't know the tango. The woman whose voice and laugh and eyes made him long for her, with nary a thought of erectile dysfunction.

He looked over Simone's back and between the louvers. The island was barely visible through the rain, the downpour hiding the secret of their lovemaking the summer before. She'd been bristly when he'd first met her, almost unapproachable, but loneliness had made her need his company, and they'd become friends and finally lovers. She was different this time around, though, a confident, cheerful woman, and he'd worried at first that she wouldn't want him anymore. Two nights of lovemaking, one on the verandah on a blanket under the full moon, had laid his mind at rest. The fire still raged.

Looking at the rumpled hair he'd once thought belonged to a goat roaming his island, he was tempted to wake her. He needed to tell her he loved her, tell her he wanted her to stay, tell her that being alone had finally lost its charm.

As if sensing his need, she turned over. "Who's that dirty old man staring at my body?" she said as she stretched.

He reached out for her. "Come to Papa."

She scooted over and snuggled into him. "It's raining, Papa."

"I know," he murmured, kissing her forehead, her cheek, her soft hair. "The August rains have started."

CHAPTER FORTY-SIX

A blindfold?" Shad said, straightening the jacket of the beige suit.

"So she said," his friend answered, and took a clean handkerchief out of his dresser drawer.

"The only time I wear blindfold was when I was a *pick-ney* and we playing blindman's buff. This time it feel like I going to the gallows." Shad laughed as his friend placed the kerchief over his eyes. "She going to execute me."

"Is hanging in the gallows you want, or execution with a gun? Make up your mind."

"Either way I is a dead man." The bartender sucked his teeth. "I don't know why you won't tell me where you taking me."

It had been the longest, hardest week Shad could remember since he'd gotten out of the Pen. Beth seemed to have enjoyed punishing him all week. He'd left her *standing at the altar*, her note had said (even though she hadn't yet arrived at the church when he left). The letter had been handed to him by his eldest child. Still dressed in her pink bridesmaid dress, Joella had been sitting under the verandah's bare bulb when Lambert had dropped him off at the house that night. She'd stood up and moved to the top of the steps, blocking his entry.

"Mamma say I must give you this."

"You can't give it to me inside?" Shad had asked wearily, squinting up into his daughter's face.

"She say you not to come inside. Read the letter, nuh?"

He'd sat on the top step and read the sloping script that belied the venom of a woman abandoned.

Dear Shadrack,

    You were not at the church when I reach and I feel like an idiot in front of everybody. You leave me standing at the altar. I do not want to see your face. Please sleep over at Frank's house. I talk to him already and he is expecting you. Do NOT come back until I tell you. Do NOT try to contact me.

    From the MOTHER of your CHILDREN.

Frank was waiting for him with a cold beer, ready to relate what had happened that afternoon at the church. Minutes after Shad had driven off with Lambert and Eric in the Rover, he said, Beth had stepped out of her brother-in-law's car (*waving like a princess*, according to Frank), only to be met by Jennifer's news about the groom's departure. Beth had sucked her teeth and uttered a curse word loudly enough for the guests inside the church to hear.

"I know he would try something," she'd added, and shouted for her brother-in-law not to park the car.

"She cry?" Shad had asked, biting his cheek.

"Two black lines from her eyes to her chin."

"Is a good thing I not sleeping there tonight, boy."

"Next thing she pour hot oil in your ear."

"What happen to the food?"

"We go back to the bar and eat everything, nuh, but we put Solomon's curry goat in the freezer at the Fishermen's Cooperative."

After describing the adventure with Zadock, Shad had gone to bed, grateful for Frank, grateful for the lumpy love seat. Sleep, however, had evaded him as he scanned his bleak future. He was certain, knowing Beth as he did, that there would be no peace, no going home, without a wedding. But there could be no wedding the next day, Sunday, with Miss Louise's funeral already planned, and nobody could come to a wedding during the week. The following weekend was out, what with the groundbreaking on Saturday and Pastor off to a church conference in Kingston. Besides, the tuxedo had to be returned and there was no money to rent another.

Shad had worked at the bar all day Sunday without going to church or the funeral, not ready to face Beth. Monday, he returned the suit after ironing it and avoided extra charges. Tuesday, he'd buried himself in his work, mopping the restaurant, doing inventory, and reading his book on wines and spirits. Yet nothing seemed to help the emptiness inside: he missed his family more than he'd thought possible.

His first time separated from them, it had felt as if one arm and two legs had been removed and only half of him were functioning. He'd wondered about Rickia's progress in the science class she hated, worried about Joella's not being supervised around boys, wanted to know if Ashante had started using the toilet, and fretted that Joshua's next tooth would pop out and he wouldn't be there to see it. Worst of all, every night when he got back to his friend's untidy bachelor house, there was no Beth to bed down with.

The only blessing was that Frank, a fisherman, slept late, allowing Shad to do the same for a change.

Sending a message to his loved one hadn't elicited a response. Maisie had taken his note on Tuesday and would only say that she'd delivered it.

"Did she say I can come home?"

"She not ready for you yet." Maisie had gone on with her dish washing.

On Tuesday evening Shannon and Eve had come to say good-bye. He and Shannon had gotten tearful when she thanked him for helping her find Zadock and for saving her life. She'd paid him in full for his services and added a tip that he hadn't expected. Eve said she'd be back next summer, but her mother had said nothing.

Simone arrived on Wednesday afternoon after Eric's apartment had been cleaned from top to bottom. Maisie had put the new sheets on the bed and placed a vase of red hibiscus on the little table. It had been almost a year since Simone had left Largo, and when she stepped out of the Rover with Eric, the bartender, remembering the skinny, angry woman he'd first met, wasn't prepared for her to look so different, so dressed up and—so American. He'd ached to tell Beth about it.

He'd kept his distance from his baby mother nonetheless, respecting her request, sure now that she was the best woman a man could have. He'd thought of the dread Zadock, who would never have been accepted by Katlyn's parents, who couldn't visit his lover in hospital, and who would probably have been charged in her death. Shad had understood very, very clearly the pain that the man had suffered living alone ever since, and he decided that this would not be his fate. He would do right by his woman. One day, if Beth would have him, he would stand before the world and say that they were man and wife. On Thursday, he'd asked Maisie if she would take another note to Beth telling her just that, but Maisie had refused, reminding him that patience was a virtue.

Jennifer had been dismissive as well. She'd held a meeting, a *briefing*, she called it, in the bar on the drizzly Friday morning. While the bulldozer flattened the land next door for the groundbreaking, Danny, Eric, and Shad had listened to her describing, yelling over the dozer, the order of events for the big day. Excited about breaking ground on his own hotel, Danny had kept nodding his big, bald head while Eric looked bored. Most of Jennifer's words had gone in one of Shad's ear and out the other because he'd kept wondering if Beth and the children were coming to the groundbreaking. When he asked Jennifer, she said she didn't know, abandoning him like everyone else.

Saturday morning had dawned hot and sunny with a breeze that dried the damp ground quickly. Jennifer had thought of everything for the groundbreaking ceremony. The big, white tent that she'd ordered in case of rain had been erected by the time he got there. Under it he set up the folding tables on which Jennifer arranged the hard hats and shovels, and Winston laid out the folding chairs as straight as he could. There was even a microphone, and Shad found a long extension cord and plugged it in behind the bar.

Lambert and Eric had helped carry a few boxes before retreating to the bar. "We have to try out the champagne Danny brought," the boss had explained.

A small crowd began to gather on the folding chairs

shortly before ten, when the printed program said they were to start. Half an hour later, the Methodist minister from Port Antonio said the invocation. After Danny poured white rum on the flattened soil to appease the spirits, there were speeches . . . and speeches. The local member of Parliament, Donovan Bailey, gave the shortest speech, his Adam's apple bobbing up and down as he praised Danny Caines for the foresight to build a new hotel in Portland. An elated Danny spoke about his childhood dreams and his grandfather, talking too much before sitting down.

Shad stood up and said he was glad about the hotel because it would mean a new life for Largo. In this first speech in his life—he hadn't expected to say anything—he found the words came easily. But Beth wasn't there to hear them. When Eric spoke, he asked Danny and Shad to come up, and a little drunk, he raised their hands high in the air, calling for three cheers, and the gathering had hip-hip-hoorayed the hotel.

The shovels came next, and Shad, the brand-new partner, had found himself in a line with the preacher, the MP, Eric, Danny, and Lambert. It felt like a dream, a bittersweet dream. Everyone in Largo seemed to be there but his family, and his heart was heavy but happy when Jennifer handed him his yellow hard hat and when the reporter from the *Gleaner* took a photograph of them holding the shovels. Feeling like an impostor as he dug into the soil, hearing Granny over his shoulder saying he was going to be a *busha* one day, Shad had kept looking for Beth, hoping she'd show up to make him feel better, maybe coming in a taxi so she wouldn't perspire.

They'd turned over the soil on the count of three, and

after the clapping had died down, Jennifer invited everyone to the bar for champagne and beer. Danny had insisted that, as a new partner, Shad shouldn't be behind the bar, so he'd had a glass of champagne with his new partners (feeling like a fraud inside, he wanted to tell Beth), trudged back to Frank's cottage afterward, and fallen asleep on the love seat.

Awakened by Frank's clanking around in the kitchen, Shad had glanced at his watch and sat up. "You should have woke me, man. I have to go to work."

"No more work today." Frank had taken eggs out of the fridge.

"Mistah Eric expecting me for late shift."

"Not this afternoon." Frank had broken three eggs and scrambled them, refusing to say anything more, except that, since Shad hadn't had lunch, he needed to eat. While Shad was finishing his scrambled eggs, Frank had gone inside the bedroom and produced his beige suit, which was now too small for him, he said, and told a bewildered Shad to put it on. It had fit perfectly.

"But you have to take a bath first, star. You smelling fresh."

Bathed, dressed, and blindfolded, Shad was now led by the elbow onto the verandah and down the steps. He could hear a car driving toward them on the dirt road, stopping in front of the house.

He heard, in an English accent, "Your chauffeur is here!" It was Danny Caines's girlfriend, Sarah. Shad pictured her, with her bright red hair and pretty mouth, calling out.

Frank guided him into the backseat and got in beside him.

"Where you taking me?"

"You'll find out soon enough," Danny said from the front.

The car drove to the left when they got to the main road, away from the church.

"Something going on at the bar, I know," Shad guessed, cocking his head to one side. He only got a *hmmm* from Sarah.

The sound of waves hitting the cliff beneath the bar came and went. Seconds later, the vehicle bumped over rough ground and came to a stop. Frank pulled on Shad's elbow again, and he felt his way out of the car, the smell of fresh-turned earth telling him exactly where he was.

"I can take it off now?" Frank asked someone.

The blindfold was removed and Shad rubbed his hand over his eyes. He was on the very spot where they'd held the groundbreaking that morning, but the tent and the chairs were gone. Frank turned him around to face a wall of people, a grinning firing squad between him and the sea. They were all dressed up: Danny in a casual suit, Sarah wearing a green gown, Jennifer in a wide hat, Lambert in a safari suit. Eric was in his good pants again, this time with a long-sleeved shirt and holding the guitar, his arm around Simone in a blue dress. Beside the petite woman sat a little dog, guarding her. It was Cammy, the little brown mutt everyone in the village (except Eric) knew belonged to the obeah man, the dog that *the doctor* had sent over to the island to protect Simone.

"What going on?" Shad protested.

"You ready to do this, bud?" Eric asked.

"Don't give him a choice, Eric," Jennifer upbraided him, "not after all my work."

"Do what?" Shad squeaked.

"Get married," Frank said. "Is your last chance to run."

"I can't get married."

"Why not?" Jennifer said.

"The church lock up and Pastor gone—"

"You don't have to worry about that," Danny put in.

"—and Beth—"

"Taken care of," Jennifer said.

"—and I don't have the ring with me."

Simone stepped forward. She held out a small, black box and opened it. "What about these?"

Shad examined the contents and looked up at her, the look they exchanged carrying the memory of last summer, when he'd rowed her groceries out to the island every week and heaved them up the cliff, and when he'd saved her from the clutches of Tiger and Sharpie. "Is *your* wedding rings?"

"I'm not using them." She laughed, all her pretty teeth showing. "And any man who wants to marry me will buy me a new set, anyway." Behind her, the boss's black eyebrows rose and fell in a flash.

Shad took the box from her and ran his finger around the square diamond of the engagement ring, over the gold band with its tiny scratches. "I can't pay you for this, you know."

"You paid me already, Shad."

"Come on, sport, let's get this show on the road," Eric said.

"Yes," the groom said, taking a deep breath, "I ready."

The wall parted to make way for him. Below them, the large white tent now sat on the beach, the silver balloons from the party blowing from its posts.

"But Beth, she know—?"

"We've been working on this since Monday," Jennifer said, linking arms with him, making sure he wouldn't run away. "She's part of the plot."

Frank put his arm around his shoulder. "Is hell to pay for us men in Largo, but if you going to do it, best to get it over."

The tent's roof flapped a welcome as they descended to the beach. Inside were rows of chairs, the same folding chairs from the groundbreaking. The people in the chairs looked up at him, everyone smiling, and he could make out a red carpet at one end, and on it the hem of Beth's white wedding dress and the shoes her sister had loaned her. Rickia popped out of the tent in her blue bridesmaid dress, waving him inside with her bouquet.

Shad clapped his hands. "Well, boy, you give me a shock now. How come nobody say nothing all week?"

"Because Jennifer would have killed them if they had," Lambert answered, and guffawed.

As they walked down to the beach on the slope of earth stripped and waiting for construction to start on Monday for the Largo Bay Grand, Shad felt a chill run down his spine. He remembered how God liked to spin people around and watch them after, and he walked as straight as he could, with a cool smile. He walked as if he weren't surprised by anything—that he was going to be a partner in a hotel, going to be a *busha*, going to be a married man. When they got to the beach, he took his time, trying not to get sand in his shoes, touching the ring box in his pocket next to his good-luck charm, the bag with Granny's grave dirt.

His woman, his Beth, was waiting for him, and she wasn't vexed with him, but looking beautiful in the long dress she'd been sewing all year, sheer lace covering the strapless top, right up to her neck and wrists. From her head flowed a veil that fell behind her to her waist, and in her hands she held a bouquet of the purple orchids that Lambert grew in his greenhouse. She was wearing the mischievous smile she kept for their special times, her eyes sparkling with happiness. Next to her, Joella was holding her own orchids, and between them was the pastor from Port Antonio who had prayed over the groundbreaking, this time in a long, black robe.

Almost all the folding chairs were filled, some people sitting in the restaurant's chairs at the back. Lambert and the others walked to the few empty seats left—except for Eric, who took up his position at the front, a teenage grin on his face, ready to play something on the guitar. Sitting in the front row were Beth's sister, eyebrows raised, and her husband and family. Miss Mac (Ashante holding on to her skirt), Tri and his woman, Solomon and Maisie (Joshua in her arms), and Old Man Job were in the second row. Carlton and Winston sat behind them, along with half of Largo, everybody happy, sharing their weeklong secret.

"Who did all this?" Shad whispered to Jennifer under her big hat.

"The people who love you," she whispered back, before handing him over to Beth.

ACKNOWLEDGMENTS

In the summer of 1989, I was the associate producer for a BBC documentary that was being filmed in Jamaica about the remnants of African culture in the Caribbean. The island's Rastafarian community was included in the film, and my memories of our visit to a Nyabinghi camp and our conversations with its leaders have never left me.

I had no idea then that my intense experience would culminate in a work of fiction, but here it is. Another contributing factor to this novel has been my growing respect for the Rastafarian lifestyle, which started long before the word *organic* became a buzzword, and for the conscious lyrics of Rastafarian singers—a refreshing alternative to some of the not-so-conscious dancehall songs.

While writing this book, I have tried to be as authentic as possible, although I have employed the more accessible acrolect form of Jamaican dialect because of the diversity of my readers. Several people and literary works have given me a better understanding of the movement. Ras Yasus Afari, dub poet, musician, and author, became my friend at a book festival in Anguilla a few years ago, and I am grateful for our friendship. Additionally, his book, *Overstanding Rastafari: Jamaica's Gift to the World*, gave me a clear explanation of his people's philosophy and language.

Another invaluable resource was the late scholar Dr. Barry Chevannes's *Rastafari: Roots and Ideology*, which traces the history of Rastafari back to the nineteenth century. Others have been *The Kebra Nagast: The Lost Bible of Rastafarian Wisdom and Faith* by Gerald Hausman, and Tracy Nicholas's *Rastafari: A Way of Life*. Leonard Barrett's *The Rastafarians* provided me with the real-life Nyabinghi scene in the novel. For Internet language resources, I used www.jumieka.com, created by Larry Chang, and so many other online Rasta dictionaries that I won't begin to list them.

It takes a village to birth a novel as much as a child, because a novelist works with the assistance and forgiveness of many, many people. I have had no greater support than from my colleagues at the University of the Virgin Islands, including President David Hall and his wife, Marilyn, Provost Camille McKayle-Stolz, former dean Simon Jones-Hendrickson, and my chairman, Dr. Alex Randall. They have done everything in their power to allow me to write, and they continue to make my teaching experience at UVI a delightful one.

Additionally, I had the great fortune of being invited back to Jamaica for five weeks, which inspired me as I completed this novel. For that invitation I thank Valerie Facey, who took care of my every need while I was on the island editing a memoir. Working in Jamaica, living in both Kingston and on a farm, not only assisted me in making the final touches to my own manuscript, but inspired my thoughts about the next.

The team who is always behind me continues to offer their support. Eric Peterson, my reader, I thank for his sage and gentle advice. Maria and Larry Earl, part of my Atlanta